KYRIAKOS

Titles available in this series

Yannis
Anna
Giovanni
Joseph
Christabelle
Saffron
Manolis
Cathy
Nicola
Vasi
Alecos
John
Tassos
Ronnie
Maria
Sofia
Babbis
Stelios
Kyriakos

Greek Translations

Anna
published by Livanis 2011

KYRIAKOS

Beryl Darby

JACH

ISBN 978-0-957452-9-5

Printed and bound in the UK by
CPI Group (UK) Ltd, Croydon, CR0 4YY

First published in the UK in 2016 by

JACH Publishing
92 Upper North Street, Brighton, East Sussex, England BN1 3FJ

website: www.beryldarby.co.uk

For Marie Baujard, my primary school teacher,
who told wonderful stories and inspired me to write.

Family Tree
for Christoforakis

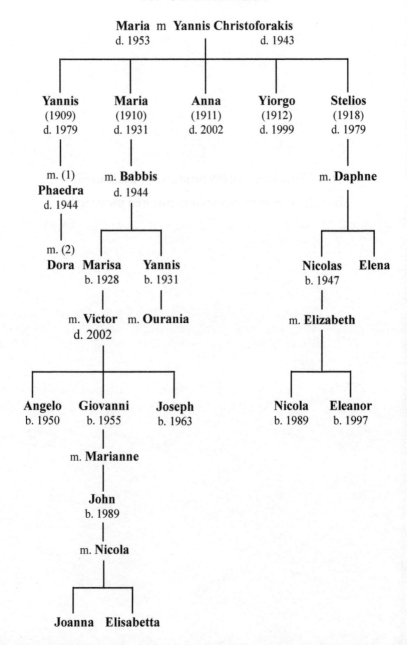

Family Tree
for Veronica Vandersham

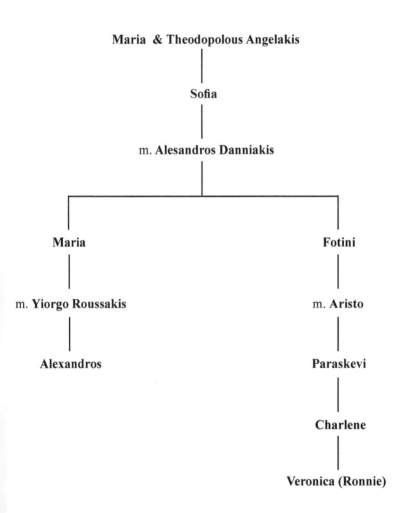

Maria & Theodopolous Angelakis

Sofia

m. **Alesandros Danniakis**

Maria

m. **Yiorgo Roussakis**

Alexandros

Fotini

m. **Aristo**

Paraskevi

Charlene

Veronica (Ronnie)

Author's Note

The old tower that served as a depository for the deceased lepers who lived on Spinalonga has been demolished due to the collapse of the roof. A new tower has been built in conjunction with the Church and Ministry of Antiquities as a lasting memorial to their suffering.

Some of the complete skulls and long bones are displayed in there. The bones that had disintegrated were removed and given a Church burial.

My description of John's activities is entirely fictitious as are the characters and any other events that take place in this book.

Week Three – August 2012

Inspector Antonakis considered the conversation he had had with Miss Vandersham and Mr Pirenzi. He was not prepared to go chasing up to Kastelli to take a statement from an old woman who claimed to have seen someone set fire to the house. It was quite likely she had made the story up to make herself appear important in the eyes of the other villagers. Even if Officer Raptakis confirmed that the fire had been set deliberately it was most unlikely to have been a building inspector who was responsible. It was far more probable that it had been caused by the carelessness of the builders.

He tapped his fingers together, it was quite possible the girl had done it herself and was trying to blame Babbis Skourlatakis. The assault that she claimed had happened was hardly serious if she only lost a few buttons from her blouse. She could have pulled those off herself. Babbis was married anyway; he had no need to go around assaulting young foreign girls. He would wait until he had received the report from Officer Raptakis, then he would interview the girl further. It was quite likely that when he questioned her again she would break down and confess to the crime.

Inspector Antonakis sighed. He did not believe the story the woman had told him about Babbis Skourlatakis starting the fire. It was ridiculous. Building inspectors did not go around setting fire to people's property. If it was proved that the fire had not been caused by the builders the crime probably lay with a careless electrician. Now he would have to decide who to visit first and see if they could shed any light on the incident. He consulted his list; the builders could know something and might be able to give him some useful information about the girl who owned the house. If there was any suspicion that Mr Palamakis and his grandsons were responsible he would make sure he elicited a confession from them.

After that he would speak to the Vandersham woman again. He knew Giovanni Pirenzi would accompany her and the man knew his way around the law. There would be no way he could brow beat her if one of the Pirenzi family was in attendance.

When he finally visited Kastelli to speak to the old woman he would need to interview her son also. He gave another deep sigh. It was Saturday tomorrow and if he wanted telephone numbers and times checked there would be no one he could ask to do that until Monday. He might just as well forget about it and enjoy his weekend off. No one had lost their life in the incident so there was no urgency.

Week One – September 2012
Monday

Kyriakos looked at Ronnie and took her hand. 'In that case Miss Ronnie will you marry me?'

Ronnie drew in her breath. She had realised how deeply she cared for Kyriakos when he had been injured. 'I'll have to think, Kyriakos.'

'What is there to think about? Either you love me or you do not. If you refuse me I'll not embarrass you by asking you again.'

'Oh, Kyriakos, it is not a question of loving you. I tried to show you my feelings at Owen and Laura's wedding, but you never made another approach to me. I thought it was drinking too much champagne that had made you kiss me.'

'So what is your problem?'

'I am an American and you are a Cretan. Will your mother accept you marrying a foreigner?'

Kyriakos shrugged. 'You are partly Cretan.'

'Only a very small part of me and remember my ancestry.'

'My mother does not have to know your family history.'

Ronnie shook her head. 'I'm not ashamed to admit that my great grandparents had leprosy. There should be no stigma attached to the illness today. I would rather your mother knew now than heard it at a later date.'

'I will tell her. She will understand,' Kyriakos said confidently.

'There are other problems to consider.'

'You think your mother would not approve?'

Ronnie shrugged. 'My mother would say it was up to me who I live with or marry. There is the house and.....'

Kyriakos held up his hand. 'The house is no problem. You say it can be put right. I can help you if you need some extra money.'

'Forget the money. I am more worried about being sent to prison.'

'I would still want to marry you even if you had been imprisoned.'

Ronnie sighed in exasperation. 'Kyriakos, be serious. I could be deported back to America. I have not said that I will not marry you, but I just feel we should give it some very serious thought.'

'I have given the matter serious thought for over a year. Please, Miss Ronnie, will you marry me?'

Ronnie placed her hands over her face. 'I cannot give you an answer now. I have to get my life back in order first. It would not be fair to say yes and then find I was going to be imprisoned and deported back to America at the end of my sentence. Even without that threat hanging over me there are so many problems that we would need to discuss.'

Kyriakos raised his eyebrows and pulled Ronnie's hands gently away from her face. 'So what are these other problems?'

'First of all I have to get permission from the Greek government to live here permanently. At the moment I am here on a visitors' work permit.'

Kyriakos shrugged. 'That is no problem. It would be changed to a permanent visa once we were married.'

Ronnie shook her head. 'I understand they look into your background quite carefully. I would probably have to declare that my father is serving a gaol sentence.'

'Your father? He is in prison? You told me he was dead.'

'My step-father is dead. I always think of him as my father. My natural father was sent to prison when I was a small child.'

'What did he do?' Kyriakos was feeling concerned now. Had Ronnie's father committed murder?

'He was a very talented artist. Far better than many others of the same era. In fact he was so clever that he was able to forge paintings done by some of the old masters and claim they were originals. For a long time no one questioned their authenticity, then he made a mistake. He sold a copy to a man whose friend had the original. They had both paintings examined and tested by experts and, of course, the one my father had sold was proved to be the forgery. I'm not sure how much longer he has to serve, but you realise that if I have to declare that on an application form the Greek authorities would have every right to refuse me a permanent visa.'

'That is not right,' Kyriakos spoke vehemently. 'Your father's crime is not your fault.'

'I know, but try telling that to immigration authorities. If Babbis does press charges against me for blackmail it could give them an added reason to deport me.'

'But you are going to charge Babbis with arson. He set fire to your house.'

Ronnie shook her head. 'I can't prove that. Old Kassie told Giovanni that she saw the man who lit the fire, but when Giovanni mentioned being interviewed by the fire service and the police for a statement she said she didn't want to be involved with the law. She was obviously hoping to be paid for her information, but Giovanni refused to give her anything. He said there could be a reward after an arrest had been made. Even if she does tell the authorities will they take any notice of her? They'll probably say she couldn't see clearly as it was at night or that she is too old to be a reliable witness.'

'You believe she is telling the truth?'

'Yes, I do. I think Babbis did it because I humiliated him before his colleagues.' Ronnie shrugged. 'It was probably foolish of me. I should have gone to the police and lodged a complaint against him, but I was so convinced they would say I was a stupid woman who had misinterpreted his actions.'

Kyriakos placed his hand on Ronnie's. 'I believe you. Giovanni believes you. That is important. He will confirm that you were very distressed and spent the night at their house as you were frightened Babbis would go to your apartment. These problems can be sorted out. The Pirenzi family has far more influence in this area than Babbis Skourlatakis.'

'More influence or more money?'

Kyriakos shrugged. 'Both; now what are these other problems that are worrying you?'

'Where would we live?'

'Here, in Elounda, of course.'

'You have no accommodation at the taverna and you live with your mother.'

'You can live there also. That will be no problem.'

Ronnie shook her head. 'That will become a big problem, no, listen Kyriakos.' Ronnie held up her hand as he was about to interrupt her. 'I do not speak Greek and your mother does not speak English. We will not be able to communicate with each other. Two women in one kitchen does not work at the best of times. Your mother would complain about me and I would complain about her. You would be continually trying to keep the peace between us.'

'So we find somewhere to live on our own. Maybe Giovanni would let us live in one of the self catering units or Vasi allow us to rent a room permanently in his hotel.'

'Neither of those ideas are practical, Kyriakos. Giovanni closes the apartments down in the winter as they have no heating and Vasi closes his hotel for maintenance and decoration at the end of the season. I wouldn't want to live in a hotel all the time anyway.'

'So, we arrange for your house to be repaired and then we live there.'

'That is not convenient for either of us. You do not close the taverna until midnight, sometimes later. I like to be up and painting early as the sun rises. If we lived in Kastelli you would not be home until at least one in the morning and I would be leaving the house at about three. We would never see each other. You would be leaving the house to come here as I returned for a siesta. That is not having a married life.'

'You come up to my taverna most days,' replied Kyriakos truculently.

'Of course. I like to come to see you and it is easy. A short walk up the road, but if we lived in Kastelli and it meant I had to drive to Elounda to see you it would not be so easy. I might want to stay at home and finish some painting.'

Kyriakos shook his head sadly. 'You are making excuses. You do not want to marry me.'

'No, I'm not making excuses, but I am trying to explain to you the problems. We need to have them settled before we make any decisions. I do not want to move in with your mother and a month later tell you I am leaving because I cannot live in the same house with her. I do not want us to live in Kastelli. You would start to complain about driving home at night when you are tired and that when I left in the early hours of the morning I was disturbing you. We would soon start to argue. I would say you should close the taverna earlier and you would say I should go to paint later.'

'I could not close the taverna earlier. I cannot ask customers to leave.'

Ronnie sighed. 'I understand that. I cannot ask the sun to rise later in the morning. I am just using these as an example of how difficult it would be to actually spend any time together if we lived in Kastelli.'

'So what do you want?'

'First I have to get the problem with the house sorted out.' Ronnie shook her head. 'I don't even know if I would be allowed to marry you as I am an American. There is no point in us trying to make plans until we know the answer to those two questions.'

'Surely you can marry whoever you please.'

'Of course, but at the moment I have to have a work permit to be here and need to renew it each year. If you were in America with a visa and work permit I'm not sure if we would be allowed to get married. America has very strict regulations to prevent marriages of convenience. Greece could have the same sort of legal restrictions.'

'You can ask Nicola and John.'

'What do you mean?'

'Nicola had to apply to the Greek Embassy before she was given permission to marry John. She could tell you what was needed.'

Ronnie smiled. 'That's a good idea, but at the moment everything depends upon the outcome of the enquiry into the arson at my house. If I was convicted of the crime I could be deported.'

'You cannot be convicted of a crime that you did not commit.'

'I wish the Inspector was as certain of that as you are.' Ronnie rose and kissed Kyriakos. 'I must go and do some painting. I'll be up again later.'

After Ronnie left Kyriakos sat outside his taverna. He would speak to his mother and tell her of his intentions. He was not sure how she would react to the news that he wanted to marry an American rather than one of the local girls. When Ronnie had visited him at the hospital his mother had always greeted her with a smile and then left them for a while to talk. Kyriakos knew it was most unlikely that his mother would have understood any of their conversation, but it was polite and tactful of her to leave them alone.

He contemplated the objections Ronnie had raised to them getting married. Were they excuses? If she did not want to marry him all he could do was to accept her decision. He could not force her. He wished he could think of a logical argument that would convince Ronnie that marriage between them would be idyllic. He scratched absently at the scabs on his arm where he had been knocked over by the young men on the motor bike. They were unsightly and he decided he must continue to wear a long sleeved shirt whilst he was at the taverna so the customers did not see them.

Kyriakos sat opposite his mother at the table in the living room with a broad smile on his face.

'Mamma, I have something to tell you. I hope to be getting married.'

'That is good news. It is time you thought about marrying and settling down. I would like to be around to see your children grow up. Who are you proposing to marry? Your cousin, Katerina?'

Kyriakos shook his head. 'She is five years older than me. I've asked Ronnie, the American lady.'

Irini looked at her son in horror. 'Why do you want to marry an American?' she asked. 'What's wrong with a Greek girl?'

'Nothing, but I happen to love Ronnie. You have met her and agreed she appeared very pleasant.'

Irini shook her head. 'Just because she is a nice lady does not mean she would be a suitable wife for you. She is a foreigner. She does not know our ways.'

'Many Cretans are married to foreigners. Ronnie has Cretan ancestry. She accepts our way of life and has lived over here for the past two years.'

'She has only lived here during the summer months. She has not experienced the cold and rain in the winter.'

'I'm sure she will manage to cope with that,' smiled Kyriakos. 'She says New Orleans often has bad weather.'

'You cannot marry her,' Irini said firmly. 'She is not Greek.'

'She has Greek ancestry.'

'She has not been brought up as a Greek. She will be no use to you at the taverna.'

'I do not expect her to help me in the taverna. She is an artist.'

'Is she of our religion?'

Kyriakos shook his head.

'Then it is out of the question. You cannot marry a heathen.'

'You have met her. You agreed she was a nice lady.'

'Many of the local girls are also nice and well brought up. One of them would be a far more suitable wife for you. Why don't I ask some of my friends in the village if they know of a respectable young girl who is not already betrothed?'

Kyriakos shook his head and smiled, determined to ignore his mother's objections. He would just have to gradually try to persuade her that Ronnie was the only girl he was prepared to marry. Irini pursed her lips. She was not happy that her son wanted to marry a foreigner.

'When do you plan to get married? I will need time to get the house organised so there is space for her belongings.'

Kyriakos frowned. Ronnie had been adamant that she would not be prepared to share his mother's house. It was going to prove a problem. Not only would his mother be offended but she would also be losing the rent money he paid her and would find it difficult to manage without.

'She has not said yes to me yet. Her mother and great uncle are arriving next week and I think she wants to speak to them first. I'd like you to meet them. They're nice people also.'

'Do they speak Greek?'

'No, although her great uncle was born over here. You won't have to spend an evening with them. It will just be a quick meeting because they will find communicating as difficult as you.'

Inspector Antonakis drew in behind Mr Palamakis's flat-bed truck. He had telephoned earlier to announce his visit and requested that Mr Palamakis's grandsons be there at the same time. He could see them standing outside smoking and smiled to himself. That could solve the case immediately. They had no doubt been smoking inside the house and left a cigarette smouldering when they finished for the day.

As he approached them they nodded briefly to him.

'Grandpa's inside. He's expecting you.'

'I'd like to speak to both of you at the same time.'

With a shrug of his shoulders Giorgos walked into the front room of the cottage, his brother following him, their cigarettes still between their fingers. Inspector Antonakis followed them, annoyed that they had not stood to one side and allowed him to enter first.

Mr Palamakis looked up from the papers he had spread out on the table before him. 'Have a seat, Inspector. Would you like coffee?'

Inspector Antonakis shook his head as he sat down on the upright wooden chair. 'I'll not put you to any trouble.' He pulled out his notebook. 'I understand you and your grandsons have been working on the house in Kastelli that has been destroyed by fire.'

Mr Palamakis shook his head. 'It hasn't been destroyed. Fortunately it is a solid stone building so the walls and ground floor are intact. The upper floor collapsed, of course, and also a part of the roof, but it has certainly not been destroyed. The work can be done again and the extension has not been badly damaged.'

'Has the young woman asked you to work on the house again to repair the damage?'

'I haven't had any instructions from her as yet.'

'So where are you working at present?'

'Nowhere at the moment. We were due to spend the next three weeks decorating and doing any finishing off that was needed in Kastelli so we had not booked in any work. No doubt Nikos will be pleased.'

Inspector Antonakis made a note on his pad. Had Mr Palamakis deliberately fired the house to ensure the work needed to be done a second time? It would obviously be very profitable for him if that was the case.

'Who is Nikos?'

'The builder who lives in Kastelli.'

'So why wasn't he working at the house?'

'Nikos is excellent when it comes to building a wall or making external repairs. He doesn't have the craftsmanship or imagination for interior work. Besides, he works alone so could not have managed much of the work on the house. He would have needed to employ.'

The Inspector made a note of Nikos's name. He would have to interview him and be satisfied that the man had not fired the house in an effort to be employed instead of Mr Palamakis. He wondered if this was the same man as the one who had raised the alarm at the Fire Station.

'So what was the work undertaken by you and your grandsons?'

'All of it. Miss Vandersham wanted an extension added to the back area and the upper floor divided to make four rooms so we put up partition walls. To ensure the access from the staircase was safe we enlarged the small landing that was there.'

Giorgos shook his head sadly as he stubbed out his cigarette in the lid of a metal tin. 'All that nice new timber; what a waste.'

'Did anyone else work on the premises besides you and your grandsons?'

'We employed a couple of men when we needed some extra help. The carpenters came and fixed the staircase they had made and then the iron workers came and welded the handrail and ornamental supports into place.'

'When did this take place, the fitting of the staircase and the welding?

'A couple of weeks ago. The carpenters came in first. I expect Greg can tell you when his workmen fitted the iron work.'

'Greg? Who is Greg?'

'The owner of the forge in Kastelli.'

'What exactly did he fit?'

'A guard rail along the upper floor to the beginning of the staircase and then a handrail down to the ground floor.'

Inspector Antonakis made another note on his pad. Welding had taken place. Welding meant a very hot jet of flame and sparks. It was possible the welders had started the fire. If a spark had gone up into the roof it may not have been noticed and if the timbers were old and dry it could have taken hold.

'Had you replaced the roof?'

Mr Palamakis nodded. 'Our building work was virtually finished. The electrician was due to come and run the cables through and connect up to the electrical supply. Miss Vandersham had ordered her sanitary and kitchen equipment and once that had been plumbed in we would make good as necessary and commence the decoration.'

'Lucky for her that none of it had arrived,' remarked Yiannis as he stubbed out his cigarette butt.

'Fortunate indeed. Now, Mr Palamakis, do I understand correctly that there was no supply of electricity at the house?'

'That's right. I just said; the electrician was due to come and install it.'

'So when you were doing all this work on the house what kind of tools were you using?'

Mr Palamakis gave the Inspector a puzzled look. 'The usual tools, of course, hammers, chisels, saws, screw drivers.'

'Quite, but did any of these need an electric supply?'

'Some of them. Others have a battery.'

'So if some of these tools needed electricity to function where were you getting the power from?' Inspector Antonakis raised his eyebrows.

'That depended upon the work we were doing at the time.'

'Explain to me, please. I am not a builder.'

Mr Palamakis sighed. 'We needed the timbers cut to size and had the roof trusses made up at the saw mill. They're pretty heavy and we had to use a small crane to get them into place. A couple of men from the saw mill spent some days up here with us. We needed extra hands to position the base plates on the outer walls and across from one wall to another. The trusses were secured to the base plates at each end of the building using a power drill; that was battery fed. Once the materials are up in position the fixing does not take that long. The additional trusses that were needed to support the weight of the roof were fixed to the wooden base plate with metal plates, again using the drill. The timbers for the rafters had also been cut to size at the saw mill and they were secured to the base plate, the cross beams and the trusses using the power drill. We then fixed the battens using a conventional hammer and nails before felting the area and nailing down the roof tiles. The ridge tiles were then cemented into place. Once that had been done we were able to move inside and plasterboard over the rafters to hide them.'

Inspector Antonakis nodded, implying that he understood. 'This power drill that you say works on a battery – how long does the battery last?'

'That depends upon the length of the job.'

'Yes, of course, what I meant was would you be able to do all the work you have described before the battery runs out?'

Mr Palamakis shrugged. 'We would not have been able to complete all that work in one day. We arranged with a neighbour across the road that we could plug in to their electricity supply when we wanted to recharge a tool or use a small electric saw or sander. We ran an extension lead across the road and paid twenty Euros for each day that we used it.'

'So why would you have needed to use a small electric saw if you had everything pre-cut at the saw mill?'

'The floorboards had to be cut to fit in the thresholds, architraves, window frames, small items like that needed to be trimmed to size and Miss Vandersham had asked us to sand the upstairs floorboards ready for them to be sealed.'

'And this neighbour was quite happy for you to use their power supply?'

Mr Palamakis chuckled. 'Of course. We were paying twenty Euros a day just to have the extension lead connected. Sometimes we only used the saw for about half an hour during the day.'

'So when you finished work and had no further need of the extension lead what did you do?'

'Unplugged it, coiled it up and put it back in the house.'

'I suppose,' Inspector Antonakis tapped his fingers together, 'That on one particular occasion you did not leave it plugged in and switched on causing a tool to overheat?'

'Certainly not,' answered Mr Palamakis indignantly. 'We are very conscientious. Before we leave any premises we always check that everything has been disconnected and everywhere is safe. We ensure that lids are firmly in place on paint pots and we bring our hand tools home with us.'

'When you left the house in Kastelli at the end of the day did you lock the door?'

'Of course. We checked that the door leading out to the yard from the extension was bolted and placed the padlock on the front door.'

'Do you know how many people have a key to that padlock?'

Mr Palamakis shook his head. 'We have two keys, but I have no idea if Miss Vandersham has given a key to anyone else.'

'I notice that both your grandsons smoke. Many fires are started by a smouldering cigarette end.'

'That may be true, but they never smoke inside a property. They always stand outside.'

'I am sure you were not at the house the whole time. Maybe if they were in the middle of a job they might decide to have a cigarette whilst working?'

Mr Palamakis looked at the boys and they both shook their heads. 'They know they are not allowed to smoke inside anyone's house.'

'They were smoking in here.' Inspector Antonakis looked pointedly at the metal lid that contained cigarette butts.

'This is my house and I permit them to smoke in here,' replied Mr Palamakis and glared at the Inspector. 'What I allow in my own house is up to me. They both know they do not smoke inside a customer's house, besides there was nothing around that they could have ignited. There were no wood shavings or paper and the walls and floor are of stone. Partition walling is treated to make it fire proof.'

Inspector Antonakis closed his notebook. 'Just one more question, Mr Palamakis. The work at the house must have cost a good deal. Have you been paid?'

Mr Palamakis nodded. 'She had paid me up to date and all she owes me now is for the time we spent clearing away the debris.'

'There was never any problem regarding the money being forthcoming?'

'Never. I gave Miss Vandersham a bill each week and we would go to the bank together where she would draw out the money and pay me immediately.'

Inspector Antonakis frowned. 'I understood the government had placed a limit on the amount of money that could be withdrawn in any one week.'

'Quite so. But Miss Vandersham has an American account and there is no restriction on the amount she can withdraw from that.'

'What about the saw mill and the forge that you mentioned; how did they receive payment?'

'I would add their bill to mine and when Miss Vandersham paid me I would deliver the amount she owed to them and obtain a receipt.'

Inspector Antonakis nodded. He would have a word at the bank and ask them to check if the woman's American account was healthy. She could have overspent drastically and set fire to the house herself, not envisaging the amount of damage that would be caused, and hope to claim on her insurance.

'You have copies of all these payments and receipts?'

Mr Palamakis frowned. 'Miss Vandersham has the receipted bills. The amounts she paid me can be checked against my books.'

'I'm sure that won't be necessary.' The Inspector placed his notebook in his pocket and rose to leave. 'Thank you for your time. I hope I won't have to bother you again.'

Mr Palamakis shrugged. The Inspector could come whenever

he wished. He knew that he and his grandsons were not responsible for the fire.

Inspector Antonakis entered the bank in Aghios Nikolaos and asked to speak with the manager. A customer advisor offered to help, but the Inspector was adamant that it was the manager he needed to speak to, adding that he was on official business. The advisor's face blanched. Had some discrepancy been discovered in the accounts? There had been the unfortunate incident with a previous employee and Mr Iliopolakis's account a few years ago.

When the manager ushered the Police Inspector into his room he also looked anxious. 'How can I help?'

'I understand that an American woman, Miss Vandersham, has been visiting the bank regularly with her builder. She would then access her own bank in America and withdraw rather large sums of money to settle her bills.'

The manager nodded. The cashier had referred each transaction to him for his sanction and she had produced her passport as identity. He hoped he had not contravened a law of which he was unaware.

'Was a withdrawal ever refused by her bank?'

'Not to my knowledge.'

'So you would be able to say if she had ample funds at her disposal?'

The manager shook his head. 'I cannot discuss a customer's financial status with anyone. In this particular case I do not have access to any details of her bank account even if you have a warrant that would force me to make a disclosure.'

'But there was never a problem if she asked to withdraw sizeable amounts?'

'As I have told you, she produced her passport for identification and the amount she requested was authorised by me. There was never any problem regarding the transactions at this branch. If you wish to have further details I can only suggest that you ask the lady in question to accompany you here and we access her American account with her permission.'

Inspector Antonakis nodded. 'Very well. I will speak to Miss Vandersham and no doubt I will be back at some time with her.'

The manager smiled. 'Provided she is with you and willing to co-operate that will not be a problem.' If the police inspector had expected to get information from him without the customer's authority he was mistaken. He opened the door. 'You are welcome to return during our normal banking hours. You may, of course, be asked to wait if I am already engaged with a customer.'

Inspector Antonakis left the bank angrily. It had been a waste of his time trying to look into the woman's accounts. He would interview the builder again. The restoration of the house at Kastelli had been a lucrative job for him and he might well have decided that he did not wish it to finish in a few weeks. He could have fired the house knowing he would be employed to do much of the work a second time. It could even be possible that the arson had been arranged between the woman and him so she could collect on the insurance money and the fire had got out of control.

He sat in his car debating whether to drive up to Kastelli to interview the woman who claimed she had seen the arsonist. It was probably going to be a waste of his time. Whoever had fired the house would not have committed the crime knowing someone was watching. His mobile 'phone alerted him to a message and he removed it from the holder. It was probably a request to return to the police station.

'Inspector Antonakis.'

'Good afternoon, Inspector. Fire Officer Raptakis here. I've had the report back from forensics. Would it be convenient to bring it to your office now?'

'You'll have to give me about ten minutes. I'm out of the office at the moment.'

'I don't wish to interrupt you if you are busy with an incident.

I could just leave it for you.'

'No, I've finished my business here and was just about to return. I'm not far away, just need to negotiate the traffic.'

'Very well. I'll make my way to the station and wait for you there.'

The Inspector looked at the line of cars making their way slowly up the hill and giving way occasionally to the traffic that was coming down. Having parked the police car right outside the bank he was causing an obstruction, resulting in a traffic jam.

He switched on the engine, flicked the switch that lit up the blue light on the roof and started the siren. The traffic began to clear immediately, driving up on the pavements, and leaving him a clear passage to the bottom of the hill. Driving a police car certainly had its advantages.

Officer Raptakis placed the report he had received from the forensic department on Inspector Antonakis's desk.

'It was definitely arson,' he announced. 'Petrol was the accelerant. Evidence of it was found all over the stone floor of the main room. There are some traces upstairs on the stone walls and on the charred floorboards that are still in situ. It is obvious that whoever did it spread the accelerant around upstairs, then soaked the staircase on their way down to the ground. Beneath the wooden staircase the decorating materials were being stored. There was quite a concentration found in that area and we can say with certainty that was the seat of the fire. Whoever started the fire knew the cans of paint would explode and the contents ignite setting fire to the staircase and the upper area '

'According to Mr Pirenzi there's an old woman in the village who claims she saw the man who set the fire.'

'Is she reliable?' asked the fire officer.

'I don't know.' Inspector Antonakis spread his hands. 'Mr Pirenzi says she saw the house was on fire and telephoned her son.'

'It was a man who called us. Are you able to get a record of the timing of the calls?'

'I expect they can be traced. Why?'

'Where does the man live? Was he at his home at the time? When we arrived the man who claimed to have called us was with the villagers trying to extinguish the fire.'

Inspector Antonakis frowned. These were the kind of questions he should be asking. 'What are you implying?'

'It has been known for the arsonist to raise the alarm and later appear to be giving assistance on the site to divert suspicion from himself.'

The Inspector nodded. 'Of course we will be questioning him. Personally I think the girl is involved. She probably didn't realise how much damage she was going to cause. I understand she has a grudge against Babbis Skourlatakis and is trying to place the blame on him.'

Officer Raptakis stood up and smiled. 'That's your problem to sort out. I'm just a fireman.'

Inspector Antonakis read the report through slowly. At the end of the report there was a record of the time the call was received at the fire station, the length of time it took the engines to arrive in Kastelli and the amount of time it took to bring the fire under control. He made a note of the times. He would certainly want to know where Mr Palamakis and his grandsons were that night and also Miss Vandersham. She could have driven someone up there and waited for them in the car. By the time the alarm was raised they could have been in Neapoli and driven back to Aghios Nikolaos by an alternative route.

He glanced at the clock on his wall. He was off duty in another hour. It was too late to drive up to Kastelli today. He would make the journey tomorrow and speak to the old lady who claimed to have seen the perpetrator and raised the alarm.

Irini had hardly slept. After the Sunday service at the church she had walked to Mavrikiano. She needed to talk to someone who had experience of their son marrying a foreign woman and the only one she was acquainted with was her second cousin, Soula. It was a hot climbing the steep hill to Pano Elounda and she was grateful to take advantage of the shade offered by the houses in the narrow streets, although the sun hit her again with renewed force as she continued along the road to Mavrikiano. She wished she had returned home after church and changed her shoes. The ones she wore to church were her best pair and they would be scuffed and dusty by the time she returned to Elounda.

She found Soula in her cool living room and was immediately offered a drink of water and a plate of biscuits. 'Fancy walking up here at this time of day; or did Kyriakos bring you in his car?'

Irini shook her head. 'Kyriakos is at the taverna. He doesn't know I've come to see you.'

'Well, I'm pleased to have a visitor. No one wanted to stop and chat after church this morning. I'm sure it's hotter now than it was in August.' She fanned her face as if to prove her assumption true.

'I wanted to ask you about your son, Thrannisas.'

Soula smiled happily. She was always willing to talk about her eldest son. 'He's doing very well. He bought a new truck recently. It's a bit larger than his old one. Said he needed the extra space as his delivery business has improved.'

'That's good to hear. Times are hard at the moment.'

Soula shrugged. 'Not as hard as they were during the war. My mother said she often went to bed hungry when she was expecting me and she was worried that I would be undernourished and not survive being born.'

Irini nodded in agreement and sympathy although she had been born some ten years after the war and was only familiar with the stories her parents had told of the deprivation suffered by the Cretans.

'Your Thrannisas, he's the son who married the English girl?'

'That's right. The other two married locally.'

'Has the marriage turned out well?' asked Irini.

'They seem happy enough. They have two children. The oldest

girl says she wants to go to University. That will mean going to Heraklion to live.' Soula sighed. 'I don't like the thought of her being in that city all by herself. You hear about bad things happening there. She may change her mind, of course, by the time she's finished her schooling in Aghios Nikolaos.'

'What does she want to study?'

'Biological diversification, whatever that might be. They have fancy names for everything these days. We were just grateful to be able to read and write. I heard there was some trouble at your Kyriakos's taverna; he was robbed and knocked down.'

'It was fortunate that he was not badly hurt. His ankle appears to be on the mend and his other cuts and bruises are healing well.'

'How is he managing? Are you going up to help him?'

'Sometimes, but he has a friend who goes up each day and sees to the tables. He has to be there as she doesn't speak Greek.'

Soula raised her eyebrows. 'Where does she come from?'

'America. She's an artist. Been here for two seasons. She owns the big house up in Kastelli; the one that was destroyed by a fire the other week.'

'I heard about that. Thranassis was surprised that anyone had bought the house. He says it had been derelict for as long as he can remember.'

'According to Kyriakos her uncle actually owned the house and gave it to her and her mother gave her the money for the restoration.'

Soula frowned. 'I thought you said she was American. How did her uncle come to own it? Did he buy it?'

'Kyriakos didn't say and I didn't think to ask him,' admitted Irini.

'I'll see if Thranassis knows. He delivers chicken feed to the farmers in the area and goods to the local shops. He'd been watching the house take shape. He said she must have spent a small fortune.' Soula shook her head. 'Terrible for it all to be ruined.'

Irini helped herself to another biscuit. 'Kyriakos says the girl's mother and uncle are coming for a visit and she had hoped to have it completed by the time they arrived. I doubt they'll be best pleased to have had all that money wasted.'

'I'll ask my Thranassis to ask around when he goes up there next week to deliver the chicken feed. He often takes up roles of wire for the farmers to make repairs to their fencing. He certainly needed that new truck as he delivers to all the villages round about. Someone is bound to know if work has started on the house again.'

Week One – September 2012
Tuesday

Inspector Antonakis drove slowly through the village of Kastelli. The journey had taken him considerably longer than he had anticipated due to having a tractor in front of him making its way ponderously up the hill. There was no point in him using his siren or light as there was nowhere the tractor could safely pull in and allow him to pass.

The burnt out house was evident as he rounded the bend in the road and it was impossible to park outside safely. He drove up to the War Memorial and parked in the space beside the cistern, receiving a curious look from the man who was working in the garden.

As he walked back up the road he realised that many of the houses looked unoccupied. He wondered just how many people actually lived in the village, probably just a few elderly residents who relied upon their children for assistance. He reached the large house on the corner that belonged to Ronnie and studied the exterior carefully. There was little sign of fire damage on the outside, only a blackening around the windows where the frames had burnt.

The house opened directly onto the toad and without a grass verge there would have been no footprints or tyre marks left by the arsonist. The amount of activity that had taken place to bring the fire under control would have destroyed any useful evidence that might have been left behind.

Cautiously he walked up the step and through the doorway where the front door was hanging precariously from its frame; the padlock that had been used to secure it was still looped through the hasp. There was a gaping hole in the roof that allowed the light in showing the charred remains of floorboards and the jagged and burnt edges of the wood that clung to the wall where the staircase had been installed showing how fierce the blaze had been.

Mr Palamakis and his grandsons had cleared the burnt timber and general debris from the stone floor. From the ground he looked up at the beams and roof supports where scorched pieces of plasterboard were hanging precariously. To his inexperienced eye they looked dangerous, ready to fall at any moment. Investigating the building further was not his job and he saw no need to risk an injury when he had the report from Officer Raptakis detailing the extent of the damage sitting on his desk.

Standing back outside he looked across the road. The woman who claimed to have seen the fire start must live in the house opposite.

Kassianae let her curtain drop back into place. She had seen the police car drive through the village and this policeman had walked down to look at the house, entering it briefly, unlike the firemen who had spent most of a day examining the building. She had been expecting a visit from the police before this.

She brushed the crumbs from her tablecloth onto the floor and rubbed her hands on her apron. She checked with her tongue to ensure that her false teeth were in her mouth and pushed some lank hair beneath her scarf. She was ready to receive him now when he knocked.

Inspector Antonakis entered the house warily, inspecting the chair he was offered before sitting down. He did not want to soil his uniform.

'You want to know who I saw entering the house and setting it on fire,' said Kassianae confidently.

Inspector Antonakis held up his hand. 'I would like to start at the beginning and ask the questions, madam. This is your house?'

'Of course.'

'And you sleep here?'

'Where else would I sleep but in my own house?' Kassianae waved her hand towards the bed in the corner.

'Quite. I am trying to ascertain how you could have seen anything taking place in the house if you were asleep in the bed over there.'

'I don't sleep well. You don't as you get older. Whatever you do during the day wears you out and you have a little rest. You go to bed at night and sleep for a while and then you're wide awake again.'

The Inspector nodded. 'So did something wake you up the night when the house was on fire or were you already awake?'

'I was awake. If I had been in bed and asleep I wouldn't have seen anything, would I? I was the person who raised the alarm,' she added importantly.

'So I understand, but we'll get to that a little later. You were awake and lying in your bed....'

'No I wasn't,' Kassianae interrupted him.

Inspector Antonakis frowned. 'You have just told me you were awake.'

Kassianae nodded. 'I was awake, but not lying in my bed. I was sitting here. When I can't sleep I sit here and look out of the window.'

'So you were sitting there and saw something. Can you tell me exactly what you saw?'

'Of course. There's nothing wrong with my memory or eyesight.'

The Inspector smiled encouragingly. At this rate he was going to be in the old lady's cottage all day trying to extract the relevant information from her.

'There's a cat that likes to prowl around at night, often catches a mouse and then torments it. I suppose I ought to go out and send it away, but it's no trouble to me and most times it lets the mouse go free. I was expecting it to appear and then a car arrived. It drove past and I took no more notice of it; just someone arriving home after a late night out. A few minutes later it came back and it wasn't making any noise. It stopped a short way from the house and the driver got out and looked around.'

'Can I stop you, just for a moment? Did you recognise the car?'

Kassianae shook her head. 'It was a dark colour, black blue, maybe green.'

'You say it wasn't making any noise. Do you mean you couldn't hear the engine?'

'Of course that's what I meant.' She glanced at the Inspector scornfully. 'Do you want me to go on?'

'Yes, please. You saw the car stop and the driver get out. What happened then?'

'He went to the boot and looked up and down the street before he opened it. Then he took some things out. I couldn't see what they were because he placed them at the side of the car out of my sight.'

Inspector Antonakis held up his hand. 'If you could see all this and the man was looking up and down the road why didn't he see you watching him?'

'Why should he? I don't sit here with the light on. Anyway,' Kassianae licked her lips, wishing she had asked the policeman to take her over to the taverna, 'he closed the door to the boot very quietly and then picked up two containers. I thought he must be delivering something. He went over to the house and unlocked the door.'

'He unlocked the door?' interrupted Inspector Antonakis. 'Did you see him use a key?'

'Well he didn't break the door down so he must have used a key.' Kassianae glared at him belligerently. The man was stupid.

Inspector Antonakis made a note on his pad. He must find out exactly who was in possession of keys to the property.

'He went upstairs,' continued Kassianae, 'and ....'

'How do you know he went upstairs?'

'I could see the light from his torch.'

'What was he doing upstairs?'

'How do I know? I couldn't see him. All I could see was the light of his torch moving around. After a little while he came back down to the ground floor. I couldn't see what he was doing there either because he had put his torch out.' Kassianae glared at the Inspector. 'A few minutes later he came outside and took something from his pocket. He lit it with his cigarette lighter and threw it inside the house.'

'Did he run back to his car then?'

'Not at once. He stood and watched for a couple of minutes, then went back to his car and drove away.'

'I understand you recognised the man. Can you tell me his name?'

Kassianae shook her head. 'No, I don't know his name. I've seen him up at the house, sometimes with the girl and other times just talking to the builders.'

'If it was dark out there how were you able to recognise him as a familiar face?'

Kassianae pointed across the road. 'The street lamp was on.'

'And when you realised the house was on fire what did you do?'

''Phoned my son, of course.'

'Where does your son live?'

'In the village, just along the road.'

'Do you know where he was when you telephoned?'

'At home, in bed,' replied Kassianae scathingly. 'Where decent people are at that time of night.'

'How did you contact him?'

'I've just told you; I telephoned him.'

'I'm sorry, I didn't make myself clear. Did you telephone him at his house or use a mobile number?'

'I used the number for that little machine he carries around with him. He told me always to use that as he would have it with him wherever he was.'

'Do you know the number?'

'I can't remember things like that at my age. It's written up there on the wall.'

Inspector Antonakis looked where she indicated and there on the wall above her telephone was a string of numbers in red paint.

'Very sensible,' he commented and wrote the number down on his pad. 'Of course, if you used his mobile number he may not have been at home when he received your call.'

'Where else would he have been?'

'Out with friends?' suggested the Inspector.

Kassianae pursed her lips. 'After a day's work he's not likely to stay out late with friends.'

'What work does he do?'

'He's a builder. The best builder in the area. He should have been asked to work on the house. He telephoned the fire brigade and then woke up the other villagers and asked them to help him to extinguish the fire.'

Inspector Antonakis nodded. This agreed with the information he had been given by Fire Officer Raptakis, but it did not mean the man did not have a hand in starting the fire. The old lady could have made up the whole scenario when she recognised the man firing the house to be her son.

'I obviously need to have a word with him, just to get his version of events, you understand.'

'Don't you believe me?'

'Of course, I do, madam, but I have to speak to everyone involved in the incident. Where can I find him?'

'He'll be at work.'

'What time will he return home?'

Kassianae shrugged. 'How would I know? When he's finished the job or done as much as he can today.'

'It might be better if I 'phoned him and asked when it would be convenient to call. I have made a note of his 'phone number and can try to contact him when I have returned to my office. I think that will be all for the time being. Thank you very much for your help.'

The Inspector rose. He had certainly spent long enough in the close atmosphere of the old lady's cottage. He wondered if she ever opened a window.

'That man who came here said there could be a reward for information.'

The Inspector sat down again abruptly. 'Which man was that?'

'I don't know. He came here with the girl asking about the fire.'

'He offered you a reward for your information?'

'He said there might be.' Kassianae was not going to admit that she had asked Giovanni if he was going to pay her.

'I imagine that would be up to Miss Vandersham,' replied the Inspector coldly. Had Mr Pirenzi bribed her to give false information? Maybe her son was involved and she was trying to divert suspicion away from him. 'I might need to visit you again at some time, just to clarify one or two things.'

Kassianae nodded. She was tired and pleased the policeman was leaving. She needed to lie down and have a rest before the taverna brought over her lunch.

Inspector Antonakis walked along the road to the taverna he had seen earlier as he drove through the village. He would call in and have a chat with the owners. They might have some useful information for him.

He seated himself in the shade and asked for a small beer. One would not hurt him, even though he was officially on duty. When the man brought it over the Inspector fumbled in his pocket, but instead of bringing out any money he took out his notebook.

'Would you be able to spare me a few minutes to answer some questions?'

The man nodded. 'My liquor licence is in order and my food certificate is up to date.'

40

'I'm sure it is or you would not have served me. I'd just like to ask you one or two questions relating to the fire that took place up here.'

'I tried with the other villagers to put it out before the engines arrived.'

'I've been talking to the old lady who lives opposite the house. How reliable is she?'

'Old Kassie? She's good for her age. Can't walk very well, but that's her only problem as far as I know.'

'Do you know who raised the alarm?'

'Nikos, I believe. He ran down the street banging on everyone's door and waking them up.'

'So I understand. When he returns from work I'll check that out with him. What work does he do?'

'He's a builder. I'm sure Kassie would have told you.'

'Of course, it had slipped my mind.' The Inspector took another mouthful of his beer.

'He's a decent chap. Looks after his mother well.'

'Does he call in here for a drink at the end of the day or come down in the evening?'

'Occasionally, but he doesn't usually stay late.'

'Did he come for a drink that evening?'

The owner wrinkled his brow. 'I think so, but he may just have called in to say hello on his way home or paid for his mother's meals.'

'You would have remembered if he had stayed late or had imbibed a little too freely?'

'Nikos!' The owner looked at the Inspector incredulously. 'He rarely has more than two beers or a half carafe of wine.'

'Did he stay late?' repeated the Inspector.

'I really don't remember. I suggest you ask his wife. No doubt she would know what time he arrived home.'

'If he has a wife in the village why doesn't she cook for her mother-in-law?'

The taverna owner grinned. 'She used to. Then she bought some fish and after they'd eaten it they were all ill. She accused Stasia of trying to poison her. Stasia took offence and said in future old Kassie would have to cook her own meals. She can't manage that so Nikos arranged for me to take a meal over to her.'

'Would she be at home now?'

'Probably.'

'Then whilst I'm in the village I might as well speak to her. Which house is theirs? Are you able to direct me? His mother simply said 'down the road' which is not a lot of help.'

'It's the next to last house before you reach the forge.'

The Inspector nodded. 'I'll remember. You say her name is Stasia?'

The owner nodded. 'Is that all? I need to get on. I'm hoping some tourists will stop on their way through and I like to have food prepared. They don't usually want to spend too long over a mid-day meal.'

The Inspector walked slowly down the narrow road. Some numbers had been scrawled on the walls beside the doors, but they meant nothing as some of the houses were obviously not occupied and looked in danger of immediate collapse. It was not difficult to find Stasia and Nikos's house. Not only was it in a better state of repair than many of the others, Stasia had obviously washed the shutters that morning and also scrubbed her front step. He knocked on the door and waited for her to answer him.

Stasia pulled open the door and then looked at him in surprise, smoothing her apron and tucking tendrils of hair beneath her scarf.

'I wasn't expecting anyone to be calling. I'm doing my washing. What do you want? Nothing happened to my Nikos, I hope.'

The Inspector removed his cap. 'To the best of my knowledge Nikos is fine. I would just like to ask you a couple of questions about the night of the fire. May I come in?'

Stasia opened the door wider and Inspector Antonakis entered into the small living room. Although crowded with furniture it was spotlessly clean; a marked improvement on Kassianae's house.

Stasia waved a hand at a chair. 'Sit down. Can I offer you some refreshment?'

'A glass of water would be very acceptable, thank you.'

He had no need of the water, having a bottle in his car and recently finished a glass of beer, but did not wish to offend the woman by refusing her hospitality.

Stasia placed the glass on the table before him and sat down in the opposite chair. 'That certainly caused some to do and excitement in the village. Given us something to talk about.'

'I'm sure it has. It isn't every day that such an event occurs.'

Stasia crossed herself. 'I'm thankful for that. Never seen a blaze like that before. Flames shooting up through the roof by the time I got there.'

Inspector Antonakis nodded. 'I understand it was your husband who raised the alarm? His mother said she telephoned him. Where was he when he received the call?'

'In bed, of course.'

'You heard the 'phone call?'

'I would have had a job not to as I was right next to him! He thought it was his mother's house that was on fire and told her to get out. Whilst he was talking to her he was pulling on his trousers.'

'Did he tell you she was safe?'

Stasia nodded. 'He pulled on his T-shirt and stuck his feet into his shoes. As he did so he told me it was the house opposite. He said he would rouse the village and see how bad it was.'

'What did you do?'

'I got up and dressed also. I could hear Nikos banging on the doors of the cottages and waking everyone up. I picked up a couple of buckets and began to go up the road. I called to the women who were coming out of their houses to bring buckets with them.'

'Is that usual?' asked Inspector Antonakis.

'Of course. It takes time for the engines to arrive from Aghios Nikolaos so if there is a fire we try to put it out or at least to contain it before they get here. We form a chain back to the cistern and there's usually a house nearby with a hose pipe that we can use.'

'Do you often have a fire up here?'

Stasia shook her head. 'We had a bad grass fire a few years back, but we stopped that from spreading into the village. Occasionally, if the wind is in the wrong direction, the sparks from the forge can blacken a bit of the garden. You just stamp them out or throw a bucket of water so it doesn't take hold.'

'But you were unable to put out this fire?'

'It was impossible. I arrived soon after Nikos and the flames were already going through the roof. A garden hose pipe wasn't going to be sufficient to tackle that.'

'Quite. I would like to speak to your husband and hear his version of the event. I understand he is at work at present. What time are you expecting him home?'

Stasia shrugged. 'When it suits him. Depends what he's doing. Sometimes he stays a bit later to finish a job, other times he comes home early and returns the following day. He should have been given the restoration job on the house; save him having to travel to other villages.'

'Where is he working today?'

'At Nofalias.'

'So it would be best if I telephoned him?'

'He won't answer if he's up a ladder. You'll have to leave a message.'

'You wouldn't know what time his mother 'phoned him on the night of the fire, I suppose?'

'I didn't stop to look at the clock. It was dark. We waited around for the engines to arrive and when we got back home it was just getting light. No point in going back to bed. We both needed to wash so I put some water on to heat. Whilst we were waiting we had a glass of raki. It's good for steadying the nerves.'

'Thank you. You've been very helpful. I'll not need to trouble you any longer.' The Inspector drank a few mouthfuls of the water.

'It's no trouble.' Once the policeman had left she would go over to her friend and describe the visit she had received. The news would soon be all round the village and neighbours would be calling to hear how she had described the fire to him and the valiant attempts of the villagers to bring it under control.

Inspector Antonakis walked back to his car and tapped in the numbers for Nikos's mobile. As the man was not working too far away it might be useful to drive over and have a word with him now. The mobile 'phone rang unanswered and the Inspector surmised Nikos was working up a ladder. He saw Stasia walk across the road and enter a neighbour's house. This was a close knit community. If Nikos had started the fire it was unlikely that anyone in the village would point a finger at him.

He wondered if the Vandersham woman had contacted Mr Palamakis and asked him to continue with the refurbishment of her house. He must have another word with him and his grandsons; if the work at the house was coming to an end they could have deliberately caused the fire to ensure they had plenty to keep them busy for another couple of months.

The Inspector drove to Nofalias. It was no more than a cluster of cottages set in a small area of farmland. The fields were almost stripped of their produce and women could be seen pulling up the dead stalks and throwing them into a heap. On one side a man was repairing a hole in the wire fence and further along still a man was building a wall. Inspector Antonakis parked on the grass verge and made his way cautiously across the uneven ground to where the man was working.

'Hi, there. Are you Nikos?'

The man looked up and scowled. 'What do you want? I need to get this section finished before my cement goes off.'

'That's quite alright. I tried to 'phone you, but there was no answer.'

'Didn't hear it.'

The Inspector was convinced the man had heard the 'phone as he could see it in his shirt pocket. He had obviously not recognised the number and decided to ignore the call.

'You continue with your work. I just have a few questions I would like to ask you about the fire in Kastelli.'

Nikos did not answer him, but placed two more large stones in position.

'I understand you were at home in bed when it started.'

'That's right.'

'Your mother said she telephoned you and you 'phoned the fire station in Aghios Nikolaos.'

'That's right.'

'What time was that? Do you remember?'

'No. I didn't look at the clock.' Nikos straightened up and looked at the wall critically, pushing a stone a little closer to its neighbour.

'I've been told that you raised the villagers and alerted them to a fire.'

'That's right.' Nikos placed some more cement on his trowel and slapped it deftly onto the wall.

'Would any of them know what time that was?'

'How should I know? Ask them.'

'The fire officer said that when the engines arrived you and the other villagers were trying to put the fire out.'

'That's right.'

'So what did you do when the fire brigade arrived?'

'Left them to it. It's their job.' Nikos placed two more large stones on the wall.

'Did you wait around to see if they were able to put it out?'

'For a while.'

'Why was that?'

'Wanted to make sure it wasn't going to spread to any of the cottages.'

'When you returned home what did you do?'

'Had a wash.'

'Anything else?

'Got ready to go to work.'

'You didn't go back to bed?'

'No point. It was near enough time to get up.'

'How do you usually travel to work?'

'Depends.'

'Depends upon what?' The Inspector was becoming frustrated. Whereas the man's mother had been garrulous it was difficult to get a reply of more than two or three words from her son.

'If it's close by I walk.'

'Did you walk here today?'

'No, I rode my bike.'

'Do you often ride your bike?'

'Depends.'

'On what?' snapped the Inspector.

'If the materials have been delivered to the site I don't need my truck to carry them.'

'Thinking back to the night of the fire, where had you been working that day?'

Nikos took his time about answering. 'I would have been finishing my work in Perambela.'

'What work were you doing?'

'Building an outhouse.'

'Did you take your car to work with you on that occasion?'

'I don't have a car. I told you, I use a truck.'

'I meant truck.' Inspector Antonakis tried to smile an apology. He had deliberately used the word car in the hope of tripping the man up. If he was caught out in one discrepancy he may well have made others. 'When you finished work that day did you visit the taverna during the evening?'

'I may have done. That's not against the law, is it?' Nikos replied belligerently.

'Of course not,' the Inspector assured him. 'I am just trying to get a correct time scale of events. Had you stayed late at the taverna you may well have seen the fire start.'

'I'd not stay that late.'

The Inspector did not reply. The man obviously knew the fire had started in the early hours of the morning. 'Any thoughts on who might have set the fire? Anyone with a grudge against the owner?'

Nikos shrugged. 'No idea. I do my job and let others get on with theirs.' He placed two more stones on the wall and tapped them firmly into place on the mortar before selecting another of a suitable size.

'Well, if you do think of anything that might be useful please contact the police station in Aghios Nikolaos. Thank you for your time.'

Nikos gave a curt nod, his eyes fixed on the wall, checking it was running straight and nothing had deviated during his conversation with the Police Inspector.

Inspector Antonakis walked back across the rough ground to where he had parked his car. It had been a wasted journey. He had gained nothing useful from the man. Driving back to Aghios Nikolaos he turned the information over in his mind.

The builder he had just spoken with seemed surly and defensive; could he have fired the house from spite for not having been offered the work? Mr Palamakis might not have any work once the house was completed; that could be a good reason for him to have set fire to the place. Then there was the old lady in the village. He did not doubt that she had seen the arsonist, but was she trying to shift the blame away from her son? She would certainly have recognised him in the light of the street lamp.

He sat at the interchange waiting for the light to go green to allow him to progress down the road to Aghios Nikolaos. He must visit Mr Palamakis again and also interview Miss Vandersham. If Mr Pirenzi had offered money to Kassianae to give a fictitious account of the happenings that night it could only be to protect the American woman. If she had run out of money to complete the refurbishment of the house she might well have thought a small fire would enable her to claim substantial damages on her insurance policy. There was also the accusation she had made against the building inspector. She might well have started the fire planning to throw the blame on him for trying to become too friendly with her.

The Inspector parked outside the builder's house and knocked on the door. There was no answer and there was a deserted air about the property. Either the builder and his grandsons had taken the opportunity to spend time with other members of their family or they had gone to work elsewhere. He decided he would visit the building inspectors' offices and see if he could speak to Babbis Skourlatakis. He would like to hear his version of the attack he was supposed to have inflicted upon the woman.

Babbis did not seem perturbed to see the Police Inspector sitting in the chair at his desk. 'How can I help?'

'Is there somewhere we could have a few words privately?'

Babbis looked surprised at the request. 'We don't have any private rooms here.'

'Then maybe we could step outside for a few moments.'

Babbis removed his name plate from his desk. 'I won't be long,' he assured his colleague, whilst Alecos smirked; no doubt Babbis's illegal parking had finally caught up with him.

Inspector Antonakis waited whilst Babbis lit a cigarette. 'May as well take advantage of having five minutes.' He sucked in the acrid smoke. 'What can I do for you?'

'I understand you were the building inspector who visited the house in Kastelli.'

Babbis nodded. 'A most unfortunate accident. I understand the house was nearing completion.'

'Miss Vandersham has intimated that you may have been responsible.'

'Me! Why would I do a thing like that?'

'I understand that you and Miss Vandersham had a rather violent confrontation a few weeks earlier. Can you tell me about it?'

Babbis seemed a little embarrassed by the question. 'I wouldn't actually say it was violent. I'd taken the lady out to dinner a few times and I thought we had become friends. I drove up the hill at Plaka to show her the lights on Spinalonga and I got a bit 'carried away'. I thought she had been leading me on during the evening. I tried to take her in my arms and realised I'd misinterpreted the situation. She hit me on the nose and then ran away down the hill.'

'Did you follow her?'

'No, I didn't think it sensible to pursue her. I waited awhile and then drove home.'

'Miss Vandersham seems to think it was a somewhat more serious attack.'

Babbis spread his hands. 'I am a big man. Had I intended to continue to attack Miss Vandersham after she protested I am sure I could have overpowered her quite easily.'

The Inspector nodded. It was as he had surmised. The woman was trying to blame Babbis for the arson as revenge for the attack she felt she had been subjected to at his hands. He wondered if Babbis's wife knew about his philandering but the man's marital relationships were none of his business. Miss Vandersham had not filed an official complaint about the incident and he had no reason to pursue the subject further.

'Well thank you for your time. That's cleared that up for me. I hope you didn't mind me asking. I'm obviously bound to follow up any information that is passed on to me that might have any relevance to the situation.'

'Quite. No problem.' Babbis drew thoughtfully on his cigarette as he watched the Inspector walk away. He re-entered the building and sidled over to Alecos's desk.

'If anyone asks where I was a couple of Fridays ago, I was with you, right?'

Alecos raised his eyebrows. 'Really?'

Babbis nodded. 'Yes. I was with you until about three in the morning. We were playing cards and I lost two hundred Euros to you.'

Alecos shook his head. 'What were you up to that you need to say you were with me?'

'Never you mind.' Babbis tapped the side of his nose. 'What do you think? My wife was away for the weekend. If anyone asks we were together that Friday night playing cards.'

Alecos smirked. 'And you think she's going to find out that you were being entertained elsewhere?'

'Something like that.'

'You lost five hundred Euros to me.'

'Five hundred!'

'At least, or the deal is off.' Alecos sat back in his chair with a self satisfied look on his face. He had done enough favours for Babbis by placing fictitious signatures on documents. It was time the man showed him some proper appreciation.

Babbis scowled. 'Five hundred is a bit steep. I won't be allowed to draw out that amount in one week.'

'I'm a better card player than you. Two fifty tomorrow and the balance by next Tuesday or I have no idea where you were on the night in question.'

'Very well. If you go back on your word you'll regret it.'

'Really?' Alecos glanced at him mockingly.

'I could easily tell the authorities about the false signatures you've placed to sign off work.'

'Prove it. I only do as I'm told. I'm only a filing clerk. Five hundred. If you get a move on you'll be able to get to the bank before they close for the day and withdraw the first instalment.'

Clenching his fists in anger Babbis returned to his desk and picked up his jacket. Five hundred Euros was an extortionate amount. It was almost half his monthly salary. He would have to tell his wife that his new car had cost more than he had anticipated.

Inspector Antonakis saw Mr Palamakis's truck in the queue of traffic ahead of him. It turned to the right and the Inspector promptly changed lanes of traffic so he would also be able to make the right turn when the traffic lights permitted. He knew the driver he had cut across in front of would be cursing him, but as he was in a marked police car they would not even dare to shake their fist at him for fear of being summoned for threatening behaviour.

'Grandpa, it's the police inspector again.' Giorgos called as he opened the door and saw the Inspector standing on the doorstep.

'Ask him in.'

Inspector Antonakis followed Giorgos through to the living room. Mr Palamakis was sitting at the table, the day's newspaper spread out before him.

'What can I do for you?' he asked wearily.

'Just a couple of questions regarding the fire in Kastelli. The work there has been very lucrative for you, no doubt.'

Mr Palamakis nodded. 'It was a good long job.'

'And you were sorry it was nearing completion.'

Mr Palamakis shrugged. 'I knew it would not last forever.'

'You could have decided to extend the work, though. A small fire resulting in work having to be done a second time; then due to the flammable substance used it spread out of control.'

Mr Palamakis glared at Inspector Antonakis. 'I take a pride in my work. I am a respected builder. I would not do anything so stupid or degrading. The work on Miss Vandersham's house was scheduled to be completed within a month and I have other work booked with Mr Iliopolakis in his hotel once the season has finished. If Miss Vandersham wants me to repair the damage and work on her house again until it is completed it is going to be inconvenient for us.'

The Inspector made a note on his pad. He would have to check with Mr Iliopolakis if the builder was due to go and work for him at the end of the season. If that was true the builder would not have had any reason to extend the work in Kastelli.

'Perhaps the builder who lives in the village would be able to help?'

'No builder likes to pick up after another. He would want to do things his way and I know how Miss Vandersham wanted it. I'll be honour bound to complete her work first if she can afford it.'

'You think she may not be able to afford to pay you to continue working there?'

Mr Palamakis shrugged. 'How do I know? She's already spent a good deal of money. She could have pulled the building down and built herself a new house for the amount she has spent, but she was insistent this one had to be repaired. I've complied with her every wish and made sure all was as she wanted to make it look the way it was originally. I'd be hurt now if she turned her back on me and employed someone else.'

'I'm sorry if I offended you. As far as I can ascertain at present you are the only person who would have benefitted from the house being burnt to ensure you had more work up there. It is my duty to investigate.'

'I can assure you that I had no hand in it. I did not even know the fire had occurred until Miss Vandersham telephoned me with the news.'

'As a formality I have to ask where you were during the early hours of that day.'

'At home, in bed, of course.'

'And your grandsons?'

'Ask them. Giorgos, Yiannis, come and speak to the Inspector.'

The two young men emerged from the kitchen where they had been eavesdropping on the conversation.

'I was explaining to your grandfather,' said the Inspector pompously, 'That I have to investigate everything regarding the house fire in Kastelli. Are you able to tell me where you were during that particular night?'

'At home, in bed,' replied Giorgos and the Inspector looked at Yiannis.

'I'd visited a night club in Aghios Nikolaos. I probably left about two in the morning and went straight home.'

'Is there anyone who can vouch for that?'

Yiannis flushed. 'My father complained that I woke him up. I'd had a bit to drink. You know what it's like. The quieter you try to be the more noise you make.'

The Inspector nodded. 'If you would both give me the addresses where you live, please. Then if it becomes necessary I can check out your statements at a later date.'

The boys exchanged glances, but both dutifully wrote down their addresses on the sheet the Inspector tore from his notebook. He folded it and placed it carefully inside. 'I don't think I need to trouble you any further today.'

'Giorgos, see the Inspector out,' ordered Mr Palamakis. 'Then I'm ready for that coffee you were making, Yiannis.'

Inspector Antonakis sat at his desk and typed up the notes he had made of his interview with Kassianae, the taverna owner, Stasia, Nikos and finally Mr Palamakis. His first job the following day would be to request Miss Vandersham to visit his office and then ask her to accompany him to the bank. He would telephone the girl in the morning and insist she came to Aghios Nikolaos to answer some further questions.

Week One – September 2012
Wednesday and Thursday

Ronnie listened to the Inspector and shook her head. 'I am unable to drop everything and come to your office at this moment. I will speak to Mr Pirenzi and ask him if it is convenient for him to accompany me to Aghios Nikolaos tomorrow. I can then telephone you back and advise you of our expected time of arrival.'

'There is no need for Mr Pirenzi to be with you.'

'I would prefer to have him with me. I do not speak Greek and I do not always understand exactly what you are asking me.'

'Very well; if you insist. I will see you tomorrow.'

'Provided that is convenient with Mr Pirenzi.'

'Miss Vandersham, I can issue a warrant for your arrest.'

'Really? What exactly would the charge be? I have not broken any laws since I have been in Crete.'

'You are obstructing the course of justice.' The Inspector closed his 'phone in irritation. He did not want Giovanni Pirenzi there with the girl, advising her that she could refuse to answer his questions or insisting that she had a lawyer present. If she was alone he knew he could intimidate her. He smiled to himself. Mr Pirenzi would not be so sure of himself when he asked him about the money he had offered to the old lady in the village as a reward for identifying the arsonist.

With this comforting thought the inspector telephoned the bank and announced that he would be calling the following day with Miss Vandersham and he would have her permission to examine her accounts.

Ronnie called Giovanni. Despite her response to the Inspector she had been alarmed by the threat of being arrested.

Giovanni chuckled when she told him. 'Take no notice. That's an idle threat. You haven't refused to visit the station. If he was serious about arresting you for any reason he would have come out to Elounda and served the warrant. I'll 'phone him back and inform him that we will be there at eleven. Does that suit you?'

'Thank you, Giovanni. I hope I haven't disrupted your plans.'

'Not at all. I'll see you tomorrow, and don't worry, you'll not be arrested.'

Ronnie settled herself into Giovanni's car. 'I do wish I knew what he wanted to see me about. It's obviously not to tell me that an arrest has been made or he wouldn't have accused me of obstructing justice.'

'Well, I suppose if he wanted you to go and identify someone he could say you were obstructing justice by delaying your visit until today.'

'If that is what he wants why didn't he say so? I really do not like him. Oh, Giovanni, do you think Babbis is accusing me of assault and blackmail?'

'If that is the problem then you refuse to answer any questions until you have a lawyer present. Even if they decide to place you in a cell you say nothing. I'll contact a lawyer and we'll apply for bail and you'll be out in a couple of hours.'

Ronnie turned distressed eyes to Giovanni. 'Would you really be able to get me out so quickly? I wouldn't want to have to spend the night in gaol.'

'They tell me the conditions have improved,' replied Giovanni gravely, then smiled. 'Ronnie, I'm sure you have nothing at all to worry about. Look at me each time he asks you a question and if I nod you can answer. If I frown and shake my head you say nothing. Speak out immediately if you don't understand what he's saying and I'll explain it to you.'

Comforted by the assurances she received from Giovanni Ronnie sat back, but throughout the journey she could not help wondering why the Inspector needed to speak to her unless Babbis had registered a complaint.

Inspector Antonakis frowned in annoyance when Giovanni moved his chair around so that he was sitting at an angle where Ronnie could see him. He knew she would be taking advice from the business man.

'Thank you for coming to the station, Miss Vandersham. If you had been able to come in as I requested yesterday this matter could have been cleared up by now.'

Ronnie raised her eyebrows. 'Inspector, neither Mr Pirenzi nor I are sitting doing nothing in case you wish to speak to me. If it was that important why didn't you drive out to Elounda?'

'It would have been a wasted journey for me. I require your permission to examine your bank account.'

'Why?'

'We need to be sure that Mr Palamakis has been truthful in his statements regarding the payments you have made to him.'

'And if I refuse?'

'I can apply for a warrant. I understand that a considerable sum has been withdrawn from your account over the previous few months. There could be money laundering involved.'

'What!' Ronnie gasped. 'That stupid accusation against Mr Iliopolakis and myself was dropped by the bank in Heraklion. My mother transferred her savings into my American account for me to use for repairing and refurbishing the house.'

The Inspector waved his hand dismissing the statement. 'Wherever the money came from I believe you spent far more than you intended and hoped to make a substantial claim on your insurance company after setting a fire at your house.'

'That is quite ridiculous,' snapped back Ronnie. 'I have no insurance on the house.'

The statement from Ronnie took the Inspector by surprise. 'You have no insurance?'

'I saw no need to take out insurance until the house was completed. Mr Palamakis assured me that if he or his grandsons caused any damage whilst they were working there he had insurance and the problem would be rectified without any cost to myself.'

The Inspector frowned. Without insurance to cover the damage there would have been no reason for the woman to fire her own property.

Ronnie looked at Giovanni. 'I really do not see the necessity for you to pry into Miss Vandersham's financial affairs,' he said firmly.

'It is a part of our enquiry. We have a legal right to pursue any avenue we think will be helpful in solving a case.'

Giovanni leaned forward. 'You have no grounds to issue a warrant for an investigation unless you have strong evidence suggesting money laundering. If you approach the bank in Heraklion you will find the accusation originally brought against Mr Iliopolakis and Miss Vandersham was proved to be groundless. If you make a further false accusation against Miss Vandersham, and when it has been proved incorrect yet again, I believe Miss Vandersham would be within her legal right to sue you.'

'If Miss Vandersham has nothing to hide she will not object to her accounts being examined,' snapped back the Inspector.

'If Miss Vandersham gives permission for her accounts to be scrutinized she has every right to be there with you. She could obviously answer immediately any questions that might arise,' answered Giovanni smoothly.

'I have spoken to the manager and he will be happy for the enquiry to be conducted in the privacy of his office this morning. Provided all is in order there will be no need to remove any papers or proceed further.' Inspector Antonakis was annoyed. The woman would never have thought of suing the police force if Mr Pirenzi had not suggested it.

Ronnie looked at Giovanni and he nodded. 'Better to get this meeting out of the way immediately. It could help the Inspector to clear his mind of unfounded suspicions.'

Ronnie suppressed a smile. She knew her accounts were in order.

The bank manager smiled at Ronnie. He had checked with his head office that allowing her to withdraw as much as she wished from her American account and converting it into Euros was well within the law. She was not subject to the same withdrawal restrictions as the Greek citizens.

'So how can I be of assistance?'

'Inspector Antonakis suspects me of money laundering. He would like to ensure that the money I withdrew to pay Mr Palamakis was for the work he had undertaken. The bank kept a copy of each bill I presented from Mr Palamakis and how much I withdrew to pay him. These bills can all be checked with Mr Palamakis and the work verified. I give you permission to disclose the balance on my American account that is used solely for the building work.'

Inspector Antonakis cleared his throat. 'I would like more than your current balance, Miss Vandersham. I would appreciate having a copy of all your transactions regarding the house at Kastelli.'

The bank manager raised his eyebrows and looked at Ronnie who nodded. 'I have nothing to hide. Maybe you can tell me the amount of recompense I can expect for being wrongly accused of money laundering?'

'You have not been accused of money laundering,' replied the Police Inspector angrily. 'I said we had to investigate to ensure there had not been any money laundering.'

'That was certainly not the impression you gave to me. You doubted my word and threatened to issue a warrant allowing you to investigate if I did not give permission for you to access my account. That amounts to an accusation in my eyes.'

Giovanni smiled to himself. Ronnie could certainly hold her own against the police inspector. When the sheets of paper ceased churning out from the printer the inspector held out his hand, but Ronnie forestalled him.

'I wish to ascertain that this is my building account before I pass these papers over to you.' She took her time running her eyes down the columns of figures and finally handed the papers to Inspector Antonakis.

'I will need to take these away with me.'

Ronnie looked at the bank manager. 'Is that in order? My financial affairs are my private concern. I would prefer the papers did not leave the bank premises.'

Giovanni leaned forward. 'Miss Vandersham is quite within her rights to say the papers should remain in the safe keeping of the bank.'

'I need to check the amounts with the bills Mr Palamakis has.'

'Then ask Mr Palamakis for the bills and bring them to the bank and check them here.'

The Inspector glared at Ronnie. 'You say this account is used solely for the purpose of rebuilding your house. Do you have a personal account?'

'Yes, there was a large sum deposited in there from the bank in Heraklion. I have used some of it to pay bills rather than continually withdraw small amounts from America as that incurs bank charges.'

'And where did this large sum come from? Was it also transferred from America?'

Ronnie shook her head. 'It was money that I found hidden away at the house by the old lady. It was all in drachma notes and Mr Iliopolakis took me to the bank in Heraklion. They investigated and decided the money was legally mine and converted the value into Euros for me.'

'How very fortunate for you,' Inspector Antonakis commented sarcastically.

'It has been a great help.'

'Have you used this to cover your living expenses?'

'I am an artist,' explained Ronnie. 'I am contracted to one of the gift shops in Plaka to supply them with paintings and I also sell to individual tourists. My work permit is in order.'

The Inspector raised his eyebrows. 'And this art work brings you in enough money to live on?'

'During the height of the season I have sufficient.'

'I would like to inspect any other accounts that are held in your name.'

Ronnie shrugged, looked first at Giovanni, who nodded and then at the bank manager. 'I give permission for you to show Inspector Antonakis my personal account. I don't have any others.'

Inspector Antonakis examined the statements that the bank manager produced. Apart from the one large sum that had been deposited there had been nothing added to the balance and only half a dozen small withdrawals within the limit allowed. That could mean that the woman had saved up the cash to pay Kassianae and her son, Nikos.

'Do you have any receipts for the payments you made with the sums you withdrew?'

'No, I wasn't given any. I paid them to Mr Skourlatakis. I needed him to provide the necessary certificate to say the house was structurally sound and the builders could safely work there. I considered the certificates were as good as receipts. Later there was other work that needed to be inspected before the builders could progress.'

Inspector Antonakis pushed back his chair. 'I need you to return to the police station with me,' he announced. 'I have some further questions I need to ask of you. I will wait for you outside.'

The manager smiled at Ronnie. 'You need not be concerned. Your affairs are in order. I will lock these papers in the safe until you authorise me to dispose of them.'

Ronnie looked at Giovanni who nodded. 'Without your

permission or a warrant Inspector Antonakis had no right to remove the papers from the bank. He knew that and I expect this will be the last you hear of the matter.'

'I hope so. I wouldn't want Mr Palamakis to be in any trouble.'

'Provided he has not altered any of the bills for less than you paid him to evade his taxes he has nothing to worry about.' Giovanni shook the bank manager's hand. 'Thank you for your co-operation.'

'Why do you think the Inspector wants us to return to the police station?' asked Ronnie.

Giovanni shrugged. 'Probably to give me a parking ticket. I left my car in the police compound which is for official police transport only.'

Ronnie giggled. 'You are awful, Giovanni.'

'Not at all. You know how difficult it can be to find a parking place in Aghios Nikolaos. If he wanted us at the police station he should be willing to provide us with a parking space.'

They followed Inspector Antonakis back down the hill to the police station and he ushered them into his office.

The inspector fixed Ronnie with an icy stare. 'I have made a number of enquiries. I think you conspired with Nikos, the builder in the village, and arranged for him to set fire to your house. You withdrew those sums from the bank to pay him and then paid a further sum to his mother to identify Babbis Skourlatakis. It was an act of petty revenge on your part for the assault you say took place.'

'That's not true. I don't even speak Greek well enough to make arrangements like that with anyone.'

'You have a number of friends whose language abilities are beyond question. Mr Pirenzi I believe you offered the old lady money on Miss Vandersham's behalf.'

Giovanni shook his head. 'Kassianae asked me if there would be a reward for her information. I said that would be up to Miss Vandersham once there had been a conviction.'

'So if I arrested Babbis Skourlatakis you would pay the woman for saying she had seen him?'

Giovanni frowned at Ronnie. 'I have never considered the possibility,' she said firmly.

Inspector Antonakis sighed. 'I'm sorry, Miss Vandersham, but I do not believe you. I have to insist that you hand your passport over to me.'

'Why? Are you arresting me?'

'Not at this stage, but I am not prepared to risk you leaving the country.'

Ronnie looked at him in amazement. 'Why would I do that? I had nothing to do with the fire.' She turned to Giovanni. 'Do I have to relinquish my passport?'

'I'm afraid so. It is an official request. It will only be a temporary arrangement. You will have it returned to you within a few days.'

'That will depend.' The Inspector spoke ominously as Ronnie took her passport from her bag and handed it across the desk.

Close to tears Ronnie left the police station with Giovanni. 'What can I do?' she asked. 'How can I prove that I had nothing to do with the fire? That I didn't ask anyone to start it or pay the old lady to give false information?'

Giovanni patted her shoulder consolingly. 'We'll go back to the house and have a word with Marianne. She studied international law and will know how best to proceed.'

Marianne listened to Giovanni's account of their visit to the police station.

'I don't think this police inspector has any evidence against you at all. He wants to make an arrest and you are an easy target being a foreigner. He knows if he accused Babbis Skourlatakis the man would talk himself out of the charge or hire a solicitor. Nikos wouldn't know where to start.'

'What do you mean?' asked Ronnie.

'Babbis is well educated and has a certain amount of knowledge of the law, particularly as it relates to building. Nikos probably left school at about fourteen. He might be an excellent builder, but that is the extent of his knowledge.'

Ronnie looked at Marianne hopefully. 'Do you think the Police Inspector is deliberately trying to frame Nikos?'

'He's a convenient person to blame – lives in the village, was not offered the work at your house, and was alerted to the fire by his mother and called the emergency services.'

'If his mother hadn't asked for a reward I doubt if the Inspector would have taken much notice of the man.' Giovanni shook his head. 'She's the kind of old woman who would expect to be paid if she told you what day of the week it was. Thank goodness I only bought her a glass of whisky.'

'You should have told her there was no reward.'

'If I had done that she would probably have denied ever seeing anyone at the house that night,' replied Giovanni grimly.

'Now the police are saying I paid Nikos to set the house alight and promised to pay his mother to say it was someone else that she had seen. I don't even know who Nikos is,' finished Ronnie desperately.

Giovanni grinned at her. 'I expect you do. He's the man whose ears stick out.'

'Oh! Him. I've seen him around up there a few times but only ever said hello to him. He just nodded to me and walked on. I don't really know anyone up there. Kyriakos visited the villagers and assured them I was not going to claim back their cottages or start asking for rent. I met the men from the forge a couple of times, but I left Mr Palamakis to deal with them once I'd approved the design for the iron work and agreed the price. I've not spent very much time actually in the village. After I finished clearing out the house last year I went up a few times to check that the ideas I had for renovation were feasible. The only time I was up there alone this year was when I first visited and found I was denied access. Since then I was always meeting Mr Palamakis or Babbis.'

Giovanni picked up his car keys. 'I'll drive up to Kastelli and have a word with Nikos. Let him know what's going on.'

'Don't be foolish, Giovanni.' Marianne spoke to her husband sharply. 'If that policeman knows you've been up there and talked to Nikos he'll probably accuse you of perverting the course of justice or some such trumped up charge. No,' Marianne shook her head, 'There must be another way to deal with this.'

'Suppose Ronnie hired a lawyer? He would have the right to speak to Nikos.'

'That's it.' Marianne smiled. 'I'll telephone Adam. I'm sure he would be willing to give us some advice.'

'Who's Adam?' asked Ronnie.

'Long story,' smiled Marianne. 'We met in Athens years ago and he sorted out a big problem. He then helped again when that idiot set fire to the chalets.'

'We did say he was welcome to come for a visit and bring his wife with him. Offer him a holiday here with us and we could at least discuss the situation with him. Don't worry, Ronnie. I'm sure everything will get sorted out. Forget your problems and go and do some painting.'

'I ought to speak to Nicola whilst I'm here. Is she around?'

'Probably down on the beach with the girls, making the most of the last of the summer weather.'

'May I go down?'

'Of course. Have you got a costume with you?'

Ronnie shook her head. 'I hadn't expected to have any time to go for a swim today.'

'Hold on, I'll find you one of Nicola's. She won't mind you borrowing it and you can change up here. She'll probably be pleased to have some help with the girls if she's on the beach on her own with them.'

Remembering how reluctant the girls had been to become

friends with her the last time they were together she was doubtful that she would be able to help Nicola with them.

Nicola was sitting close to the sea in the secluded cove watching the girls carefully as they ran in and out of the gentle waves. She turned her head briefly and raised her hand to Ronnie.

Ronnie sat down beside her. 'If you want to go in and have a swim I'll keep an eye on them for you.'

'I'd love to, but they'll try to follow me and if you stop them all hell will be let lose.'

'Why don't we take them in together? Then when they've decided I'm not going to drown them they'd probably be happy enough to stay with me for a while.'

'You take Lisa. She's not as brave and fearless as Jo.'

Ronnie sighed. 'Fine, but just tell me which one is which. I have problems knowing them apart when they're dressed. In their costumes and with wet hair they look identical to me.'

'Lisa,' called Nicola and they both looked round at their mother. 'Lisa come here a moment and let me speak to you.'

One little girl began to walk towards Nicola, followed by her sister.

Nicola put out her hand. 'Why have you come, Jo? I asked for Lisa.'

'Why?' asked Joanna.

'Do you remember the lady who played at being a big bear and was looking for someone to make her a cup of tea?'

They both nodded and looked towards Ronnie.

'She would like to go in the sea, but I said she could only go for a swim if we went in with her. If Lisa held her hand and I held Jo's hand we could go a long way out.'

'Up to my chin?' asked Lisa.

'Up to my eyes,' said Jo immediately.

'The sea water would make your eyes hurt. We'll only go out as far as your chins.'

The girls exchanged glances and then nodded in unison.

'That's good,' said Nicola, rising to her feet. 'Lisa, you take Ronnie's hand and I'll look after Jo.'

Ronnie felt a small hand clutching her own and then another holding her other hand. She looked at Nicola in despair. 'I definitely need help.'

'They've just realised how they can confuse everyone and think it's a great game.' Nicola walked into the sea and then knelt down. 'I'm up to my chin,' she declared.

Joanna let go of Ronnie's hand and strode towards her mother. 'I'm not,' she announced and Nicola stood up.

'This is Jo,' she said to Ronnie, 'so you have Lisa.'

For over half an hour they played with the girls in the water, allowing them to hold onto their shoulders as they swam, jumping up and down so the sea reached their chins and whirling then around whilst both girls emitted shrieks of laughter. Finally Ronnie felt Lisa give a little shiver and called to Nicola.

'I think Lisa is getting cold.'

Nicola nodded. 'Come on, girls. Time for a drink and a biscuit.'

Swathed in towels, a drink in one hand and a biscuit in the other the girls sat happily between their mother and Ronnie.

'It's my turn to have a swim now,' declared Nicola. 'You two are to stay here with Ronnie. You are not to come into the sea. Understand?'

The girls looked at each other. There were other ways to alarm their mother's friend who did not understand when they spoke to her.

As soon as Nicola had swum a short distance from the shore the girls shrugged off their towels and stood up. One ran to the right and the other the left, giggling as Ronnie called their names ineffectually. Ronnie caught one easily, but was unable to catch the other being hampered by the child she had in tow. She had no option but turn their mischievousness into a game. She ran first to one and caught her, then let her go whilst she caught her sister, repeating the process until neither girl was able to run any more as they were laughing too much to get their breath. Nicola had watched the antics that were taking place on the beach, knowing full well that she could swim strongly enough to reach the shore before either girl managed to get more than a few steps into the sea.

'That was a good game,' commented Nicola as she emerged from the sea.

'It was hot and exhausting. I'm handing them back to you now whilst I go and have a swim to cool down.'

Ronnie ran the few steps down to the sea and waded into the cool water gratefully. She was pleased to have been able to look after the girls and allow Nicola to have a swim, but it was not something she was prepared to repeat every day. She floated on her back and squinted up at the sun, then looked towards Spinalonga. The island was no longer sunlit, but a short distance away the sun was glinting on the water and she wondered if she would be able to reproduce that effect in a painting.

Ronnie allowed herself to drift back to the beach and sat down beside Nicola. 'I actually came down to talk to you.'

'Oh, I forgot. You had to go into see that police inspector with Giovanni. How did it go?'

Ronnie shrugged. 'He's now trying to say that I paid Nikos to start the fire and offered his mother money to implicate Babbis. He also made me relinquish my passport.'

'The man's a fool,' announced Nicola. 'What did Giovanni say?'

'We came back here and he spoke to Marianne. She suggested that she 'phoned someone called Adam and asked his advice.'

Nicola nodded. 'He's a nice man and knows what he's doing. He won't let that inspector bully him. Don't worry. I'm sure you'll get your passport back within a few days.'

'Well I'm not planning on going anywhere at the moment. I wanted to ask you about getting married.'

Nicola raised her eyebrows.

'Kyriakos has asked me to marry him.'

'And ?'

Ronnie shook her head. 'That's what I wanted to ask you about. What did you have to produce in the way of paper work to get permission to marry John?'

'Oh, loads of unnecessary stuff. I had to go up to Heraklion to the American Embassy, fill in forms and answer questions, produce my birth certificate and passport. I needed a certificate from America to say there was no impediment to me getting married.'

'Like what?' asked Ronnie.

'Well, if I was still married to someone else I would be acting illegally so I would have had to produce my divorce papers. If I was a wanted criminal and stupid enough to apply to get married they could have arrested and extradited me. After they had investigated there had to be an Affidavit in Greek and English saying there was no reason why we shouldn't marry. We both had to sign that before a Consular Officer then all the papers had to be submitted to the priest who was going to officiate at our wedding. We had to publish in the newspapers the details of our parents along with our mother's maiden names and where we planned to get married.'

'That just sounds time consuming, but would be no problem to me.' Ronnie felt reassured by Nicola's words.

'It became a bit complicated with us as John was born in America and I was born in Athens. There was no problem regarding John's parents. They were married here and Giovanni adopted John officially. My side was more difficult. Dad had to send copies of his birth certificate, their marriage certificate and all the papers relating to him becoming an American citizen. Would you believe they wanted to know what his father did during the war? Fortunately Dad was able to produce Grandpa's death certificate and also his discharge papers from the Greek Army due to ill health.'

'Suppose your Greek grandfather had worked for the Nazis or been involved in the black market?'

'I don't know. I suppose they could have refused me permission to live here permanently and I would have had to go backwards and forwards to the States to renew my visa.'

'Do they always look into your family background?'

'As far as I know. It's time consuming and frustrating but I doubt if you would have any real problem.'

'Mmm. I'm not sure.'

'Not sure whether to marry Kyriakos or not sure if you would have a problem?'

'Both He seems to think that we could go and live with his mother and I've said I won't contemplate that. I've told him I need to get the fire at the house sorted out before I give him an answer.'

'Is that delaying tactics?'

'Yes and no. I need to be sure that Babbis is not going to sue me for assault and blackmail and I need to make certain he is prosecuted for the arson he committed. I don't feel I can make a sensible decision until that has been sorted out. I wouldn't want to agree to marry Kyriakos and then find out I was being deported or sentenced to a term of imprisonment.'

'That's not likely to happen,' Nicola assured her. 'I'm sorry I've not been much help to you.'

'I just hope this friend Adam can sort out the truth and the police inspector believes him.'

'I'm sure he will. Do you want to come back and have a quick shower or are you going in for another swim?'

'I'd love a shower; then I can dress properly and go up to see Kyriakos.' Ronnie frowned. 'I should have gone up earlier and told him about the police visit.'

'You don't have to tell him you came for a swim. You could have been kept waiting for hours in Aghios Nikolaos.'

'Better that I tell him. I can make the excuse that I was waiting to hear the result of Marianne's 'phone call.'

Nicola began to pack away the beach items.

'Buckets and spades,' she said to the girls in English.

'I can take them,' offered Ronnie, but Nicola shook her head.

'They have to be responsible for whatever they bring down to play with. If I was willing to carry everything most of their toys would be down here along with their bikes and dolls' pushchairs.' Nicola reverted to Greek. 'Come along, girls. Time to go home and have a shower and your tea and when Daddy comes home you can tell him about the game you played with Ronnie.'

'Caught you,' said Joanna and placed her arms around Ronnie's legs.

'Caught you,' echoed Lisa and tried to push her sister out of the way.

Nicola spoke sternly to both of them and Joanna released Ronnie's legs.

'This is when I'm lost,' admitted Ronnie. 'I don't know how to tell them in Greek when I want them to do something.'

'They understand English pretty well. We tend to speak Greek at home and explain something to Marcus if necessary. John and I play a game with the girls; we ask them to fetch toys or food using the English word. They'll learn it when they go to school, but there's nothing like being brought up speaking both languages from when you're a baby. They're beginning to be able to string a few words together. My mother was so envious of Marianne when they visited Greece. Even when Mum had lived here for a couple of years she still hadn't picked up more than the odd word or two. Dad was determined that I learnt and I'm certainly grateful to him now.'

Ronnie shook her head. 'Now you tell me!'

Nicola ushered the girls into the bathroom whilst Ronnie went into the kitchen to speak to Marianne.

'Were you able to speak to your friend Adam?'

'All sorted. He's arriving on Friday and bringing his wife with him. I didn't tell him the whole story, just that you were an

American friend whose house had been set on fire and was now being accused of doing it herself. I thought it better to let you tell him the details.'

'Do you think that police inspector will take any notice of him?'

'Adam is a legal representative at the American Embassy in Athens. If he agrees that you are being falsely accused and acts on your behalf the police have to take notice of him.'

Ronnie swallowed. 'His fee must be enormous. I'm not sure if I can afford to have him as my lawyer.'

Marianne shrugged. 'I doubt that will be a problem. Once he's sorted everything out you can start to claim compensation from the police and the arsonist. You should have more than enough to pay Adam.'

'If you say so,' replied Ronnie doubtfully. 'I am very grateful to you, Marianne.'

Ronnie walked up the hill to Kyriakos's taverna deep in thought. Nicola saying that her grandfather's activities had been looked into before she was given permission to marry John and live permanently in Crete gave her no reassurance. If she concealed that her father was in prison by using her stepfather's death certificate her true father's name would be on her birth certificate and her duplicity would be discovered immediately. She was in enough trouble at the moment without adding to her problems.

Kyriakos greeted her with relief when she arrived at the taverna.

'I thought you had been arrested. I expected you to return from Aghios Nikolaos early this afternoon.'

Ronnie smiled shakily at him. 'I began to think they were going to arrest me. I have had to surrender my passport. The police are now saying that I paid Nikos to set fire to my house and bribed his mother to say she saw Babbis.'

'That is ridiculous,' stated Kyriakos. 'Why would you want to set fire to your own house?'

'As revenge for Babbis attacking me. As far as I was concerned I had my revenge by taking his car keys and humiliating him before his colleagues. Giovanni says I'm not to worry and Marianne has 'phoned someone she knows at the American Embassy. He is coming over next week and she says he'll sort everything out. Whilst I was at their house I went for a swim and helped Nicola with the girls for an hour.'

'So you had some pleasure from the day. That is good.'

'I should have come up here and helped you. I feel guilty now about going for a swim and leaving you to manage on your own.'

'It was no problem. My mother came up and helped carry out the dishes and clear the tables afterwards.'

'That was kind of her.'

'She is a kind lady.' Kyriakos looked at Ronnie meaningfully.

'I'm sure she is,' smiled Ronnie. However kind Kyriakos's mother might be she had no intention of living with her.

'What would you like to eat later?'

'Whatever you have left.'

Kyriakos shook his head. 'You do not eat the leftovers. Tell me what you would like to eat and the chef will prepare it for you with fresh food.'

'You cannot waste food, Kyriakos.'

'It will not be wasted. If it cannot be saved for tomorrow I will eat it.'

'So if you can eat it, why can't I?' Ronnie smiled.

'Because, Miss Ronnie, only the best is good enough for you,' he said earnestly.

Ronnie felt herself blush and tears coming into her eyes. If only her life had not been complicated by her father's criminal activities it would have been easy for her to give Kyriakos the answer he wanted.

Inspector Antonakis visited Mr Palamakis and insisted that he handed over all his paid bills relating to materials and labour for the house in Kastelli. Grudgingly Mr Palamakis acquiesced and the inspector carried the thick folder down to the bank and demanded the use of the manager's office to check the amounts against Ronnie's bank statements. To the Inspector's annoyance, after two hours work, he could not find any discrepancy in the amounts withdrawn from America and the sums paid to the builder.

Week One – September 2012
Friday, Saturday and Sunday

Adam and his wife, Melina, arrived in Heraklion and hired a car to drive down to Elounda. As they drove down the hill Adam slowed to enable his wife to admire the spectacular view.

Melina caught her breath. 'I could never have imagined anywhere to be so beautiful. What is the island over there? Is there a hotel on it?'

'Not that I know of, unless, of course, Yannis has expanded his business. It was originally a leper colony and it has become a tourist attraction.'

'Really?' Melina raised her eyebrows. 'Are the lepers still there?'

'No, they were sent back to the hospital in Athens over fifty years ago. It's completely abandoned and deserted, except for the hundreds of tourists every day, of course.'

'What is there to see?'

'I don't know. I've never spent long enough down here to visit.'

'Well, we're here for two weeks and you are supposed to be on holiday so maybe we could go over one day.'

Adam smiled. 'I'm sure it can be arranged. I've only been asked to give this American woman some advice in exchange for their hospitality so when I've spoken to her tomorrow the rest of my time should be at your disposal.'

'That will make a change. Even on a day out in Athens you seem to have to abandon me and rush off on urgent business.'

'It won't happen this time,' Adam promised her. 'Once I've heard the full story from this American and given her whatever advice I can offer it will be job done. We'll spend a few days here, then drive up to Heraklion and then on to Chania. You'll have to look in the guide and see where you want to visit en route.'

Melina glanced at her husband doubtfully; somehow she found his assurances hard to believe.

Marianne and Giovanni greeted Adam effusively. 'Why haven't you come over here for a holiday before?' asked Giovanni. 'You know we said you were always welcome.'

Adam shrugged and looked at his wife. 'I met Melina and devoted most of my spare time to courting her. We went over to America for our honeymoon and to enable her to meet my relatives. Our return flight was delayed due to a thunder storm. You know what it's like, a ten minute delay in take off means you have to wait another hour to get a slot. We were about two hours into our flight when we had to turn back as there was an engine malfunction. That delayed us for another thirty six hours. By the time we arrived in England we had missed our connection of course and had to wait to be allocated space on the next available flight.'

'Weren't you frightened when they said there was an engine malfunction?' asked Marianne. 'I would have been petrified that we were going to crash.'

Adam smiled. 'We had three other engines and they assured us we were perfectly safe. We were only turning back as a safety precaution. It was just an annoying waste of time. When we finally arrived back in Athens the Embassy were not amused that I had returned to work almost a week later than scheduled, despite having a good excuse. Work had piled up and I didn't even have a weekend off for a couple of months. I was expecting Melina to divorce me.'

Melina touched her husband's hand and winked. 'It was a

near thing. My parents were becoming most upset. I would visit them on my own and they were convinced there was some big rift between us that I wouldn't admit to. Fortunately once Adam was able to have some time to himself we visited them together and they realised the problem had been all of their own making.'

'So why didn't you give us a call and ask to come here for a holiday the following year?' asked Giovanni.

'We had to spend part of that holiday visiting Melina's relatives so we went to Volos and stayed with her aunt and uncle. They were very good and took us around the area. We were able to go to Meteora and visit the monasteries. That is an experience that I can recommend if you are ever over there.'

'They are amazing,' added Melina. 'So dramatic, perched up on the top of mountain peaks they look as if they are floating in the clouds and the views from them are spectacular.'

'Do the monks still live there?' asked Giovanni.

'A few, but mostly the monasteries are just tourist attractions. You can drive most of the way up a road to them. You don't have to be hauled up in a basket any more. I had to go to Lesbos for a few months and Melina was able to join me there. No sooner was I back in Athens than I was being sent away to another island. When I finally had some leave we decided to spend our time quietly in Athens and renovate our apartment. This is our first real holiday since our honeymoon.'

'And we have to ask you to come and sort out a problem! That doesn't seem very fair,' observed Marianne.

'From your telephone call it sounds quite straight forward; just a rather officious policeman that needs to have indisputable facts presented to him. Who is this lady that has a problem?'

'You'll meet her tomorrow. I've asked her to come down in the morning. She couldn't come this evening as she was helping her friend at his taverna.'

Adam nodded. He was quite pleased to have the evening free to enable him to renew his acquaintanceship with the family. 'Tell me what you have all been doing since I was here last. Did John make a full recovery from his burns?'

Marianne smiled. 'Well, we thought he had; then he began to have a problem with his eyesight. Fortunately Saffie had contacts at the hospital in England and was able to have him seen by a specialist. A small piece of his skull was fractured and affecting his optic nerve. The surgeon sorted that out and put in a metal plate. The day he was discharged from hospital he was involved in a car accident and ended up in hospital again with a fractured cheek bone and eye socket. Poor Nicola was going frantic.'

'She didn't go to England with him?'

'She didn't want to leave the girls.'

Adam raised his eyebrows.

'John and Nicola have twin girls. They're absolutely delightful and we are all besotted with them. We have to be very strict with ourselves so we don't spoil them. They decided it would be best to keep them quietly in their rooms when you arrived so we could sit and talk. Once the girls are in bed and asleep John and Nicola will join us and you can meet their children tomorrow.'

'The rest of the family? Are they well?'

'Grandma died. It was rather a shock although she was a hundred. She had appeared quite fit and well the day before, just complained that she was a little tired. Aunt Ourania is becoming very confused, but most of the time she seems contented enough when Uncle Yannis is with her. Grandma Marisa is very patient with her.'

'You may have to excuse Aunt Ourania if she makes some strange remarks and behaves rather oddly,' added Marianne. 'As Giovanni said, she's becoming very confused. We tend to just agree with her otherwise she often becomes quite angry. I know Uncle Yannis is worried that she may end up the same as her mother; she had to have specialist care towards the end.'

'Are your other relatives still living with you?' asked Adam, preferring to move away from Ourania's problems.

'You mean Bryony and Marcus? They are still here. I don't think either of them would want to go back to New Orleans now. Hurricane Katrina was a blessing in disguise for them.'

'And the business?'

'Going from strength to strength, thanks to you,' Giovanni assured Adam. 'I'll have to show you the new apartments we built after the fire. It was due to you that we were able to get back on our feet. If you hadn't managed to get so much compensation money from that American we would have ended up with nothing.'

'Your uncle would still have had his shop.'

'He only spends a few hours up there each day and doesn't buy new stock. He said he planned to retire when he was eighty but he can't quite let go. He insists on going over the accounts with me each month to ensure everyone has paid their rent up to date on his other shops.'

'Surely he trusts you to keep accurate accounts?'

Giovanni smiled. 'I know he does, but it's his way of letting me know that he is still in charge of his financial affairs and making sure that I am doing everything the way he wants. I tried to give him a spread sheet one month and he said it was gibberish and he needed to see hand written figures in a ledger.' Giovanni sighed. 'I always did have a problem making him keep up with the latest technical progress.'

Bryony looked out from the kitchen. 'Shall I begin to set out the food?' she asked. 'I doubt that John and Nicola will be much longer and if I tell Uncle Yannis we are ready it will give him time to remind Aunt Ourania that we have visitors.'

'Let Grandma Marisa know also, please Bryony.'

Bryony smiled. 'No need. She's been sitting in the kitchen with me for the last half an hour.'

'How do you cope with such a large family?' asked Melina. 'My grandparents lived with us when they were old, but there were never more than six of us in the house.'

'I'm just used to having a house full, I suppose. Uncle Yannis realised his aunt and uncle needed to be cared for so he made sure they had their own rooms here. You'll have noticed that your room has a wide doorway and there are grab rails in the bathroom. We have disconnected the alarm system as it isn't really necessary now. I don't think Uncle Yannis was expecting to end up with such a houseful of people. Giovanni and I arrived with John so he added on our suite, then when Bryony and Marcus came he added their rooms on upstairs. We can all be private if we wish. The only thing we do have to share is the kitchen.'

'Don't you get under each other's feet?' asked Melina.

Marianne shook her head. 'It means there is always someone around if the older people need anything or to keep an eye on the girls. We all have designated jobs and share the cooking and the housework. Marcus is invaluable. He cleans all the windows inside and out every month and keeps the patio and driveway clean, along with the same work at the self catering.'

'Don't you have chamber maids?'

'Of course, but they really only deal with the rooms. If someone has spilled a bottle of wine on the patio they let Marcus know and he will go and scrub the tiles. The girls don't find it easy to reach to the top of the windows and it isn't practical for them to carry a step ladder around. Marcus can usually reach from the ground.'

'I could do with Marcus,' grinned Melina mischievously. 'Do you hire him out? I have a man called Adam around, but I've yet to see him clean a window or scrub a floor.'

Marianne pretended to consider the suggestion. 'That could be difficult. At least once each week he's needed to drive up to the airport to meet our guests or take them to catch their flight at the end of their holiday. It isn't practical to run the mini bus for just two passengers. That leaves Giovanni free to drive at a different time to the airport or to do any other essential jobs. Marcus is always willing to take a turn up at the taverna to give John a break. Somehow I don't think we could manage without Marcus.'

'I thought John wanted to be a photographer?' frowned Adam.

'He had so much trouble with focusing after his head injury that he gave up that idea. He's taken hundreds of photos of the girls, of course, and has never lost his interest. Needless to say we don't encourage wildlife at the taverna and John is forbidden to put any specimens in the fridge up there. If the Health Inspector walked in and found them we'd be closed down immediately.'

Adam smiled. 'I'd love to see his face if he opened the fridge and found John had filled it with his little plastic cases of insects.'

'Insects – in the fridge?' Melina could hardly believe her ears.

Giovanni smiled at her. 'Don't worry. They are always captive in little boxes and John always leaves a note on the door of the fridge. Putting them in there for about an hour means their body temperature drops and they become lethargic. Once he's photographed them he sets them free and within a few minutes they've recovered.'

Melina shuddered. 'Please ask him not to put any in whilst we are here. I can't bear creepy crawlies.'

'I'll tell him,' promised Marianne. 'Bryony helps out for three days at Saffron's shop. Do you know Saffie?'

Adam wrinkled his forehead. 'I think I've met her.'

'She's Bryony's half sister and lives over here with Vasi. Bryony was marvellous when the girls were tiny and John wasn't able to give Nicola any help. She often has the girls for a few hours in the afternoon to give Nicola a break. She's found out that being a mother is a full time job, particularly with twins.'

'I can only think that triplets would be worse,' observed Melina seriously.

'I'm certainly glad that John was not one of twins. He was a nightmare as a small child. Into everything. It could have happened as I have a twin sister.'

'Is she over here as well?'

Marianne shook her head. 'She doesn't like Crete at all. She says it's too hot and if she goes for a swim it ruins her hair. She can't understand what I love about the country, besides Giovanni, of course.'

'So how do you spend your day?' asked Melina. 'You seem to have everyone else organised.'

'I deal with all the advertising for the apartments with the travel agents, take the bookings and ensure that I have all our certificates up to date for when we have a surprise inspection. In the meantime I keep an eye on Grandma Marisa if she hasn't gone to the shop with Uncle Yannis and I'm always available to run any errands.'

'Shopping, you mean?' commented Melina

'No, I do very little shopping. Each week I give Giovanni a list and he goes to the Cash and Carry to re-stock the taverna and also any items we need. Nicola takes the girls down into Elounda each day and buys fresh fruit and vegetables, meat or fish. My errands consist of rushing into Elounda to buy bread for the taverna when John has run out, or taking him up salad items. Uncle Yannis will wave his toothbrush at me and tell me he is out of toothpaste and forgot to ask me to add it to the shopping list. Things like that. I take the ladies in to the hairdresser each week and if a visit to the doctor or dentist is needed I accompany them.'

'You all seem to be so busy I'm surprised that you welcome visitors.'

'Not at all,' smiled Marianne. 'We have my mother and uncle coming over in a few weeks. A couple of extra people around don't make any more work. It's actually easier to have them during the tourist season. Once that finishes there are repairs and redecoration to be done on the apartments, general maintenance on this house and updating the advertising for the following year.'

'You don't really get a break, do you?' remarked Adam.

Marianne smiled easily. 'Once we only have to think of ourselves we can change our work itinerary around. Provided there is someone at the house to keep an eye on the elderly we can always arrange a day out or go to visit our friends.'

Ronnie walked round to the patio where Melina and Adam were talking to Nicola and John whilst the girls rode their tricycles around. On seeing Ronnie they left their bikes and rushed over to her, grabbing her around the legs and nearly toppling her over.

'Caught you. Caught you,' they chanted in unison.

Ronnie placed an arm around each girl. 'Caught you, too,' she smiled and began to remove their hands from her legs.

'Play?' asked Lisa and Ronnie shook her head.

'Later.'

Elisabetta repeated her request in Greek and Ronnie looked at Nicola for interpretation.

'She didn't understand the word "later". I'll explain that you are busy at the moment and will play again another day. I'm going to take them into town now. The shop keepers make a fuss of them and they enjoy being the centre of attention.'

Nicola turned to her daughters and spoke to them in Greek. 'Ronnie is busy today. We are busy also. We have to go into Elounda for our shopping. Put your bikes away and come and help me make out the shopping list. We'll do it in the kitchen so we can check what is needed.'

Joanna looked at her mother. 'Later. Play now.'

Nicola shook her head. 'Later is not a game. I've told you; Ronnie is busy now. If she is not busy when we have done the shopping she may be able to play, that will be later today.'

The girls looked at each other and appeared to accept that Ronnie was not going to play with them. They returned to their bikes and rode them around to the patio door that led to the rooms that Nicola and John occupied. Nicola followed and John smiled in relief.

'I was expecting a tantrum,' he explained. 'Help yourself to a drink and come and be introduced to Melina and Adam.'

The introductions over, Ronnie sat with Adam, Giovanni and John on the patio. Melina had indicated her desire to accompany Nicola on her shopping expedition with the girls. Ronnie felt nervous; would Adam believe her or think she was just trying to get revenge on Babbis?

'So, Miss Vandersham, if you could tell me the whole story. You won't mind if I take a few notes? Start at the beginning and if I have any questions I'll stop you. How did this house come into your possession?'

'Please, call me Ronnie.' Ronnie took a mouthful of her drink and leaned back in her chair. She related to Adam her first visit to Crete and her decision to return to the area and paint. How she had taken her mother and great uncle to Kastelli where he had recognised the house as being his childhood home.

'Some coincidence,' murmured Adam.

'There's far more to the story, but it isn't pertinent to my current problem. My uncle was the only direct descendant of the family and as such he inherited it.'

Adam held up his hand. 'I seem to remember something about that; the proof that the house did belong to him and the subsequent transfer of the deeds to his niece as a gift.'

Ronnie nodded. 'He said he was too old to deal with it now and had no wish to come to Crete to live so I could have it. My mother, unbeknown to me, had been saving for years for such time as I was married so I would have some money as a deposit for a house. She transferred the money to me so I could repair the Kastelli house.'

'Very generous of both your relatives,' remarked Adam. 'Are you paying your mother any interest on the money?'

'Interest?' Ronnie looked at Adam in surprise. 'No, it was a gift.'

'Sorry, I interrupted, please continue.'

'I cleared out all the rubbish from the house, saving anything of interest. Whilst I was doing that I found a tremendous amount of money hidden inside the old mattress.'

Adam raised his eyebrows. 'Where had that come from?'

'John talked to an old lady in the village who had taken care of the woman who lived there. Incidentally she was my great great grandmother. She owned many of the cottages in the village and she had been hiding away the rent in the mattress. She knew her husband had borrowed money from a bank to send their daughter and her family to America before the war. She was waiting for someone to come from the bank and claim it.'

'Why didn't she take it to them?'

Ronnie shook her head sadly. 'She couldn't read or write. Her daughter wrote from America and when she received no reply she assumed her parents had died during the war.'

'So what happened to this money?'

'I declared it at the bank. Records had been lost or destroyed during the war and the debt outstanding could not be traced. Eventually the money was declared legally mine and converted into Euros. I've used some of it to pay Babbis to provide me with the certificates to say certain work had been completed and complies with the building regulations.'

Adam nodded. He knew the only way to obtain your building certificates within a reasonable amount of time was to pay to go to the head of the queue.

'The building inspector I dealt with seemed a very pleasant and helpful man at first. He invited me out to dinner and foolishly I agreed to accompany him. I had no idea he was married or I wouldn't have accepted his invitation.'

'You found him attractive?' asked Adam.

Ronnie shook her head. 'No, but I thought if he believed us to be friends I would get my certificates more quickly. On the third occasion he became far too friendly. He insisted on taking me up on the hill to see Spinalonga floodlit. As soon as I stepped out of the car he grabbed me and said he would accept payment for the certificates in another way.'

Adam raised his eyebrows. 'Was his assault serious?'

'Not really,' smiled Ronnie. 'I kneed him and blacked his eye. I then snatched the car keys so he couldn't drive after me and ran down the hill to a friend's taverna. He telephoned Giovanni and I came here for the night.'

'Did you press charges?'

'No. I didn't think I would be believed and apart from losing a couple of buttons from my blouse no harm was done.'

John inched forward on his seat. 'Can I tell my part now? I took my dog up on the hill for a walk that morning and his car was still parked up there. I had a look around it, just in case Ronnie had actually knocked him out and he needed medical treatment,' added John with an innocent look. 'There was no sign of him, but on the way back down my dog found some car keys.'

Ronnie had a job to stop herself from smiling. She knew John had taken Skele to the car for him to pick up the scent of Babbis in the hope of finding the keys, not out of concern for the man's health.

'I went down to the building inspector's office and there was a man sporting a very painful looking black eye. Having made a note of his name I went to the Town Hall and pretended to be him. I asked the clerk to check that my address was recorded correctly as I had moved recently. I told Ronnie I knew where he lived and that his wife lived there with him. I took Ronnie into the offices and she spoke very loudly to Babbis, telling him she had his car keys and showing him the blouse with the missing buttons. She said unless her certificates were produced immediately the work on her house was completed she would tell his wife and press charges for assault.' John gave a satisfied smile. 'His face was a picture, enhanced by the black eye.'

'And now he is accusing you of assault?' Adam turned to Ronnie.

Ronnie shook her head. 'I haven't got that far yet.'

'I'm sorry, please continue.'

'A few weeks ago my house was set on fire. The interior has been gutted. Giovanni took me up to see the old lady who lives across the road and she said she saw the person who did it. She couldn't put a name to him, but she had seen him up there on occasions and he was a building inspector.'

Adam raised his eyebrows. 'Can her information be relied upon?'

'I believe so,' replied Giovanni. 'We went down and spoke to the police but Inspector Antonakis seems to think Ronnie made the story up to get revenge on Babbis for the assault. The Inspector has accused her of blackmailing Babbis to get the certificates signed and has said that Babbis could sue her.'

Adam looked from Giovanni to Ronnie.

'And there's more,' said Ronnie sadly. 'At first the Inspector accused me of setting the fire myself for the insurance money. That is ridiculous as I haven't any insurance on the house. Now he is saying I paid the old lady's son to set fire to the house and have bribed her to implicate Babbis. I've had to surrender my passport to him.'

'That's partly my fault,' admitted Giovanni. 'Kassianae asked if there would be a reward for her information and I said there might be once the arsonist had been arrested.'

Adam finished his drink and sat back in his chair. 'What exactly are you asking me to do?'

Ronnie looked helplessly at Giovanni and John. 'Is there anything you can do?'

Giovanni nodded. 'If you are willing, Adam, we'd like you to conduct a complete examination of the situation. I believe old Kassie and I'd like to see Babbis brought to justice. It's one thing accepting a bribe to complete a certificate more quickly; we all know that happens, but you don't set fire to someone's house because they've rejected your advances.'

'Well, you've given me the overall picture. When I've thought it over I'll probably have to ask you for more details. Now I will go and ask my wife what she would like to do this afternoon. I know she wants to go to Spinalonga.'

John shook his head. 'It's not a good time to go over in the afternoon. It will be full of tourists. I'd be happy to take you over later when most of them have left or tomorrow morning before they arrive. I can give you a special tour and also fill you in on the family relationships. My great uncle lived over there and so did Ronnie's great grandparents.'

Adam looked from one to the other. 'So are you distantly related?'

'No,' smiled Ronnie. 'I found some old diaries up at the house and John and Nicola translated them for me. They found out that my great grandmother had been sent over there and my grandmother was born over there. They even found that the old lady, Kassianae, in the village had worked for the family and persuaded her to talk to them. It's rather a sad story.'

'I'd like to hear it at some time and I'm sure Melina would be interested.'

'Come for a meal this evening, Ronnie, then you can entertain us,' offered Giovanni.

Ronnie shook her head. 'I can't. I've promised to help Kyriakos. It's still difficult for him to run in and out with orders and serve at the tables. If your offer is still open I can tell him I'm not able to help him tomorrow. That will give him a chance to ask his mother to go up.'

'Who is Kyriakos? Is he also a part of your problem?'

Ronnie blushed. 'He's a good friend and helped me when I was turning out the rubbish from the house. When Vasi was accused of money laundering Kyriakos confirmed that he had seen me find it hidden in the mattress.'

'And we will have visited Spinalonga by then,' announced John.

John led Adam and Melina through the tunnel and into the square. 'I wish there was a block of stone for me to stand on,' he said ruefully. 'Old Uncle Yannis used to stand here and talk to the villagers. Everywhere was pretty ruinous and he finally persuaded them to help him to repair the old houses and build some others so everyone had somewhere to live. He lived in that one with his wife and his adopted daughter.' John waved his hand at the house opposite.

'Unfortunately due to the clearance that has taken place the stairs have been removed along with the back wall. Once visitors began to come over here in large numbers the government realised that many of the structures were unsafe; roofs or walls could fall at any minute. They've also cleared the rubbish and the weeds so you can now walk up the side streets and go to the hospital without risking injury. Follow me up these steps and I'll show you where Ronnie's great grandparents lived.'

'Look at the view,' remarked Melina. 'I would love a view like that. From our apartment all we see are the apartments across the road.'

John smiled. 'Earlier this year a man came over from Australia. His mother had had a liaison with a man who had been sent here and he was the result. She was convinced that everywhere would look as she remembered it and Ronnie used her imagination to paint some pictures for her. Whilst she was up here she did a bit of research of her own and decided that her relatives had lived there.' John pointed to the foundations of a house.

Adam raised his eyebrows and John grinned. 'They certainly lived up here, but I wouldn't like to claim that it was in that house. There's only one person I know of who is still alive and when I next visit him I'll ask if he remembers which was their house. He escaped from the island. That's another story you'll enjoy hearing. I'll tell you this evening. If I start now it will be dark before we've walked around and seen everywhere.'

John led the way back down the steps to the square and up the main road, explaining how the inhabitants had received a pension from the government that enabled them to buy items from the mainland and have their own small businesses.

'Very enterprising of them,' remarked Adam.

'Old Uncle Yannis was determined they should be like any

other village. Had the war not intervened they could be living here now, well, their descendents and others who were afflicted. It was due to Old Uncle Yannis that they were finally tested to see if they were suitable for the new treatment that had been developed and it was found that many of them were "burnt out". It caused a bit of a dilemma for the government. They had no reason to keep them here any longer and finally sent them back to the hospital in Athens or to relatives who would accept them. Old Uncle Yannis was devastated. He had wanted to stay here, but it worked out well for him eventually.'

'Another story?' asked Melina.

'Definitely. You'll have to arrange to go to Uncle Yannis's shop. He has copies of Old Uncle's book there along with the sketches that were done on the island. I'll ask him if he'll show you those in his private collection that have not been reproduced for the public to buy.'

'You know, when Adam said we were coming here for a week I wondered how I would manage to occupy myself. I know what Adam's like; once he starts working on a problem he's in a world of his own. From all you've told me so far I think I will be happy to sit and listen to stories whilst I'm here.'

'There is plenty to see,' John assured her. 'I can give you a list and you'll not need the car to go to all of them if you're happy to walk for an hour or so.'

He waited patiently whilst they looked inside dilapidated houses and neglected gardens, finally walking up to the hospital building and peering through the windows.

'It looks thoroughly miserable in there,' announced Melina with a shudder.

John shrugged. 'It probably was by our modern standards, but at least there was someone to look after you if you were bedridden, give you a wash or bring you a drink. You didn't have to rely on your neighbours remembering to call in to see if you wanted anything.'

'So those who were not bedridden; how did they pass their time?'

'Well, they were either helping with the rebuilding, tending the little gardens they had made or in their shops. There was a barber, seamstress, cobbler, baker; all the usual sorts of shops that you would find in any village. In the evening you could either visit your neighbour or go to a taverna, just as you would have done if you were on the mainland.'

'It doesn't sound a bad life,' remarked Adam.

'Once they had organised themselves into a proper community they were happy enough most of the time. Old Uncle Yannis taught many of them to read and write. That facility would not have been available to them if they were still in their home village.'

'Was that the school?' asked Adam as they reached the apartments at the top of the hill.

John shook his head. 'Those were built after the war for the people who were sent over then. The original inhabitants refused to move from their houses. There isn't anything more of interest to see up here so we'll walk around to the other side of the island to the graveyard.' As they walked John told them how the dead had been placed in a grave for three years before being exhumed and placed in the tower.

'Of course, during the war so many people died that they ran out of graves so the people were placed directly into the tower without a prior burial.'

'Are they still there?'

John nodded. 'They're just a jumble of bones now; but you can peer through the opening and see them.'

Melina shuddered. 'Rather an ignominious end.'

'There was always a church service for them before internment and services were held in accordance with the Greek Orthodox religion. They were not discarded like rubbish the way they had been in the hospital.'

On reaching the graveyard John stopped in consternation.

Across the entrance was a length of yellow tape.

'Who put that there?' he exclaimed in annoyance. 'Duck underneath and walk carefully in case there has been some subsidence.'

As they neared the tower the reason for the tape became clear. A large section of the roof had collapsed. John tried to look down into the darkness.

'Where's Old Uncle Yannis? I can't see him.'

'What do you mean?' Adam looked around as if expecting to see a man walking towards them.

'Old Uncle Yannis died over here and my father and Uncle Yannis along with some others placed him in the tower. I always knew it was him as he was wrapped in a sheet and having been interred so much later than the others he was on the top.'

'Was that legal?' asked Adam with a frown.

John shrugged. 'I've no idea, but it would have been his wish to be here. I'll have to find out what they intend to do about repairing the damage. I'll come over on Monday morning and speak to the workers.'

Ronnie joined the family for a meal on Sunday evening, ensuring she arrived after the girls had been put to bed. She looked hopefully at Adam, but he was not forthcoming.

'Have you visited Spinalonga?' she asked.

Melina nodded. 'It was so interesting. John knows so much about the island and the people who once lived there.'

'That's the advantage of having a relative who lived there and wrote about his experiences. Ronnie was also fortunate that her great great aunt kept a diary. If she hadn't discovered that she would never have known the truth about her grandmother.'

'Tell us more,' urged Melina.

John shook his head. 'No that's Ronnie's story. I'm sure she'll tell you all about it when we've eaten. Red or white wine for you, Melina?'

John walked around the table pouring glasses of wine for everyone except Bryony and Marcus who would only be drinking fruit juice.

'Which would you prefer, Uncle Yannis?'

'I'll have red, please, and only a little for Ourania.'

John complied and only half filled Ourania's glass, leaving Yannis to add water to weaken it.

Ourania looked around the gathering at the table. 'Who are our visitors, Yannis?'

'Melina and Adam from Athens,' answered Yannis patiently. He did not remind her that she had been introduced when they arrived and he had already told her twice that evening.

Ourania frowned. 'Are they relatives?'

'No, just friends.'

Ourania pointed at Ronnie. 'I know her.'

'Of course you do. Ronnie often comes to visit us.'

'She's my hairdresser,' announced Ourania to no one in particular. 'That's how I know her.'

Ronnie did not contradict her, but hoped Ourania would quickly forget that she had been mistaken.

'You must be tired at the end of the day. You spend all your time on your feet and I know how exhausting that can be. I work in the shop and by the end of the day my feet are quite sore from standing. Yannis says I'm invaluable to him.'

Yannis patted his wife's hand. 'You certainly are. Now, shall I help you to some salad? There are pork chops or chicken breasts and Marianne has cooked some chips.'

'I like chips.'

'Marianne knows that and cooked them specially.' Yannis placed a chicken breast on Ourania's plate along with some chips.

'My Mamma cooked good chips.' Ourania fell silent for a moment; then smiled brightly. 'We went to see my Mamma today. We couldn't stay long as she was busy in her shop. We'll go again tomorrow.'

Adam looked at Giovanni in surprise. He did not expect Ourania's mother to still be alive. Giovanni shook his head.

'Tell us more about your visit to Spinalonga, Adam,' said Marianne hoping to deflect attention away from Ourania's imagined outing.

'I found it hard to conceive how so many people once lived there. We were just about to leave when a boatload of tourists arrived. There were probably about two hundred, but suddenly the island seemed awash with people.'

'Now you know why I said to go early in the morning or late at night,' grinned John. 'Later in the day you can hardly walk along the road. I'm sure it wasn't as congested when it was inhabited. People would have been engaged in their daily occupations in their houses, not all wandering along the main street at the same time.'

'It was like rush hour in Athens,' remarked Melina.

'Athens?' Ourania looked up from her plate. 'I've been to Athens.'

'I had a hotel there, remember?' asked Yannis gently. 'We used to go over and stay there and you used to go shopping with Dora.'

Ourania smiled. 'Of course I remember. Dora and I would go and buy clothes. We would often spend most of the day in one shop, trying on different outfits. Why doesn't Dora come to visit us here?'

'She would find the journey too difficult. She had a bad leg, remember.'

'You could go and fetch her,' replied Ourania truculently. 'Your friends come here to visit, but you don't ask mine to come.'

'Melina and Adam are here on business. There isn't the space for any more visitors at the moment. When they have left you can ask any friends you wish to come to stay.'

Mollified Ourania turned her attention back to her meal and Yannis spread his hands in an apologetic gesture.

'No problem,' Marianne assured him, 'Just tell me when they are arriving!'

Yannis smiled at her. Marianne was very understanding about the difficulties he had with his wife.

'Tell me where you visited in America. I'd only ever lived in New Orleans until I came here.' Nicola felt it advisable to talk about a country that Adam knew well so that he and Melina could rejoin the conversation.

John refilled their glasses whilst Adam talked and Melina made comments about the various cities they had visited and the hundreds of miles they had driven.

'Sometimes it took all day just to drive from one town to the next. I admit I began to get bored and after a while everywhere began to look the same to me. I'd rather stay in one place and explore it thoroughly.'

Ourania had eaten most of her meal and now she was tired. If she began to clear the table maybe all these people would go away and she could go to bed. She picked up her plate and went to remove Yannis's.

'No,' he placed a restraining hand on her. 'I haven't quite finished. There's no need for you to clear the table.'

'I don't know who'll do it if I don't,' she replied querulously.

'I'll see to it, Auntie,' offered Bryony. 'Would you like to go and sit in an easy chair until we have all finished?'

'No.' Ourania pushed her chair back. 'I want to go home.'

Yannis rose. 'Yes, it's time we left. I'll take you home now, Ourania.' He sighed. He had been looking forward to the raspberry roulade Bryony had made.

'There will be plenty in the fridge if either of you want anything later,' Marianne assured him. This was not the first time Ourania had decided she wished to go home during a meal and once Yannis had settled her down he usually returned for a short while, to make apologies for his wife and also to finish his wine.

'I'm sorry,' apologised Marianne after they had left the room. 'It's very difficult. I feel guilty if I don't ask them to join us, but Aunt Ourania doesn't seem able to cope with visitors.'

'We understand,' said Adam. 'I was just a little worried that I might say the wrong thing and upset her. Yannis seems able to deal with her very well.'

'I'll save some roulade for them. If Aunt Ourania decides not to eat hers I'm sure Uncle Yannis will manage two portions. If John refills your glasses whilst I'm serving Ronnie can tell you how she found out about her grandmother.'

'Should I wait until Uncle Yannis returns?'

'No,' Giovanni assured her. 'He knows your story, but I'm sure Adam and Melina will find it interesting.'

'It was really all due to John and Nicola deciphering Maria's diaries. Then they talked to old Kassianae and found out even more about my family. Certainly not all good, I'm afraid,' Ronnie smiled.

Irini returned home after church and changed into her old shoes before walking up the hill and along the path to Mavrikiano. She had cleaned her best pair carefully and they seemed no worse for wear, but she did not want to risk walking up to the village in them a second time. New shoes were expensive. It did not seem to be quite as hot this week, but she was grateful when she arrived at Soula's house and was invited into her cool living room.

Once coffee, water and a plate of biscuits had been produced and the polite enquiries about each other's health and that of their families were concluded, Irini felt she could broach the subject of Thranassis's latest visit to Kastelli.

'Did your Thranassis find out anything when he went to Kastelli?'

Soula nodded. 'Why are you so interested?'

'My Kyriakos helped the girl get rid of the rubbish from inside. When she returned this year she was told the building was structurally dangerous.'

'In that case it should have been pulled down,' said Soula firmly. 'Suppose a wall had collapsed on somebody as they walked past.'

'It was inspected and they found the building was safe enough.'

'Apparently the old man who lived there was the local tax collector. Married to a woman young enough to be his daughter, but he managed to give her two children. According to the villagers he was shot by the Italians, but his wife stayed on there alone after the war.'

'What about her children?' asked Irini.

'They'd left.'

'Moved to another village you mean?'

Soula shook her head. 'According to what my Thranassis has heard one of the daughters ran away and never returned. The other one was married with a child and they went away also.'

'So the old lady was left completely alone after her husband died?'

Soula nodded. 'That's what my Thranassis says.'

'How sad.' Irini crossed herself, hoping that such a fate would never befall her. If Kyriakos did marry the American woman would he want to go to live in America?

'And neither of her daughters came back to claim the house?'

'They might have done, but if they were living in Aghios Nikolaos or Heraklion it's doubtful they would have wanted to return to a tiny village. I'll ask my Thranassis if he can find out any more when he goes up there again.'

Week Two – September 2012
Monday

John drove over to Spinalonga in his motor boat and moored at the old port entrance. He did not want to risk damage to his boat from the larger craft that used the new landing place. He walked up to the graveyard where two men were lifting the grave slabs. He ducked beneath tape that was cordoning off the area.

'Hey, you can't come in here,' called the nearest workman.

John ignored him. 'What are you doing?' he asked, standing a short distance away.

'Filling in the graves, then we'll pave them over and make the area safe. Left as it is people could trip over the lifted paving stones and hurt themselves.'

'What about the occupants?'

'They've been removed.'

'Placed in the tower you mean?'

The man shook his head. 'No, we've had a directive from the Church. The bodies that remained in these graves have been sent to Aghios Nikolaos. All the remains from the tower are to be removed as well.' The workman pointed to the charnel house where there was a gaping hole in the roof. 'It isn't safe any longer. Once the bodies are elsewhere it will be demolished.'

'What will happen to them?' asked John

'They'll be washed, sorted and stored until the tower has been pulled down and a new one built.'

'Then you'll put the bodies back?'

'As I understand it once the new tower has been built there will be shelves where their skulls can be displayed and wooden cages down below for their long bones. A stairway will be built to provide access.'

'What!' John gasped in horror. 'You can't do that. My great uncle is in there.'

'So are many other people's relatives. They're all jumbled up together.'

'My great Uncle Yannis won't be jumbled up. He's on top.'

'How do you know? He's probably moved by now or been covered over by others. One skeleton looks like another.'

'He was interred much later than the others and wrapped in a sheet.'

The workman looked at him sceptically. 'I doubt we'd be able to distinguish him. They'll be removed sympathetically. We've been told they have to be cleared by hand, not just shovelled up and a priest will give our work a blessing before we start.'

'I don't want my great uncle's bones put on show for everyone to gawp at.'

'Then you'd best contact the church as soon as possible and see if they're willing for you to make a separate burial. It's not my decision.'

'Which church?' asked John eagerly.

'I don't know. The bones are going to be stored at Aghios Nikolaos church, but the instructions came from Athens.'

John looked at the number of graves that would need to be filled and paved over. It should be a weeks' work at least.

'When will you start to dismantle the tower?' he asked.

'Probably next week.'

John groaned. There was no way he could go to Athens and plead for his uncle's remains to be released to the family before the work was due to start.

'May I have your 'phone number? I'll give you mine,' he said.

'Please don't touch any of the bodies in the tower until I have spoken to you again.'

The man looked at John and shook his head. 'Can't make promises like that.'

John dug in his pocket and pulled out all the Euro notes he had in there. He held them up and moved closer to the man. 'I will make it worth your while,' he assured him. 'Just give me your word you'll not touch them until I can be here with you.' He pressed the notes into the workman's hand. 'Make sure your mate understands,' he cautioned.

The man looked at the small bundle of notes he held. 'I'll need more than this,' he stated.

'That's all I have with me at present. That's just for you to call me on my mobile. I'll bring over some more money the next time I come.'

Elias shrugged. What difference would one body make if he was going to be paid to ignore its removal?

John motored back to the mainland. He was not at all sure how his father and Uncle Yannis would feel about his idea, but he was convinced they would not want their relative's remains on show to the public.

'So what do you plan to do today, Adam?' asked Melina.

'I'm hoping either Giovanni or John will be free to drive up to Kastelli with me. I'd like to have a look at the house and also talk to the old lady. It might be better if I had someone she was familiar with to accompany me. If her son is around I could have a word with him at the same time.'

'John did say he wanted to go to Spinalonga and have a word with the workmen about the graveyard.'

'In that case I'll ask Giovanni to come with me. Later I'll need to speak to the Fire Officer and ask if I can see his report.'

'You won't need me with you, then?'

Adam shrugged. 'You're welcome to come, but you could find it a very boring day.'

'I'd like to see the house and I can always wander around the village until you're ready to leave.'

'Actually it would be practical if we took two cars. Once I've been introduced Giovanni could always return here and you could come back with him if you've had enough wandering. I could then drive into Aghios Nikolaos to the fire station.'

'Will you take Ronnie with you?'

Adam shook his head. 'It's far better that she keeps a low profile at the moment. If Ronnie's with me I'll have to admit that I'm working on her behalf. Depending upon my findings I'd rather the Police Inspector was unaware of my involvement with her at the moment. I have to keep an open mind until I've investigated the evidence.'

'She's a nice girl and the story she told us about her grandmother was interesting. Fancy going all through your life and not knowing you had been adopted and why.'

'That's another thing,' mused Adam. 'The friend she mentioned, Kyriakos, I ought to have a word with him.'

'You don't suspect he had anything to do with the fire, do you?'

Adam shook his head. 'No, but he helped her turn out the house and spoke to the villagers. He might know if anyone bore a grudge against her great great grandparents going back to when they lived at the house.'

'As I understand there's only the old lady in the village who remembers them.'

'That doesn't mean a grudge hasn't been passed down. You know what some of these villagers can be like. A feud can be carried on for so long that no one really remembers how it started. Maybe they got to hear that their rent money had been found and felt it should have been returned to them.'

'Ronnie said she asked her friend to tell them that she considered the cottages belonged to them now. It would have been somewhat greedy of them to ask for the return of rent money that was legitimately paid years ago,' argued Melina.

'I'm only speculating. Maybe they thought the money she was spending on the house should have been spent on their cottages. They could need repairs or modernising and were resentful that she hadn't thought of them before spending a small fortune on her own house.'

'If the cottages belong to them surely any repairs are their responsibility?'

'They are now, but apart from patching up the roof if there was a hole it's unlikely they would have done anything more than that previously. They obviously didn't understand that they could be considered to be the legitimate owners as ten years had passed since the old lady died and no one had come forward during that time to claim her property.'

'But her great uncle did claim the big house. Why didn't he claim the cottages as well?' Melina frowned.

'You obviously weren't listening properly last night,' her husband chided her. 'He had no idea he owned the cottages. He inherited the house through proving his lineage and the fact that there were no other living relatives. It wasn't until John and Nicola translated the diaries and then visited the old lady that the full story emerged. I certainly would not have wanted to try to take his case to court and ask for a retrospective judgement for possession of the properties.'

'I wonder what kind of condition they are in? If people are still living in them they must be reasonable.'

'Well, you'll be able to judge for yourself if you're coming up there with me. Are you ready? I really need to speak to Giovanni before he goes off to the airport or disappears on another errand somewhere.'

Melina looked at the surrounding countryside with interest as she rode with Giovanni in his car, followed by Adam up the steep road and around numerous bends.

'Although Elounda is in the Lassithi Prefecture once you

drive up these hills you are on the Lassithi Plateau. It's good farming country. Being relatively high it catches the rain that often bypasses the coast.'

'What do they farm? All I can see are olive trees.'

'That is their main product, but there are grape vines and they export both the fresh and dried fruit There are orange, plum, lemon and pear trees along with tomatoes, courgettes, aubergines, onions, melons.' Giovanni shrugged. 'More or less anything you care to name as well as the herbs that grow wild. The village where we are going is known mostly for the chicken farmers. Just about everyone has some along with a few goats. Fifty years ago I doubt if the villagers ever went outside Kastelli; they had everything they needed on their doorstep.'

'What about meat and fish?'

'There would have been a travelling man who went around to the villages with fish. Some people would have kept a pig and slaughtering it was quite an occasion. The meat was then shared out between the households and would last them through until the following year when another slaughter would take place.'

'I can't imagine never going into town. Suppose you wanted a new dress?'

'You would have made it. There were pedlars travelling everywhere and they would have a cart containing just about everything you could imagine. Pots and pans, needles and cotton, knitting wool, material, tools, screws, nails – why would you need to make a journey into town?'

Melina pondered the question. 'I suppose I am a town person and also of the modern age. We go to the shops for our produce, not the fields, and expect to have a vast choice of clothing. Surely the people who live up here now go into the town?'

'Most of them have some form of transport. The women drive now as well and that would have been unheard of at one time. The women didn't even ride a donkey, the men rode and the women would walk beside them.'

'So living on Spinalonga would not have been such a hardship. In many ways it would have been no different from living in a village in the countryside,' said Melina thoughtfully.

'Once Old Uncle Yannis got them organised and their living conditions improved the only hardship they really suffered, apart from their disease, was being unable to visit the mainland whenever they wished.'

'John said that later they were allowed visits from the mainland.'

'Quite true, and they must have relished seeing their family and hearing all the news. It was hard for them if they knew a family member was nearing the end of their life and they were unable to go over and say goodbye or pay their respects at the funeral. Of course, those who had come to Spinalonga from further away were unlikely to have a visitor or have any news of their family.'

'That's sad.'

'That's life.' Giovanni shrugged.

'So if the villagers did not travel outside their village there must have been a good deal of inter-marriage?'

'They would have had visitors coming from the outlying villages to have their donkeys shod at the forge and would meet people when they took their produce to the market in Neapoli. Occasionally someone married and went to live elsewhere, but most of them are related. The marriage would have been arranged between cousins when they were young and it was accepted. Just occasionally one would rebel, like Ronnie's great great aunt who insisted on marrying the man of her choice. It is different now, of course.'

'Thinking of my own cousins that is an awful prospect. I would not have wanted to marry any of them.'

Giovanni grinned at her. 'How did you and Adam meet?'

'I was teaching English and giving private lessons. Adam wanted to learn Greek and asked me if I could teach him. He wasn't able to come on a regular basis and it took quite a while before he had a grasp of the grammar. Once he was proficient we didn't see each other again for years and then we literally bumped into each other. He drove into the back of my car when I had to stop suddenly. We both got out ready to argue about responsibility and it ended up with Adam asking me out to dinner with him. I only had a small dent in the bumper, along with others, so it seemed like good compensation. We just progressed from there.' Melina smiled to herself. 'My parents weren't very happy about it at first. He was a foreigner with an outlandish and unpronounceable name. Once they got to know him they realised that he was a decent, unmarried American.'

'There's nothing wrong with Americans. Half our family come from New Orleans, although they are of Greek origin.' Giovanni drew in beside the water cistern and Adam parked his car beside him.

Melina looked at the cistern curiously. 'Surely the villagers don't get their drinking water from there?'

Giovanni shook his head. 'They have water piped into their houses now. At one time they had to use the wells for fresh water. The cistern supplies the water to irrigate their fields during the summer. They block up the drainage channels during the winter and the rain and snow accumulates. If it gets too high and there is a danger of it overflowing they just unblock a channel and let some of the water out.'

'Ingenious. Is there a taverna here where I can meet Adam later? I'm planning to walk around the village whilst you're talking to the old lady but I need a convenient meeting point.'

'Up the road. We'll walk up to the house together and it's just a little further on from there around the corner. I'll suggest to Kassianae that we go to the taverna to talk. She'll be happy with a glass of whisky in front of her.'

Melina looked at the house in admiration. 'It really is beautiful. No wonder Ronnie wanted to restore it.'

'Thankfully being built of stone the structure is still sound.

Surprisingly the rooms she had added at the back weren't too badly affected and she hadn't had any of her white goods delivered. It will cost her a good deal to refurbish again, but it could be worse. Do you want to go inside, Adam?'

Adam shook his head. 'No, I'm sure the forensic team did a good job. If I have any queries I'll ask the Fire Officer when I've read the report.'

'I'll go and ask Kassie to come to the taverna. I'm sure you'd rather meet her there than sit inside her cottage.'

Kassianae had watched the group looking at the house and when Giovanni knocked she opened with alacrity. 'Have you come to pay me my reward?'

'I never offered you a reward,' Giovanni said firmly. 'You asked me if there would be one and I said that would be up to Miss Vandersham if there was a conviction.'

Kassie went to close her door, but Giovanni held on to it.

'I'd like to take you to the taverna to meet a friend. He's a very important man from Athens and would like you to tell him exactly what you saw on the night of the fire.'

'I've told you. Why do I need to tell him?'

'I may have forgotten something, or you might remember a detail whilst you are telling him that had slipped your mind earlier.'

'There's nothing wrong with my mind,' replied Kassianae indignantly.

'I'm not implying there is, but we all forget things occasionally. Get your stick and we'll go and have some refreshment at the taverna.'

'I'll have a whisky,' announced Kassianae and Giovanni smiled.

Adam sat quietly whilst Kassianae savoured her whisky, smacking her lips in appreciation. Finally she looked at Adam.

'What do you want to know?' she asked.

'I'd like you to tell me exactly what you saw on the night of the fire. I know you've told Giovanni, but he can't answer any questions I may have. You are the only person who can do that.'

'If I know the answers,' muttered Kassianae.

'You won't mind if I make a few notes?'

Kassie shook her head; the man could make as many notes as he liked, but they would not alter the facts.

'Just tell me what you were doing and how you came to see the house on fire.'

Kassie took another mouthful of whisky and sat back. 'I don't sleep well nowadays so I often sit at my window during the night.'

Adam nodded understandingly and Kassianae related how she had seen a man arrive at the house, go inside and move around, then throw a lighted paper into the living room. 'Then I 'phoned my son, Nikos.'

'Can we stop there for a moment? I'd like to ask you a few questions.'

Kassianae looked at her empty glass and Giovanni hastily signalled to the taverna owner that a refill was needed.

'You live opposite the house that was burnt, I believe. The fire happened in the early hours of the morning so it would have been dark. How were you able to see someone go into the house?'

'There's a light up on the wall just across from the house. Don't know why they bothered to put one there. We never had one in the past. Didn't need it. The cars have headlights. They can see there's a bend in the road.'

'And it was from the light of this lamp that you saw the person?'

'That and the moon. That gives plenty of light unless the sky is overcast, but that's usually in the winter.'

Adam consulted his notes. 'You saw a car drive past the house and along the road. You then saw the same car return a few minutes later and stop outside the house. Is that right?'

Kassianae nodded. 'Driving slowly, not making any noise like some of them do.'

'Did you notice the colour of the car?'

'It was a dark colour; black, blue, green; certainly not white.'

'You're certain that it was the same car as the one that had driven past earlier?'

Kassianae regarded Adam suspiciously. 'It looked the same.'

'Did you recognise it as belonging to anyone who lives in the village?'

Kassianae shook her head. 'If they lived in the village they'd know better than to park on that corner, besides, they'd park outside their own house or down by the water cistern.'

'So having parked; what happened then?'

'The man got out.' Kassianae sighed. She had told him this.

'Did he get out immediately?'

Kassianae considered. 'He looked around for a minute or two and then he got out.'

'Can you tell me about him?'

'Tell you what?'

'Was he tall or short, fat or thin, dark or fair?'

Kassianae shrugged. 'Quite tall, but not fat or thin, just average looking and he had dark hair.'

'Could you tell what he was wearing?' Adam prompted her. 'Was he wearing a suit, or just a shirt and trousers? Were they jeans or lightweight trousers?'

Kassianae wrinkled her forehead. 'He wasn't wearing jeans. I think they were light coloured trousers. His shirt was white.'

'Having got out of the car what did he do then?'

'Went to the boot and took out some things.'

'Could you tell what these things were?'

'When he picked them up they looked like petrol cans. He placed them on the ground and closed the boot lid very quietly. He didn't slam it down like most people do. He lowered it and then pushed it a bit further to latch it. He checked his pockets, then picked up the cans and walked to the door. It was always padlocked when there was no one working there. He must have had the key in his pocket as he opened it easily.'

'Did he close the door behind him?'

'He may not have shut it, but he pushed it so that it looked closed.'

'So you don't know what he did when he was inside?' frowned Adam.

'I kept seeing a light flickering across the window openings. He must have been using a torch. First it was upstairs and then downstairs, then it went dark.'

'What happened when it went dark?'

'He opened the door and came back outside.' Kassianae finished her second glass of whisky and tilted her empty glass meaningfully towards Giovanni.

'When he came out was he carrying anything?'

'Some paper.' Kassianae's eyes were on the glass that Giovanni was refilling.

'So then what did he do?'

'He stood there for a moment; then folded up the paper.' Kassianae took a paper napkin and demonstrated the way she had seen the paper folded. 'It was quite a big piece, bigger than this. Then he took a lighter from his pocket and lit the end of it before he threw it inside the house.'

'How did you know it was a lighter?'

'Must have been. He didn't stand there and strike a match.'

'Did he shut the door?'

'No, he left it open; stood there for a minute or two looking inside and then hurried over to his car and drove away.'

'Which direction did he drive in?'

'Back the way he had come. The road to the other villages around here and the turn off to Aghios Nikolaos.'

Adam smiled at her. 'You've been very helpful. Now I'd like to move on to what you did when you saw the house was on fire.'

'I've told you; I called my son and he called the fire brigade. He roused the other villagers and they tried to bring it under control before the engines arrived. It takes quite a while for them to get here.'

'Why didn't you call the fire brigade before calling your son?'

'I always call my son first if there is a problem,' answered Kassianae firmly. 'That's what family are for; to help if you have a problem.'

'He's a builder, I understand.'

Kassianae nodded. 'Best builder there is around here.'

'So why hadn't he been asked to work on the restoration of the house?'

Kassianae looked sourly at Giovanni. 'Told the girl to use the builders he always used.'

'It would have been too big a job for Nikos to tackle on his own,' Giovanni tried to mollify her. 'Mr Palamakis had both his grandsons working there full time for months. They had to call in additional help for the roof and to erect the supports for the balconies.'

Kassianae pursed her lips. 'Didn't give him the chance to refuse,' she muttered.

'You told Giovanni you recognised the man who went inside that night. Who was he?'

'He'd been up here on occasions, sometimes with the girl and other times just to speak to Palamakis. He's a building inspector. They have to come and check that the regulations have been adhered to and the work done satisfactorily.' Kassianae was pleased to be able to impart this knowledge that she had gained from Nikos.

'You've been a tremendous help,' Adam assured her. 'I'd like to have a word with your son. I imagine he's working so where could I find him?'

'He's gone to Sirmeso. He wants to finish that job today; then he was going to Fourni to look at another. You'd best 'phone him.'

'Do you have his number?'

'Of course.' Kassianae looked at Adam scathingly.

'If you could tell me it, please.' Adam took out his mobile 'phone ready to add the number.

'I don't have it with me. It's back at the house.'

'Well, there's no rush. I'm meeting my wife here when she's finished looking around the village. When she arrives we can go across the road and you can tell me your son's 'phone number then.'

Giovanni smiled to himself. If they were going to wait for Melina to arrive he would have to refill Kassianae's glass again. He hoped she would not be away too much longer or he doubted that Kassianae would be capable of walking back to her house.

'Is there anything else you can think of to tell me?' asked Adam.

'I used to work at the big house. Looked after the old lady when she could no longer care properly for herself. My mother worked there before me. She knew the old man and his wife who lived there and their girls.' Kassianae drank the remains of her whisky and pushed her glass towards Giovanni. 'I can tell you some tales.'

Adam nodded and Kassianae began to reminisce about life in the village when it was occupied during the war.

Giovanni gave a sigh of relief when Melina finally joined them at the taverna. Adam introduced her and Kassianae extended a grubby hand that Melina dutifully shook.

Adam spoke to his wife in English. 'I'm sure you're hot and would like a drink. I have to go back to the old lady's house to collect her son's 'phone number. It could take us quite a while to get her there as the whisky bottle has certainly been depleted.'

Melina raised her eyebrows. 'By whom?'

'Who do you think?' Adam inclined his head towards Kassianae. He reverted to Greek. 'I was telling my wife how helpful you have been. She is going to have a drink whilst we return to your house for your son's 'phone number.'

'I'll settle up with the taverna owner; then we really should leave.' Giovanni rose and indicated that he would like to pay their bill. He held up the bottle of whisky and four fingers.

The taverna owner grinned and nodded. Kassianae was certainly his best and most regular customer.

Once back at his car Adam tried the 'phone number he had been given for Nikos, only to find it was engaged. 'Probably his mother telling him about our visit,' surmised Adam. 'I'll give him another call later.'

They followed Giovanni as he drove to Fourni and drew in a short distance away from the taverna. 'Once we managed to get Old Kassie back to her house I thought it better to come here rather than stay in Kastelli. I'm sure whatever we discussed there would be relayed to the whole village within the hour and she would have expected to drink the rest of that bottle. I didn't fancy having to carry her back.'

'I'm so pleased you suggested we went over to the taverna. I don't think I could have sat in that stuffy little room for very long without feeling ill,' remarked Adam.

'I agree. You'd think her son would arrange to have her house cleaned up a bit.'

'He's probably used to it and his might not be any better,' smiled Adam.

'Did you find out anything useful?' asked Melina.

'One or two details that could be helpful. Was there anything you picked up on, Giovanni, that was inconsistent with the story she originally told you?'

'Only the description of the man and what he was wearing. I didn't ask her those questions.'

'No reason why you should. I wonder if the Police Inspector asked her?'

'Somehow I doubt it. He was sure Ronnie had set the fire until he found out she had no insurance and then he made up his mind that it was Nikos and his mother had been paid to make up the story and implicate Babbis.'

Giovanni considered. 'Old Kassie is not stupid by any means, but I think if she had been asked to make the story up she would have identified Babbis Skourlatakis from the start.'

'What do you plan to do now?' asked Melina.

Adam smiled at her. 'I'll try to contact Nikos again. We could have some lunch here. If Nikos is supposed to be coming to this village to look at a job it will save us chasing around the countryside after him.' Adam looked at his mobile 'phone in frustration. 'He's not answering.'

'Tell us about your walk around Kastelli, Melina. Did you find anywhere interesting?' asked Giovanni.

Melina nodded. 'The little back streets are fascinating. I'd love to see behind their doors.'

'Not if they're anything like Old Kassianae's you wouldn't,' observed Adam.

'I walked to the churchyard and looked around. So many of the surnames are the same. You're obviously right, Giovanni, about the families marrying relatives.'

Adam raised his eyebrows.

'I was telling Melina about the village as we drove up. The occupations of the people and how they lived generally,' explained Giovanni.

'I had a look in the forge. No one appeared to be working in there, but there were a group of men sitting on a bench beneath a tree. They looked at me very suspiciously and stopped talking as I approached. I waved to them and said "good morning" but I didn't get a response. I saw plenty of chickens, though, and a couple of goats. There was a donkey tethered somewhere near as I could hear it braying. Apart from that everywhere appeared to be deserted.'

'Many of the villagers would have returned to their homes by then. They would have started work at dawn before it became too hot, then they'll have a siesta before going back later when it has cooled down and probably work until dusk. It's not much fun being a farmer and you get scant rewards.'

'In that case this man Nikos we're hoping will turn up may have returned to Kastelli for a siesta if he's finished his other work,' frowned Adam.

Giovanni shrugged. 'It's possible, but I would expect it more likely he would come to Fourni from Sirmeso. It would make sense to come here first and then return home. He may not even finish his other job until late today and decide to come here tomorrow.'

'I don't think I could ever get used to the unreliability there seems to be here. If I arrange to meet someone in Athens I know they will be there.'

'We haven't arranged to meet Nikos,' Giovanni reminded Adam. 'We can't complain if he decides not to come to Fourni today.'

'Why don't you ask the taverna owner if he is here?' suggested Melina. 'He might know who is expecting him to call or he may even have arrived earlier and we will have missed him.'

'Which Nikos do you mean?' asked the taverna owner when Giovanni enquired. 'I'm Nikos and there are three others with that name in Fourni.'

'Nikos, the builder, who lives in Kastelli. We were told he was coming here to look at a job.'

Nikos, the taverna owner, shrugged. 'He might be. What would you like to eat?'

'Just salad for me,' declared Melina.

Giovanni considered. 'How about some pita bread, humus, taramasalata and olives along with a large bowl of salad?' and Melina and Adam nodded in agreement.

They lingered over their meal, hoping Nikos would appear, but there was no sign of him.

'Right,' said Giovanni finally. 'I really should get back home now. John should have been back from Spinalonga in plenty of time to relieve Marcus at the taverna so he could do the airport run, but there's another run needed later this afternoon. If I'm not back it will mean Marcus has to drive up and back a second time. Do you want to drive back to Kastelli and see if Nikos is there or go on to Sirmeso?'

'What do you want to do, Melina?' asked Adam. 'Go back with Giovanni or come searching for the builder with me?'

'I'll come with you. I'd be interested to see what this Nikos is like and if we go to Sirmeso it will be somewhere new for me to see.'

'Don't get excited,' Giovanni warned her. He took out his wallet and Adam waved him away.

'I will get this. I doubt if our food will cost as much as you paid for filling that old lady up with whisky.'

Adam followed Giovanni's directions back to the main road and halted at the turn off that was signed for Sirmeso to call the 'phone number Kassianae had given him for her son for a third time. There was still no answer and he shook his head.

'He's not answering. Either he's driving and can't hear the 'phone or there's no signal in the village. We'll drive down to Sirmeso and see if we can locate him.'

As they drove past the olive groves and vineyards, interspersed with small fields they were passed by a three wheeled farm vehicle, a hire car, two scooters and a couple on a motor bike going in the opposite direction. The village was so small that they had driven through before they realised and Adam turned their car and drove back slowly along the main street.

'Look for a taverna,' he instructed his wife. 'We can ask the owner if he's seen Nikos and if he knows where he's working.'

'Over there. That looks a likely place.'

Adam parked and leaving Melina in the car he walked over to the taverna. There were two tables outside that were unoccupied and the owner looked up hopefully as Adam entered the open door.

'What can I get you? Our meals are freshly cooked. Cold drinks can be taken away.'

Adam shook his head. 'I'm sorry, we have already eaten. I've stopped to ask if you could help me.'

'You are lost?'

'No. I understand that Nikos, the builder from Kastelli, is working in the village. I was hoping you might be able to tell me where I can find him.'

'He left a while ago. Saw him drive past.'

Adam clicked his tongue in annoyance. 'Any idea where he was going?'

The man shrugged. 'Home, I expect.'

'Thank you.' Adam returned to his car whilst the taverna owner glared after him. He could at least have bought a bottle of water.

'Back to Fourni,' Adam announced to Melina. 'He must have been on one of the scooters that passed us.'

'Well, I don't think Sirmeso had much to offer in the way of tourist attractions.'

'It's like most of the small farming villages in this area. Just a few houses, a church, taverna and general store. They all look very much the same.'

'Fourni is larger. How are you going to find him if he is there?'

'I'll try the taverna where we had lunch. The owner may have seen him pass by. If he doesn't know then we'll have to return to Kastelli and wait for him there. I'm sorry, Melina. You should have returned to Elounda with Giovanni. Driving around in circles must be very boring for you.'

'I would only have been sunbathing. Being with you I'm seeing something of the area away from the sea.'

'Not exactly exciting. Maybe we could go into Aghios Nikolaos tomorrow and we can look around the town.'

'You mean I can whilst you pursue your enquiries.'

Adam shrugged. 'They shouldn't take me too long.'

'Really?' Melina raised her eyebrows, disbelieving her husband's assurance.

The taverna owner in Fourni was surprised to see them return so quickly. He greeted them with a broad smile. 'Welcome. It is good to see you again. What would you like? Something more to eat or just some drinks?'

Adam shook his head. 'I'm still trying to contact Nikos, the builder. I think he drove past us on the road to Sirmeso, probably coming here. Have you seen him?'

'I saw him, but I don't know where he was going. Why don't you have a seat and a drink? When he drives back I could wave and stop him.'

'Will he drive back this way?'

'Bound to; only road to get back to Kastelli unless he goes down to Finokalia and drives back that way.'

Adam nodded. 'Thank you. I'll have a frappe and I'll check with my wife to see what she would like.' Adam signalled to Melina and she joined him at a table outside the taverna. 'I'm having a frappe. What would you like?'

'I'll have the same.'

Adam went to the doorway. 'Make that two frappes please. How are you going to see if Nikos drives past if you are inside?'

'If you see him you can stop him,' replied the owner logically.

'I don't know what he looks like.'

The taverna owner sighed and called out to a small boy who was playing with a toy car on a table at the rear. 'Yiorgos, go outside and look for Nikos. Wave to him to come in and call me.'

Obediently the boy went outside and stood watching the road, whilst Adam stood beside him. A scooter could be seen coming down the road and the boy squinted and raised his hand, only to drop it again and shake his head.

'Not Nikos.'

The frappes were brought to their table and Yiorgos returned inside whilst the taverna owner stood where he had a good view of the road and mopped his brow. It was cooler inside where he had the air conditioning running. He wished some other customers would arrive so he would have the excuse to call his son back out to watch the road.

Finally he raised his arm and waved frantically at the man who was approaching on a scooter. Nikos stopped, but continued to sit astride the machine with the engine running. Adam immediately went over to him.

'Are you Nikos?' he asked.

Nikos nodded. 'What's the problem?'

'There's no problem. I'd just like to have a few words with you. I spoke to your mother this morning.'

'That's right,' said Nikos.

'She gave me your 'phone number but you haven't answered any of my calls.'

'I was busy.'

'I've been asked to make a few enquiries about the fire in Kastelli and I understand you alerted the fire services.'

'That's right.'

'I'd just like to check a few facts with you. Please, join my wife and myself for a drink. I won't keep you for more than a few minutes.' Adam studied the man's appearance. He was of average height and was wearing a stained beige T-shirt and jeans that had streaks of cement on them and there were splashes of cement on his bare feet that were pushed into open sandals.

Grudgingly Nikos parked the scooter at the edge of the road and switched off the engine. 'A small beer,' he said to the taverna owner and inclined his head towards Melina as he took a seat at their table.

'I told the police all I know. No need to go over that again.' He drank half of the beer in one gulp and wiped his mouth with the back of his dirty hand.

'Quite,' said Adam. 'Your mother said she 'phoned you and you called the fire brigade. You also roused the other villagers and together you tried to bring the fire under control before the engines arrived.'

'That's right,' agreed Nikos.

'What were you wearing at the time?'

Nikos looked at Adam in amazement. 'My clothes, of course.'

'I believe you were woken up. Do you sleep in your clothes?'

'Of course not. I put my trousers on whilst I was talking to my mother.'

'Which trousers were they?'

'What do you mean?' Nikos was bemused. What difference did it make which trousers he was wearing? 'I put my working trousers on of course; wouldn't want to get my decent ones ruined.'

'Of course not. May I ask what colour your decent trousers are?'

'Black.'

'Do you have any others?'

'A couple of pairs of jeans.'

'You don't have any light coloured trousers?'

Nikos shook his head. Why was this man obsessed with his trousers? 'I wear the black ones when I go to church on a Sunday and jeans when I go to work. I don't have money for fancy trousers.'

'You wear a white shirt when you go to church?'

'Of course.'

'And when you are working you wear a T-shirt like the one you have on now?'

Nikos nodded. 'I wear a pullover in the winter.'

'I'm sure you need one if you're working outside. How many white shirts do you have?'

'Two. No need for any more.'

'And you would not have put a white shirt on that night when you went to fight the fire?'

Nikos regarded Adam scornfully. 'You don't put on a white shirt to go and do a dirty job.'

'I just thought you may have been wearing it earlier and it was the first one that came to hand.'

'I took off my working clothes when I went to bed, left them on the floor ready for the morning. Why would I bother to get out a clean shirt?'

'You didn't change and go out to the taverna that evening?'

'No. There was basketball on the television. Sat and watched that.'

'Good game?' Adam had no interest in the sport.

'Not bad. Seen better.'

'If you had gone to the taverna that evening what would you have been wearing?'

'Jeans and a T. Why? What's it to you what I was wearing?'

Adam leaned forward, sure the taverna owner had been listening to their conversation. 'There's some talk that you may have been involved in setting the house on fire.'

Nikos's face turned red in anger and he balled his fists. 'Who said that? It's not true.'

'It's just a rumour that I heard and I don't believe there is any truth to it.'

'It was the building inspector who did it,' insisted Nikos. 'My mother saw him.'

'She described the man she saw, but couldn't name him. I'm just trying to make certain the culprit is arrested for the crime and not an innocent man.'

'I didn't do it. Why would I? If the American woman didn't ask me to do the work the first time why would she ask me to repair the house now?'

'You were aggrieved that she did not ask you?'

Nikos shrugged. 'At first I was; then when I saw the amount of work Mr Palamakis was doing, the balcony supports, new roof, building the extension at the back, I realised it was far too much work for one man.'

'Your mother seems to think you should have been asked.'

'Yes, well, she would, wouldn't she? She's my mother.' Nikos emptied his glass. 'Is that all?'

'You've been very helpful. Thanks for your time.'

Adam watched as Nikos rode off down the road and Melina raised her eyebrows. 'So?'

'At present I'll keep an open mind, but unless Nikos and his mother are far cleverer than I imagine I cannot believe either of them are criminally involved.'

'In the best detective stories it is always the person who appears innocent who has committed the crime,' observed Melina.

'This is not a story, so I think we can disregard that theory,' said Adam dryly. He placed the money on the table for their drinks and raised his hand to the owner. 'Thanks for your help.'

John waited impatiently for his father to return from the airport. Immediately upon his return from Spinalonga he had sought out Nicola and told her that the tower was to be dismantled and the bones of the dead lepers were to be put on show.

'Wouldn't you have to get permission to bring them back and have them buried along with the other members of the family?'

'Probably, but I have a better idea,' smiled John. 'We let the workers believe we have brought Old Uncle Yannis back for burial here, but then we take him back and bury him beneath the floor of his house.'

'John! You can't.'

'Why not?'

'Well, it isn't sacred ground.'

'Nor was the tower.'

'But Father Minos used to hold a service for them before they were placed in the tower.'

'According to Dad, Aunt Anna insisted that Old Uncle Yannis would have wished to remain on Spinalonga. The island was closed by then, so a service and burial was arranged at the church here. The family went over to Spinalonga and Father Andreas, Old Uncle Yannis's cousin, held a service in the graveyard, then they placed Old Uncle Yannis into the tower and brought back the empty coffin.' John smiled triumphantly.

Nicola shook her head. 'You're not going to know his bones from the others, John. If you persist in this crazy idea you could end up with bones from half a dozen different people.'

'Aunt Anna washed his body and sewed a sheet around it. He would have been the last person placed in the tower so he should be on the top of everyone else. Provided the sheet hasn't decayed it should be simple to identify him.'

'And if the sheet has disintegrated and his bones have become mixed with the others? What then, John?'

John shrugged. 'Then I would have to give up the idea.'

'Suppose your father disagrees with you?'

John looked at Nicola and shook his head. 'If Dad disagrees I'll say no more about it. I'll then go over there on my own and bury him in his house.'

'You have to get him from the tower first,' Nicola reminded him.

'I've arranged that with one of the workmen. He said it would be at a least a week before they began to demolish the tower and I've arranged that he will 'phone me before they start.'

'Can you rely on him?'

'I've given him a down payment.'

'So assuming he does 'phone you and tell you the demolition is about to start what do you plan to do?'

'Go over and claim my great uncle.'

'Will they let you take away a body?'

John grinned sheepishly. 'I don't think they'll protest.'

'You mean you're paying them to turn a blind eye?'

'Exactly. I've got to provide him with some more cash and after that it should be straightforward enough. All I will need is a large strong box. I'm sure I can find something suitable at the stationery suppliers in Aghios Nikolaos. If not they're bound to have some over there to place the bones in when the time comes.'

Nicola raised her eyebrows. 'Have you really thought this

through, John? Would you be happy handling the bones of a dead person?'

John swallowed. 'I'll manage,' he muttered unconvincingly.

Giovanni waved John away when he tried to talk to him upon his return from the airport. 'Not now, John. However important you may consider your conversation to be I do have other things to deal with. I need to talk to Marcus about the airport run he did and ensure there were no problems then speak to your mother about tomorrow's agenda. Once I've done that Melina and Adam will be joining us and we will have to talk with them. They are our visitors. I'm sure whatever you wish to tell me will keep until tomorrow.'

Week Two – September 2012
Tuesday

Giovanni listened to John patiently; then he shook his head. 'I agree, I don't want Old Uncle Yannis's bones put on display, but I don't see how you are going to rebury him in his own house.'

'It will only be a question of taking a pickaxe to dig a hole and then we can place him in it.'

'A grave is generally dug six feet long and six feet deep.'

'There will be no need to dig a hole as large as that. There shouldn't be any flesh remaining on his bones after all this time. We will have his skeleton placed in a casket, the way you are supposed to do according to the Greek Orthodox religion.'

'The bones will still have to be washed and who is going to do that?'

John looked at Nicola and she shook her head. 'I can deal with the children if they are ill, but I'm not game for washing bones. I'd like to see you try and do it, you're far too squeamish.'

John frowned. He did not like to be reminded that he had fainted whilst watching Nicola give birth to their twins. 'Saffie,' he announced. 'I'm sure Saff wouldn't worry. She used to deal with bones and he's not really her relative so it would be impersonal.'

Giovanni sighed. He had an idea that whatever objections he raised to the reburial of Yannis Christoforakis his son would sweep them aside. He wondered if he should ask Adam about the legality of such an enterprise, but thought better of it. If Adam said it was totally illegal and John went ahead with the idea he could well end up in prison.

'What are your plans for today?' asked Giovanni as Melina and Adam appeared in the kitchen ready for breakfast.

'Well, after Melina putting up with us driving around the countryside yesterday I thought we'd go and have a word with Ronnie. I'd like her to show me exactly where the assault on her took place. Then I'll drive into Aghios Nikolaos. Melina can look around the town whilst I speak to Mr Palamakis,' smiled Adam. 'I might even visit the building inspectors' office.'

'Shall I 'phone Palamakis and arrange a time for you to visit?' asked Giovanni. 'You don't want to call unannounced and find he's out working.'

'Will Mr Palamakis answer his 'phone? I'm sure Nikos's mother had called him and said I wanted to question him so he was deliberately ignoring me.'

'Very likely. He's a bit of a strange one.'

'Is he married?'

'I believe so.'

'I might well go back to Kastelli at some point and see if I can speak to his wife. That taverna owner should know where she lives. If I ask his mother she'll probably 'phone her daughter-in-law and tell her not to answer the door to me. I don't understand why they should be so unwilling to talk to me.'

Giovanni grinned. 'You're a stranger. You don't talk to strangers apart from giving them directions. You managed to get some information from Nikos, though.'

'He answered my questions, but I wasn't able to lead him on to give me anything useful to work on. The only time he really opened up was when I mentioned that he might be considered responsible and hoped to be given the repair work. He was reasonable in his assumption that the job would have been too big for him to tackle in the first place and thought Ronnie would be unlikely to ask him to take over now.'

Ronnie was easily found sitting at her easel in the small square at Plaka. Melina wandered over to the shops and looked at the goods on display. In Yannis's shop there were pots of different sizes and designs, all labelled as genuine museum copies, and a note on the door with a telephone number where he was able to be contacted. She looked at the tables placed outside Saffron's shop with attractive souvenirs laid out and a large ginger cat looked back at her from a basket.

'Are you for sale?' she asked with a smile as she bent and stroked him.

Saffron appeared at the doorway and placed a guide book to Spinalonga on the table. 'Can I help you?' she asked.

'I'm really just browsing and waiting for my husband. He's talking to Ronnie.'

'Are you interested in Ronnie's paintings? I have a good selection in the shop.'

Melina shook her head. 'Not today. I'll be back at some time to have a proper look at your goods. Bryony has told me that if I want souvenirs I should come here. I gather your cat is not for sale?'

Saffron smiled. 'You must be the friends who are staying with Giovanni. No, our cat is not for sale, although I'm not sure we can really claim him as ours. He adopted us. If you do want a cat I can direct you to a lady who rescues them. She's always looking for someone to give one a good home.'

Melina shook her head. 'I don't think an apartment in Athens would be suitable for a cat. I've even resisted having a bird as we are both out each day.'

Ronnie collapsed her easel and packed away her paints. She walked up to Saffron's shop, allowing Adam to carry the easel for her.

'Adam wants me to go up the hill to show him the view of Spinalonga,' she explained as she took her easel from Adam and carried it through to the small back room.

Saffron raised her eyebrows. No one needed a guide to take them up the hill to see the view of Spinalonga. There were various vantage points where a car could draw in and visitors could take a photograph.

'He wants to see exactly where Babbis took me,' she added in an undertone and Saffron nodded. Bryony had told her that Adam and his wife were visiting and hoping to ascertain the perpetrator of the fire.

Adam smiled at Saffron. 'I'm still trying to get relationships sorted out. I believe you are Bryony's half sister and your partner is Vasi Iliopolakis?'

'That's right. From believing I was alone in the world apart from my step mother I came here for a holiday and found all my relations and Vasi.'

'I'd like to have a quick word with both of you at some point, just to corroborate some information Ronnie has given me.'

'Vasi is in Heraklion at the moment.'

'You can probably answer my question. I understand from Mr Palamakis that he has been contracted by Vasi to work on refurbishing his hotel once the season is over. Is that correct?'

'Mr Palamakis usually does any work that is necessary at the hotel so I expect he will be working there during the winter months, but you'd have to ask Vasi. He'll know the arrangements he's made. He should be back by Friday at the latest.'

'There's absolutely no urgency. I'll give you a call and arrange to meet when it is convenient for both of you.'

Melina shook her head; so much for Adam saying they would only be staying for a few days and then travelling around the rest of Crete.

Ronnie directed Adam and Melina up the hill to where Babbis had stopped his car.

'You do get a wonderful view of the island from here. I've even done some paintings here so that I can show the island from a different perspective. They're not as popular as the ones I do from the square as the tourists who are on an organised coach visit don't have time to come up the hill. They have about an hour on the island, time for lunch and then they're taken back to Aghios Nikolaos. Those who take the boat tour from Aghios Nikolaos don't get the opportunity to come over to Plaka or Elounda.'

'So tell me again exactly what happened between you and Babbis. Which way was his car facing when you got out?'

'He had turned so he was ready to drive back down the road.'

'So as you ran past the driver's side you grabbed the keys from the ignition?'

Ronnie nodded. 'The car window was open and it was just instinctive. I realised as I ran down the road that he may well have had a spare set in the glove compartment or his pocket.'

'Quick thinking on your part. Incidentally, what colour is his car?'

Ronnie looked at Adam in surprise. What difference did the colour of the car make? 'It's a dark blue.'

'Do you know the registration number?'

Ronnie wrinkled her forehead. 'I think there were the numerals two and four. I never really took any notice of it.'

She gave Adam a detailed account of the evening she had spent with Babbis, culminating in her temporarily disabling him and running down the hill to Kyriakos's taverna. 'It was fortunate he was still there. I was sure Babbis would come after me and I would not be able to get away from him a second time.'

'I'd like to meet Kyriakos. Could we stop there and have a drink as we return?'

'He may not be open yet. His ankle is still in a plaster cast and he has to rely on the chef for transport up and down from Elounda.'

'How does he normally get there? Has he a scooter or a car?'

'A car, he allows me to drive it when I go up to Kastelli.'

'What colour is his car?'

'Dark blue.' Why was Adam so interested in the colour of the cars that people drove wondered Ronnie?

'Do you know the registration number?'

'Yes.' Ronnie recited it immediately.

Adam took a last look at the view and returned to his hire car.

'Do you want to drive further up?' asked Ronnie. 'There are a couple more places where you can stop and you can drive right to the top of the hill and there's a marvellous view from there.'

'I'd like to,' said Melina immediately.

Adam nodded. 'That's fine. On the way back down would you be able show me where you threw the car keys?'

Ronnie looked doubtful. 'I'm really not sure. It was dark. John will be able to tell you where he found them.'

'Does he still have them?'

'I believe so.'

Kyriakos had only just arrived at the taverna when Adam drew up. He greeted Ronnie with delight.

'What would you like? A drink or are you here for an early lunch?'

'Just a drink, please. I'll get them. We've been up to the top of the hill to look at the view. There's a plot of land for sale up there.'

Kyriakos shook his head. 'Who would want to live up there? You need more than a view for a comfortable life.' He sat down at the table with Adam and Melina. 'You are staying with Giovanni, I understand. Miss Ronnie said you are here to help her prove that Babbis set fire to her house.'

Adam smiled. News certainly travelled fast in the area. 'I'm hoping to ascertain who committed the crime. I won't accuse this man Babbis until I have absolute proof.'

Kyriakos looked at Adam derisively. 'Of course he did it. Miss Ronnie told me the old lady in the village saw him.'

'She saw someone who may have been Babbis. He drives a dark blue car, so do you and many other people around here. At night, by the light of the moon and street lamp, she may have thought it was Babbis she saw.'

Kyriakos shrugged. 'He tried to assault Miss Ronnie. She gave him a black eye and ran down here to me for help. Of course it was Babbis,' he declared.

'When she arrived at your taverna and asked for help, what did you do?' asked Adam.

'Once I had made sure she was not truly hurt I telephoned Giovanni and asked if she could spend the night at their house. I did not think she should go back to her apartment. Babbis knew where she lived. He may have tried to force his way in during the night.'

'Very sensible of you. Ah, here comes Ronnie with our drinks.'

'She has been a great help to me since my accident.' Kyriakos scratched at his arm and then withdrew his fingers hurriedly. He did not want to take the scab off and get blood on the sleeve of his shirt.

'How did it happen?'

'I was run down by two young men on their motor bike. They had tried to rob me. A customer threw a bottle at them and they lost control of the bike. I do not think they deliberately tried to run me down.' Kyriakos scratched at his arm again as he spoke. The abrasions he had suffered to his arms were taking a long time to heal completely.

'A frightening experience.'

'It was awful,' said Ronnie as she placed a beer in front of Adam and lemonade for herself and Melina. 'Kyriakos was lying there and I thought they had killed him.'

'The ground is hard when you hit it with your head.' Kyriakos tried to make light of the incident.

'I called the police, Saffie and John.'

Adam raised his eyebrows. 'The police I understand, but why Saffron and John?'

'I wanted Saffie to help Kyriakos. She used to be a doctor so would know what was best to do for him and I needed John to act as an interpreter. The boys on the motor bike were English and so was the customer who had stopped them. My limited Greek would certainly not be good enough to explain the situation.'

'And they both came up?'

'At once. They both arrived before the police.'

'What happened to the boys?'

'They are in custody. They had been systematically going around the island robbing people.'

Adam nodded. If the two young men were in police custody they could certainly not have set fire to Ronnie's house, even if they had known it belonged to her. Although Kyriakos's car was dark blue he was in hospital at the time and he would have had no reason to damage her house.

'Would you like us to drive you back to Elounda or are you planning to stay up here with Kyriakos?'

'I ought to go back and remove my materials from Saffron's shop,' replied Ronnie. 'I'll come up this evening, Kyriakos and help out.'

Kyriakos smiled. He would have liked her to stay for the afternoon. It would probably have been quiet and he would have been able to talk to her seriously in the hope of persuading her to marry him. He knew that it would be impossible in the evening as she took orders from the customers and he relayed them to the chef in Greek. Although he was able to walk around in the plaster cast now he could not move as swiftly and easily as previously and he hoped it would be removed on his visit to the hospital in two week's time.

'Will you join us for lunch, Ronnie?' asked Melina.

Ronnie hesitated. 'We could have had some lunch with Kyriakos.'

''I'm sure we could, but would he have charged us or insisted on giving it to us as he's a friend of yours?'

Ronnie blushed. 'He would probably have said it was in exchange for me helping him in the evenings.'

'He doesn't pay you?'

'Of course not. Once he's had his plaster off he won't need me to run in and out any more. I wouldn't expect payment for a favour.'

Adam shook his head. 'That doesn't sound very Greek to me. Favours are either expected to be reciprocated or a payback will be expected of you later.'

Ronnie blushed even more deeply. 'He has done me many favours in the past. This is my turn to repay some of them. If he hadn't confirmed that he saw me find the money in the mattress when he helped me turn out at Kastelli I could have been convicted of money laundering with Vasi as an accomplice. I'll return to my apartment, thank you. I made a salad earlier and if I don't eat it now it will be wasted, although it's in the fridge.'

Adam was secretly pleased that Ronnie would not be joining them. If they ate at a taverna it would be a leisurely meal taking most of the afternoon. If they returned to the house for a snack he could ask Giovanni to telephone Mr Palamakis and arrange a time to meet him and that could leave time to visit the building inspectors' office later.

Mr Palamakis was quite willing for Adam to visit him and having arranged where he would meet Melina later, Adam knocked on the builder's door. He was ushered into a small front room and introduced to Giorgos and Yiannis.

'Mr Giovanni said you wished to discuss the Kastelli house so I thought you might want to speak to the boys at the same time.'

'That was very thoughtful of you.' Adam sat down at the table. 'I'd really just like to ask you about the work you did up there. I understand it was quite a big job.'

Mr Palamakis nodded. 'We needed some additional help with some of it. How that Nikos thought he would have done it all single handed is beyond me.'

'I think he realises that now. Tell me exactly what your work entailed.'

Mr Palamakis was only too happy to sit and explain to Adam the requests Ronnie had made. 'She agreed the exterior was to remain exactly the same. Good job, as she would never have had permission to alter any of it. That inspector is a stickler for the rules and regulations. I told Miss Vandersham that we had to comply with whatever he said and once the work had been passed and the house signed off as completed she could make alterations inside if she wanted.'

'What alterations would they have been? Do you know?'

'She wanted a couple of the doorways arched, all the pipes and electrical work hidden away, and she planned to have the storeroom at the end of the extension as her workroom.'

'And the building inspector objected?'

'He said altering the doorways could make the walls unsafe. Rubbish. We would have made sure they were well supported. He tried to make a fuss about the drain runs not being at the correct angle. We knew they were so we ignored him.'

'Did this often happen?' asked Adam.

'What? The drain runs?'

'No, him saying the work was not of a sufficient standard and would have to be done again.'

Mr Palamakis snorted. 'That man is just a crook. He often failed work and demanded that it was done a second time so the customer had to pay for him to make a second visit.'

'Was the work done a second time?'

Mr Palamakis shook his head. 'I've never done my work a second time whatever he has said. I always knew it was up to standard and complied with the regulations. The next time he came out he passed it without question.'

'Is there only one building inspector?'

'No, there are two of them; Panos Lamanakis and Babbis Skourlatakis, along with the crippled man who works in the office, but he's not an inspector.'

'Which of the inspectors was in charge of signing off your work?'

'Skourlatakis.'

'Did you ever have any problem regarding payment for your work?'

'No, Miss Vandersham and I had an agreement. I would present her with a bill for materials and labour at the end of the week and we would go to the bank together. She had an arrangement to draw whatever she wanted from her American account and always paid me in full whilst we were in the bank.'

'What about the work on the roof and the iron work? Did she pay for those separately?' asked Adam.

'No, everything went through me. She said she would be charged each time she withdrew money so would prefer to pay one large bill to me and she trusted me to settle with the other suppliers. There was never any problem.'

'Does she owe you for any work now?'

Mr Palamakis shook his head. 'Paid me for clearing the place out after the fire and we've not done any work since up there. We were so close to being finished and I was proud of the job we'd done. Wasn't that so, boys?'

All the while Mr Palamakis had been speaking to Adam his grandsons had nodded their heads in agreement with his words.

'We were all proud of our work,' agreed Yiannis. 'We'd done straight forward rebuilding before, but never tackled restoration like that.'

'Hoped to use it as an advert,' added Giorgos. 'I'd enjoyed myself and would have liked to have been asked to do something similar in one of the other villages.'

'Do you have any other work at present?'

'Not really. We'd turned work away. Wanted to finish everything up in Kastelli; then have a week or two off before starting Mr Vasi's decoration and refurbishment when the tourist season finished. Once the visitors have left there's always plenty of work getting the hotels and tavernas ready for next year.'

'Just one other question. Do any of you have a car?'

Both the boys shook their heads. 'We have scooters,' answered Yiannis. 'Can't afford to run a car.'

'And you, Mr Palamakis?'

'The truck that is outside. More useful than a car. We can put all our tools and materials in the back without causing any damage to upholstery.'

Adam checked his watch as he left the builder and his grandsons. He had an hour before he was due to meet Melina. Enough time to visit the building inspectors' office and see if Babbis Skourlatakis was there.

He looked at the name plates on the desks, noting which one said "Babbis Skourlatakis". Both men were busy and there was another man waiting and Adam took a seat beside him.

The man smiled sympathetically. 'Waste of time having to come here to ask the building inspector to come out and check a job. My builders know what they're doing.'

Adam nodded. 'Which inspector are you dealing with?'

'Skourlatakis unfortunately. He's a stickler. Refused to sign off the work done on my drains. Says the run is not steep enough. It's no different from the way it was before. The pipe that was cracked has been renewed and it works perfectly whenever the cistern is flushed.'

'Have you had the work done a second time?'

'No,' the man shook his head. 'No need. When I've paid him to make another visit he'll pass them.'

Adam frowned. This was the second time he had been told that Skourlatakis would condemn satisfactory work and have to make a return visit for which he would be paid again.

'What about Mr Lamanakis?'

'He's fair enough. If the work is substandard he asks for it to be done again, but if it's satisfactory he will always sign it off on his first visit. What are you asking to have checked?'

'Nothing, actually. I just want to have a word with Mr Skourlatakis.'

'You'd do better to deal with Lamanakis.'

'Do you have a choice of which inspector checks out work?'

'No. You're expected to use whichever one is free when you arrive.'

The man at Mr Lamanakis's desk rose and the inspector looked up expectantly at the two waiting men. Both of them shook their heads. Mr Lamanakis handed some papers to the man sitting behind him who then limped into a back room out of sight.

Adam sat patiently whilst the man he had been speaking with went up to Babbis and arranged a date for the inspector to make a further call on his property. Mr Lamanakis looked again at Adam.

'Can I help you?'

'No, thank you. I have to see Mr Skourlatakis.'

Mr Lamanakis removed his name plate from the desk. 'I'll take a break now as we're not busy,' he said to Babbis.

Once the man had made his appointment and was leaving the building Adam rose and took his place in the chair in front of Babbis's desk.

'Good afternoon. I was hoping I could have a few words with you privately.' Adam looked meaningfully at Alecos.

'There's some filing needs doing.' Babbis tipped his head towards Alecos who rose obediently. He would have liked to remain and hear the private conversation that was about to take place. Even with his ear to the door it could be difficult if the men spoke quietly.

'So, what do you want to see me about?' asked Babbis.

'Well,' Adam appeared to be diffident. 'It's really about an incident that took place with Miss Vandersham.'

'What has that to do with you?'

'Miss Vandersham is considering whether she should take any further action, maybe bring proceedings against you.'

'That's ridiculous. It was weeks ago. She has no grounds to make a formal complaint against me.'

Adam smiled. 'I thought that might be the case. Could you just tell me about the events that took place that evening?'

'We'd had a pleasant evening together and I suggested that I took her up the hill to see Spinalonga floodlit. She agreed. We got out of the car and I placed my arm around her shoulders. Nothing more. She screamed, hit me and ran off down the road as if the devil himself was after her.'

'Did you follow her in your car?'

Babbis shook his head. 'She was unlikely to come to any harm and if I'd caught up with her she may have used her mobile to call the police.'

'How long did you wait before you drove away?'

Babbis shrugged. 'I'm not sure. Probably about fifteen minutes. I was angry that she had misunderstood and hit me. I needed to calm down so I smoked a cigarette before leaving.'

'Did you see her as you drove back down?'

'There was no sign of her on the road. I can only imagine she had reached her apartment and locked herself inside.'

Adam nodded. 'Well, I think that's all. Oh, by the way, what colour car do you drive?'

'A white one.'

Adam raised his eyebrows. 'Really? Miss Vandersham told me it was dark blue.'

'I traded that one in recently. Cars don't last that long when you have to drive over the country roads.'

'You don't have a car supplied for your work?'

Babbis shook his head. 'Condition of employment, clean driving licence and you use your own car.'

'Bit unfair. What about parking tickets? Do they take those into account?'

'No, only accidents where you've either injured someone or claimed on your insurance.'

'Do they at least provide you with a parking space?'

'Yes, round the back. Certainly saves having to go around searching for somewhere when you return from a job.'

'I'm contemplating changing my car. Where did you use?'

'The large garage on the outskirts by the roundabout. Plenty of cars on their forecourt to choose from.'

'Did you get a good deal on yours?'

'Couldn't complain.'

'I'd want a five door. My wife and I travel a good deal so we need a decent sized boot. Is yours large enough to take a couple of suitcases?'

'Never had occasion to put a suitcase in there, but I would think so. I just use it for a box of tools, the red triangle and a jack in case I have to change a tyre.'

'And are the cars covered by a warranty?'

'Six months on any repairs that have been done if you buy a second hand, full year if it's a new one you purchase.'

Adam rose. 'Thank you for your time, you've been very helpful. I'll take a run out to the garage you recommend and take a look.'

'No problem,' smiled Babbis, confident that Ronnie would be told to forget the incident ever took place.

Adam sat back down. 'I was so busy talking to you and getting advice about a car that I almost forgot. I have to ask where you were on the night of the Kastelli fire '

'Why? I had nothing to do with it.'

'It's just a formality. I have to ask everyone who had any dealings with the property. I've spoken to the builders and they say you were the inspector who visited the house to sign off their work. If I haven't asked everyone I'll be in dereliction of my duty. It's just for the records.' Adam smiled disarmingly at Babbis.

'I was with a friend; playing cards. We played until the early hours of the morning.'

'Where were you? At a club?'

'No, I was at his house.'

Adam took out his notebook. 'The name of this friend, please, and his address?'

'He lives in Aghios Nikolaos.'

'His exact address, please, as I will need to speak to him.'

'There's no need for that. He works in the office with me. You can speak to him here. He'll confirm that we were together.'

'Are you referring to the young man who went into the back room?'

Babbis nodded. 'Alecos Vikelakis. I'll ask him to come out and speak to you.' It suddenly occurred to Babbis that he had no idea of the identity of the man who was questioning him. 'Who are you, anyway? Have you come from an insurance company?'

Adam smiled. 'I've been asked to make a few enquiries.' He evaded answering Babbis's question directly.

Babbis walked to the door leading into the back room. 'Alecos,' he called. 'You're needed here.'

Alecos limped out and looked in surprise at Babbis. 'What's the problem?'

'This man is from an insurance company and he's asking where I was on the night that the house in Kastelli caught fire. I've told him I was with you.'

Alecos smirked. This was even better than he had anticipated. If Babbis needed him to confirm they were together the man must have had a hand in setting the fire. To give him an alibi would cost Babbis far more than the five hundred Euros that had originally been agreed.

'How can I help you?'

'Mr Skourlatakis claims that on the night the house in Kastelli was set alight he was with you, playing cards until the early hours of the morning.'

'That's right,' agreed Alecos much to Babbis's relief.

'Where were you playing this card game?'

'At my house.'

'You live alone?'

'With my parents in Aghios Nikolaos.'

'Who won the card game eventually?' asked Adam with a smile.

'I did,' announced Alecos. 'Won just over a thousand Euros.'

Babbis gave an audible gasp and glared at Alecos as Adam raised his eyebrows. 'Some game! You must be quite an accomplished player. I don't think I'd want to pit my chances against you.'

Alecos smiled. He was no expert at cards, but willing to take the compliment.

'Thank you both for your help. If I could just make a note of your names and addresses.' Adam looked at both men expectantly.

'Is that necessary? You know where we work.'

'Officialdom can take a tremendous amount of time. If anyone decided to speak to you again in the future you could both have moved on to work elsewhere.'

Alecos shrugged and gave his address which Adam wrote down. 'And yours, Mr Skourlatakis, if you please.'

Grudgingly Babbis gave his address. Inwardly he was seething. Alecos had agreed five hundred Euros for giving him an alibi and now he had raised it to a thousand!

'What time do you close today?' asked Adam as he rose a second time.

'Lunch break is from one until three and then we are here until six. Why?'

'I doubt that I'll need to call again, but a good idea for me to know your working hours just in case.'

'They're on the door.' Alecos offered the information.

'Of course,' agreed Adam. 'Silly question. I should have thought before I asked you.'

Babbis rounded on Alecos angrily after Adam had left. 'We agreed on five hundred Euros.'

Alecos shrugged. 'The price has just escalated. You can afford it. You've just bought a new car. I thought I was keeping you out of trouble with your wife. What were you up to that weekend?'

'None of your business.'

140

'Oh, I think it is. If you expect me to say you were with me I need to know where you actually were at the time.'

'I had some business in another village.'

'Really?' Alecos raised his eyebrows. 'That wouldn't have been the village of Kastelli, would it?'

Babbis turned away and set his mouth in a grim line. He had no intention of confiding in Alecos.

Adam walked around to the rear of the building where there was a small car park marked "Government Employees Only". The registration numbers of the cars allowed to use the area were painted on the ground between white lines that delineated their allotted space. Adam surveyed them and walked across to where there was a white car parked. He looked at the registration details painted on the ground and checked the number plate. They were not the same.

He made a note of the painted registration gratified to see a two and a four amongst the numbers. On show in the windscreen was a hand written notice saying the car belonged to Babbis Skourlatakis who was entitled to use the parking space and across the back window was a sticker with the name of the garage. He would pay them a visit on their way back to Elounda.

Adam walked back to the coffee bar where he had agreed to meet Melina. If Babbis had lost that large sum of money to Alecos why had he seemed surprised and annoyed when Alecos mentioned the amount? He had not wanted to appear too inquisitive and put both men on their guard, but it could be worth his while to call on Alecos's parents and see if card games were a regular occurrence at the weekends. He would do that now before the young man had the opportunity to return home and ask his parents to confirm the story.

Melina was waiting for him and raised her eyebrows. 'How was your visit to the builders?'

Adam nodded. 'They seem like decent young men and are happy to work for their grandfather. I want to make a quick visit to an address in Aghios Nikolaos and then I'd like to stop at a garage on our way back to Elounda, if you don't mind.'

'Is there a problem with the car?'

'Not at all. I called into the building inspectors' office on my way here. I understand that Babbis Skourlatakis traded in his old blue car for a new white one. I'm hoping they might still have it there.'

Melina looked at her husband doubtfully. 'How are you going to know which one was his? They could have any number of blue cars.'

'I do have the registration.'

'What are you hoping to find?'

Adam shrugged. 'Probably nothing at all. He's not likely to have left a bill for the petrol or an empty can in the boot.'

'They've probably given it a thorough cleaning by now ready to sell. If you do find anything that you think links him with the crime what will you do?'

Adam smiled and tapped his pocket. 'I'm sure they wouldn't mind looking after it for me for a few days.'

Adam drew up before the small house in Aghios Nikolaos and hoped Alecos's parents would be at home. He knocked and waited, finally hearing shuffling footsteps and the door was opened.

'Yes?' A man stood there, his hand on his chest.

'Mr Vikelakis? I'm sorry to bother you, but may I ask you a few questions?'

'I'm not a well man.' He tried to close the door.

Adam produced his identification. 'I'll not keep you more than a few minutes. Would you prefer to go inside and sit down?'

Mr Vikelakis nodded and led the way into the living room where he subsided into a deep arm chair. 'Heart, you know,' he said by way of an explanation and waved Adam to a chair at the table. 'Means I can't get out and about as I used to. Stuck inside the house all day.'

'Very worrying. As I said, I'll not keep you very long. Are you Alecos's father?'

'What's he done?'

'Nothing to the best of my knowledge,' Adam spoke reassuringly. 'He works at the building inspectors' office I believe.'

'Only job he was able to get after his accident. Wonder he wasn't killed. They never have brought the driver who ran him off the road to justice. My son should have received enough compensation to keep him in luxury for the rest of his life.' The man paused, panting for breath.

'He has a colleague in the office, name of Babbis Skourlatakis?'

Alecos's father nodded and clasped his chest again.

'They're good friends as well as colleagues?'

'How would I know?'

'I was under the impression that he came here some weekends and played cards with your son.'

'Never. I wouldn't allow card games in my house. Quickest way to make enemies and lose all your money.'

'They wouldn't have been able to play cards here without your knowledge?'

'Impossible. My wife and I sleep in here, Alecos's bedroom is behind this room and the kitchen and bathroom are out the back.'

Adam rose from the hard chair he had been sitting on. 'I must have made a mistake. Maybe Alecos goes to Babbis's house to play cards.'

Alecos's father pursed his lips. 'I can't stop my son going to a gambling club, but he knows his mother and I disapprove.'

Adam pretended to look alarmed. 'Please, don't mention my visit to him, Mr Vikelakis. I may have completely misunderstood and I wouldn't want to get him into trouble. No, don't get up. I can see myself out.'

Adam was anxious to leave the man before he began to question him further about the interest that was being shown in his son.

Melina was surprised to see her husband return so swiftly and placed a marker inside her book. 'I've only read a couple of pages.'

'I told you I wouldn't be more than a few minutes. You'll be able to catch up on your reading whilst I'm at the garage.'

The garage was easy to spot as they drove towards the roundabout and turn off for Elounda. There was a banner stretched along a high wire fence advertising their name and proclaiming new and used cars for sale.

'Do you want to come with me or stay in the car?'

'I'll stay here and read until you get back. If you're more than half an hour I'll come looking for you. It would be nice to be back in Elounda in time for a quick swim.'

Adam parked in front of the main building and began to wander through the lines of parked cars. As he had surmised within minutes a salesman had approached him.

'How can I help you, sir? Are you looking for a new car?' The salesman looked at the hire car Adam was driving.

'I'm looking for a specific car. I know it is blue and I have the registration number. I believe the owner traded it in with you for a new white model.'

'I can assure you the paper work will have been in order. We are very particular about checking. We certainly do not want to trade in a stolen vehicle.'

'I'm sure there was no question of it being stolen. I believe the owner may have left something inside.'

The salesman frowned. 'Had we found anything we would have contacted the person and returned it to them.'

'I'm sure you would. If you still have the car in your possession I'd be very grateful if you would allow me to examine it. Here's the registration.'

Adam handed a slip of paper to the salesman who shrugged. 'I think you should speak to the manager. I can't say without consulting the records. If you would like to come to the office with me I can see if we still have the keys. If they have gone then the car will have been sold.'

'If that is the case I'd appreciate you giving me the name and address of the new owner.'

'Has this car been used in a robbery or do you suspect stolen goods hidden inside it?' The salesman looked at Adam warily.

'Nothing like that, I can assure you.'

Still clutching the piece of paper and feeling doubtful the salesman made his way to the office with Adam following him. The office was sparsely furnished with four plastic work desks and matching chairs. In front of each desk two chairs were placed, obviously intended for prospective purchasers and there were four more placed in a corner. At one desk sat a very large woman stabbing ponderously at the keyboard of a computer. As the salesman explained Adam's errand she ceased typing and listened curiously.

The manager ignored her and went to the back wall where there was a peg board with literally hundreds of keys hanging, each with a tag recording the registration number of the vehicle. The man worked his way along the line, checking each tag and finally lifted a set of keys from the hook.

'I believe these belong to the car you are looking for.'

'Do you know if the car will have been cleaned since it was left with you?' asked Adam.

The manager shook his head. 'It will depend where it is parked. We only put them out on the forecourt and advertise them when they have been thoroughly checked over by our mechanics and cleaned inside and out. We want them to look at their best. According to the date on the tag we've only had it for a few days.'

'It could save time if we looked at those awaiting attention first,' said Adam firmly and the manager led the way around to the rear of his office.

A large concrete building sprawled across the area. Metal doors were open and Adam could see a car raised up above a pit and various others with their bonnets raised and the engines being examined. At the far end was a hose pipe and judging by the amount of water that was on the ground it had been used recently. The manager pointed to where half a dozen cars were parked with a low wire fence and a gate keeping them separated from the vehicles on show.

'This is where we keep them until they have been worked on. When the mechanics declare them sound they bring them down to the finishing area where they are washed and polished before going out on the forecourt. If there's insufficient space on the forecourt we store them here and work on them at a later date.'

'Do you leave them exposed on the forecourt all the time?'

The manager shook his head and pointed to some wooden supports. 'When we close we erect the polythene protection along the sides and up to the awning. It's mechanised so only takes about half an hour. Keeps them protected if the weather changes.'

'You don't have any problem with vandals or people looking for a free ride?'

The manager grinned. 'We padlock the front gates and let the dogs roam around. It would be a bit foolish for anyone to try to get in.'

'Where are the dogs now?' Adam looked around nervously.

'Locked in their compound. We make sure everyone is off the premises before we let them out. That includes the employees. Once we see Manolis arrive we know it's time to shut shop for the day. He's the only one who can deal with them. Now, the car you say you are looking for is blue, right?'

Adam nodded. There were four blue cars and he began to check their number plates. 'Here it is,' he said. 'Would you be good enough to unlock all four doors and the boot, please? I'd like you to stay with me and ensure that I do not put anything in the car or remove anything without your knowledge and agreement.'

Looking thoroughly bemused the manager unlocked the doors and raised the lid of the boot. He stood back as Adam peered inside the back, first from one side and then the other and sniffed at the floor covering. There was a slight smell of petrol in the area of the foot pedals. He slipped his fingers down between the backrest and the seat, finding nothing except a scrap of sweet paper. He repeated the procedure on the driver's side and found nothing. Taking his clean handkerchief from his pocket he wiped the steering wheel and collected a residue of grease and general grubbiness.

'Who parks the car here when you have purchased it?' he asked the manager.

'We get the owner to do so.'

Adam nodded. The grease would have come naturally from Babbis's hands, along with the dust and grime that was in the air. He folded his handkerchief carefully, ensuring the marks were inside, and placed it in his pocket

He moved around to the passenger side and as he slid his hand down the back of the seat he could feel something wedged down there. He knelt on the seat and a faint waft of perfume came up. He wondered if that was from Ronnie or Babbis's wife. Having made a slightly larger gap he managed to grasp whatever he had found between two fingers and drew it gradually upwards and between the back rest and seat. It was a handkerchief, similar to his own, but when he held it up to the light he could see translucent marks and there was a smell of petrol adhering to it. He turned to the salesman.

'When we return to the office I would like you to record that you saw me find this wedged down the back of the front seat on the passenger side.'

'Is that what you were looking for?'

'Maybe.' Adam held the cloth carefully between two fingers and walked to the boot of the car. The base was covered in coarse carpeting, but the sides were bare metal. Adam sniffed. He was certain he could smell petrol.

'I'm sorry to be a nuisance, but could we return to the office so I can place this handkerchief into a bag? I'd then like to return to examine the boot more thoroughly.'

'We'll be closing soon.' The manager, having been intrigued at first, was now bored with watching Adam.

'As soon as I have dealt with the handkerchief I'm sure I will not need more than a few minutes longer to finish my inspection.'

Once back in the office Adam asked for two clean paper bags.

The manager shook his head. 'I haven't any paper bags. Anything we sell comes pre-packed.' He waved his hand airily towards a miscellaneous selection that included windscreen wipers, light bulbs, upholstery cleaning kit and key fobs.

Adam clicked his tongue in annoyance. 'Then take a couple of items out from their bags and I'll use those.'

'Can't do that. The customer won't know they're new if they're not in their packaging.'

'I'll buy them.' said Adam in exasperation. 'Two windscreen wipers, please. Just open the bag at one end and take them out. Try not to touch the inside of the polythene.'

Carefully Adam inserted the handkerchief he had found in the car into one bag and then turned to the salesman. 'Please write down that you saw me find this pushed down the back of the passenger seat of the car you traded in for Mr Skourlatakis; then I would like you to sign and date it.'

'Who are you?' The manager suddenly realised he had no idea of Adam's identity. 'Are you a policeman?'

'Something like that. When we've dealt with this I can show you my identification.'

Dutifully the man wrote as Adam had directed and Adam then placed his own handkerchief where he had wiped the steering wheel in the other polythene bag. 'Another note, please. You saw me take this from my pocket and wipe the steering wheel of the car you had traded in for Mr Skourlatakis, with your signature and date.'

Once the notes were written Adam asked for a stapler and sealed each bag, attaching the hand written notes appropriately. He laid them on the counter in front of him.

'How much do I owe you for the windscreen wipers?'

The manager hesitated. 'If you're a policeman I'll not charge you.'

Adam withdrew his wallet and held up his Embassy identification card. 'I'm relying on you to keep our meeting to yourself. I'm working undercover at the moment so no one must know I have been here and taken any possible evidence away from the car.'

Round eyed, the manager nodded.

'That includes telling your wife or your mates in the taverna tonight,' added Adam sternly. 'You would be committing an offence.'

The manager reddened. He had had every intention of telling his wife and visiting the taverna with the story of the strange man who examined the interior of a car and kept smelling the carpets.

'Now, if we could just return to the car for a few minutes so I can have a proper look in the boot.'

'I'm not in any trouble, am I?' he asked anxiously.

'None at all, provided you act exactly as I say.'

Adam smelled the carpet again. There definitely was a smell of petrol on the carpet in one area. Gingerly he tried to lift the corner, but it was firmly stuck down. He turned back to the manager.

'This car is not to be touched in any way until I give you permission. No maintenance or cleaning inside or out. I believe it has been used at a crime scene and until it is proved otherwise the evidence must be preserved. Do you have a tarpaulin that can cover it for a few days?'

The manager nodded. He hoped that he would eventually be told the reason the car held so much interest.

'Did you find something useful?' asked Melina as Adam returned to the car and placed the two polythene bags into the glove compartment.

'I think so. I'll need to go back at a later date, but the manager has agreed not to have the car touched until I give permission.

Now we'll go straight home and you can have your swim. Once I've locked these bags safely away in my briefcase I'll take a walk up to the taverna and have a word with John.'

'Why don't you have a swim first and see John when he comes home?'

Adam shook his head. 'I want him to show me where he found the car keys. If I wait until he returns I'll only have to ask him to walk back up there with me.'

Adam timed his walk to arrive at the taverna just as John was closing for the day. Skele was sitting outside and wagged his tail at Adam.

'You've still got your dog, I see?'

'Wouldn't part with him for the world. He still lives down with Dimitris, but I collect him each morning and bring him here. He runs along at the side of my scooter. I take him up on the hill for a quick walk when we arrive and after that he's generally content to lie in the shade with a bowl of water.'

'Do you take him for another walk when you close?' asked Adam.

'Not usually.'

'Would he like one tonight?'

John raised his eyebrows. 'I've never known him refuse a walk. What do you have in mind?'

'I'd like you to show me where you found Babbis's car keys.'

'I'll do my best, but I didn't take a lot of notice of the actual location.' John locked the padlock on the taverna door and whistled to Skele. 'We're going for a walk.'

Skele loped over to John's scooter and stood waiting patiently. John shook his head. 'No, I said "walk".'

As Adam and John walked up the hill away from Plaka Skele alternately ran ahead or behind them, sniffing at the grass and often following a scent for some distance before returning to them. John looked across at Spinalonga and then stopped a few yards further up the hill.

'I reckon it was about here that Skele found them.'

Adam looked up the hill. The viewing area where Ronnie said Babbis had parked was clearly visible.

'When you found the keys the car was still up there?'

John nodded. 'I'd been up and had a look around it. Shortly after Skele found the keys a taxi came up the hill. I carried on walking down and within a few minutes the taxi drove back down the road. Almost immediately afterwards the car came down. Just to make sure I went back up until I could see the viewing area and the car was gone. I'm certain it was Babbis arriving in a taxi to collect it.'

'Sounds likely,' agreed Adam. 'Ronnie said it was dark blue.'

'That's right.'

'Interesting that he's bought a new car and it is now white.'

'Bit stupid,' commented John. 'White shows the dirt and dust even more than the other colours and when the sun is bright it tends to reflect off the bonnet back into the windscreen.'

'I don't think Babbis is quite as clever as he would have everyone believe. I've a few more enquiries to make and then I'll visit the police station and have a chat with Inspector Antonakis.'

'Have you read the forensic report?'

'Not yet. If I went to the fire station and asked to look at it I expect the officer would tell the Inspector. I want to keep everything to myself for the time being.'

'Dad said that police inspector is pretty officious.'

Adam smiled. 'As I am officially from the American Embassy and working on behalf of an American citizen I can pull my rank over him. I believe you have Babbis Skourlatakis's address. Could you give it to me, please?'

'Of course. I can give you the keys to his house as well. They were with the car keys. Are you planning to pay him a surprise visit at his home?'

'I just need to be sure of all my facts. I don't want to be made to look a fool by missing something obvious.' If John had seen

Babbis collect his car in the morning following the assault on Ronnie the man had been lying when he said he drove back home after about fifteen minutes. He would be interested to know if Babbis had a separate set of house keys or if he had to spend the night in his car.

'Well, I'm willing to swear an oath that I saw a man arrive in a taxi and drive the car away. I can't say with any certainty that it was Babbis driving, but from a distance it looked like him and the registration number of the car was the same as the one that had been parked up.'

'Would you write out a statement to that effect? I could take that with me when I visit the police. They'll probably want to question you about it, but it could save you an initial visit and having to give a statement at the station.'

'No problem. I'll take Skele back to Dimitris and write it out when we've put the girls to bed. No point in starting whilst they're still up and causing mayhem.'

Week Two – September 2012
Wednesday

John telephoned Saffron and asked if she would be willing to call on him at the taverna before she opened her shop.

'I can do. What's the problem?'

'I can't discuss it on the 'phone. I'll explain when I see you.'

Feeling concerned by John's request and his unwillingness to speak about it over the telephone Saffron drove to the taverna and arrived shortly after John.

'What is it, John? Is your sight troubling you again?'

'No, that all appears fine, thanks to you. It's more like a favour in your past professional capacity.'

'What are you talking about, John?'

'You know about bones, don't you? The structure of the skeleton.'

'Yes, it was part of my training when I was a limb specialist. Has Kyriakos got a problem with his ankle? I couldn't possibly give any medical advice without seeing an X-ray. I'm sure they'll examine him thoroughly when he goes to have his cast removed.'

John shook his head. 'It's about Old Uncle Yannis.'

'Uncle Yannis?'

'No, Old Uncle Yannis. My great uncle who is in the tower on Spinalonga.'

'What about him?'

'He's being moved. They're building a new tower. All the old skeletons are being taken out, washed and put on display. I'm not prepared to have Old Uncle Yannis's skull stuck up on a shelf for visitors to look at.'

'What do you expect me to do about it?'

John lowered his voice, although there was no one in the vicinity. 'I'm planning to bring his body back over here. Aunt Anna sewed him into a sheet before they interred him so he should still be complete, not all jumbled up with the others. He'll need to be washed and placed into a container ready for a reburial. Would you be willing to do that?'

Saffron swallowed. 'Is it legal? You won't be accused of body snatching or anything?'

'He's our relative.' John's mouth set in a determined line. 'We have every right to say where he should be buried. If the sheet has rotted and I can't say for certain they are his bones I'll have to forget the idea. I'm not interested in anyone else. Ideally I'd like to be able to find Phaedra as well, but that would be impossible. Will you wash him, Saff? There shouldn't be any flesh left on him after all this time.'

Saffron considered. 'I'm not squeamish or anything, but what are you planning to do with him?'

'I'm going to dig a hole in the corner of his house. Then I'll place the casket in there and cover it up. It's what he would want. Throughout his diaries and publications he always said he did not want to leave the island. He has a right to stay there.'

'Have you spoken to your father? What does he say?'

'In theory he agrees with me, but doesn't see how it can be accomplished. I've arranged to be there when the workmen start to demolish the tower and I'll bring his bones back to the mainland. Once I have them in my possession there's no rush to re-inter them. We'll know they are safe.'

'Suppose the authorities find out?'

'How will they know? I'm sure they have no idea how many bodies were placed in the tower over the years. Some of the bones at the bottom will have been crushed or totally disintegrated.'

'What about the workmen? They'll know you've removed a body.'

'I've already made an arrangement that they'll not touch any of them until I'm over there. I drew some money from the bank and they've given me their word that they won't remove any bones from the tower until I'm there. They're filling in the graves in the old graveyard at the moment and think they'll be ready to start dismantling the tower on Monday.'

'Who's going to run the taverna whilst you're on Spinalonga?'

'Well,' John hesitated, 'that's another bit of the favour. Could you spare Bryony from the shop so she can come up here? I'd ask Marcus, but I know he and Dad have airport runs booked. Nick can't manage the taverna and the girls and Mum needs to be on hand to deal with the oldies if necessary.'

'If you're going to dig a hole in the floor of Old Uncle Yannis's house won't you be seen?'

'I'll go over at night. I'm sure Dimitris will help me. It shouldn't be that difficult. We'll take a pick axe so we should be able to break up the earth fairly easily. I'll have a spade with me and once we've loosened the earth we can dig it out. As soon as the hole is deep enough I'll place some stones in there and cover it up. When we take the casket over we loosen the earth, dig down and remove the stones and place the casket in the cavity. Once we've covered it up and tamped the earth down hard we can sweep up any excess soil and bring it back in a sack. Once a few visitors have walked over it no one will notice that the floor has been interfered with.'

Saffron shuddered. Memories of her Indian husband came rushing back and the horror she had felt when she discovered he had buried his previous wife under the kitchen floor. She shook her head to drive the unwanted recollections away. This was not a murder being covered up; this was the secondary internment of a man who had died naturally years earlier.

'You have it all worked out, don't you? If you bring the bones back I'll wash them, but I'll need a large sink to be able to immerse the long bones and they will have to be dry before you place them in a casket. I can't wash and dry them at home. I think Vasi would have a fit. Could we do it up here at the taverna?'

John looked doubtful. 'I'm not sure if Dad would allow that. Why don't I tell Ron our plans and she can ask Ackers if we can use his kitchen? He'll do anything for Ron.'

Inspector Antonakis was feeling pleased with himself. He had written out his conclusions regarding the fire at Kastelli and was satisfied that the perpetrator was the builder, Nikos. The old lady's description of seeing a car and a man she could not name committing the offence was rubbish. The whole affair had been planned by the American woman and she had paid both the builder and his mother to do her bidding.

'I am planning to make some arrests later this afternoon,' he announced pompously to his junior colleague. 'I'd like you to come with me as I may need some assistance.'

'Are you expecting the suspects to be violent?'

'No, but one is an old lady and I may need help to get her into the car. Then we'll pick up her son from wherever he's working and bring them back here. Once they're safely locked away I'll go up to Elounda for the American woman. When she sees her accomplices are under lock and key she'll more than likely admit to instigating the crime. We'll take their statements and agree to them being released on bail, provided they are able to raise sufficient funds.'

On reaching her shop Saffron could see Ronnie sitting down by the sea wall painting. She hesitated, should she go down and talk to her now or wait until Ronnie brought up her paintings? As she considered she saw a couple approach Ronnie and stop to speak to her. Now was not a good time. It might be better to wait until she had closed the shop and arrange to visit Ronnie at her apartment later.

Adam was feeling pleased with the progress he had made so far. Today he would visit the area where Babbis lived and have a few words with his wife and the neighbours. After that he would go to the fire station and ask to see the forensic report. He did not invite Melina to accompany him, sure she had seen enough of Aghios Nikolaos, and would appreciate some time on the beach or wandering around Elounda.

He asked directions to the suburb and when he arrived he was pleased to see that Babbis's car was not in evidence. He had been tempted to call in at the inspectors' office and check that he was there as usual, but that could alert the man that he was suspicious.

Adam checked the address, walked up to the apartment block and into the large hallway where he scanned the names that were beneath the bell pushes. He would speak to Mrs Skourlatakis first. When she answered his ring he asked if he could go up or if she would prefer to come down and speak to him on the doorstep.

'What's it about? I'm not buying anything.'

'I'm not trying to sell you anything. I've been asked to make some enquiries about some incidents that have taken place in the neighbourhood recently.'

'I'll come down.' The entry 'phone clicked back into place and Adam hoped she would come to the main door and he would not have to try a second time to speak to her. He waited patiently until he saw the lift descending and finally the door opened. She looked at Adam suspiciously.

'Are you the man who spoke to me in my apartment?'

'That's correct. I only need a few minutes of your time. I understand there have been some disconcerting events taking place in the area during the early hours of the morning. Have you heard any disturbances?'

'No.'

'There was an incident reported that took place in the early hours of the twenty seventh of July. I wondered if you heard anything that weekend.'

Mrs Skourlatakis shook her head. 'I was away visiting my parents. You'd do better to ask my husband. He would have been here.'

'Is he at home now?' asked Adam, knowing full well that Babbis should be at work.

'He's at work. I suggest you come back after six. He'll be home then.'

'Thank you. I should be off duty by then, but I can ask a colleague to give him a call. I'm sorry I had to bring you down unnecessarily.'

'It was no problem. I'm going shopping,' she announced as she walked out of the main door.

Adam took out his notebook and pretended to make an entry whilst ensuring that she did not return for something she had forgotten. He then rang the bell that was marked "Caretaker" beneath the man's name.

'Hello. What's the problem?'

'I'd be grateful if you could come to the door. I have a few questions I would like to ask you.'

'Do you live here?'

'No, I've been asked to conduct an investigation. It will only take a minute or two of your time.'

Before the click of the entry 'phone Adam could hear the man grumbling to himself and the door was opened abruptly.

'Yes? What do you want?'

'I've been asked to enquire about some disturbances in the area; particularly in the early hours of the twenty seventh of July.'

'What kind of disturbances?'

'Youngsters being a nuisance, playing football against the side of the building, ringing the tenants' bells and running away when they were answered; that kind of a problem.'

'If they play football against the walls I go out and chase them off.'

'Has anyone rung your bell in the early hours?'

'Only Mr Skourlatakis when he had lost his keys and was locked out.'

'Was that on the twenty seventh of July?'

The man scratched his head. 'Probably. His wife goes to visit her parents for the weekend at the end of the month. She must have been away or he would have woken her up instead of me.'

'Did it take him very long to rouse you?'

'How would I know? He could have rung any number of times before I heard the bell.'

'Oh dear; I have a feeling that he may have disturbed other residents whilst he was trying to contact you. If it took a while to alert you he may have thought your bell wasn't working and banged on your door. I'll check with Mr Skourlatakis and I am sure that will be the end of the matter.' Adam smiled. So much for Babbis saying he had driven home; he had no car keys and no keys to let himself into his apartment.

Adam drove to the fire station in Aghios Nikolaos and asked to see Officer Raptakis.

'Have you got an appointment?' asked the young woman who was at the desk.

'I wasn't sure when I would be able to visit. I've come from Athens. I would be very grateful if he could see me now or make an appointment for later in the day.'

'I'll see what I can do. Have a seat, please, Mister ...?'

'Kowalski. I doubt if he will know my name.'

Adam watched as she spoke animatedly into the telephone. Obviously saying he had come from Athens had made her assume he had made a special trip over to Crete.

She smiled at Adam as she replaced the receiver. 'Officer Raptakis will be able to see you in about ten minutes. He's just finishing a report.' The information was completely untrue. Officer Raptakis was actually having his morning break, enjoying his coffee and cigarette and unwilling to be disturbed.

Once ushered into Officer Raptakis's office Adam took the chair in front of the desk and took out his identification.

'I am a criminal investigator attached to the American Embassy in Athens. I have authority to investigate any situation that involves an American citizen and I do not need the permission of the local police.'

Officer Raptakis frowned. 'How can I help you? I am not a part of the police force.'

'I would like to see the forensic report relating to the house fire in Kastelli. Once I have familiarised myself with the details I will be visiting Inspector Antonakis and requesting that he issues a search warrant.'

'There is little left to search in Kastelli. The main house was virtually gutted.'

'So I understand, but I also believe I know who committed the crime.'

'I believe Inspector Antonakis is aware of the perpetrator.' Officer Raptakis smiled smugly.

'Then I hope we will agree and an arrest can be made. May I see the report, please?'

Adam read the report through slowly and entered some observations into his notebook. He handed the report back to the Fire Officer. 'I have a few questions, if I may?'

The officer nodded. His team had been thorough in their search of the debris and everything had been recorded honestly in the report.

'According to your investigation the seat of the fire was beneath the wooden stairs where there were paint cans stored.'

'That is correct.'

'Does that mean that is actually started there or was that where there was the most flammable material?'

'According to our findings petrol had been used as an accelerant. There were traces of it upstairs on the remains of the floorboards. It is our opinion that a quantity was splashed around upstairs, on the stairs, across the ground floor and over the paint cans. There were scorch marks on the stone floor and we believe that a trail of petrol was then laid from beneath the stairs to the entrance and subsequently set alight.'

Adam nodded. 'I would surmise that from your report. Have you any explanation why the extension suffered very little?'

Officer Raptakis shrugged. 'I can only assume that having sprayed the petrol around upstairs the perpetrator did not feel he or she,' he added hurriedly, 'had sufficient left to ensure that the amount leading from the front door to the stairs would burn with enough ferocity to heat the paint cans sufficiently to cause them to explode. The objective appears to have been to do as much damage as possible in the main body of the building.'

'So if someone was splashing petrol around from a can would he have splashed himself?'

'Assuming we are talking about a man then I would expect his shoes and the bottoms of his trousers to have received splashes.'

Adam nodded. 'That is my thinking exactly. Is it likely that when undoing the cap on the petrol cans that some of the petrol would have been transferred to his hands?'

'Very likely, unless they were new cans.'

'It has certainly been my experience that filling the petrol tank on a car from a can is a messy job. However careful you are your hands need a good wash afterwards. I think it unlikely anyone would have bought new cans if they were planning to destroy them. Terrible waste of money. Assuming they were not new there could have been old petrol residue on the exterior?'

'It's possible.'

'So if you placed them on the carpet in the boot of a car you might well leave traces of petrol behind,' mused Adam. 'Do you have facilities in Aghios Nikolaos to test for petrol residue on fabrics?'

'Basic facilities. Nothing sophisticated. You'd have to go to Heraklion or even back to Athens if a more detailed analysis was required.'

Adam handed back the report and closed his notebook. 'You've been incredibly helpful. Now I will go to the police station and ask to see Inspector Antonakis.'

Ronnie took her completed paintings up to Saffron's shop, pleased to find that for once she was not busy with customers.

'Quiet day?'

'It was busy earlier, but the first group of coaches have just left and the next ones have arranged for their passengers to go to Spinalonga. I should have enough time for a coffee before they return. Will you join me?'

Ronnie nodded. 'Actually I wanted to ask you something.'

Saffron raised her eyebrows. 'I have something to ask you also. Let me make the coffee then you can ask first.'

Ronnie placed the cup of coffee safely on the floor and Saffron placed hers on the shelf below the counter.

'So what do you want to ask? Are you thinking of increasing the price of your paintings?'

Ronnie shook her head. 'No, it's rather personal and if you don't want to tell me I'll understand. You and Vasi are not married, are you? May I ask why not?'

'I've been married before and we decided it would be less complicated if we just lived together.'

'Oh, does that mean that you are not divorced?'

Saffron smiled. 'I'm actually a widow under rather unpleasant circumstances. I don't really want the authorities investigating into my background.'

Ronnie felt embarrassed. 'I'm sorry. I didn't mean to pry into your affairs.'

Saffron shrugged. 'It's a good excuse to return to England every so often. It gives me a chance to visit Marjorie whilst I apply to renew my working visa. Why do you ask?'

Ronnie blushed. 'Kyriakos has asked me to marry him.'

'Is that a problem?'

'There are a number of practical problems that would have to be overcome, but I asked Nicola what the procedure was for getting married to a Greek. She said they look into your background and you have to produce your birth certificate. If they found that I had a relative who was in prison do you think they would refuse me permission?'

'It could depend how close the relative was to you. I'm fairly certain that a second cousin would not be considered detrimental.'

Ronnie pulled a wry face. 'My natural father is in prison. He's not a murderer or anything awful like that, but he's serving a sentence for forgery.'

'Well in that respect you're fortunate.' Saffron took a breath. 'I don't usually tell everyone this, but my husband had murdered his first wife.'

'How awful!' Ronnie's eyes opened wide in horror and astonishment.

'It certainly was at the time. He was convicted and whilst he was in prison he was set upon by the inmates and met his death at their hands. I'm sure if I asked for permission to marry Vasi my application would be refused and I might even be banned from entering the country. It isn't worth taking the chance.'

'Does Vasi know?'

'Of course. My family here also know and they have placed the knowledge in the cupboard along with the other skeletons that are hidden away in there.'

'They know about my father.'

Saffron smiled. 'Then no doubt they have added your information to the family secrets. Have you told Kyriakos?'

'Yes, he says it makes no difference to him. I think he would accept us living together, but I'm not sure how his mother would react to that. She's a devout church goer. The fact that I'm not a member of the Orthodox religion will probably go against me as well.'

Saffron shook her head. 'I'm sorry I haven't really been much help to you. I can only suggest that you have a long and serious talk together and then he explains the situation to his mother.'

Ronnie nodded. 'I'll talk to my mother when she arrives next week before I speak to Kyriakos again. I'm sure it will be no problem to her whatever I decide. If he tells his mother that mine has no objection it may help.' Ronnie drank some of her coffee. 'What did you want to ask me?'

'Well, it concerns Kyriakos.'

Ronnie raised her eyebrows.

'John took Adam and Melina over to Spinalonga earlier in the week. He says the authorities are going to dismantle the tower and remove the bodies. They will then build a new tower and place the skulls and long bones on display. He doesn't want that to happen to his Old Uncle Yannis and is arranging to bring his bones back to the mainland.'

Ronnie sighed. 'If I knew which bones belonged to my ancestors I'd do the same. They could then be buried in the local cemetery. How will he know which ones belong to his relative?'

'He says his Aunt Anna washed the body originally and sewed him into a sheet before they placed him in the tower. He's hoping the sheet is still intact with the skeleton inside.'

'How does this affect Kyriakos?' asked Ronnie.

'John has asked me if I will wash the bones. That's no problem to me, but I can't take them home and wash them there. John knows his father won't let him take them up to the taverna or wash them at their house and he wondered if you could ask Kyriakos if he would allow me to use the sink at his taverna.'

Ronnie frowned. 'That is some ask. Couldn't you bring them to my apartment? I wouldn't mind you using my sink, provided you didn't ask me to help you.'

Saffron shook her head. 'It wouldn't be large enough. I need one where I can submerge the long bones. I also need some large trays to lay them out on and a bowl where the skull can sit until they have dried out. I would obviously do it at night when the taverna was closed.'

Ronnie gave a little giggle. 'I can just imagine the reaction of customers being invited to inspect the kitchen and seeing the sink full of human bones. They would probably report Kyriakos for serving human flesh and making them cannibals.'

'Most people wouldn't know human bones from animal, but I wouldn't take the chance.'

'How long will they take to dry?'

'At least twenty four hours. I couldn't leave them lying around at the taverna. Would you be willing to store them at your apartment, just for a day or two?'

Ronnie looked at Saffron doubtfully. 'I suppose so, but I wouldn't want to be looking at them every time I went in.'

'They could be covered with a cloth or you could come and stay with us for a few days. Once they're dry they can be packed into a casket and John plans to take them back to Spinalonga and bury them under the floor of Old Uncle Yannis's house.'

'Is it legal?'

'John says that as he's their ancestor they have a right to say where he is buried.'

Ronnie shrugged. 'I'll speak to Kyriakos, but if he refuses then John will have to make some other arrangements.'

'Provided the bones are taken there after the taverna has closed and are removed before it opens no one will be any the wiser.'

Adam walked to the police station and asked if he could see Inspector Antonakis. The duty officer shook his head.

'The Inspector is at lunch at present.'

'I'm willing to wait. What time are you expecting him to return?'

'He will be out this afternoon. I suggest I make an appointment for you for tomorrow.'

Adam frowned. 'It is quite urgent that I speak to him.'

'If you would like to tell me the nature of the problem I may be able to help or pass the message through to him later.'

'You wouldn't happen to know where he is going to be this afternoon?'

'He will be on official police business; more than that I am unable to disclose.'

'I understand. I will leave you my card and I would be grateful if you could ask him to telephone me when he returns from his lunch break.'

The duty officer nodded and without giving Adam's card a second glance he placed it on his desk. He had no intention of delaying the Inspector and earning his wrath. Once his superior had left that afternoon he would place the card on his desk with a written request to telephone at his convenience.

Adam returned to where he had parked his car and drove back to the police station. He drove around the block a number of times before a parking meter became free and he hurriedly parked in the space. From there he could see who entered or left the police station along with the two cars that were parked outside. If a parking warden tried to move him on he would plead ignorance as a tourist and ask where he could buy a ticket.

A number of cars passed and signalled to Adam, obviously asking if he was leaving so they could occupy his space. He shook his head at them and continued to watch the door of the police station, his patience at last being rewarded when he saw the Inspector walk inside. Adam straightened up and took his mobile 'phone from his pocket, waiting for it to ring. After half an hour he ground his teeth. It was unlikely there would be more than one officer of that rank stationed in Aghios Nikolaos; either the duty officer had not passed on his message and card or the Inspector had ignored his request.

Just as Adam was about to enter the police station again he saw the Inspector accompanied by a young officer coming out and climbing into a car. There was no point in him returning inside the station and asking for a meeting; the excuse he had been given was obviously genuine. He followed the police car down the hill and onto the main road leading up towards the roundabout and the turn off to Elounda. The police car carried on the main road towards Neapoli and on impulse Adam decided to follow.

It was with a feeling of foreboding that Adam saw the car take the road down to Kastelli and he decided to go down to the taverna and see if he could find out the reason for the Inspector's visit. Before he reached the taverna he saw the Inspector had pulled up outside Kassianae's house and was hammering on her door. He watched with some amusement as Kassianae lifted the corner of her dirty lace curtain, shook her head and dropped the curtain back into place again.

'This is the police,' called the Inspector. 'I demand that you open your door.'

Silence greeted him and he banged on the door again. Further along the road a woman opened her door.

'What do you want?' she called.

'I need to speak to Kassianae.'

The woman shrugged. 'She'll not open her door unless she wants to speak with you.'

'Then I will have no choice but to break it down.'

A look of horror came over the woman's face and she began to run along the road calling for help. Doors opened and the villagers looked out curiously. Shrilly she told them the police were going to break down Kassianae's door. A young woman took to her heels and ran to the forge, returning within minutes with the men who worked there and the old men who used to sit beneath the tree each day.

They shouldered their way through the gathering of women who had now been joined by the taverna owner and two other men.

'What's the problem?' asked the taverna owner, placing himself between Kassianae's door and the Inspector, whilst the men from the forge lined up beside him.

'Move aside. You are obstructing me in the course of my duty.'

The men stood their ground, one of them talking animatedly on his mobile 'phone.

'What do you want with Old Kassie?' asked the taverna owner again.

'I have a warrant for her arrest. Now move out of my way or I'll be forced to arrest you also.'

'Her arrest?' The taverna owner looked at the Inspector incredulously. 'What are you arresting her for?'

'Perjury and perverting the course of justice. Now stand aside.'

'You're not going to lay a finger on Old Kassie until her son is here.' The man closed his mobile 'phone and glared at the Inspector. 'I've called him and he's on his way. You can tell him exactly why you plan to arrest his mother.'

Adam smiled to himself. Due to the commotion outside of Kassianae's house no one had noticed him parking and listening. Now he felt it would be time for him to intervene. He withdrew his identification from his pocket and, walked across to the gathering and elbowed his way through to the Inspector's side.

'If I could just have a quiet word with you, sir?'

'I'm busy. I'm in the midst of making an arrest.'

'I think you are about to make a disastrous mistake. If you would spare a few minutes to listen to me I'd be grateful. If you still wish to arrest this old lady afterwards I'll not interfere.'

'Who are you?' The Inspector eyed Adam up and down and Adam offered his identification for inspection.

'This has nothing to do with the American Embassy.'

'On the contrary. The young lady who owns the house that was set on fire is an American citizen. As such she has asked me to represent her and investigate the facts surrounding the arson.'

'We know the facts. The woman paid Nikos to set fire to the house and paid his mother to say she had seen someone else do it. I shall be arresting Nikos as soon as he arrives and once he and his mother are back at the station I will be going to Elounda to arrest Miss Vandersham.'

Adam shook his head. 'I fear if you proceed you will be sued for wrongful arrest by all the parties. I have collected evidence and I believe I know the perpetrator. It was certainly not Nikos and I believe his mother spoke the truth when she identified the man she saw.'

'Rubbish,' muttered the Inspector.

'It is not rubbish. I tried to see you earlier today but I was told you were at lunch and would not be able to see me until tomorrow. I left a message asking you to telephone me, either it was not given to you or it was ignored.'

The crowd had subsided into silence, straining to hear what Adam was saying to the Inspector whilst the junior officer stood embarrassed by the side of the police car.

'I can conduct my business here with you or we can return to the station in Aghios Nikolaos.'

'I have an arrest to make.'

'Then arrest me.' Adam held out his hands.

'I have no grounds to arrest you.'

'If I pushed you, you could claim I had assaulted you. That would be grounds for arrest. At least then I would be able to make a full statement to you and you would have to take notice of the evidence I can produce and investigate further.'

The men had gradually moved closer to Inspector Antonakis and he realised that he was suddenly in a very insecure position. If they decided to molest him no one would admit to having seen anything at all and he was not in a position to arrest everyone in the village, despite having a junior officer with him. He looked around warily.

'You will leave your car here and I will drive you to the police station in Neapoli. It is closer than Aghios Nikolaos and I am sure they will allow us to use one of their interview rooms. In the meantime I will leave my officer here. I do not want to return and find the old lady and her son have disappeared. I will then drive you back here when I return to make the arrests.'

'That's agreeable to me,' replied Adam. 'Shall we go?'

As Adam was driven away in the Inspector's car the watching crowd clapped. Kassianae lifted her curtain and waved to him and the villagers as if she were royalty. Adam was forced to smile. The old lady was certainly a character.

The Inspector drove as swiftly as possible away from Kastelli. 'If you were not an Embassy official I would arrest you for causing a disturbance.'

Adam did not deign to reply. If the Inspector thought he could be intimidated by threats he was wrong.

The duty officer at the Neapoli police station looked at Inspector Antonakis in surprise when he strode into the building and demanded an interview room placed at his disposal.

'Are you arresting this man?' he asked.

'I need to interrogate him,' replied the Inspector pompously. 'I may well need to arrest him; in which case I would like to avail myself of one of your cells until he can be transferred to Aghios Nikolaos.'

Adam smiled to himself. There was no way the Inspector could arrest him; he had not committed a crime and he was of a far higher rank than the policeman. He followed the officer meekly down the corridor and into a small room, furnished with a table and two chairs.

'Do you wish to have the interview recorded?'

'Yes,' said Adam immediately. 'It may be needed as evidence at a later date.'

Inspector Antonakis scowled. He knew that all interviews should be recorded, but he had hoped to avoid the procedure. He would then have been able to send the man away claiming his purported evidence was invalid and irrelevant and proceed with the arrests of his suspects.

Adam sat silently until he saw the light on the camera at ceiling height begin to glow and the tape recorder that the officer had produced was switched on.

Inspector Antonakis began to speak and Adam interrupted him. 'You have not tested the recorder to ensure it is functioning correctly. Please do so before you start to conduct my interview.'

The Inspector jabbed at the "off" switch; then pressed "replay". Both the Inspector's voice and Adam's objection could be clearly heard.

'Satisfied?'

Adam nodded. 'Certain procedures have to be followed,' he said smugly as the Inspector pressed "record".

Before the Inspector could speak again Adam gave his full name and rank, adding that he was at the police station in Neapoli with Inspector Antonakis to give a voluntary statement regarding the fire in Kastelli.

'I would like to start with the assault on Miss Vandersham. It was more frightening than physically damaging. She hit Mr Skourlatakis, temporarily disabling him, snatched the keys from his car and ran down the road for assistance from a friend.'

'I do not see that incident has any relevance to the fire,' interrupted the Inspector.

'I am about to prove that Mr Skourlatakis did not tell the truth. He said he had driven home shortly afterwards. He had no spare car keys; nor did he have the keys to his apartment. He had to awaken the caretaker to gain access. The following day he was seen arriving at his car in a taxi and subsequently driving away. Both the caretaker and the witness, who also happened to discover the discarded bunch of keys, are willing to make statements to this effect.'

'No doubt the man was embarrassed to admit that he had lost his keys.'

'Embarrassment is no excuse for lying to a police officer,' said Adam firmly. 'Miss Vandersham and Mr Pirenzi confronted Mr Skourlatakis in his office and humiliated him before his colleagues. I believe that Mr Skourlatakis decided then that he would revenge himself on Miss Vandersham for both her rejection of him and the humiliation he had experienced.'

'Pure speculation,' commented Inspector Antonakis.

Adam continued unperturbed. 'In the early hours of the morning when Miss Vandersham's house was set on fire the old lady who lives opposite was sitting at her window. She witnessed a man driving a dark coloured car arrive at the house. Had she been bribed or coerced to give this information she would also have been given the name of the man. She only knew she had seen him at the house before and he was a building inspector. If Mr Skourlatakis was innocent of the crime, why did he trade his car in for a white vehicle the following week?'

'People trade their cars in for a newer model all the time. There is nothing suspicious in that.'

'I visited the garage and requested permission to examine the dark blue car that had previously belonged to Mr Skourlatakis. I noticed there was a faint smell of petrol in the area of the pedals. Upon further examination I found a rag stuffed down the back of the passenger seat that smelled of petrol. I removed this and the garage salesman witnessed the removal and provided me with a bag in which to place it. I also wiped the steering wheel with my handkerchief. There was soiling visible, but this could be just the natural grease residue left by the hands of the driver. I also have this in a bag, again duly witnessed.'

Inspector Antonakis shrugged. 'There is often a slight smell of petrol in a car due to refuelling.'

'There was also a smell of petrol on the carpet in the boot. I have arranged that the car is not cleaned until it has been thoroughly examined. I would request that you take a sample of the affected area and send it to forensics for testing, along with the rag and my handkerchief.'

'Forensic testing by the fire service is expensive. It might even have to be carried out in Heraklion.'

Adam nodded. 'I spoke to Officer Raptakis and he said they had the basic equipment here. I would also request that you issued a search warrant for Mr Skourlatakis's apartment and removed all his light coloured trousers and shoes. Again, they need to go to forensics to be tested for petrol residue.'

'This is preposterous. Everything you have told me is pure supposition.'

'I have proved that Mr Skourlatakis did not give a true account of the events that took place after his assault on Miss Vandersham. When I asked where he was at that particular time he claimed to have been involved in a card game with his colleague Alecos Vikelakis. Mr Vikelakis confirmed this and claimed Mr Skourlatakis has lost one thousand Euros to him. Mr Skourlatakis reaction to the monetary claim was "interesting". He appeared both surprised and annoyed at the amount mentioned.'

'There is no law against men gambling. If Mr Skourlatakis lost more than he intended that is not a criminal matter.'

'I agree. I asked where this card game took place and Mr Vikelakis said it was at his house. I checked his information with his father and he denied that Mr Skourlatakis was there that night and he and his wife disapproved of gambling and would not have allowed a card game with monetary stakes to take place in their house. I believe Mr Vikelakis to have been paid to give Mr Skourlatakis an alibi.' Adam leaned forward. 'In view of this statement that I have given voluntarily to you I request that you delay making any arrests until you have the results of forensic tests and made further investigations.'

Inspector Antonakis hesitated. The account Adam had given him was plausible. If he ignored it and it was subsequently proved that he had arrested innocent people he would probably be sued and also stripped of his rank.

'I'll consider your statement.'

'Thank you. Before we leave I would like a copy of the tape. You can then take one away with you and I will have possession of the other. Now I would appreciate being returned to Kastelli to collect my car. No doubt your officer would also like to be relieved.'

Inspector Antonakis felt thoroughly aggrieved. Even Adam's request for a copy of the tape had been recorded and he would be unable to lose it or claim it had been accidently erased by the police at Neapoli. He drove back to Kastelli in silence. He needed to listen to the taped interview Adam had given and consider his actions. He was still not convinced that Babbis had started the fire.

As they entered Kastelli Kassianae could be seen sitting at the taverna surrounded by the villagers and Adam smiled. The Inspector may have been able to persuade her to leave her house if he had held up a bottle of whisky. Nikos was also in attendance and when he saw Inspector Antonakis arrive he stepped up to the car angrily.

'I am going to complain about the treatment you meted out to my mother. She is an old lady. You threatened her. You had no right to do that.'

'I did not threaten her,' protested the Inspector.

'You were heard banging on her door and threatening to break it down if she did not open it. The whole village is a witness, including the officer you left here. It's a wonder she did not drop dead with fright.'

'Had she opened her door there would have been no need for me to bang and shout. She is a stupid old lady.'

Nikos stepped forward his fists clenched. 'How dare you call my mother stupid!'

Two men caught hold of him and pulled him back. 'Leave it, Nikos. We'll back you up in your complaint for police harassment. There's no reason for you to argue with the Inspector now.'

Adam caught Kassianae's eye and she winked at him. She was enjoying every moment of her notoriety.

'Nikos, do as your friends say,' urged Adam. 'I am going to Aghios Nikolaos with the Inspector and then I will return and speak to you and your mother. I also witnessed the events.'

Inspector Antonakis glowered at him. 'There is no need for you to return to Aghios Nikolaos.'

'I need to hand over the evidence I have and receive an official receipt. I would not want it to be mislaid in transit.'

The Inspector beckoned to the officer. 'You can drive me back. We are leaving now.'

Once again as the Inspector drove away the villagers clapped vigorously.

Week Two – September 2012
Thursday

Adam had relayed the events of the previous afternoon to the family whilst they were having their evening meal.

'Have you told Ronnie about your adventures in Kastelli?' asked Giovanni as Adam arrived in the kitchen to help himself to some breakfast.

'I thought I would speak to her later when I've had another confrontation with that Inspector.'

'I'm sure she'll be relieved that the problem has been dealt with. Her mother and great uncle are arriving next week and it will mean she can enjoy being with them without wondering if she will be arrested.'

'It's such a shame about her house. I know she was hoping it would be finished so they could all stay there,' said Marianne. 'I was going to speak to Kyriakos and see if he was willing to help me with the cooking so we could throw a surprise party up there for them.'

'Where's the party?' asked John as he arrived with his daughters. 'No, Lisa, only one piece of fruit. When you've eaten that you can have a second piece.'

Marianne repeated her idea of a party to John.

'No reason why we shouldn't have one up there anyway. It could be in celebration of getting the culprit brought to justice. The villagers would love it.'

'Do you think so?' asked Marianne with a frown.

'Why don't we arrange a date and then I'll go up there and tell everyone,' suggested John. 'I'm sure they'd all agree to bring a dish so all we would need to take was plenty of wine.'

'And a bottle of whisky,' added Adam with a smile. 'Let me visit Aghios Nikolaos this morning and find out the conclusions Inspector Antonakis has come to. He may have decided to ignore the information I gave him.'

'I don't see how he can ignore it. You have the tape of your interview with him and he has to ask Officer Raptakis to carry out some forensic tests on the rag.'

Adam shrugged. 'That could be circumstantial. It's quite possible that when Babbis was filling his car with petrol he had some residue on his hands, wiped it off and pushed the rag down the back of the seat. That could have been at any time in the past few months. Without finding traces of petrol on his trousers and shoes he could still claim his innocence.'

'Bit of a coincidence, changing his car so soon afterwards and asking his colleague to alibi him at a fictitious card game.' John cut a slice of Madeira cake in half and gave each girl a portion along with some grapes.

'Where's Nicola?' asked Marianne. It was unusual for her not to be in the kitchen supervising her daughters' breakfast and checking what shopping was needed that day.

'Said she wanted to wash her hair,' replied John easily, not admitting that he had left his wife sitting in their bathroom feeling decidedly queasy. 'What are you planning for today, Melina?'

'I want to walk up to Mavrikiano, on to Pano Elounda, down to Kato Elounda and then into Elounda. I can catch a taxi back from there if I've had enough walking by then.'

'Make sure you take some water with you,' cautioned Marianne. 'If the taverna isn't open when you arrive there will only be the general store and if their supplies haven't been delivered there'll be nowhere to get a drink.'

'I'm sure I could knock on a door and beg a glass of water from someone, but I will take a bottle with me, just in case. It would be my luck that everyone would be down in Elounda doing their shopping.'

'I could 'phone you when I've finished in Aghios Nikolaos,' suggested Adam. 'You could have an ice cream in Elounda and I could meet you there.'

Melina smiled wickedly at her husband. 'That's a lovely kind thought, Adam, but I know what you're like. Once you have sorted out the Inspector you'll want to go to Babbis's house with him to collect the shoes and trousers. After that you'll go to the garage and supervise the removal of the carpet, then on to the fire station to deposit everything. I'll be surprised if I see you before late in the afternoon. I don't think I could manage to eat that much ice cream.'

Adam smiled back. 'Sometimes these things take a little longer than I anticipate.'

Ourania could be heard coming from their rooms towards the kitchen. Her voice raised in protest.

'Time to go, I think,' said John. 'Come along girls. You've both eaten enough to keep an army going for the day.'

'Yes,' agreed Adam. 'I ought to make a move. I don't want to find that Inspector has gone out on another case or couldn't wait any longer for me.' He had no wish to witness the family's personal problems.

'I want to see my Mamma. When can we go and see her, Yannis?'

Yannis sighed. Ourania had woken him in the night, asking what he was doing in her room and who he was. Having calmed her he slept fitfully until Ourania rose and began opening the drawers and cupboards, muttering to herself.

'What are you looking for, Ourania?'

'My purse. I shall need it when we go out.'

'You get dressed and I'll help you look for it after breakfast.'

Ourania looked at her husband in confusion. 'Haven't we had breakfast yet? We'll have to hurry or we'll be late.'

'What will we be late for, Ourania?'

'To visit Mamma, of course. She will be expecting us.'

'We haven't arranged to go today.'

Yannis dressed himself, watching Ourania to ensure that she put on the clothes he had laid out for her the night before, finally helping her with the buttons on her blouse, ensuring all were fastened in the correct order. The whole time Ourania kept reminding Yannis they would be late and it was not fair to keep her mother waiting.

As they walked to the kitchen Yannis spoke firmly. 'We are not going to see your Mamma today, Ourania.'

'Why not? You never take me to see my Mamma. You're cruel and heartless, Yannis.'

'It isn't a day when she would want to have visitors.'

'Why not? Mamma would always be pleased to see me. You're just being selfish, Yannis. You have your family here and you don't care about my Mamma.'

'Of course I care, Ourania, but it is not possible to visit her today.'

Ourania glared at her husband and began to walk up and down, wringing her hands.

'Come and sit down. What would you like for your breakfast? Shall I ask Marianne to make some toast and a scrambled egg?'

'I don't want to sit down. I don't want any egg. I want to see my Mamma.'

'Maybe we could go for a walk this afternoon?'

'And see Mamma?'

Yannis nodded. To make the hollow promise was the only way to calm Ourania. 'You must have some breakfast first.' He had already suggested the walk twice before, but he knew that in a short while she would have forgotten the conversation and return to her demand to visit her mother.

Marianne looked at her uncle in concern. He looked tired and worried.

'Can I help at all?'

'I doubt it, Marianne. You know how it is when Ourania gets an idea fixed in her head.'

'Why don't you go up to the shop for a while? Take Marisa with you. I'll keep Ourania occupied for an hour or so. It will give you a chance to relax a bit and by the time you return she may well have forgotten about visiting her mother.'

'She may go to sleep for a while. She was up in the night rather disorientated.'

'You look as if some sleep would not come amiss for you, Uncle Yannis.'

Yannis shrugged. 'I'll probably have a nap after lunch.'

Marianne shook her head. She was worried about her uncle and the situation with Ourania was gradually worsening.

'I'll speak to the doctor and ask if there is any medication that would help her to sleep.'

'I don't want Ourania drugged up all the time.'

'I'm not suggesting that. If he prescribed a mild sleeping draught for her so she would sleep through the night and that would enable you to get a decent night's sleep. It might even have a beneficial effect on her during the day as she would not have been up in the night.'

Yannis nodded. It made sense to speak to the doctor and see if there was any medication that would be effective for Ourania. He was not sure how much longer he would be able to cope with disturbed nights

Inspector Antonakis listened to the recording of Adam's statement for a third time. He had certainly presented a plausible case and it would need further investigation. The man was an interfering nuisance; just as he had decided he could make an arrest he had been made to look a fool in front of his junior officer and the villagers of Kastelli.

Knowing Adam had already visited Officer Raptakis and questioned the facilities available for testing for petroleum residue on fabric he would have to visit the garage and remove the carpet from the boot. He tapped his pen on the table. If those articles came back negative there would be no need to issue a warrant and remove Babbis's clothing and shoes. He still found it hard to believe that a building inspector would commit such criminal vandalism.

The Inspector's intercom buzzed and announced the arrival of Adam Kowalski. With a sigh Inspector Antonakis agreed to admit him. He might have guessed the man would arrive early before he could claim he had other cases that demanded his attention.

'Good morning, Inspector. I trust I am not too early for you? I have thought about procedure and I suggest we visit Mr Skourlatakis's apartment and serve the warrant for the removal of his trousers and shoes and deposit them at the fire station along with the items I bagged up before we proceed to the garage.'

The Inspector shook his head. 'You are moving too fast, Mr Kowalski. The search warrant has not yet been authorised.'

Adam frowned. 'Why not? You could have contacted a Magistrate or Judge yesterday evening and obtained their signature.'

'Unfortunately those I tried to contact were not available,' replied the Inspector smugly.

Adam shrugged. 'In that case I will sign it myself.'

'You cannot do that.'

'As an Embassy official I have the authority. I am only acting as an advisor; I am not the investigating officer.'

Inspector Antonakis pursed his lips. He could not refute Adam's signature as invalid, although he had not tried to contact anyone to authorise the warrant the previous evening.

'I believe it is essential that certain items of clothing are removed from Mr Skourlatakis's premises as soon as possible. If he has any suspicion that we are investigating him he could dispose of them. Although that would prove his guilt in our eyes there would be no material evidence to corroborate our claims apart from the rag I found and any petrol on the carpet in the car boot. Both of which could easily be explained away by an astute lawyer. Shall we go?'

Inspector Antonakis scowled. 'The man is probably at work by now.'

'Quite likely, but it is doubtful that his wife will have left the apartment yet to go shopping or socialise with friends. No doubt she will attempt to contact her husband immediately after our visit. I think it would be advisable for an officer to request that both Mr Skourlatakis and Mr Vikelakis come to the station immediately to assist us with some further enquiries. They can be questioned whilst we await the results of the tests from the fire station. I think Mr Vikelakis would very soon admit that the card game he claimed took place was fictitious. Mr Skourlatakis will then have to think of another alibi if his clothing is confirmed as contaminated.'

'If Mr Skourlatakis is innocent he could sue for wrongful arrest.'

Adam shook his head. 'Neither of them are being arrested at this stage. You are merely asking them to come to the station to answer some questions and make a statement. Mr Vikelakis can probably be accused of perjury in an attempt to pervert the course of justice as it appears Mr Skourlatakis was not with him until the early hours that weekend. Mr Skourlatakis may be able to prove he was elsewhere that evening. It is possible he spent the night with a lady friend and is trying to protect her or prevent his wife knowing about his infidelity.'

'Suppose they refuse to come to the station? I cannot force them unless I issue a warrant for their arrest.'

Adam sighed. 'I will sign a warrant that will permit your officer to arrest them if they refuse to come here voluntarily. I hope it will not be necessary for him to produce it. If you would like to give me the forms, please.'

Reluctantly Inspector Antonakis produced the two blank forms and Adam inserted one man's name on each and signed them.

Adam was formally introduced to the officer who had accompanied the Inspector to Kastelli the previous day and handed him the forms.

'I would like you to go to the building inspectors' office. You will tell Mr Skourlatakis and Mr Vikelakis that the Inspector has to go out in about half an hour and he would like them to come down to the station immediately to make a statement regarding their movements on the night of the fire. It is just a formality so their statement can be added to the file along with the others. They must switch off their mobile 'phones as they must not be used in the police car or at the station until you give permission due to interfering with the police radios. Should they refuse to come voluntarily you will have a warrant for the arrest of each man, but I hope it will not be necessary for you to enforce them.'

The officer looked at the Inspector who nodded in confirmation. 'Please carry out Mr Kowalski's instructions to the letter. We are at a very important juncture of our enquiries and will be relying on you to have both men here when we return. They are not to have access to any telephone calls, mobile or otherwise.'

Inspector Antonakis and Adam drove to the apartment where Babbis Skourlatakis lived with his wife and rang the bell on the intercom. A woman answered them promptly.

'Mrs Skourlatakis? This is Inspector Antonakis from the police here. There is nothing for you to worry about, but I would like to come up to your apartment and speak to you.'

'Has something happened to Babbis?'

'No, to the best of my knowledge he is at his office. We will take the lift and meet you at the door of your apartment.'

The lift travelled slowly and when they reached the floor where the apartment was situated Mrs Skourlatakis was standing there, her mobile 'phone pressed against her ear.

'I've been trying to call my husband to ask him to come home, but his 'phone is switched off.'

'He's probably busy. His presence here is not necessary. If you would just be good enough to show us where he keeps his clothes, madam.'

'His clothes? Has he been in an accident and needs a change of clothing?'

The Inspector shook his head. 'No, we just want to examine his trousers and shoes. It may be necessary for us to take them away with us.'

Mrs Skourlatakis shook her head. 'You can't do that without his permission.' She tried to close the door and Adam placed his foot firmly in the doorway.

From his pocket Inspector Antonakis withdrew the search warrant and held it out to her. 'This gives us permission to enter your apartment and look for anything that we think could be helpful in our enquiries. It is an offence to obstruct us and refuse entry. Can you tell me where you were two weekends ago?'

Mrs Skourlatakis paled and stepped aside. 'What has Babbis done?'

'I am not at liberty to disclose the nature of our investigation. Where were you at the weekend in question?'

Mrs Skourlatakis frowned. 'I would have been visiting my parents. I go once a month, travel down on the Saturday and stay overnight with them. I then return on the Sunday after church.'

'So Mr Skourlatakis would have been alone in the apartment during that time?'

'Of course.'

'Your husband's clothes, please, then we will have no need to impose on you further.'

'In here.' Mrs Skourlatakis led the way into the bedroom and pointed to the large double wardrobe.

Adam opened the door and saw an array of feminine outfits neatly hung up and shoes placed in pairs below. He closed the door and opened the one next to it revealing suits, trousers, shirts and shoes.

'I am sure you have washed some of your husband's clothes during the previous two weeks. Have you washed any of his trousers?' asked Adam.

Mrs Skourlatakis shook her head. 'I only wash his jeans. He usually wears those at the weekends. The others go to the cleaners.'

Adam nodded and leaned into the wardrobe, sniffing at the trousers, lifting each pair out and examining them before placing them in a paper evidence bag. A light tan pair had faint stains on the legs.

He turned his attention to the shoes that sat on the floor of the wardrobe and looked at them carefully. They were none of them new, one pair needed to be re-heeled, but they were all polished and he felt disheartened. If Babbis had been wearing highly polished shoes it was unlikely that any petrol would have penetrated into the leather. He turned each one to the light and looked inside, noticing that along with the general wear that was to be expected, there was also a dark mark on the interior of the scuffed lining of a pair of casual brown shoes. If you were wearing light brown trousers you would probably choose a pair of brown shoes, rather than black.

He nodded to the Inspector who once again produced a number of paper bags and Adam placed each pair of trousers separately inside, followed by the shoes in individual bags. Before declaring himself satisfied Adam removed the shirts from the wardrobe, returning them after a careful examination.

Mrs Skourlatakis looked on thoroughly puzzled. Why would the police be interested in some of her husband's clothes? 'What are you going to do with them?' she asked.

'We want to have a few tests carried out on them. We will explain the procedure to your husband later.'

'Will you be bringing them back?'

'Not today. There will be no need for you to wait in for us.' Adam smiled at her. 'We don't need to trouble you further. Thank you for your help. If we could go into your living room for a moment the Inspector will give you a receipt for these items and then we will be on our way.'

Whilst Inspector Antonakis wrote out the receipts for the trousers and shoes Adam marked the bags with the location, signed and dated them, asking the Inspector to add his signature.

'I'd better let my husband know.' Mrs Skourlatakis picked up her mobile 'phone as she closed the apartment door behind her unexpected visitors.

'We'll drop these in to Officer Raptakis and then continue to the garage,' announced Adam. 'He should have the preliminary results for us within a couple of hours and the carpet can be tested later. Assuming a pair of trousers and shoes come back positive the carpet will only add to the evidence.'

'Even if the test results show positive for traces of petrol that will still not be proof that Skourlatakis fired the house,' argued the Inspector.

Adam smiled. 'I'm hoping that when Mr Vikelakis has admitted that the alibi he gave is false and Mr Skourlatakis is confronted with that along with the results of the tests and the old lady's sighting of him he will realise that we can prove his guilt and admit to the crime.'

Officer Raptakis viewed the bags that held the trousers, shoes and section of carpet that Inspector Antonakis handed to him.

'I can confirm that the rag had traces of petrol on it. It was more or less the amount I would expect from someone who had filled his tank from a container and wiped his hands afterwards.'

'Have you any idea how long ago that would have been?' asked Adam.

'Not really. The stains remain for a considerable amount of time, but the density of the substance reduces. That means we can identify the source, but unless they were very recent it is difficult to put a time limit on them.'

Adam nodded. 'Do your best, please, and the Inspector would

appreciate a telephone call from you with the results as soon as possible. We will be at the station and leave instructions that your call is to be put through to him immediately.'

Officer Raptakis looked at the Inspector who nodded in confirmation. 'We will be interviewing a suspect and when the chemical results come through from you they could be the final thing we need to gain a full confession.'

As Adam and Inspector Antonakis entered the police station Babbis rose from the hard chair where he had been sitting. 'How much longer am I going to be kept waiting? I have work to do.'

'All in good time, sir. I had to follow up on some enquiries this morning and they obviously took me a little longer than I imagined. I had expected to be here when you arrived and able to go about my duties after I had spoken to you.'

'Well now you are here, maybe we could get this formality over and done with as rapidly as possible.'

'I can assure you we are as anxious as you are to have the statements so we can close the file. I will have to ask you to wait just a little longer as we want to speak to Mr Vikelakis first.'

'It is more important that I return to the office. He only answers the telephone and does the relevant filing. I need to speak to people who are applying for planning permission.'

'Quite so, sir. I will deal with Mr Vikelakis as swiftly as possible and then you will have my undivided attention.'

Alecos slouched in the chair in front of Inspector Antonakis and Adam. 'I really do not understand why I could not have given a written statement to the officer who drove us down here. It would have saved a considerable amount of time.'

'The officer had his instructions from me to request that you and Mr Skourlatakis came to the station. Unfortunately I was out when you arrived and I apologise if you have been kept waiting for any length of time.' The Inspector switched on a tape recorder.

'You have no objection to your interview being recorded? It speeds the process up considerably.'

Alecos shrugged. 'If you say so.' He knew the interview would be recorded anyway by an officer using speed writing or shorthand and if mistakes were made he would have no way of proving the error.

Inspector Antonakis tested that the recorder was working and prepared the recording with his usual introduction of his name, rank, the date, time and the name of the suspect he was interviewing.

'I would like you to tell me about the evening a couple of weeks ago that you spent with Mr Skourlatakis. You were playing cards I believe.'

Alecos nodded.

'You need to speak, Mr Vikelakis. Yes or no?'

'Yes.'

'You were playing cards with Mr Skourlatakis until what time?'

'I don't know for sure. The early hours of the Sunday morning.'

'When you finished your game what was the outcome?'

'What do you mean?'

'Had either of you won or lost a large amount?'

'I told him,' Alecos pointed towards Adam. 'I won a thousand Euros.'

'A very sizeable sum. Where did this game take place?'

'At my house.'

'You have your own house, Mr Vikelakis?'

'I did have until my accident and losing my job at the bank. I live with my parents now.'

'They do not mind you having a friend there playing cards until the early hours?'

'Why should they?'

Adam sat forward. 'Mr Alecos Vikelakis is now being questioned by Adam Kowalski. Mr Vikelakis, I called on your parents to verify your story. I spoke to your father. He denied categorically that you were participating in a card game at the house that evening. Your parents do not approve of gambling. They sleep in the living room and you have a bedroom behind that room. Had you been playing cards in the living room they would probably have wanted to go to bed and asked Mr Skourlatakis to leave.'

'We played in my bedroom.'

'Are you sure of that, Mr Vikelakis? Your father said no one called that evening.'

Alecos looked from Adam to the Inspector. 'Maybe I'm thinking of the wrong evening.'

'Maybe you are,' agreed Inspector Antonakis. 'I suggest we leave you for a while and you can think about the evening in question.'

'Are you arresting me?' asked Alecos in alarm.

'No, sir. We are simply holding you pending further enquiries. We will be back. The interview has been temporarily suspended.' Inspector Antonakis switched off the tape recorder and he and Adam left the room. The Inspector locked the door behind them.

'Now we will hear what Mr Skourlatakis has to say. They may have concocted the story between them, but it will be interesting to hear Mr Skourlatakis's version.'

Once again Inspector Antonakis apologised for keeping Babbis waiting. He ushered him into an interview room and went through the same procedure about recording the interview.

'Is that necessary?' asked Babbis. 'I thought I had come down here to make a statement.'

'A recording is the equivalent. It also gives us the opportunity to ask you any questions during the proceedings and could save having to ask you to visit us again. Mr Kowalski has agreed to conduct the interview on my behalf. Shall we proceed?'

'I would like you to tell me about the evening a couple of weeks ago that you spent with Mr Vikelakis. You were playing cards I believe.'

'That's correct.'

'Where did the game take place?'

'I told you originally, at Mr Vikelakis's house.'

Adam nodded. 'Which room did you use for your game?'

'Room? The living room, where else would we play?'

'Of course. Were Mr Vikelakis's parents present during the evening?'

Babbis hesitated. 'Probably.'

'When you say "probably" does that mean that you did not see them?'

'I don't remember.'

Adam raised his eyebrows. 'Do you remember how much money you lost that evening?'

'A thousand Euros.'

'Rather a large amount. Now I would like you to think back to a previous evening; the one where you took Miss Vandersham for a meal and subsequently drove up the hill for her to view Spinalonga floodlit. I understand there was a misunderstanding between you and Miss Vandersham ran back down the hill. Can you tell me again what you did after she left you?'

'I waited a while and then drove home.'

Adam shook his head. 'I don't think that is entirely accurate. Would you care to think about your movements and tell me again?'

Babbis looked from Adam to the Inspector and decided to try to bluff it out. 'What else would I have done? Had I followed Miss Vandersham immediately I would probably have distressed her further. I had no wish to do that.'

'So you insist you waited a while and then drove home to Aghios Nikolaos?'

'Yes.'

'Mr Skourlatakis, you are lying. You did not drive your car home. Miss Vandersham had taken your car keys and you did not have a spare set with you. Nor did you have a key to the door of your apartment. When you finally arrived back in Aghios Nikolaos; I imagine you took a taxi for the journey; you had to rouse the caretaker and ask for the spare keys to allow you access to your home.'

Babbis shifted uncomfortable in his chair.

'Not only did you have to wake the caretaker to enable you to enter your apartment, you also took a taxi the following day to recover your car,' continued Adam. 'You were seen arriving on the hill and driving your car away. Your car keys were also found amongst the grass lower down the hill. I suggest you are lying about your movements, Mr Skourlatakis.'

'I was embarrassed. I didn't think it would make any difference if I said I drove home or returned the next morning for my car.'

'No difference at all, except that it proves you to be untruthful. What else have you not told the truth about?'

Babbis's eyes swivelled between the Inspector and Adam again and he swallowed nervously.

'Let us return to this supposed card game. You say it took place in the living room, but you did not see Mr Vikelakis's parents. Not only do they sleep in that room they disapprove of gambling and would not have sanctioned a card game.'

'Maybe they were away.'

The Inspector shook his head. 'Mr Vikelakis has a heart condition that keeps him confined to the house. Another lie, Mr Skourlatakis. You were not at Mr Vikelakis's house playing cards that night. Where were you?'

'I don't remember; probably somewhere in Aghios Nikolaos.'

'I think you know exactly where you were. On that particular night you were seen entering the house in Kastelli carrying two petrol cans. When you came out some time later you threw a lighted spill through the doorway and watched the petrol ignite before you drove away.'

Babbis paled. 'Rubbish. Utter rubbish. I was nowhere near the house that night.'

'Why should I believe you, Mr Skourlatakis? You have lied about returning home after assaulting Miss Vandersham, you have lied about participating in a card game and I believe you are lying now.' Adam looked at his watch. 'The Inspector and I are expecting an important telephone call within the next few minutes. We will terminate this interview and return later. When you have had time to think about the web of lies you have told you may feel more inclined to tell us the truth.'

Adam and Inspector Antonakis returned to the room where Alecos was waiting for them. The Inspector smiled at the nervous man as he switched the tape recorder back on.

'Now you have had a while to think about the evening when a supposed card game took place you may feel more inclined to tell us the truth.'

Alecos licked his dry lips. 'Are you going to prosecute me?'

'That will very much depend upon the answers you give us. There was no card game, was there?'

Alecos shook his head.

'Please answer yes or no.'

'No,' muttered Alecos.

'Why did you say you and Mr Skourlatakis had spent the time together?'

'He asked me to say that.'

'It must have meant a good deal to him to have you give him an alibi for that night if he was willing to pay you a thousand Euros. What do you think he had been doing?'

'I thought he'd been somewhere with a woman. His wife goes away each month and he often finds someone else to spend his time with.'

'If this is common knowledge to you why do you think he was prepared to pay so much on this occasion?'

'He said it was important and I thought he must have been seen and someone had probably told his wife. I asked for five hundred, but then he,' Alecos pointed to Adam, 'came around asking questions so I upped the price.'

'Why was that?'

'I knew about the encounter with Miss Vandersham. She came into the office and held up her blouse for all to see and described how the buttons had been torn off. She said if Babbis did not give her the completion certificates for her house she would tell his wife. Babbis was furious. When Babbis asked me to say we were together that night in August I realised it was the night of the fire. I asked Babbis where he had been and he said he'd had business in another village. I decided to take a chance and ask him double and although he didn't like it he didn't argue. I honestly don't know where he was.'

'Has he paid you?'

'Some of it. He can only take so much out of the bank each week and he's just bought a new car so he's probably a bit stretched at the moment.'

The Inspector nodded. 'Thank you, Mr Vikelakis. I will ask my officer to take an updated statement from you. This will give you the opportunity to say that Mr Skourlatakis bribed you to give him an alibi and that you were not together that night.'

'Are you going to charge me with anything?' asked Alecos anxiously.

'We would be within our rights to charge you with perjury and attempting to pervert the course of justice, but once we have your revised statement we may well reconsider prosecution proceedings.'

'And I'll be free to go?'

'We will not be holding you, but you are not to leave Aghios Nikolaos until we give you permission. No sudden visits to another city and trying to disappear. I would also ask that you do not discuss your visit here with anyone.'

'Babbis is sure to ask me.'

'You were asked to verify your statement. No need to tell anyone more than that.'

Adam smiled to himself. It was unlikely that Babbis Skourlatakis would be at liberty to question Alecos Vikelakis. 'I think we can leave Mr Skourlatakis contemplating for a little longer. I would like to have the forensic report through before we talk to him.'

Inspector Antonakis nodded in agreement. 'I'll telephone Raptakis and find out how much longer we will have to wait for the results.'

Mrs Skourlatakis was worried. She had tried unsuccessfully to telephone her husband and each time she was told that his mobile was switched off. She could only think it had developed a fault. Polishing her furniture would have to wait. She must visit her husband's office and tell him that the police had called and taken away an old pair of trousers and his brown shoes. She must also alert him to the fault on his mobile.

Mr Lamanakis shook his head when she approached his desk and asked to speak to Babbis. 'I'm sorry. He isn't here. He went down to the police station to make a statement hours ago and hasn't returned yet.'

'Why would he have to go to the police station? What do they think he has done?'

'I've no idea. Mr Vikelakis was asked to accompany him and he returned a short while ago. He may be able to help you.'

Alecos scowled and shook his head at Mr Lamanakis. 'I've no idea why Babbis is still there. They kept me waiting so I can only think they've made him wait as well.'

'I'll go down to the station.' she said. 'I need to let Babbis know his mobile isn't working.'

'We were told we could not have our 'phones switched on in the police car or at the station. Interferes with their radios apparently.'

Mrs Skourlatakis hesitated. 'That would explain it, then. I'll go back home and wait until Babbis calls.' She was not going to mention that the police had removed some of Babbis's clothes from the house earlier that day. Had a girl accused him of rape?

She knew her husband would always find himself a companion when she was visiting her parents. Since he had blacked her eye when she had confronted him after the first occurrence came to her knowledge she had ignored his philandering. He was ready to use his fists on her at the slightest provocation and she did not want to end up with broken bones and bruises that she would have to try to explain away to her neighbours.

Office Raptakis was cautious over the telephone when he spoke to Adam and the Inspector. 'The results came through about ten minutes ago. I can confirm that the stains you found on the trousers and inside the shoe were caused by petrol, but I can't say when they happened. It may have been any time during the last month.'

'Did you subject the whole shoe to a test or just the spot inside?'

'Both shoes. There was petrol residue on both of them. At a rough guess I would say it had splashed up from a hard surface and spotted his shoes across the toes.'

'And the carpet from the boot of his old car?'

'Definitely a petrol stain on it, but again I can't be specific about the length of time it has been there.'

Adam smiled. 'Thank you. That information will certainly be useful to us. I believe the Inspector could well be able to make an arrest very shortly.'

Inspector Antonakis nodded. 'Thank you, Raptakis. I'm very grateful.'

Adam and the Inspector returned to the room where Babbis was waiting.

'I hope you've come to tell me I can leave now. I ought to sue you for wrongful imprisonment.'

'You have not been imprisoned, Mr Skourlatakis, merely detained. Mr Kowalski has some more questions he would like to ask you.'

'I thought you were the police inspector, not him.' Babbis indicated Adam with his thumb.

'Mr Kowalski has a far higher position than me. He is employed by the American Embassy.'

'It's that American girl, isn't it? Because you work for the Embassy she thinks you'll accept her story of the incident rather than mine.'

'Mr Skourlatakis,' said Adam patiently, 'I am only interested in getting at the truth regarding the arson at Miss Vandersham's house. If you recall in our earlier conversation I proved that you had told us a tissue of lies. This morning the Inspector and I visited your house and removed a pair of brown trousers and brown shoes.'

Babbis sat forward, his face red with rage. 'What right did you have to go to my house? No doubt you terrified my wife.'

The Inspector shook his head. 'We had a search warrant and your wife was most co-operative. I am sure she will have no complaint against our behaviour. We also went to the garage where you exchanged your car for a new one and removed a section of the carpeting from the boot. We have just spoken to Fire Officer Raptakis and he confirmed that traces of petrol were found on all the items.'

Adam looked at Babbis. 'In view of the fact that petrol stains were found on your clothes and in your old car and that we have a witness who saw you setting light to the house maybe you would now like to give us a true statement of events?'

Babbis's face was ashen. 'I need a lawyer,' he mumbled.

'You are entitled to make one telephone call. You have permission to switch on your mobile. When the call is terminated we will be taking possession of your 'phone until a later date. I suggest you request your lawyer to come to the station as soon as possible. No doubt you would like him to apply for bail on your behalf.'

'You mean you're going to lock me up?'

'Mr Skourlatakis, we believe you have committed a serious crime and have tried to cover your tracks by bribing an associate.

Unless your lawyer can convince us that you are innocent I am afraid that we have no alternative but to keep you here until bail has been applied for and approved.'

'How long will that take? My wife will be expecting me home. She'll be worried.'

'Mr Kowalski will call on your wife and explain the situation to her. If your lawyer arrives speedily and you are able to raise the sum of money agreed for your bail before the banks close for the day you could be home by this evening.'

Adam left the police station feeling satisfied. However adept and crafty Babbis Skourlatakis's lawyer might be there was no way he would be able to talk his client out of a gaol sentence. He would impress upon Ronnie the need to demand excessive financial compensation, knowing that the figure would be negotiated downwards to a reasonable amount. The only thing he did not relish now was calling on Mrs Skourlatakis and breaking the news of her husband's whereabouts.

Week Two – September 2012
Friday – Saturday – Sunday

Ronnie walked up to Kyriakos's taverna. Adam had called on her late the previous afternoon and related the events of the day. She had looked at him with a mixture of relief and delight.

'I'm so pleased old Kassianae was telling the truth. I didn't want to find that her son had done it out of spite as I hadn't employed him. I'll make sure I have some work for him in the future.'

'You're planning to start again with your renovation?'

Ronnie shook her head. 'I can't possibly afford it unless I do get compensation from Babbis and goodness knows how long that would be arriving in my bank account. I had planned to have everything ready for my mother and great uncle to stay up there and now they have to go to Vasi's hotel.'

'I'm sure that's no hardship.'

Ronnie smiled. 'No, his hotel is superb. I'm just disappointed that my plans for them have had to change. Can I tell Kyriakos when I visit the taverna?'

Adam considered her request. 'You can tell him that Babbis is in custody, but it would be better not to claim anything more than that. If Babbis was subsequently declared innocent and word had been spread around that he was in gaol for the crime he would be the one demanding compensation.'

'Oh, do you think his lawyer will be able to have his case

dismissed?' Ronnie looked alarmed at the thought.

'I think it most unlikely, but I wouldn't want to take the chance. I happen to know that he has not been strictly honest in his dealings as a building inspector. He often refused to issue completion certificates for work that had been carried out perfectly satisfactorily. He would tell the customer the work had to be undertaken a second time and they would have to pay him to make another visit. Once he has been charged with arson we may well add some other offences.'

Ronnie shook her head sadly. 'I'm a very bad judge of character. He seemed quite a nice and helpful man until the incident on the hill. Oh, did you collect my passport from the Inspector?'

'I am not allowed to do that. You have to collect it yourself and sign to say it has been handed back to you. It is a security precaution.'

'I'll ask Kyriakos if I can borrow his car and go in this afternoon. I really would like my passport back as soon as possible.'

'Kyriakos, I need to speak to you about something.' Ronnie sat down under the umbrella outside Kyriakos's taverna.

'Yes?' Kyriakos looked at her hopefully.

'It's to do with John and Saffie, well mainly John, I suppose. Even if you cannot agree please do not tell anyone else or John may be in trouble.'

'What is this mysterious something you need to talk about?'

Ronnie proceeded to tell Kyriakos about the bodies being remove from Spinalonga. 'They're not really bodies now. They will be skeletons. John is convinced he can find his great uncles bones as they were wrapped in a sheet and the last ones deposited in the tower some years after the island was closed.'

Kyriakos frowned. 'What are they going to do with the bones?'

'They are planning to build a new storage room where they

can be on display and those that are virtually dust will be taken to a graveyard on the mainland and buried. John and his family do not want their relative's remains on display.'

Kyriakos nodded. 'It would not be dignified.'

'Exactly. John has arranged with the workers over there that when they start to dismantle the old tower he will remove the body on the top that has been wrapped in a sheet.'

'Suppose the sheet has disintegrated?'

Ronnie shrugged. 'He will have to forget the idea, but assuming he can find Old Uncle Yannis's body he plans to bring it back to Elounda.'

'And then it will be buried in the church yard here.' Kyriakos smiled. 'That is more fitting than being placed on display.'

'Not exactly. John has asked Saffie if she will wash the bones and they will then be placed in a casket. At a suitable time they will be taken back to Spinalonga and reburied under the floor of the house where Yannis lived.'

Kyriakos looked at Ronnie and shook his head. 'I do not think the authorities will allow that.'

'The authorities are not going to be asked for permission. That is why you must not tell anyone, even if you refuse to help.'

'Help? How?'

Ronnie took a breath. 'Saffie needs a large sink in which to wash the bones. Can we bring them here and use your kitchen sink?'

Kyriakos looked at her in stunned silence. 'You want to use the sink in my taverna to wash human bones?' he said finally.

'There isn't another that would be large enough for the long bones. It shouldn't take very long as all the flesh should have disintegrated long ago.'

Kyriakos shuddered. 'Human bones in my sink! What will my customers think if they see them?'

'We would do it at night. If you trust me with the keys you don't even have to be here. Saffie will wash the bones and then take them to my apartment and lay them out to dry. We would disinfect your sink afterwards and leave everything spotless,' Ronnie assured him.

'You are going to sleep in your apartment with a dead body?' Kyriakos was aghast.

Ronnie shook her head. 'They are only bones, not a body. I have arranged I will go to stay with Saffron and Vasi for a couple of days.'

'Suppose the germs stay in your apartment?'

'Don't be silly, Kyriakos. There will be no germs on the bones; they are too old. If there was any danger of being infected I would certainly not have agreed to the idea. Saffie used to be a doctor. She knows about these things and she has no qualms about dealing with them.'

'She is not having them washed in her sink or stored in her house,' observed Kyriakos darkly. 'What happens if the authorities find out? My taverna would be closed down.'

'John will take full responsibility. He will say he brought the bones over and washed them at his house.'

'Suppose I refuse?' Kyriakos was wrestling with the horror of having his taverna closed and the reason being known by the villagers along with his wish to please Ronnie and agree to her request.

Ronnie shrugged. 'I don't know where else the bones can be washed, but please, do not tell anyone; not your mother or your chef. I will understand if you say no, but then you must forget that I ever asked you.'

'You would wash the bones at night?'

Ronnie nodded.

'And there would be no sign left that you had been here?'

'Absolutely nothing.'

Kyriakos gave a deep sigh. 'Tell me when you wish to be here.'

Ronnie looked at him in delight. 'Really? Oh, Kyriakos, John will be so grateful and so am I.' She rose and placed her lips on his. 'I love you, Kyriakos.'

'Does that mean you will marry me?' Kyriakos held her tightly.

Ronnie shook her head and wriggled away from him. 'You know I cannot give you an answer yet. I still need to sort out some other problems. May I borrow your car? I want to collect my passport from the police station in Aghios Nikolaos and then drive up to Kastelli.'

'Of course, you may consider my car to be yours until I am able to drive again. Are you sure you want to go to Kastelli? It must be so distressing for you after all the work you had completed.'

Ronnie smiled. 'I'm not expecting a magic wand to have been waved and it is all rebuilt. I want to think about it in a practical way and to do that I need to be up there and looking at everything.'

Ronnie arrived in Kastelli and walked down the road to her house. As she passed the old men sitting on the seat beneath the tree she waved to them, but only one returned her wave and then they huddled together talking. Ronnie was certain she was the subject of their conversation.

She stood outside her house and could not help the tears coming into her eyes. It looked little different now from when she had first started work on it, although she knew the balconies had been strengthened and the ironwork on them renewed. Cautiously she entered through the doorway. Mr Palamakis had said the structure was safe and she was not worried about the walls collapsing on her, but she could see the ceiling joists were sagging and some roof tiles looked in imminent danger of falling. She hoped she was not risking one landing on her head.

Taking a deep breath she hurried across the stone floor and into the old scullery. The door that led to the new extension was scorched, but looked reasonably sound. Carefully she withdrew the bolts and pulled it open. The door frame and the adjoining wall also showed marks from the fire, but the rest of the room she had planned to use as a kitchen only appeared to have a layer of sooty deposit.

Ronnie looked around the large kitchen she had originally designed. It would have been in keeping with the spaciousness of the house when everything had been completed, but she certainly did not need such a big area. She took out her sketch pad. If she had a combined fridge freezer rather than two separate appliances there would still be sufficient space for a washing machine. The kitchen could be made smaller by having a dividing wall erected with an arched entrance at the end of the worktop area and just before the yard door.

If she gave up her proposed workroom her latest idea might be possible. She could have patio doors installed and extend the wall outwards and down to join the wall that she had intended to be her workroom.

The wall that marked the present boundary for her workroom would have to be removed, making one large room. A dividing wall, once erected at the far end, would leave her with a reasonable size lounge and dining area. She could have a bedroom with an en-suite and a small bathroom next door. The drain runs had already been dug so it would only be a question of running a couple of extra pipes into them. She would have to discuss ventilation and a drain run in the bathroom with Mr Palamakis if he approved of her idea.

The biggest alteration she would have to make was to the retaining wall that ran around the property. She would need to have an entrance made; she could not use the front door of the derelict house as her main means of access. No doubt the work would be expensive and she would have to gain permission from the building inspectors.

She sighed with frustration. She would have to speak with Giovanni and ask him to accompany her to Mr Palamakis and discuss her ideas with him and also find out the cost involved and the amount of time it would take to complete the work. If it could be completed by the end of the season it could solve the problem of somewhere to live during the winter months.

Eyeing the damaged roof warily she returned to the front of the house and began to walk up the side road. She stopped and shook her head. There was no need to make a hole through the stone wall at the side; there was the wide wooden gate that had originally led into the courtyard and she had blocked it from inside with the wall of her extension.

Ronnie studied her original plan. The only alteration she would need to make would be the removal of a section of the newly erected wall in the kitchen. The main entrance to the house could be where the blocked gateway was now and would lead directly into her lounge. She would not need permission to knock a hole in the wall. She walked back to Kyriakos's car deep in thought. Provided she could afford the additional building work having a home there could solve another problem for her.

Vasi arrived back in Elounda feeling relaxed and satisfied. The hotel in Hersonissos was sold, the contract signed and the money deposited in the bank. He now needed to visit the bank and arrange for the Hersonissos loan to be repaid and then he could decide how much he could afford to repay off the loan on the Imperia. He would not want to find that he was asking for a further loan to enable him to make the necessary repairs.

He knew that underpinning the structure to ensure it did not collapse further down the hill was an essential priority and would have to be undertaken before he could consider refurbishing the inside. Mr Palamakis would not be able to undertake the work and he thought it likely he would have to employ structural engineers from Aghios Nikolaos. Christos Palamakis would have plenty to occupy him during the winter months making necessary repairs and redecoration to the hotel.

Once the Imperia had been declared safe, work could commence on the interior. If he concentrated on the ground floor initially, once completed, it could be opened as a bar. Yiorgo would be quite capable of running that when the daily trips to Spinalonga had finished.

Buying Manolis's boat when he died and asking Yiorgo Palamakis to be responsible for taking groups of tourists to Spinalonga had been the saving of Yiorgo's marriage when his wife had threatened to leave him. She was tired of being left alone, often for months at a time, whilst her husband was at sea on a naval vessel, but the winter always presented a problem as the only option then was for Yiorgo to return to work for his father doing the most menial and unskilled building work that he hated.

Saffron greeted Vasi with delight, and could tell by his broad smile that his negotiations had been successful.

'It really is a weight off my mind,' he confessed. 'The hotel in Hersonissos was making money, but the loan I had was horrendous due to the amount of work I had to do after it was used as a brothel. What with that and the Imperia sitting there gobbling up money every week I was beginning to think I would have to ask my father for a loan.'

'Oh, Vasi, why didn't you tell me how stretched you were financially? I would never have asked you to pay for more stock for my shop.'

Vasi shrugged. 'That was a minute amount compared with everything else, and you always repaid me at the end of the season.'

'So that I could borrow it again! I have a bottle of champagne chilled. Shall we sit out on the patio and have a drink whilst you tell me all your plans?'

'I think the champagne could wait a little. I really need a shower and it's been quite a hot day. You probably need one as well.' Vasi raised his eyebrows at her.

Saffron giggled. She knew exactly what he was suggesting.

'So what did you find out at your house?' asked Kyriakos when Ronnie returned his car.

'I'll tell you later. I need to speak to Giovanni. I've had an idea and I want to ask if he thinks it will work. If he agrees I need him to telephone Mr Palamakis for me so we can arrange a discussion. Ideally I'd like him to speak to Mr Palamakis this afternoon so I cannot stay up here now.' Ronnie placed a kiss on his forehead. 'Thank you for lending me your car. I'll be back soon.'

Kyriakos looked after her departing figure in both longing and despair. He was not able to take Ronnie back to his mother's house and the taverna was certainly not suitable for a romantic liaison. Once his plaster cast had been removed he would suggest they spent a weekend in a first class hotel in Aghios Nikolaos.

Ronnie found Giovanni and Marianne sitting on the patio overlooking the bay with Adam and Melina.

'Come and join us,' called Marianne.

Ronnie looked doubtful. 'I don't want to interrupt anything. I really wanted to have a quick word with Giovanni about my house.'

'You're not interrupting. Adam and Melina are leaving tomorrow so we were just having peaceful drink before Nicola returns with the girls and they start demanding attention. They'll want to tell us exactly what they have been doing; then they will argue between themselves and start the story all over again. It's quite tiring,' smiled Marianne.

'Oh, I was hoping to introduce you to my mother and uncle when they arrive. You've been so helpful, Adam. I'm sure Babbis would have got away with his crime if it hadn't been for you.'

Adam shrugged. 'I just asked a few questions that had not occurred to the Inspector; the advantage of being an outsider and not having prejudged opinions of people. Did you get your passport?'

Ronnie produced it from her bag. 'There was no problem, nor was there an apology for taking it in the first place.'

Giovanni was secretly relieved that Adam and Melina would not be with them during the following week when John planned to remove Old Uncle Yannis's remains from Spinalonga. 'What did you want to ask about your house? Are you in a position to ask Mr Palamakis to start work on it again?'

'Not exactly. I went up there today and had a look at the extension. That is hardly damaged and I thought that with a few alterations I could make it into a habitable apartment. I don't need a grand house to live in.' Ronnie presented the page of her sketch pad where she had drawn out her ideas. Adam and Giovanni sat forward, and Marianne touched her husband's shoulder.

'Move back. I can't see a thing with you in my way.'

Ronnie laid the pad on the table and began to indicate the alterations that would need to be made. 'It's really taking down a wall and erecting another, then dividing the room and installing an en-suite. The bathroom on the other side might be more of a problem, but it will only need an extra drain run and some form of ventilation.'

Giovanni nodded. 'What about light?'

'I can have windows placed in the side wall and front wall of the room I plan to have as a lounge. I know there will be very little light coming into whatever is left of the yard, but I can have a skylight in each room. I'd planned to have one put into my workroom and Mr Palamakis said that would be no problem once the building had been signed off by the inspector. My kitchen will have to be a little smaller if I'm going to make a doorway through from the side wall, but I'm not planning on doing mass catering.'

Giovanni frowned. 'What about an entrance or are you planning to walk through the old house and into the kitchen?'

'No, I'll have that doorway blocked up and have an entrance that leads directly into the lounge area.'

Giovanni shook his head. 'You won't get permission to knock a hole through the wall.'

'I don't need to,' Ronnie smiled triumphantly. 'The old entrance to the yard is there. I had blocked it with the wall of the kitchen. It would be a five minute job to remove the plaster board. After that it would just be a question of taking away the new brickwork and making a new door frame.'

Adam studied the sketch. 'It looks feasible to me.'

'What would you know?' asked Melina. 'You can't even knock a nail in straight.'

'At least I can take a measurement and get it right. Melina decided to make some new curtains for our bedroom. One ended up a good six inches shorter than the other,' he explained with a smile. 'I may not be any good at the practical work, but I can understand potential when I see it.'

'What happened to the curtains?' asked Marianne.

'We bought some,' answered Melina. 'I was being too ambitious. I'd never made anything larger than a cushion cover before.'

'Would you be able to telephone Mr Palamakis for me?' asked Ronnie anxiously. 'If you could arrange a meeting for tomorrow or Monday morning and come with me I'd be terribly grateful. He and his sons would talk about it in Greek, nodding and shaking their heads and I would have no idea if he agreed that the work could be done.'

Giovanni picked up his mobile. 'Better do it straight away, before Vasi decides he has some work for him.'

'Vasi's work isn't scheduled to start until the end of the season. He thought my house would be finished by then.'

Giovanni shrugged. 'Things change. Mr Palamakis can't afford to be out of work for too long so he'll take anything that comes along between now and when Vasi's job is due to start.'

Ronnie looked at him in alarm. 'I'm hoping this work can be completed by the end of the season. It would give me somewhere to live during the winter months. I don't really want to spend five months back in New Orleans again.'

'You might not find it particularly pleasant living up at Kastelli,' smile Marianne. 'They quite often have snow up there.'

'Snow?'

Marianne nodded. 'Mostly it's quite light, but sometimes there's a heavy fall and they become cut off due to the snow and ice on the roads. It would be a good idea for you to have a wood burning stove in your lounge in case you have power outages.'

'Electrics! I hadn't really thought about those. Will Dimitris be able to do them for me as we arranged originally.'

'I imagine he'll be grateful for the work. He's had a few small jobs and we can always find him something useful to do. He's always willing to keep the apartment gardens neat and tidy during the season.'

Giovanni waved his hands as he talked on his mobile, making Marianne move his glass of wine further away from him. He continually pointed to Ronnie's sketch and nodded in response to Christos Palamakis's replies. Finally he ended the call and smiled at Ronnie.

'I think we 'phoned him just in time. I've arranged for us to visit him tomorrow morning at ten. He has Vasi visiting him in the afternoon as he has decided he wants work done on the Imperia.'

Ronnie looked at Giovanni in alarm. 'That could mean he does Vasi's work first, then he's scheduled to work in the hotel at the end of the season.'

Giovanni shook his head. 'I pointed out to him that if he was still working on your big house Vasi would have to wait until it was finished. The Imperia has been empty for so long that I don't think a week or two will make much difference.'

Ronnie smiled at Giovanni gratefully. 'Thank you. I couldn't possibly manage without your help.'

Giovanni shrugged. 'No problem. Are you going to join us for a meal this evening?'

'I wish I could,' said Ronnie regretfully. 'I've promised Kyriakos I'll go up to the taverna and help this evening. I can't let him down now. He let me use his car to go to Kastelli and he's agreed to John's request.'

'We'll talk about that another time.' Giovanni indicated Adam and Melina with his head and Ronnie nodded. 'When does he have his plaster cast removed?'

'Two more weeks, provided he hasn't become so impatient that he's cut it off himself before then. He says it makes his leg itch and he can't wait to have a proper shower.'

'I've found a large enough box,' announced John as he walked onto the patio. 'It's really meant for an artist so it isn't terribly deep and I won't be able to get a lid to fit.'

'Not now, John,' said Giovanni sternly. 'This is Melina and Adam's last day with us. Come and join us for a drink and we can talk about other things tomorrow.'

Ronnie looked at John. It was obvious that Giovanni did not want the subject of the removal of Old Uncle Yannis's body to be discussed in front of Adam.

'Come and show me the box, John. I'll be able to tell you if it's suitable.' Ronnie smiled conspiratorially at John and he grinned.

'I've got it in the lounge. It's really a question of whether you think it is long enough and wide enough.'

Ronnie followed him and looked at the cardboard box that was lying on the floor. 'Let me get in and we'll see if I fit.'

She lay down in the box and there was just enough space for her arms at her side. 'I think it's ideal,' she said, sitting up. 'You can always put a cover over as you haven't got a lid.'

'That's what I thought,' agreed John. 'Dad seems a bit uptight about it at the moment.'

'I don't think he wants Adam to know. If he thought it was against the law he would have to report you. Let them think the box is for me.' Ronnie lowered her voice as she regained her feet. 'I've spoken to Kyriakos. He's not very happy about it but has agreed we can use the taverna kitchen at night.'

'Really? I knew he would agree if you asked him.'

Ronnie blushed. 'He's a bit worried that the taverna might be contaminated. I've assured him that we'll disinfect everything afterwards.'

'Actually,' John hesitated, 'would you be willing to come over to Spinalonga with me and Dimitris on Saturday evening?'

'What for?'

'Well I'd like to have a go at digging up the floor in Old Uncle Yannis's house. I'm going to ask Dimitris to come to help. With two of us working we should be able to loosen the soil underneath fairly quickly and make the hole deep enough. I don't expect you to help, but if you came with us you could sit and paint Elounda at night. If anyone asked why we were over there at night I could use you as an excuse.'

'What time would you want to go over?'

'After the visitors and workers have left, probably about eight as it should be dark by then and no one will see me carrying a pick axe and shovel.'

'I'll have to tell Kyriakos I can't go up and help him on Saturday and promise to go up on Sunday.'

'So all I need to do now is ....' John stopped speaking as Melina came through to the lounge. 'All I need to do now is have a quick wash and then I'll join you on the patio,' he said quickly and winked at Ronnie.

'I'll say goodbye to you, Melina, and thank you for coming; then I must go and thank Adam again and say goodbye to him.'

Ronnie sat with Giovanni in Mr Palamakis's living room, her sketch and the original plans for the extension on the table in front of them. Christos Palamakis studied them carefully and made some notes on a pad.

'It all looks feasible but I'll need to go up to the house and take some measurements. The sky lights will have to be installed after the extension has been signed off as completed.'

'Will the plans have to be redrawn?' asked Ronnie and Giovanni interpreted for her.

Mr Palamakis shook his head. 'The only exterior alteration is extending the wall from the proposed workroom. Everything else is internal.' He held up the original plans and handed them to Giorgos. 'Go and get these photocopied so I can work on them.'

'What about my ideas for the en-suite and separate bathroom?' asked Ronnie anxiously.'

Mr Palamakis shrugged. 'The en-suite is no problem. We go into the existing drain run.' He pulled the plan of the drains towards him. 'These have been signed off as completed.' He picked up a black pen and rule and drew a line from the intended bathroom to where the main drains ran outside in the road. 'We will have to go underneath the wall, but as the pipe is already agreed on the plans that will be no problem.'

Ronnie gasped and Giovanni smiled. The builder knew how to overcome obstacles.

Giorgos returned with the photocopied plans and Mr Palamakis handed the originals to Ronnie. 'It is better that you keep those. I do not want to make a mistake.'

He took some ink remover and began to paint it over the lines that showed where the kitchen ended. Checking with Ronnie's sketch he then removed various other lines and finally decided he had succeeded in giving himself a new plan to work on. Once again Yiorgos was sent to copy the amended plan.

'Is this all legal?' asked Ronnie. 'I don't want to end up with a large fine and being told to remove walls and have to start again.'

Giovanni shrugged. 'If the new plan is ever queried you ask to have the alterations passed in retrospect. There should be no problem. It has the architect's signature and date at the bottom along with the stamp of approval from the building inspectors' office. Final constructions often differ from the original design and arrangements can be made so they are overlooked.'

Mr Palamakis offered them coffee whilst they waited for Giorgos to return, and called out to his wife who complied with his request. Ronnie eyed the small cup of strong black coffee warily and was pleased to see that a glass of water had also been provided. She hated getting the coffee grounds in her mouth.

'With the new design there will be no problem hiding the electrical work or the trunking for the air conditioning,' continued

Mr Palamakis. 'Do you plan to have a wood burning stove or an open fire for use during the winter?'

Giovanni translated and Ronnie frowned. 'I hadn't really thought about either. I thought the air conditioning could also be used for heating.'

'It can, and it will keep the whole area comfortable most of the time. It will not be sufficient during the worst of the winter if you wish to sit in your lounge unless you have it turned up very high. That becomes very expensive.'

'In that case please tell Mr Palamakis that I would like a stove. I don't think I could cope with an open fire.'

Mr Palamakis spread out the plan on the table before him. With swift, confident strokes of his pen he decreased the length of the kitchen and made an arched entrance through to the living room area. He enlarged the doorway that led into the yard and then re-drew the walls from the proposed workroom, placing windows along the length. Measuring carefully with his rule, he blocked off an area at the far end and made four rooms.

'Bathroom, bedroom, en-suite, bedroom.' He pointed with his pen and looked at Ronnie with a smile of satisfaction. 'Is done.'

Ronnie and Giovanni pored over the redrawn design and finally Ronnie nodded. 'There is only one thing missing,' she said. 'Where is the entrance from outside into the lounge?'

Giovanni asked Mr Palamakis who shrugged and drew a line in the lounge wall.

'I hope it will be there, but I will need to see exactly where the gate is that has been blocked. It is possible the kitchen wall will have to be moved a little. Miss Vandersham will have to decide where she would like her wood burner positioned as there will be the need for a chimney. I will take measurements of the new walls and insert them on the plans. There will be no problem.'

John returned Skele to Dimitris's house after he had closed up the taverna. 'How's work going, Dimitris?'

Dimitris shrugged. 'I was relying on the electrical installation in Kastelli for money to pay my sister. She never presses me for payment during the season, but once the tourists leave she'll need the money to see us through the winter months.'

'I'm sure Dad will want you to check out the electrics in the apartments and Vasi will probably have some work for you. In the meantime if you were willing to give me a hand I'd pay you.'

Dimitris raised his eyebrows. 'At the taverna?'

John shook his head. 'It's a bit more complicated than that and strictly confidential. Have you heard the government are planning to build a new tower on Spinalonga and put the bones on show there?'

'No. Who wants to go and look at old bones?'

'The tourists according to them. My old uncle is over there in the original charnel house. The family deposited him there after he died. They were sure he would have wished to be on the island rather than buried in the churchyard.'

'Are you going to ask for his body to be returned so he can have a proper burial?'

'He did have a proper burial,' replied John. 'His cousin was a priest and he conducted the service. He even returned to Elounda and went over to Spinalonga to say prayers on the obligatory days. We were all happy that Old Uncle Yannis was resting peacefully on Spinalonga, but now the charnel house is going to be dismantled he is going to be disturbed. The last thing we want is to have his bones put on show so I've arranged to bring him back to the mainland.'

Dimitris smiled. He would not want the remains of one of his relatives to be put on show. A reburial in the local churchyard would be far more fitting.

'The thing is, I need a bit of help to dig a hole. Provided his bones are still all together in the sheet he was wrapped in I'm bringing him back for Saff to wash. We plan to place him in a casket and then rebury him in his house on Spinalonga.'

Dimitris looked at John in disbelief. 'You're not serious?'

'I certainly am,' replied John firmly. 'I've discussed it with Dad and he agrees with me. Saff has no problem dealing with the bones as she used to be a doctor. I've looked at his house and there's only one possible place that could be dug up and a deep enough hole made. I need someone to help me so I thought I would ask you.'

'You'll not be allowed to dig a hole over there without permission from the ministry. Have you asked them?'

'There's not enough time to go through the procedure. You know what it's like. I'd have to approach the church authorities; they would consider it and then pass the request on to the ministry. They would probably still be discussing it this time next year and the charnel house is due to be dismantled within the next few days. It will be my only opportunity to retrieve Old Uncle Yannis otherwise he'll be muddled up amongst the other bones.'

'We'll be arrested.' Dimitris shook his head. 'I don't want to end up in prison.'

'We'll go over at night taking some tools with us. When the hole is large enough we can fill it with stones and some earth. Once Old Uncle Yannis was ready to return it would be quite easy to remove the earth and stones and then fill the hole in again above the casket. No one except the family would know he was there.'

'Suppose someone saw us over there and reported us?'

'Who is going to see us?' asked John scathingly. 'I've asked Ron to come over with her artist materials. If by any chance the coastguard was alerted or a fisherman decided to investigate she will be able to see them coming and let us know. We then go down to the jetty and are sitting there fishing. The gate will be locked so they will have no reason to assume we have been through it. There's no law against sitting there fishing, even at night. If they insist we leave we meekly agree and return again later when they have left the area. Either that or I say Ron was accidently left behind and we came out to rescue her.'

Dimitris pursed his lips. 'It sounds risky to me. Suppose the workers discover the hole? If we've been spoken to by the coastguard we will be the immediate suspects.'

'No one will see us,' announced John confidently. 'If by any chance the hole was discovered I would say I had been on the island alone. I promise I'll not incriminate you.'

Dimitris scratched at Skele's ears. 'When would you want to go over?'

'Saturday night.'

Dimitris walked to the quay to meet John who was already aboard his small motor boat with Ronnie sitting in the stern with her artist's materials. Two fishing rods were in evidence and stowed beneath the seats were a pick axe, fork, shovel, brush and some sacks.

John raised his eyebrows. 'Ready for our night time adventure?' he asked as he started the engine and Dimitris nodded unhappily.

Ronnie giggled nervously 'Suppose someone spots us and reports us to the authorities? Surely they'll send someone out to investigate.'

'That's your job to keep a lookout for any boat that approaches the island. If it is a coastguard vessel Dimitris and I will be innocently sitting next to you watching you paint when they arrive or we'll be sitting in the boat fishing'

'I hope no one does come. I've had enough dealings with the police out here to last me a long time.'

'At least thanks to Adam you're not in gaol,' grinned John. 'I doubt that your mother would have wanted to visit you there every day. Keep a look out for any fishing boats that might be returning to port. I'm not going to put my lights on unless there's one coming our way.'

'This must have been how the smugglers travelled over when they went to retrieve the goods that had been stored there.'

'To the best of my knowledge no smuggling takes place over there now. The only people we are likely the encounter is some stupid tourist who hid from the officials with the idea of spending the night over there.'

'Do you think that's possible?' frowned Ronnie.

'Stupid tourists do stupid things. Remember you said you'd like to be out there to experience a storm.'

'I still would,' she answered defensively. 'I'm glad it's this year we are coming out at night. Last year I would have been frightened that Fotini's ghost would appear to me.'

'She still might,' grinned John.

'You won't do anything silly like coming up behind me and pretending to be a ghost, will you?' asked Ronnie anxiously.

John shook his head. 'I'm on serious business tonight and frightening people isn't my idea of a joke. You'll not be far away from us and if anything scares you shout for me or come and join us.'

Ronnie nodded. Somehow she did not feel so brave and unconcerned about being on Spinalonga in darkness.

John moored the boat securely, helped Ronnie ashore and passed up her easel and bag of paints. Dimitris followed her carrying the shovel, brush and sacks whilst John checked he had his torch and spare batteries in his pocket before shouldering the pickaxe and fork. Dimitris glanced nervously over his shoulder as John unlocked the gate and locked it again when they had passed through. He led the way up past the old disinfection room and along the main street towards the house where Old Uncle Yannis had lived with Phaedra.

'Where do you want me to sit?' asked Ronnie.

'How about up there.' John pointed to the flight of steps that led to the area above the tunnel. 'You'll have a good view of Elounda and the lights and also be able to see if a boat approaches.'

Apprehensively Ronnie picked up her easel and began to climb the irregular steps carefully, avoiding the crumbling edges and tree roots. She placed her easel so she could sit facing the shoreline and attached a sheet of paper to it, then looked around nervously. This was the area where Fotini and Aristo had lived.

'Hello Fotini, hello Aristo,' she said softly. 'I'll not be here long and I won't disturb you.' She gave an involuntary shudder, remembering her previous strange experiences when painting on the island.

She looked across at the lights she could see along the shore line and spreading up into the hills above Elounda. With the moonlight on the dark sea it would make a dramatic picture. Provided she concentrated on her painting she should have no problem and could also look out to see if any boat was approaching.

As she opened her box of paints she heard a slight rustle in the grass behind her and turned swiftly seeing nothing. 'Don't be silly,' she told herself sternly. 'It was either the wind or an insect that made the noise.'

Ronnie tried to concentrate on painting the coastline. It seemed that every time she placed her brush on the paper another rustle came from behind her making her start and look around.

'Fotini, if that is you, please stop trying to frighten me.'

There was no sound and Ronnie began to paint the dark sea, adding darker lines to denote the ripples. Once she had accomplished that successfully she could always add the lights on the shore and maybe a small fishing boat returning at a later date.

'Where do you want to dig?' asked Dimitris.

'In that corner. The rest of the floor has been metalled at some time in the past and would be almost impossible to dig through. Hold the torch for me whilst I sweep away the sand and dust into a pile over there. I'll need to replace it later to hide the traces of our work.'

Dimitris continued to look around nervously as John cleared the small area in the corner of the house.

'Provided I don't find this corner has been metalled lower down it shouldn't take me too long to loosen the earth. Place the torch on the ground over there and begin to shovel the earth into a sack as I dig it up. Once I've found out how deep I can dig you can go and collect some of the large stones from the pile we passed on the way here.'

'How will I know what size stones to bring?' asked Dimitris.

'Any size that you can manage will be fine. There'll be enough light from the moon for you to be able to see which ones are suitable.'

Reluctantly Dimitris left John alternately swinging the pick axe and shovelling out the loosened earth. Despite the moonlight the walls of the houses cast deep shadows over the path and Dimitris shuddered and crossed himself. What must it have been like living over here before the electricity was installed?

He bent over the pile of stones that had been placed in an open area by the workmen and selected a number that he thought he would be able to carry. He should have asked John for the spare sack and could have loaded twice as many in there. Between them they would be able to carry it back and it would save him from making a considerable number of journeys.

As he straightened up he was sure he had seen something move on the opposite side of the path. He strained his eyes in that direction, but could not make out anything further and decided it had been a trick of the moonlight and his imagination. He managed to carry five large stones and made his way back to the house where John was working.

'If I loaded up the sack with stones we could carry it back between us,' he suggested, but John shook his head.

'It's better that I continue digging. If anyone asks you can honestly say you did not dig a hole anywhere. Put the stones over there and then hold the mouth of the sack open for me whilst I put some earth into it.'

As John returned to digging Dimitris went to bring back some more large stones from the pile. He looked around warily, but could see nothing to alarm him.

'I should have brought some more sacks to put the earth in,' said John as Dimitris returned. 'That's about as deep as I can dig down, but I think it will be large enough now. I'll just have to pack the earth back down as tightly as possible or dump it somewhere else. Can you start passing me the stones?'

John inserted a layer of stones into the hole and shovelled some earth around them, stamping it down with his feet. 'We'll need more stones,' he observed and Dimitris dutifully returned to the pile of discarded stones.

Ronnie's hand jerked and a blob of yellow paint splashed onto her paper. She was sure something was moving towards her through the grass. Stifling a scream Ronnie jumped to her feet and ran back to the steps hurrying down them as fast as she dared.

'John,' she entered Old Uncle Yannis's house where John was shovelling earth back into the hole and stamping it down.

'What's wrong?' he asked.

'There's something up there. I saw the grass and a bush moving and I'm sure it was coming towards me.'

'Probably a mouse,' answered John nonchalantly.

Ronnie shook her head. 'A mouse would not have made the bush move the way it was doing.'

'I thought I saw something move when I was sorting out the stones,' added Dimitris.

'Probably just the wind blowing the grass and bushes around.' John was totally unconcerned.

'I can't go back up there,' declared Ronnie, 'besides there's hardly a breeze.'

John straightened up. 'I'll go back up there with you to collect your materials and you can show me where your ghost is hiding.'

He led the way up the steps with Ronnie gripping his hand tightly. They stood together and Ronnie pointed to an area. 'It was over there,' she whispered, 'behind that low bush.'

John stepped towards the area that Ronnie had indicated. When he had nearly reached the bush a cat sprang out and leapt up onto a wall where he sat and glared at them balefully, his fur standing on end in anger.

'I think we disturbed his hunting,' smiled John. 'When I come again I'll bring a bit of meat for him.'

'Where did it come from?' asked Ronnie.

'There are some cats that live over here. There's a woman on the mainland who comes over to ensure they have food and water. They've probably stowed away on a boat at some time and then come ashore.'

'I do feel foolish,' admitted Ronnie.

'No need. It made me jump when it suddenly sprang out. We should have brought Skele with us. He would soon have chased him away. Let's collect your materials. I've nearly finished the hole and I don't think anyone is going to come to disturb us now.'

John and Ronnie returned to the house where Dimitris was waiting for them. 'It was only a cat,' smiled John. 'It was probably on its way up there when you thought you saw something move earlier.'

'Is that hole going to be big enough?' asked Ronnie. 'I thought you were going to place the box down there.'

'That's only to bring Old Uncle's body back in. I'm hoping I can leave him wrapped in the sheet and leave him in the box for Saff to deal with.' John wiped his forehead with his hand. 'I'll go and collect some stones with Dimitris. You can keep the torch here.'

Ronnie picked up the torch from where John had placed it on the ground. It was comforting to have some light, although the moon was nearly full it was casting deep shadows and it was impossible to see across the road to the house opposite.

Ronnie held the torch whilst John knelt down and tipped some of the earth from the sack into the hole, packing it around the stones. Another two layers of stones were placed inside and John finally shovelled earth over the top of them and stamped it down hard.

'We'll have to make it pretty firm. If someone stepped on it and it subsided so the authorities found out we'd not have the chance to dig anywhere else.'

He swept up any excess earth and then brushed the sand and dust back into the corner. John took the torch from Ronnie and swung the beam over the area and eyed his handiwork critically. 'I don't think it will be noticed. Once the first visitors tomorrow have walked into the room no one will realise we've been digging around.'

'What about the workers? Won't they check in every house?'

John shook his head. 'They might poke their head inside the doorway, but they're not going to start checking the floors to see if anyone has dug them up. I'll come back and check on it before we bring the casket over. Let's get everything back to the boat and become innocent fishermen.'

'If the coastguards are waiting for us and search the boat they'll want to know why we had those tools on board and no fish.'

John grinned at Dimitris. 'Stop worrying. I'm sure I could come up with some excuse and they would have to prove that I was lying. Thanks for your help. I certainly couldn't have managed it all on my own.'

Irini sighed. She did not relish the thought of walking up to Mavrikiano. She had not slept well all week and nearly fallen asleep in church which would have been humiliating and disgraceful. Kyriakos had not mentioned his plans to marry the American again and she hoped he had realised such a liaison was not practical.

She climbed the hill slowly, taking frequent sips from her bottle of water and thankful that she did not live up in the village. Soula was obviously expecting her as there was already a plate of biscuits on the table and it took no more than a few minutes to produce some coffee.

'Did your Thranassis find out anything when he went to Kastelli?' she asked anxiously.

'When they first appeared in the village the older residents thought it was the man who had married the old tax collector's

222

daughter. The villagers were not pleased. The old lady had owned a number of cottages and once she had died they no longer paid their rent.' Soula spread her hands. 'There was no one to pay it to any longer and when no one came to claim the house they stopped saving it. They didn't want these foreigners demanding rent from them again and asking for all they must owe over the years.' Soula shook her head. 'You know how it is, one of these foreigners arrives with money in their pocket; they turn the occupants out of their homes with a measly sum that they call compensation and then spruce up the inside and sell it as a holiday home. It isn't right.'

Irini nodded in agreement. 'They've done that further up the road from me. New people arriving every other week during the summer. They spend all their time on the beach, buy their food and drink from the supermarket and never go to the tavernas. We can do without them. Has she been asking the villagers for rent? Is that where she's got the money to spend on the house?'

'At the end of the season they all went away again and no one saw anything of them until the following summer when the girl cleared out the house. Thranassis said Greg told him the girl had given the villagers the cottages. You can ask your Kyriakos about that. Apparently she asked him to go and explain to them that she was not going to claim their cottages.'

Irini sucked in her breath. Kyriakos had not mentioned anything to her. The girl was either very foolish or had so much money that the rents were of no consequence to her. Irini helped herself to another biscuit. Maybe marriage to the American woman would be to Kyriakos's advantage after all.

'By then word had gone around that she owned the house and they were expecting her to sell once she had finished clearing out the rubbish but instead builders were up there every day. Pity the house didn't burn down as soon as the builders started work. It would have saved her a good deal of money and killed the germs.'

Irini looked at her friend with a puzzled frown. 'What germs?'

Soula took a mouthful of water and warmed to her story. She leaned forward and lowered her voice. 'According to what my Thranassis was told the old man who lived there had leprosy. Kept quiet about it and no one knew until he died. Rumours say that he infected one of his daughters. According to Nikos's mother the girl was taken away by her father and never returned. Nikos's mother said her mother had told her she overheard him telling his wife that the girl had leprosy. She was told to scrub out the girl's room to ensure that all the germs were gone.'

'What about the rest of the house? There could have been germs everywhere.'

'No one else appeared to be sick.'

'Surely his wife must have known?'

'She may have had it as well. You're not going to tell the authorities that your husband is sick if you are as well. The old man managed to keep it hidden, claimed the deformation of his hands was arthritis, shuffled around with a stick and always wore a hat. When the Italians shot him his hat came off and exposed the sores on his head for all to see.'

Irini sucked in her breath in horror. 'So what happened to the other daughter?'

'The older daughter and her husband suddenly appeared in the village with a little girl. They said they had adopted her. Nikos's mother said the family resemblance was so strong that she had to be the younger daughter's child. They never admitted it, but just before the war they left for America, taking their son and the adopted girl with them.' Soula sat back. 'That's all I know.'

Irini felt herself go cold. 'You mean this American girl is directly descended from a leper?'

Soula shrugged. 'I only know what my Thranassis found out when he was in Kastelli. The girl they adopted may not have been a relative and the likeness was a coincidence.' Soula hesitated. 'He spoke to Greg at the forge. He said she appeared to be a nice lady and he had made her new railings to go on the balconies. He also made the hand rails inside and fitted them. Greg said that Nikos had told him that his mother had met her along with a Greek man and he had asked her questions about the house and the family who had lived there. Her mother had worked at the house and later she looked after the old lady until she died.'

'You mean the girl knows there was leprosy in her family?'

Soula nodded. 'Must do.'

Irini felt her head swimming. She as not sure if it was due to her walk in the sun or the information that Soula had imparted. She had only come originally to ask if Soula's son's marriage to a foreigner was a success. She would have to call in to the church again on her return to Elounda and say a prayer for the health of Kyriakos. She wondered if her son knew that the old man who had lived at the house had been a leper. Surely the American woman must know, but she may well have kept the information to herself. There was no way Kyriakos should marry the girl. It was too dangerous; her own father had spent his remaining days on Spinalonga, although no one outside of their immediate family had been made aware of his condition. When Kyriakos had been a small boy she had examined him daily to ensure he had no signs of the deadly disease and never confided in him the fate that had befallen his long dead relative. If he married someone who also had a history of leprosy in their family was there any guarantee that the sickness would not reappear?

Week Three - September 2012
Monday

John was surprised when his father announced that he would be accompanying him to Spinalonga that day.

'If there is anyone over there supervising the removal of the bones they might take more notice of me than you. I can claim to be a closer relative than you and I was actually over here at his original internment.' Giovanni sighed. 'I'd better take some extra money with me.'

John smiled gratefully at his father. Despite bribing the workmen to turn a blind eye it could be more difficult if there was anyone from the Ministry of Antiquities there or the priest objected to the unauthorised removal of the bones.

'Besides,' continued Giovanni, 'there's no way you are going to be able to manage moving Old Uncle Yannis's body on your own. Even if he is still wrapped in the sheet as you try to lift one end you'll probably find it disintegrates or half of him will fall out.'

'I realised his sheet might be in tatters and I thought I would take an old sheet with me to wrap around him.'

'Good idea, but you'll still need help. If you lay the sheet on the ground we can take one end each and then wrap it around him before we try to lift him. At least all his bones will be together even if they get a bit jumbled up.' Giovanni frowned. 'You would have thought they would have closed the island to visitors whilst they removed the bodies from the tower. When we carry him to your boat we'll probably have to thread our way through the tourists.'

'If we take one end each and place the box on our shoulders no one will be able to see what is in there. If anyone asks we just say it is equipment.' John shrugged complacently.

John and Giovanni placed the box and sheet into the boat and motored round to where the workers alighted. A small motor boat was moored there and John frowned.

'I bet that's the priest,' he muttered. 'Once we've sorted things out I'd like to take the boat round and tie it up at the old jetty. Once the tourists start arriving my boat will be in their way and they'll probably just mow it down regardless.'

'Why don't you do that now? We can go in through the other entrance and down the main street.'

John shook his head. 'We need to get to the tower before they start removing bodies otherwise Old Uncle Yannis will get muddled up with the rest of them.' He picked up the sheet and jumped ashore.

'What about the box?' asked Giovanni.

'We can collect that later. It's more important that we get there as quickly as possible to see how much progress they've made.'

John hurried up the path to the graveyard, his father following behind. To John's immense relief the workmen were placing metal uprights into the ground and stretching blue plastic sheeting between them to stop visitors from viewing any activity that was to take place. As the last piece of plastic sheet was fixed into position John and Giovanni lifted the corner and entered the restricted area.

'There's the workman I spoke to.' John pointed to Elias who was rolling a cigarette. 'Obviously the no smoking rule on the island does not apply to the workmen.'

'Don't get into an argument over that,' warned Giovanni. 'We just want to complete our business as quickly as possible and leave.'

'Don't worry. I'm only going to make sure he knows why we're here.'

Elias acknowledged John with a nod of his head. 'You're early. We can't start until the men have cordoned off the area above so we don't have onlookers. Once that has been done the priest will say some prayers and then we'll be able to begin the demolition.'

'That's no problem. We'll be happy to wait.'

John relayed the message to his father and announced his intention of moving his boat round to the old jetty. It could also be a good excuse to have a quick look inside Old Uncle Yannis's house to check that no one had interfered with the hole that had been dug. 'I'll bring the box back with me and a couple of bottles of water. By the sounds of things this could be a long process.'

As John returned the priest could be heard intoning a prayer and he walked forwards quietly to join his father. To John's immense relief the workmen were standing around respectfully with their heads bowed. The priest looked their way and frowned when he saw he had intruders. John and Giovanni stood in silence, only joining in with the fervent responses that were expected of the small congregation. With a final swing of the incense burner, the priest raised his hands to the sky and said a last 'Amen'.

Giovanni greeted the priest with a smile. 'It was very gratifying to hear you saying prayers for those poor souls who perished over here.'

'It was a private ceremony. It was not meant for visitors.'

'We're not casual visitors. A member of my family is in the tower.'

The priest crossed himself. 'Knowing that he is now going to be removed must be a great comfort to you.'

Giovanni shook his head. 'We were quite happy for him to stay there until we heard that some of the bones will be put on display. We certainly don't want that to happen to him so we have come to take him back to the mainland.'

The priest gave a thin smile. 'That's impossible. You will not know which bones belong to him.'

'We're hoping he will be on the top and sewn into a sheet. He was placed in the tower long after the island was closed.'

The priest raised his eyebrows. 'Who gave permission for his interment?'

Giovanni shrugged. 'I have no idea. His brother and sister were alive at the time. They would have dealt with the formalities.'

'Do you have any papers giving you authority to remove him?'

Giovanni spread his hands. 'By the time we heard about the removal it was far too late for us to apply to Athens. Obviously if the sheet my uncle was wrapped in has disintegrated and his bones are amongst the others we will just have to accept that he leaves here with the others.'

'And in the event that you are able to identify his bones what do you plan to do with them?'

'We have a sheet with us to wrap around him and a large box. We will take him back with us and his bones will be washed and placed in a casket before he is reburied. All our family are buried in the churchyard at Elounda. We do not want his bones put on show to the public.'

The priest stood there hesitantly and Giovanni pulled some notes from his pocket. 'In the event that we can identify him we would like you to say a special prayer for him.'

The priest eyed the money greedily and finally stretched out his hand and placed it in the pocket of his robe. Giovanni smiled in relief. He had yet to meet anyone who could not be bought for a bundle of notes.

John greeted his father excitedly. 'I had a quick looked through the opening and I'm sure Old Uncle Yannis is on the top. There's definitely a sheet or material of some kind in there. The men are pretty certain that the rest of the roof is safe. They're going to knock out some of the lower bricks from the opening so they can put a ladder inside. A couple of them will climb in and move that section of fallen roof to one side and shore up the roof as an added precaution. They plan to make a hole lower down on the other side of the tower so the bodies can be brought out.'

Giovanni nodded. 'The priest is going to say a special prayer for our uncle before we take him over to the mainland,' he said loudly and winked at John.

John smiled. 'I'm pleased to hear it.'

John watched anxiously as a workman reached through the small entrance in the wall of the tower. Carefully he knocked at a brick on the inside of the aperture and once loosened caught it deftly in his hand before passing it to Elias who threw it onto the ground.

Giovanni looked at his watch. 'At this rate we'll be here all day,' he grumbled.

'You can go back home if you want, Dad. I can always 'phone when I need the boat to come to collect me.'

Giovanni shook his head. 'We've discussed the difficulty of one person managing to keep the bones intact and getting them into the box. I agreed to help so I'll stay until we can take him away.'

'I'll go and help with moving the rubble. That may speed the process up a little.'

Whilst John moved the largest chunks of stone to an area well away from the tower two of the workmen turned their attention to preparing the supports for the roof. Finally the workman agreed that the hole he had made was large enough for him to place a ladder inside and for the men to climb through.

'Be careful not to disturb the bodies,' John cautioned him.

Elias gave John a scathing glance. 'Hold the ladder for me, Makkis. I don't want to fall off and end up on top of them.'

Watched by the other workmen Elias climbed carefully down inside the tower, followed by Makkis.

'Pass me the supports,' he ordered, 'then shine your torches inside so we can see what we're doing. It smells down here and the quicker we can get some fresh air the better.'

John looked anxiously at his father. 'Do you think they have actually decayed and that's the smell?'

Giovanni shrugged. 'The flesh will have decayed originally. That could account for the smell or it may be just where there's no air circulating in there.'

Once the supports for the roof were in place Elias and Makkis could be heard knocking at the wall lower down and the other workmen hurried to a safe area, followed by the priest. Large chunks of masonry began to fall to the ground and Elias stuck his head through the hole and took a deep breath.

'That's better. How's it looking?'

A workman squinted at the upper part of the wall. 'There's a crack developing. You'll need to shore it up before you go any further.'

Elias and Makkis waited whilst their companions manoeuvred a length of wood into position across the new opening and wedged it firmly into place.

'That should be safe enough for the time being. We'll keep an eye on it and if we see any movement we'll shout at you to stop.'

John held his breath, longing to look inside and see if the sheet that had been wrapped around Yannis was still intact. He kept looking at the makeshift support that was holding up the higher section of the wall and the roof. If either should collapse the man who was working inside would be trapped, injured, possible killed.

Both Giovanni and John were relieved when Elias declared they were almost down to the ground and climbing out for a rest.

'Does that mean we can collect our uncle?' asked John.

Elias shook his head. 'The opening needs to be enlarged before we can start anything like that. It will be a while. Once we've had a break we'll get back on with the job.' He sat down a short distance away, took a mouthful of water from his bottle, rinsed his mouth around and spat it out before lighting a cigarette.

The other workmen hurried back to the tunnel entrance and walked through to the room in the main square where they were storing their equipment. A short while later they returned with brooms and shovels.

'Fancy making yourself useful?' asked one of John and he nodded.

'Come with us and collect some boxes. They've been flat packed, but an extra hand carrying them would speed things up.'

'You're not going to shovel them up, are you?' asked John as he walked along beside the men.

'The bones that are intact we'll put into the boxes, but by the time we get to the bottom of the pile I doubt there'll be more than bone dust. We'll sweep that up and keep it separate.'

'Then what will happen to it?'

'I understand there will be a church service and then it will be reburied along with the other limbs that have almost disintegrated. They'll only put on show the ones that are virtually complete. No good putting out bits and pieces; they won't mean anything to anyone.'

'Will they be examined before they are reinterred or put on show?' asked John.

'What for?'

'Well I would have thought some of the doctors would have been interested in seeing how the leprosy had developed amongst people who had little or no medication. They might find something useful that could help present day sufferers.'

The man shrugged. 'No idea.' He unlocked the door to the storeroom and began to pass out flat packed cardboard boxes, tied together in bundles of twenty.

'How many do you need?' asked John as he picked up two bundles.

'That will depend upon how many bodies there are. We want to get them moved as quickly as possible and before any tourists become too curious. We can store the boxes back down here as we fill them and then take them all to the mainland at the same time. It will mean an early start before the boats begin arriving.'

'I'm happy to cart as many boxes as you think you need,' John assured him and waited whilst the door to the storage room was locked again.

'Kyriakos, I need to speak to you seriously.' Irini stood with her arms folded before her, barring way to the front door of their house.

'Not now, Mamma. My chef will be collecting me any minute to go up to the taverna. I need to make sure all is in order for Ronnie's relatives when they come for a meal this evening. Would you like to join us? It would be a good opportunity for you to meet them.'

Irini shook her head. 'You cannot marry that girl.'

'Why not? Just because she isn't Greek doesn't mean she won't be a suitable wife for me. Why are you so set against her?'

'I visited my cousin Soula in Mavrikiano after church and talked to her. Her son visits Kastelli regularly and gets to know all the latest gossip. You know this American girl's great grandparents came from there, but do you know where they ended up?'

'Yes, I do. Ronnie told me.'

'And you weren't planning to tell me!' said Irini bitterly. 'This girl you want to marry has tainted blood.'

'Mamma, that was years ago. Ronnie has no signs of leprosy and I had planned to tell you about her relatives. There is no cause for concern about her health. I'm sure there are any number of other people around this area who had a sick relative and they have no hesitation about getting married. Just because one person in the family was afflicted it does not mean that any of the others were.'

'In her case it was more than one member,' stated Irini grimly. 'Her great great grandfather passed it to his daughter. The villagers were sure the family had adopted their daughter's child. That means that both this Ronnie girl's great grandparents were leprous. The child would have lived over there amongst them and goodness knows what she brought back to the mainland with her. No wonder they went away to America.'

'Mamma, you are worrying unnecessarily. Ronnie is fit and healthy.'

'Have you slept with her? Have you seen her undressed?'

Kyriakos flushed with embarrassment. His mother had no right to ask him such a personal question; he was not a little boy. 'She hasn't agreed to marry me yet.'

'She might look clean now, but the disease could always come back. Suppose you had a child together and found you had passed the infection to them?'

Kyriakos frowned. 'I don't think it can be passed down like that.'

'You don't know. You cannot take the chance.'

Kyriakos shrugged. 'So we agree not to have any children. Does that satisfy you?'

Irini shook her head. 'Married people should have children. She could pass the disease on to you. Have you thought of that? Good thing that house has been burnt down. At least the germs in the walls will have been destroyed.'

'I don't think leprosy germs can live in stone walls.'

'What about the rubbish you helped her clear out? How do you know that was not contaminated? Had I known that was what you were doing I would have forbidden you to go near the place.'

'Mamma, be reasonable. The house had stood empty in Kastelli for years. If it was contaminated surely some of the villagers would have become sick.'

'They may have done. How many people have moved away? Where have they gone? Do you know?'

Outside the house a car hooted. 'Mamma, please move away from the door. Costas is waiting and I have to go. If you are so concerned then we'll sit and talk about this sensibly when I have time.'

'I'll not be coming up to the taverna this evening,' Irini called after her son.

Ronnie waited anxiously for her mother and great uncle to land at Heraklion airport. Kyriakos had insisted she borrowed his car to collect them provided she took them to his taverna that evening for a meal. They both looked tired and hot as they dragged their cases through passport control. How she wished she was going to drive them to Kastelli and install them into her new house.

'How was your journey?' she asked as she loaded their cases onto a trolley.

'Not too bad,' replied her great uncle. 'We stopped in Washington for a couple of days and then spent a night in London. It's too exhausting to try to fly all that way without a proper break.'

'We did think we were going to be delayed. There was something wrong with the air con when we first boarded at Gatwick and they said we couldn't fly until it was fixed. Fortunately we only had to sit on the runway for about ten minutes, then we were told all was in order and they had been allocated a slot and could take off.'

'You're safely here, that's all that matters. Once you are in Elounda you can have a shower and a siesta.'

'I'm sure we won't need a siesta,' said Charlene. 'The shower sounds like a good idea, but I'm longing to hear all your news. Has anyone been charged with arson?'

Ronnie nodded. 'I think someone will be very soon. I have a good deal to tell you, but it can keep until later. I need to concentrate on driving to get through this traffic.' She pressed her hand on the horn. 'What does that idiot think he's doing? Just because he's driving a hire car and is a visitor does not mean he can change lanes just as he fancies without indicating.'

They threaded their way through the traffic and finally left the suburbs of Heraklion behind them. Ronnie was amused to see that both her visitors had their eyes shut and her great uncle was snoring gently. So much for not needing a siesta!

It was mid afternoon before John was told he and Giovanni could move the body they believed to belong to Old Uncle Yannis. Giovanni spread out the sheet they had brought with them on the ground and with the help of Elias and Makkis they carefully inserted their hands beneath the rotting sheet that shrouded the body. There was an indefinable smell coming from the remains and as John's hands touched bones that lay beneath it he felt the bile rising. Thank goodness Saffron had agreed to wash the bones and no one expected him to handle them.

He was sweating when the body was laid on the new sheet and it was certainly not from exertion. The bones were far lighter than he had envisaged. Giovanni and John wrapped the new sheet firmly around the old one and then with the help once again of Elias and Makkis the bones were carefully placed in the long box that John had purchased. He was relieved to see that they fitted easily.

The priest, since his initial prayers to encompass all the bones in the charnel house, had spent the day sitting beneath a tree in the shade. Now he stepped forward and began to intone more prayers over the body that had been placed in the box and John and Giovanni waited respectfully, both longing to be back on the mainland, their objective accomplished. Once again Giovanni pulled some notes from his pocket and handed them to Elias.

'Share them out between you. I'm very grateful to you all.'

'We'll give you a hand taking it to your boat. I suggest you wait half an hour or so. You don't want to have to walk through crowds of curious tourists to get to the jetty. The big boats will leave about five and there will be far fewer people around.'

Although both Giovanni and John were anxious to leave Spinalonga with the bones as quickly as possible they realised it would be far easier to wait for the visitors to thin out.

'I'll 'phone Nick,' announced John and his father nodded. A disconcerting thought had occurred to Giovanni.

'Where are you planning to store the box until the bones go to be washed?'

John stopped scrolling down his mobile for Nicola's number. 'What do you mean?'

'Well, they can't be stored at the house. Suppose the girls

found them? They would probably think they were toys. If your Aunt Ourania came across them she'd probably scream the house down or drop dead from shock.'

'It should only be for a couple of days.'

Giovanni pursed his lips. 'I'm not comfortable with that. Suppose for some reason there's a delay and they have to be stored for longer?'

'Leave it with me,' replied John airily. 'I'll think of something.'

'Well you have about an hour to come up with a solution.'

John pressed the key on his mobile to bring up Nicola's number and waited until she answered.

'All accomplished,' he told her. 'We're just waiting for most of the tourists to leave and then we'll be home. There's just one problem. Dad says we can't have the box in the house. Any ideas?'

There was silence on the end of the 'phone. 'Are you still there?' asked John anxiously.

'I'm thinking,' replied Nicola tersely.

'Ron doesn't mind them being left in her apartment over night to dry, but she's not prepared to stop there and has arranged to go to stay with Saff. Saff can't have them because Vasi's at home. Where else is there?'

Again there was silence on the 'phone. 'Nick?'

'I told you, I'm thinking. We'll solve the problem of storage when you've got them over here. Could you leave them on the boat?'

'I wouldn't want to do that. Suppose we had a freak storm and the boat was swamped or a tourist took it for a joy ride?'

Nicola gave a giggle. 'They'd get a shock.'

'Nick, be serious.'

'I am, it was just the thought of a tourist taking the boat and finding there were bones on board. They'd think they were on Charon's boat and going to the River Styx. I'll give it some serious thought, John. There's bound to be a solution.'

Ronnie sat downstairs outside the bar of the hotel waiting for her mother and great uncle to appear. They had both slept for most of the drive from the airport to Elounda and woken bleary eyed and yawning.

'I think my sleep pattern is awry,' declared Charlene.

Ronnie smiled. 'I'm not surprised. You've travelled half way across the world. I'll settle you in and then wait downstairs for you. Take as long as you like. I can spend my time making a few sketches which I would have been doing anyway this afternoon.'

From her vantage point beside the sea Ronnie could see across to Spinalonga and she wondered if John had managed to retrieve Old Uncle Yannis's body. The large tourist boats were leaving the island and within a short while they were followed by a number of small boats returning to Plaka or Elounda. She decided to wait a short while and then call John.

She did not think it advisable to tell her mother and great uncle that at some point she would be spending the night with Saffron or the reason why. She was not sure if they would approve and the reburial of Old Uncle Yannis was nothing really to do with her. She would be giving them plenty of other news to consider.

Able to curb her impatience no longer she pressed in John's number. 'Yes?' he answered eagerly.

'It's me, Ronnie. Did you manage to do what you wanted?'

'Oh,' John sounded disappointed. 'I'm sorry, Ron, I was expecting Nick to be calling me back.'

'Is there a problem?'

'Everything went well, but we have a problem now. Dad says we can't take the box into the house because of Aunt Ourania and the girls and we can't take it up to Ackers ready for Saff to deal with. Nick said she'd think of something and 'phone me back.'

Ronnie frowned. Should she offer to have the box in her apartment until Saffron was able to wash the bones? She would not want to sleep there with a skeleton for company.

'What about Saffie's shop? Would she be willing to store the box there? No, wait, I know. Uncle Yannis's shop. That would be the ideal place. He doesn't open every day and it would not be in his way. He has a number of large boxes with vases and statues inside so no one would notice another one.'

'Ron, you're brilliant. I'll call Dad and ask him to speak to Uncle Yannis and borrow his keys. I'm sure he'll agree. When we deliver it we can ask Saff when she can wash the bones.'

'Have you examined them? Is he complete?'

John gave a shudder. 'I've not unwrapped him. I thought it better for Saff to do that. I might do some damage.' John was not prepared to admit that he did not want to have to handle the bones at all. He did not understand how he could deal with any insect or reptile, allowing them to crawl all over him, but could not bear the thought of touching human bones.

'Let me know what you arrange. I'll be up at Kyriakos's taverna this evening with Mum and Uncle Alex.'

'I'll bring Skele up for a quick walk,' promised John. 'He will have been down with Dimitris's sister all day and probably feeling hard done by.'

Charlene settled herself beside her daughter. Although she had been devastated by the news of the fire at the Kastelli house she was not sorry to be staying in the seafront hotel. She would have felt obliged to make her bed and clean the bathroom each day, along with helping Ronnie with any other household chores.

'So what is the latest news about the fire?'

'Wait until Uncle Alex arrives or I'll have to tell you everything a second time. Would you like something to eat? We're going up to Kyriakos for a meal this evening, but that won't be for some while yet.'

'Maybe a snack of some sort. Some pita bread, taramasolata and olives, oh, and some humus. Alex if particularly fond of that.'

Ronnie smiled. Her mother always asked for the same items for a snack or light lunch and told her each time how much her great uncle liked humus. As she walked over to the bar area to place the order she saw her great uncle arriving and mimed eating and drinking to him. He nodded in agreement and she increased the amount of pita bread and added a tomato salad.

'So,' he said as Ronnie took her seat, 'I'm longing to know who has been arrested for setting fire to your house.'

'Well,' smiled Ronnie, 'I was nearly arrested. It was quite frightening. The police insisted that I handed over my passport.'

'Why would they think you had fired your own house?' asked Charlene.

'First of all they said I had done it to claim insurance money. When I told them it was not insured they said I had conspired with the village builder and his mother to frame Babbis in revenge for assaulting me. Fortunately Giovanni had a friend who is attached to the American Embassy and he came over from Athens and investigated. It seems pretty conclusive that Babbis Skourlatakis was the culprit and he has been arrested.'

'And charged?' asked Alex.

'I'm not sure. Adam said all the evidence he had provided against Babbis could be explained away by a clever lawyer so it really depends upon Old Kassie being believed.'

'Hmm.' Alex felt dubious that the man would be brought to justice. 'So what is happening with the house now? How much is it going to cost to put right?'

'I don't know and I'm not going to have any more work done on it at present.'

'Why not?' Charlene looked at her daughter in surprise.

'Two reasons. One, of course, is the amount of money it would cost to renew the roof again and have a new staircase built along with doing most of the other interior work. I could not afford it and I would not expect you to give me more money towards the repairs.'

'I'm sure we could manage something.'

'Thank you, Uncle Alex. It's reassuring to know you are in the background and willing to help if I become destitute. If I do manage to rebuild the house a second time I think I will turn it into a local folk lore museum. I had thought of that earlier, but I think the idea of being the grand lady of the village with the big house had turned my head. The second reason,' continued Ronnie, 'is that I've arranged with Mr Palamakis to have the extension altered so it can become separate living accommodation.'

'That won't be very big, will it? You had designed the area as your kitchen with a workroom on the end.'

'I wanted a large kitchen originally to be in keeping with the rest of the house. I don't need a kitchen that size and I don't actually need a separate workroom. It would probably end up filled with rubbish. I've spoken to Mr Palamakis and it's just a question of moving a few walls and I will have a perfectly acceptable apartment. I'm hoping it can be completed by the end of the season so I can live there during the winter.'

Charlene frowned at her daughter. 'Does that mean you won't be coming to New Orleans for Thanksgiving?'

'Of course I will come over, but I won't be staying more than a few weeks.'

'What will you do with yourself over here during the winter months?' asked her uncle. 'I understand it can be pretty cold and wet.'

'Well,' Ronnie hesitated, 'there's something else I need to talk to you about. Kyriakos has asked me to marry him.'

'And you have agreed, of course,' said Charlene with a smile.

Ronnie shook her head. 'I've not given him an answer yet, but I don't think it's possible.'

'Why ever not? He's a nice young man and you both seemed fond enough of each other last year.'

Ronnie flushed. 'There's no problem with Kyriakos. I actually encouraged him when he was too shy to approach me and still insisted on calling me "Miss Ronnie", but there is his mother to be taken into account. She would obviously like him to marry a local Greek girl and have them live with her. I can't do that.'

'Couldn't you live nearby? If she had three or four sons she surely wouldn't expect them all to take their wives to live in her house.'

'It isn't that simple. Kyriakos pays his mother rent and she probably couldn't manage without the money he gives her. He rises late and returns in the early hours of the morning from the taverna. I get up as the sun rises to go and paint. If I feel in need of a sleep during the day I return to my apartment and have an hour or so. He suggested we shared my apartment, but we would be continually disturbing each other and they are closed down in the winter anyway. Once the tourists have gone home we might be able to find a small apartment to rent, but we don't need to be in Elounda then. That's why I have come up with a new idea for my house.'

'If you lived up there permanently it would be quite a long drive to Kastelli each night after he had closed the taverna,' remarked her uncle.

'We would only live up there during the winter. That way there would be no rent to pay and Kyriakos can continue to help his mother.'

'How does Kyriakos feel about that?' asked Charlene.

'I haven't spoken to him about it yet. He may not agree. He's hoping those two young men who ran him over will be made to pay him compensation. He lost money when he had to stay in hospital for a few days and the taverna was closed. He still had to pay the chef and the overheads, of course, but word got around that he was closed and it took a while for the customers to return.'

'Will you be receiving compensation for the fire damage to your house?' asked Uncle Alex.

Ronnie shrugged. 'I hope so, but it could be a long while before I receive it. Babbis has been allowed out on bail, but no date has been set yet for him to appear in court. If he is convicted Adam said he would represent me and ask for an outrageous sum in compensation that would be decreased to a reasonable amount, but that doesn't mean I won't have to keep taking him to court to get it.'

'Just make sure he pays down to the last cent.'

'Greek law can be terribly slow. At least I have a little money left that will cover the alterations to the extension and I can keep myself afloat with the money from my paintings. I've done some of Elounda at night from Spinalonga and Saffie was quite impressed.'

'What were you doing over there at night? I thought the island was closed then.'

'I went over with John when it was dark. I certainly couldn't be over there alone at night. A cat that was prowling around nearly frightened the life out of me.' Ronnie smiled at the recent memory, but did not enlarge on the real reason for their nocturnal visit.

'Never mind cats and the island,' interrupted Charlene. 'Provided Kyriakos agrees to live in Kastelli during the winter when do you two plan to be married?'

Ronnie shook her head. 'I don't think we can. I've made some enquiries and I would have to produce my original birth certificate. Once my parentage had been looked into and they found out my father was in prison it is very unlikely that I would be granted a residency permit. I might even be refused permission to work over here.'

'That's outrageous! Your father's crime had nothing to do with you. I thought he was just a successful artist when I first met and married him. I had no idea he copied old masters and passed them off as genuine.' Charlene was indignant.

'I know, Mum, and I'm not blaming you in any way. I'm pleased I inherited his artistic talent. Think of the positive; I will have to return to New Orleans each year to reapply for a permit to work in Crete so I will be with you for Thanksgiving. The only solution I can see is that we live together, but that's something else I haven't discussed with Kyriakos yet.'

'And his mother will certainly not approve of that arrangement,' observed Charlene.

'I know,' answered Ronnie miserably. 'There has to be a lot of compromise on his part.'

John collected Skele from Dimitris and walked up to Kyriakos's taverna. He greeted Ronnie's mother and great uncle and then accepted a place at their table.

'I'll just have a beer, thank you. If I eat with you I won't be able to eat any of the meal my mother will have prepared and then she'll think I'm ill.'

Charlene pushed a plate of taramasalata closer to John along with some pita bread. Automatically he broke off a piece and dipped it into the cod's roe. There was definitely something wrong. Both Ronnie and Kyriakos seemed ill at ease and he wondered if Ronnie's mother had objected to their union.

'What has Ronnie planned for you whilst you are staying here?' he asked.

'Tomorrow she is taking us to Kastelli and will explain her new idea for the extension to us. I had been looking forward to staying up there, but now I'm actually down in Elounda I realise how much more convenient that is for us.' Charlene pushed a bowl of olives towards John.

Kyriakos looked at Ronnie with a pained expression on his face. She had told him she had spoken to Mr Palamakis about making alterations to the extension, but not disclosed the nature of them to him. Ronnie frowned at her mother.

'I have plans to take you to other places. Marjorie, Saffie's step mother arrives on Wednesday evening so I thought we could take her on some of our outings. I talked to Saffie about her visit and Saffie always feels guilty that she has to leave her alone at the house or down in Elounda whilst she is at the shop so I have invited her to accompany us. Not every day, of course, only when Saffie is busy or we are going somewhere interesting. I was going to arrange to hire a car for a couple of weeks, but Kyriakos has insisted I use his car every day. He's been so generous allowing me to use his car at short notice whenever I've needed transport in a hurry.'

'It will be no problem,' Kyriakos assured her, and Ronnie smiled gratefully at him.

'That was a kind offer on your part,' remarked John to Kyriakos. 'The younger people who visit are usually happy to spend most days on the beach and stay out in the tavernas until late. That's not the kind of life style you appreciate when you get older. You want to see something of the surrounding area.'

'Quite true,' agreed Alex. 'Besides I doubt if I could keep my eyes open much after eleven nowadays.' He sighed. 'That is definitely a sign of growing older.'

John winked at Kyriakos. 'I stopped off and spoke to Saff on the way up here. I said Dad and I had completed our business and she said tomorrow would be most convenient for her, before Marjorie arrives on Wednesday. She suggested you phoned her when you were ready to close.'

Kyriakos nodded. He was still not happy at having human bones washed in his sink at the taverna and then having them laid on his trays whilst they dried.

Ronnie accompanied Kyriakos into the taverna to collect the plates of food the chef had called were ready for them.

'What's this about the extension?' asked Kyriakos. 'I know you wanted to meet with Mr Palamakis, but you haven't told me anything about any decisions you made.'

'I haven't had a chance. We can't talk about it now. I have to sit down and have a serious chat with you without my relatives around. When Saffie is up here tomorrow night I'll be with her and we can talk then.'

'Did you tell your mother that I had asked you to marry me?' asked Kyriakos anxiously.

Ronnie smiled. 'She thinks you're a very nice man – and so do I,' she added as she placed a quick kiss on his cheek. 'That's another thing we need to talk about together.'

KYRIAKOS

Kyriakos did not mention the acrimonious words his mother had spoken before he left the house that day.

Week Three – September 2012
Tuesday

Ronnie slowed as they passed the house in Kastelli and finally parked beside the water cistern.

'This is certainly not the way I wanted you to see the house this year,' she apologised. 'It was so close to being completed and was looking magnificent.'

Charlene shuddered. 'At least it happened before you had moved in. Imagine what could have happened if you had been living here when the fire started.'

'It could have been worse,' agreed Ronnie. 'I'm afraid we have to use the front entrance and walk through to the extension at the moment, but I'm having an entrance made at the side that will open straight into the lounge area. You may have to use a bit of imagination as I describe what I plan to do, but I can show you my drawings later.'

As Ronnie led the way across the main room towards the extension she could hear loud hammering and the door from the old kitchen into the extension was open.

Mr Palamakis greeted her with a wide smile. 'Is good. Come, see.'

He spoke to his grandsons who paused in their labours.

'Grandpa said it would be most practical if we made the new entrance way before we started anywhere else,' Yiannis informed her. 'That way we can block up the doorway where you have entered and make everywhere secure. Once that is completed we can knock down the wall we built outside and make a start on rebuilding it the way you want.'

'Don't you need the plans to work from?' asked Ronnie.

Yiannis shrugged. 'The plans for the extension were passed. You've told us what you want altered and Grandpa has made notes. If you want to have new plans drawn up by an architect it will cost you more money and it could be weeks before they are passed.'

Ronnie looked nonplussed. 'But how will you know how long or high to make the new walls or where the drain runs should go?'

'We are builders. We can work without detailed plans. It is common sense.'

'Oh, well.' Ronnie turned away. 'I just have to trust you. We won't delay you for very long. I just wanted to show my mother and uncle how I plan to use the area now.'

'No problem. We will take a short break and continue knocking out those bricks when you leave. No need for you to be choked with the dust.'

Ronnie smiled at him gratefully. 'This is where the new main entrance will be. Because we had built up to the perimeter wall we didn't bother to remove the old entrance to the yard. When that is complete you will walk into the lounge. There will be an arch leading through to the kitchen area which will be considerably smaller than it is now and the doorway we have just walked through will be blocked off.'

'Will you have enough space for a fridge, freezer, washing machine and cooker?' asked Charlene.

'I've measured it and all I need to do is buy slightly smaller appliances. I've spoken to the suppliers and cancelled my original order. They were very understanding. Over here,' Ronnie pointed, 'the wall is going to be extended out to where my workroom wall is. The side wall will be knocked down and that will make the lounge considerably bigger and squarer in shape. Instead of having one door leading out to the yard I will have patio doors. I'm also having glass high up in the walls and windows that I can open in the lower part of the roof. They will provide more light and I can have blinds fitted to keep out the sun when necessary.'

'What about heating in the winter?' asked her uncle.

'I will have air con that doubles as heating and a stove for when it is really cold.'

'And your flooring?'

'Tiles in the kitchen and bathrooms, of course, and then wood everywhere else. If I find that cold in the winter I can always get some carpet squares to put down.'

Ronnie walked to the other end of the room she was calling her lounge. 'There will be a dividing wall about here with a bedroom and bathroom en-suite. Next to that Mr Palamakis says he can make another bedroom and then a separate bathroom. It will be a wall of doors.'

'What about ventilation?'

'I'll have windows in the lower part of the roof again. If I put up some trellis work no one will be able to see them from the road. I might even manage to get a grape vine to grow and spread along. Imagine, waking up in the morning, opening the window and picking a bunch of grapes.'

'Do you have enough money to pay for all of this?' asked Charlene.

Ronnie gave a rueful smile. 'I should have. I don't need to buy the kitchen appliances until everywhere is finished and the only furniture I need to start with is a bed, table and chairs. I could probably borrow those and anything else I found I needed from Giovanni's apartments over the winter, but I haven't actually asked him yet.'

'He'll miss having you in his apartments over the summer.'

Ronnie shook her head. 'Provided Kyriakos is agreeable we will be living down there in the summer.'

'That was a very enjoyable meal last night,' remarked Alex. 'Are we going there again tonight?'

'No, I thought I would take you somewhere else; then I will go up there and help him later.'

'Has he got a group booking?'

'Something like that.' Ronnie did not want to enlarge on her proposed activities for later in the evening. 'Have you seen enough? I don't want to hold the workers up for too long.'

'We go back out the way we came in, I presume,' said Alex.

'I'm afraid so. I hope by this time next week I can ask you to come in at the new entrance. Now, would you like to stay in Kastelli and have some lunch or drive on to Neapoli?'

'It's a bit early for lunch. Why don't we drive on and look for a taverna in an hour or so?' suggested Charlene.

Ronnie deposited her mother and great uncle back at the hotel just after four. 'I have a few jobs that I have to do and then I'll be back to meet you at seven. How does that sound?'

Neither Charlene nor Alex were sorry to be back at the hotel. They had both enjoyed visiting Ronnie's house and hearing her new plans for the extension, followed by a drive to Neapoli where they spent a short time wandering around in the square before deciding they would stop there for lunch. As they drove back to Elounda Alex could feel his eyes closing and began to think longingly of a short siesta before showering and preparing for their evening.

Ronnie drove back to her apartment and packed a bag with the essentials she would need for a short stay at Vasi and Saffron's house before walking down to Saffron's shop. To her surprise she found Bryony there.

'Where's Saffie?' she asked.

'She 'phoned me and asked if I could come down for a couple of hours as she had some jobs she needed to complete before Marjorie arrives tomorrow. It was a bit inconvenient at such short notice, but she said her errands were urgent. I offered to come in all day, but she said just the afternoon would be sufficient and then we could arrange some full days later so she can take Marjorie out whilst she's staying. I suggest you call her if you need to speak to her.'

Ronnie shook her head. 'It can wait. I'll catch up with her some time later.'

Ronnie escorted her mother and great uncle back to their hotel after a meal at a local taverna and arranged to meet them for lunch the following day.

'I have to complete some paintings tomorrow,' she lied. 'Saffie needs her stock replenished.' She was not going to admit that she would probably be up half the night and would want to catch up on her sleep.

'I'm sure we can find something to occupy us. We don't expect you to devote all your time to entertaining us,' said Alex. 'We can always walk into the town or visit that taverna over the causeway.'

'That's a good idea. I could meet you there for lunch.'

Relieved that her excuse had been accepted so readily, Ronnie returned to her apartment and parked Kyriakos's car. There was plenty of time before she needed to go to the taverna and she sat and examined the paintings she had completed the previous day, adding a touch of colour or extra detail to them until she felt satisfied. Finally she decided it would probably be no more than another half an hour before Kyriakos closed and she did not want him to think she and Saffron were not planning to arrive after all.

She placed the bag she had packed earlier into the boot of the car and drove the short distance to the taverna. Kyriakos's mother was there and she glanced at Ronnie sourly.

'My mother insisted that she came up to help tonight,' explained Kyriakos.

Ronnie nodded. 'That's no problem provided the chef will take her home when you close. When Saffie has finished and we've cleaned everything I'll take you home. Then I'll follow Saffie up to Vasi's house.'

'Would you like something to eat?' asked Kyriakos and Ronnie shook her head.

'I ate earlier so I'll just have a drink, thank you. It would look rather strange if I just sat at a table with nothing in front of me.'

The time passed slowly until the last of the diners finally called for their bill and Kyriakos waved them away and Ronnie called Saffron with the information.

'There's probably no need to rush. Kyriakos has to persuade his mother to leave with the chef and she could be difficult. She's obviously not happy that I have arrived. I want to sit and have a serious talk with him whilst you work and there's no one else around.'

Saffron agreed that she would telephone John. 'I need to meet him at Uncle Yannis's shop to unlock and also to help me place the box in the car. It shouldn't be heavy, just unwieldy. I'll put the passenger seat down and then I'll ask you to help me to get it out.'

Ronnie could see Kyriakos arguing with his mother whilst the chef waited patiently until she finally agreed to climb into his car for the ride back to her house.

Kyriakos sat down beside her and shook his head. 'She wanted me to ask you to leave and return home with her. I told her we wanted some time alone together. You are going to tell me about your new plans for your extension.'

Ronnie nodded. 'I will, as soon as Saffie has arrived and I have helped her with the box. Once she has started washing the bones we shouldn't be interrupted.'

'You could start now.'

Ronnie sighed. 'Very well. When I've finished telling you I want you to think very seriously about the proposals I am going to make. I will understand if you refuse.'

Kyriakos looked at her perplexed. 'Why should I be unhappy with the plans you have for the extension? It is your house. You can do as you please.'

'My ideas involve more than alterations to the extension.' Ronnie proceeded to explain how she had decided to make the kitchen area smaller and remove her proposed workroom to enlarge the lounge.

Kyriakos listened carefully and nodded. 'So you will have your workroom at the end of the lounge?'

'No, I'm planning to make bedrooms and bathrooms in that area. They won't be very big, but Giovanni came with me to talk to Mr Palamakis and I have decided they will be large enough.'

The lights from a car could be seen as Saffron arrived at the taverna. 'I'll tell you some more when I've finished helping Saffie.'

Kyriakos smiled. So far all the proposals Ronnie had described were practical and he saw no reason to object.

Ronnie helped Saffron manoeuvre the long box from her car and carry it into the kitchen of the taverna where they placed it on the floor.

'Can you take one end of the sheet and then we'll place it on the floor beside the box. I may still find that all his bones have disintegrated and if so I'll just put them back in as they are.'

Somewhat dubiously Ronnie took hold of the sheet and helped Saffron to place it gently on the floor. She stood back as Saffron pulled the sheet back to reveal the discoloured shroud below.

'Can you pass me a sharp knife?'

Ronnie selected one from the block and handed it to her, watching as Saffron deftly cut the rotten stitches that were still holding it together. Ronnie gasped as the complete skeletal remains were exposed.

'That is amazing. I've never seen a real skeleton before.'

'Not feeling queasy, are you?'

'No, but I'm not sure I would want to touch it, I mean him.'

Saffron looked around. 'The lids from those three large containers should be ideal to lay the bones out on whilst they dry and that bowl for the skull. Do you think Kyriakos will object?'

'I don't think we should ask him. Once you have used them it will be too late for him to say no.'

'Can you take the box out of my way? I don't want to trip over it and land on him. I'll work as fast as I can, but I'll probably be at least a couple of hours.' From her shoulder bag Saffron took some labels and a pen.

'What are they for?'

'I'll need to label some of the bones from the right and left side. Some are obvious, of course, but fingers and toes look exactly the same, as does most of the spinal column.'

'Is that necessary? They're all going to be bundled up and placed in a casket.'

Saffron shrugged. 'I don't know, but I wouldn't want to make a mistake that was offensive.' She pulled on a pair of surgical gloves.

'Why do you need those?'

'If I have any bacteria on my skin I could transfer it to the bones and it could cause decay. I'm trusting that the chef is scrupulous about hygiene when he finishes each night.'

'I'm sure he is.'

Saffron nodded. 'I'll start with the skull, that's easy.'

Ronnie swallowed, not sure that she wanted to stay in the kitchen any longer. 'I'll take the box out and wait with Kyriakos until you give me a shout.'

Ronnie sat down outside at one of the tables with Kyriakos. He raised his eyebrows. 'All is well?'

'The skeleton appears intact. Saffie says she will probably be a couple of hours and will call me when she's ready for me to help her take the bones to her car.'

'So we have plenty of time to continue with our conversation. You were telling me you planned to have bedrooms and bathrooms at the end of the new lounge.'

'That would make it into a proper apartment. I'm hoping Mr Palamakis will have finished by the time Giovanni closes the apartments and I can live there during the winter months.' Ronnie took a deep breath. 'I thought we could live there together.'

A broad smile crossed Kyriakos's face and he hugged Ronnie to him. 'So you will marry me?'

Ronnie pulled herself away. 'There's more we need to talk about first.'

'There is no need to talk further. You have given me the answer I have been hoping and praying for. If the fire had occurred earlier and you had thought of this good idea for the extension we could have made arrangements to be married whilst your mother and uncle were here. Now they will have to return.'

'Kyriakos, I am only proposing that we live there in the winter.'

'That is no problem. During the summer season we can live with my mother.'

'No,' Ronnie declared vehemently. 'I cannot live with your mother. She doesn't like me. That was obvious when I arrived up here this evening.'

'She will become used to the idea of me marrying an American girl. It will be no problem.'

'Kyriakos, please listen. In the season we rent an apartment from Giovanni. That way you will be close to the taverna and I will be able to continue with my painting.'

Kyriakos frowned. 'That will mean we have to pay rent to him. My mother relies upon me paying rent to her. She placed her savings as a guarantee against the loan for my taverna and cannot touch them until I have repaid my debt. She has no other income and I cannot afford to pay two rents.'

'During the winter I won't expect you to pay any rent to me, just share the expenses for the heating and light. I have always managed to earn enough from my painting to pay Giovanni. You will still have the money from the taverna and can help your mother by giving her the same as you do now. I would not want her to suffer, but I cannot agree to live with her.'

'It is customary for a couple to move in with their relatives whilst they save up enough to rent a place of their own.'

'Kyriakos,' said Ronnie patiently, 'we do not have to save up money to enable us to rent an apartment. I will have one for the winter months. I realise Kastelli is not the most convenient place for us to live during the summer but could we at least try the arrangement I'm proposing for one year?'

'Hello. Hello. Is there someone there?'

Both Ronnie and Kyriakos started violently as the voice came out of the darkness. Kyriakos lifted the small lantern that stood on the table and held it up.

Ronnie lifted her mobile 'phone from her handbag and switched it on. If necessary she would call the police.

A man walked closer, followed by a woman and two children. He gave a big sigh of relief. 'Do you speak English? Can you help us?'

'What is your problem?' asked Kyriakos.

'We were driving back to Aghios Nikolaos and must have taken the wrong road. I decided to turn and go back the way we had come, but we hadn't gone very far when the car broke down.'

'If it is a hire car you should have telephoned them. They are obliged to come to your aid.'

'I thought my wife had the papers and she thought I had them. They must be back in our hotel room. We've been walking in the dark for hours trying to find someone to ask for help. Can we at least sit down?'

Ronnie hurried across to the taverna and looked into the kitchen. Saffron looked up in surprise.

'I haven't finished yet.'

'Some people have arrived who appear to be lost. We'll get rid of them as quickly as possible.'

Ronnie collected two chairs and took them back to the table where she and Kyriakos had been sitting. 'Sit down there. Would you like a drink?'

'Yes, please,' they answered almost in unison.

'I suppose you haven't anything we can eat?' asked the man.

Ronnie frowned and looked at Kyriakos who nodded.

'I'll have a look and see what is available. We can't cook

anything as some kitchen maintenance is taking place. That's why we're still up here.'

'Thank goodness you were.' The woman kicked off her shoes. 'Just before it got really dark Max thought he saw a path leading down towards the main road and expected it to be a short cut. We couldn't see the way down or back once darkness closed in.'

'You didn't have a torch?' asked Kyriakos in surprise. Everyone always kept a torch in their car for a night time emergency.

'We hadn't planned to be walking around in the countryside,' answered the man grimly.

'You should still have thought to put one in the car,' answered his wife. 'You always say you are organised and prepared for anything, yet you forget the car hire papers and don't bother to bring a torch.'

'I'll see what the chef has left in the fridge.' Ronnie had no wish to become embroiled in the argument between the couple.

'Can I come with you?' asked the girl and Ronnie shook her head.

'If you need the toilets they are at the side and I can put the lights on for you. I can't let you into the kitchen as there is work going on in there. What would you like to drink?'

'A cup of tea,' answered the woman promptly and Ronnie shook her head.

'I've told you I cannot use the kitchen. I can offer you beer, a soft drink or water.'

The woman sighed deeply. 'I suppose I'll have to settle for a beer.'

'I'll be right back.' Ronnie went to the fridge that stood inside the kitchen area and pulled a face at Saffron. 'I told them the kitchen wasn't available and the stupid woman asked for a cup of tea! I'll take these drinks out and then collect some bits from the fridge as they say they're hungry. They probably expect me to cook them chicken and chips.'

Ronnie handed the bottles to Kyriakos to remove the caps,

placed a straw in the mouth of the soft drink bottles before pouring the beer into the glasses.

Ronnie placed some bread, taramasolata, tsatziki and olives on a tray and carried it across to the table. 'This is all that is available, I'm afraid.'

The man eyed the food disparagingly. 'We could have done with something a bit more substantial.'

'You're fortunate we had anything to offer you. As soon as you've eaten we can call a taxi for you and they can take you to wherever you're staying in Aghios Nikolaos.'

'You couldn't take us in your car? It's quite a long journey and I'm not sure if I'll have enough on me to pay them.'

'That is your problem. I'm sure they will stop at a cash point in the town for you. We need our car to drive home, besides there would not be room. It only seats four.'

'We wouldn't mind squashing in a bit and you actually have two cars standing there.'

Kyriakos shook his head and Ronnie scowled. 'As soon as the maintenance work is completed we will be locking up and leaving so I suggest you help yourselves to whatever you want and Kyriakos can call a taxi for you in about ten minutes. You can always take what you haven't eaten with you.'

'You're not very welcoming,' commented the woman.

Ronnie sighed in despair. 'We have had a busy day and would all of us like to be at home in bed and asleep.'

'I can't eat that muck,' said the girl pointing to the taramasalata. 'It smells fishy and I'm vegetarian.'

'Then eat the tsatziki or olives,' snapped back Ronnie. 'There's no meat or fish in them.'

Slowly the girl inserted an olive into her mouth. 'Ugh, it still has the stone in.' She spat it onto the ground.

Ronnie turned to Kyriakos in despair. 'I suggest you 'phone for a taxi now. The food is obviously not to their liking so they should be ready to leave as soon as they have finished their drinks.'

Kyriakos nodded, scrolled down on his 'phone to the local taxi number and began an animated conversation with the operator who answered him. 'They are on their way. The bill for the drinks is twelve Euros, please.'

'Twelve – for a couple of beers and lemonades! That's extortionate.'

'I would be within my rights to charge you the same again for the food.'

'But we haven't eaten it,' protested the man.

Kyriakos shrugged. 'We took it from the fridge for you. Once food has been served we cannot put it back and offer it to another customer. It will have to be thrown away tomorrow morning.'

The man took out his wallet and slapped a ten Euro note down on the table. 'That's all I'm prepared to pay. Take it or leave it.'

Ronnie scooped the note up quickly and placed it in her pocket, willing the taxi to arrive quickly.

'I need the toilet,' announced the girl.

'You know where it is.'

'I suppose I ought to go also,' said her mother standing up. 'What about you, Terry?'

Ronnie collected together the untouched plates of food and empty bottles and walked into the taverna. As she placed the food back into the fridge and the bottles into the rubbish she realised the boy was right behind her.

'I told you the toilets are at the side. I've put the lights on.'

'I just wanted to see what was going on in the kitchen.'

'That's none of your business,' snapped Ronnie.

'What's that?' he asked. 'It looks like someone's head.'

Ronnie looked at Saffron in horror. Old Uncle Yannis's washed skull was sitting in a bowl and looked as if it were grinning at them.

'You are to return outside,' Ronnie spoke sternly. 'You have no right to try to enter the kitchen when I have told you it is closed. I did not even invite you to step inside the taverna. You are actually trespassing.'

'So what are you going to do about it?' The boy looked at her insolently. 'Wait 'til I tell my Dad you've got a body in here.'

'Don't be ridiculous,' retorted Ronnie.

'Dad, Dad, there's a body in the kitchen. I saw it. These people are murderers. I bet they poison their customers. There are lots of bones in there.' The boy shouted across to his father from the taverna and Kyriakos paled.

The woman fanned herself gently. 'Oh, my, thank goodness we didn't eat any of their food.'

'Quite right,' agreed her husband. 'I'm notifying the police as soon as we arrive back at our hotel and tomorrow I'm informing Health and Hygiene that you are serving human remains to your customers. I'll make sure you're closed down and you'll probably be put in prison.'

Ronnie shrugged. 'You can do as you please. I can assure you that Health and Hygiene will have no problems with the establishment and the police will probably think you were drunk.' She placed her hand reassuringly on Kyriakos's shoulder.

The man glared at her. 'We'll see about that when I tell them what is going on up here. Where's that taxi? It's taking its time.'

Ronnie tilted her head and listened. 'I'm sure I can hear a car approaching. It's probably your taxi.'

Kyriakos limped over to where the car had stopped and could be heard talking to the driver who grinned and replied with a nod of his head as the family climbed into the car.

'What did you say to him?' asked Ronnie.

'I told him they wanted to go to Aghios Nikolaos and were not sure if they had enough money. He's going to stop at the cash point in Elounda and tell them the amount of the fare. They either pay him in advance or he leaves them there and lets the other drivers know the situation.'

Ronnie giggled. 'Serve them right if they have to walk from Elounda to Aghios Nikolaos.'

'Do you think he will report me? I do not want any trouble with the police or my taverna closed down.' Kyriakos spoke anxiously.

'Saffie has nearly finished. Don't worry. Once we have moved the bones to my car we'll make sure the kitchen is spotless. Neither Health and Hygiene or the police will have anything to complain about. If they should call on you, and I doubt that man will carry out his threat, you can confirm that the kitchen was closed for a thorough cleaning. You usually do it yourself, but due to your broken ankle you've not been able to complete it to your satisfaction and asked Saffie and myself to come and help.'

'I am still worried,' replied Kyriakos. 'What will my mother think if the police come calling on me?'

'You explain to her that because you refused to cook a meal for our unwelcome visitors they complained to the police. You need to go home and get some rest, Kyriakos. Saffie and I can stay in bed late tomorrow, but you will have to be ready when the chef comes to collect you.'

Kyriakos nodded. 'I would like to finish our talk.'

Ronnie shook her head. 'Not tonight. We'll arrange another time when we can talk some more. I want you to have time to think seriously over my proposal that we live in Kastelli over the winter. I don't want you saying I rushed you into a decision that you regret.' Ronnie pulled the ten Euro note from her pocket and handed it to Kyriakos. 'This belongs to you. I'll go and check with Saffie and find out how much longer she will be.'

Saffron had folded up the rotten shroud as best she could and stuffed it into a carrier bag along with her gloves.

'Just about done,' she announced. 'Actually I found something interesting when I had finished removing the shroud. It was a wonder I didn't miss it. Look.'

Saffron held a silver chain with a small blue stone set in silver hanging from it. A similar talisman was worn by many men and women to ward off misfortune and ensure good luck.

'That's amazing. I wonder if he was wearing it when he died?'

'Probably, as the chain is snapped. Uncle Yannis or Giovanni may know how it came to be placed in the shroud with him.' Saffron placed it carefully to one side. 'Shall I put it in my purse for safe keeping and give it to Giovanni or John? I'm sure they'll be delighted. I'll go and unlock my car then we can start loading up and then come back and clean the sink and drainers.'

'We'll have to make sure everywhere is spotless. Kyriakos may be getting a visit from Health and Hygiene or the police. That man said he is going to report him for serving human flesh.'

Saffron looked at Ronnie in disbelief. 'That's ridiculous.'

'I know, but Kyriakos is worried. That boy who followed me in saw the skull sitting in the bowl.'

'I'm sorry. I wasn't expecting anyone to come in. I had washed the skull first and replaced his false teeth before I moved it over there out of my way.'

'Don't worry about it. We'll make sure they cannot find anything to substantiate the story. If they find they're abandoned in Elounda by the taxi driver they'll probably accuse him of kidnapping them. If that man is foolish enough to go to the police he could find himself in trouble for wasting their time.'

Week Three – September 2012
Wednesday and Thursday

Kyriakos had not slept well, despite being tired. He was worried that if a Health and Hygiene inspector did call on him they would find something incriminating that Saffron and Ronnie had overlooked in the kitchen. He would have to check everywhere thoroughly. Even a dead fly or spider could be enough to close him down temporarily.

Irini eyed her son suspiciously. She had tried to stay up until he returned so she could question him about his conversation with Ronnie but when he had not arrived by two thirty she had given in and gone to bed. She had a nasty suspicion that he might be spending the night somewhere with the girl.

'You look tired,' she remarked.

'I was late getting in.'

'What kept you up at the taverna?'

'Some tourists arrived. Their car had broken down somewhere up on the hill. They'd walked down looking for help. I gave them some drinks and then 'phoned for a taxi for them,' answered Kyriakos honestly.

'I wouldn't have expected that to keep you out so late.'

'They arrived just as we were about to leave. I felt I should help them.' Kyriakos looked out of the window, hoping he would see his chef arrive so that his mother could not question him further. He was annoyed by his mother's animosity towards Ronnie. It was due to her silly cousin, Soula, feeding her the local gossip.

He determined to pay the woman a visit and tell her to stop such nonsense.

Kyriakos walked into the kitchen at the taverna and inspected the sinks and work tops. They were spotless. The oven and hot plates, although old and discoloured, showed no sign of food residue. He checked the cupboards where the china and cutlery were stored along with the glasses. Inside the fridge were a number of chickens, sausages, some slabs of pork and joints of lamb. More frozen meat was in the freezer and each pack was well within the date whereby it should be used. There was nothing in there that could be mistaken for human bones. He gave a sigh of relief. If a Health and Hygiene inspector did arrive he had nothing to worry about except the large cardboard box that was sitting outside and he set about systematically breaking it up to take to a rubbish bin.

His mind at rest, Kyriakos began to consider Ronnie's proposal of the previous night. If she was asking him to live in Kastelli with her it must mean that she was willing to marry him and his heart soared in delight.

Ronnie had slept fitfully. She was not concerned about Kyriakos having a visit from Health and Hygiene or the police, but wished she had been able to explain that she did not feel able to marry him, but was prepared to live with him. The disapproval of his mother to such an arrangement could influence his decision regarding her proposal that they spent the winter months in Kastelli. It had appeared to be a simple answer to their problems when the idea had first come to her, now she was not so sure.

Saffron had slept well. She had enjoyed washing the bones and was looking forward to having some time to examine them further. They should give clues to the extent that the leprosy had affected the man. She had noticed that Old Uncle Yannis's skeleton had a broken arm along with two broken ribs. No doubt that had happened when he was originally placed down in the tower as they were not fresh breaks and there was no sign that the fractures had begun to heal. Although she was completely happy living with Vasi and having her shop to keep her occupied she realised that she had missed diagnosing and treating skeletal problems. She wondered if it would be possible for her to be given permission to inspect the other bones that were planned to be placed in the new tower when it had been constructed.

Saffron consulted her watch. She had two hours before she would have to drive up to Heraklion to meet Marjorie and decided to see if Ronnie was awake.

John waited anxiously for Ronnie to telephone him and let him know that Old Uncle Yannis's bones had been washed and were now drying off in her apartment. His father had visited the undertaker and purchased a casket to accommodate the remains. It looked ridiculously small compared with the cardboard box that had been used to transport the skeleton back to the mainland and John was concerned that the long bones would not fit inside. He hoped Saffron would be willing to pack them and he would not be expected to handle them.

The police car drew up outside Kyriakos's taverna and he looked at it with trepidation. Inspector Antonakis climbed out and regarded the neatly laid tables with the umbrellas over them to protect customers from the sun. There was nothing to suggest anything out of the ordinary.

Kyriakos limped forwards to greet him. 'Good morning, Inspector. How can I help you or have you just stopped for some refreshment?' He hoped his voice did not betray his nervousness.

Inspector Antonakis removed his hat and mopped his brow. 'Mr Mandakis, I received a rather strange report this morning from a tourist. I feel sure the man was imagining things, but I'm duty bound to investigate because of the seriousness of the accusation.'

The Inspector eyed the surrounding area as he talked.

'I can assure you that my licence to serve alcohol is up to date and also my Safety and Health and Hygiene certificates. They are all displayed inside if you wish to check them.'

'I will check those whilst I am here, but that is not the reason I have called. Can you confirm that a man and his family came here in the early hours of the morning?'

Kyriakos nodded. 'They said their car had broken down and they did not have the hire firm's 'phone number with them. They had decided to walk down the hill in the hope of finding someone to help them.'

'Why were you open so late?'

'I wasn't open. As you know I have a broken ankle due to the incident with the two Englishmen. The chef is responsible for leaving the work surfaces clean each night. Usually I clean the kitchen floor each morning along with the more inaccessible areas. It has been difficult for me to kneel down and complete this. I cannot expect my mother to help or ask my chef to do additional cleaning. I had arranged with some friends to come and do the work I have been unable to do efficiently recently. I would not want Health and Hygiene to make an inspection and say that my taverna was dirty.'

'So you were closed when these people arrived?'

'I was certainly not open for customers. I gave them some drinks and called a taxi for them.'

'So I understand. I believe you also offered them some food.'

'I provided them with some cold items from the fridge. I explained that the kitchen could not be used for cooking due to the maintenance that was taking place.'

'Were they happy with the food you provided?'

Kyriakos shook his head. 'They didn't eat any of it.'

'Why was that?'

'I can only imagine it was not to their liking.'

The Inspector looked at Kyriakos speculatively. 'The man told me that his son had entered the kitchen and seen a body in there.'

'A body? Why would there be a body in my kitchen?'

'I would like to know that also. You have no objection to me inspecting your kitchen I hope?'

'None at all. The chef is in there preparing vegetables ready for later. May he continue or shall I ask him to step outside for a moment or two?'

'Provided he does not hinder me in any way he can continue.'

Kyriakos limped into the kitchen followed by the Inspector. 'Sorry to interrupt your work, Costas, but the Inspector would like to have a look around the kitchen. He has had a report that we have a body in here.'

The chef looked at Kyriakos in disbelief.

'A body? Who told him that? The only bodies we have in here are chickens.' He swung open the door of the refrigerator where four chickens were sitting along with some pork and two joints of lamb. 'There's more in the freezer.'

The Inspector looked cursorily at the meat products in the fridge and turned his attention to the freezer. He ignored the chickens and sausages, but checked each leg of lamb and pack of pork. The name of the supplier was on the label along with the "use by" date.

Inspector Antonakis opened the cupboards finding only culinary items; he peered into the sinks and scrutinized the work tops. There was no sign of any blood.

'May I see your butchering knives and chopping boards, please?'

'Certainly. The boards are over there and the knives are kept in that drawer. I am very strict about them being returned to that drawer after they have been used and washed. I would not want my chef to cut his hand where a knife had been placed in an unexpected place.'

Inspector Antonakis was unable to find any trace of blood or flesh on the boards or knives. He scratched his head and mopped his face again.

'Do you think the man was drunk?'

Kyriakos shrugged. 'Not noticeably. I think he wanted a free meal. I asked him for twelve Euros to cover the cost of the drinks and he would only pay me ten. He also asked if we could take him to Aghios Nikolaos and was annoyed when I refused. I offered to call a taxi and he said he was not sure if he had sufficient money with him for the taxi fare.'

The Inspector raised his eyebrows. 'So what did you do?'

'I 'phoned the taxi station in Elounda and arranged for a car to come and collect them. I also warned them that the man might not have enough money and suggested the driver asked for the fare in advance. If the man was unable to cover the cost they could stop in Elounda and he could use the cash point.'

'And what was the outcome?'

'I have no idea. You would have to ask at the taxi station. The driver is probably asleep now, but he would have logged his journey.'

'I'll check with them when I return. I see no reason to pursue this enquiry any further. Thank you for your co-operation.'

'It was no problem.' Kyriakos sighed in relief.

'I'll take a quick drive up the hill and see if there is a car abandoned up there. Of course the hire firm may have recovered it by now; then I'll have a word at the taxi station when I return.'

The Inspector shook Kyriakos's hand and returned to his car. Kyriakos walked into the kitchen and helped himself to a beer from the fridge. His legs were shaking and he leaned against the fridge to steady himself as he drank.

'What was that all about?' asked Costas.

'Some people arrived last night after you had left. I refused to cook them a meal and the man made up a stupid story for the police saying he had seen a body in the kitchen.'

Costas snorted in derision. 'No one would store a body in their kitchen!'

Kyriakos telephoned Ronnie. 'I've just had a call from the police. That man had told them I had a body in the kitchen.'

'Well that shows just how ignorant that boy was if he couldn't tell the difference between a body and a skeleton.'

'Ronnie, please, be serious. I was worried that you or Saffie would have overlooked something and I would be hauled off to the police station.'

'We assured you that we would leave everything spotless.'

'I know, and I had checked around before he arrived, but I was still worried.'

'I gather the Inspector couldn't find any evidence to support the story. I would be more concerned if Saffie and I had been seen moving the bones into her car or my apartment. I will be pleased when they have been safely reburied.'

'Have you spoken to John?'

'Not yet. Saffie said the bones will need at least a day to dry off properly. They none of them had any flesh still attached so she only had to immerse them for a short space of time just to ensure they were clean. They didn't need to be soaked. After she has collected Marjorie and settled her in she said she would make the excuse that she had to call up at the shop to make sure all was well there with Bryony. She'll telephone me first and I'll go up to let her in. If she's satisfied that the bones are dry they could be placed in the casket tomorrow and then it will be up to the family to look after them until they take them over to Spinalonga.'

Kyriakos gave a shudder as Ronnie mentioned that the bones had no flesh to be removed. He was quite happy butchering and jointing an animal for food, but was not sure he could cope with human remains, particularly if he knew the name of the person.

'Are you coming up to the taverna?'

'Maybe. No promises. I'm meeting my mother and uncle at the Kanali for lunch and will probably take them for a drive afterwards. I'll see what time Saffie phones.'

Kyriakos sighed. Ideally he would like to have discussed

Ronnie's idea for living in Kastelli further and before he made any decision he would want to find out when she would marry him. It did seem to be an ideal solution, but he was not looking forward to the difficult conversation he envisioned having with his mother in the future.

Saffron collected Marjorie from the airport and drove her to Vasilis's apartment.

'We won't stay long,' she assured her. 'Cathy and Vasilis just want to say hello and no doubt you could do with something to eat as there was only a sandwich available on your flight.'

Marjorie nodded. Ideally she would have liked to have driven straight to Elounda and had a rest, but if she refused both Cathy and Vasilis would be hurt and offended that their offer of hospitality had been rejected.

Vasilis opened the door to them as Saffron drew up outside, a broad smile on his face.

'Cathy will be delighted to see you. I offered to meet you at the airport but Saffie wouldn't hear of it. She wanted to be the first to greet you.'

'How is Cathy?' asked Saffron as Marjorie walked into the lounge.

Vasilis frowned and shrugged. 'In herself she is well, but she now needs a walking frame to move around in the apartment.'

'Thank goodness Vasi agreed to sell his apartment to you. It would have become impossible or you to live in your house.'

'I am sure we would have managed. We could have made a bedroom downstairs and I have a car that is large enough for Cathy's wheelchair to fit inside. Anyway, come in and sit down. Cathy has prepared a late lunch for you.'

'That is very kind of her. I hope it was not too much trouble.'

'Of course not. Provided Cathy can prepare food whilst she is sitting down it is no problem.'

'We cannot stay too long. Marjorie will be tired after her flight and we still have an hour's drive before we get home.' Saffron did not add that she was also anxious to return to Elounda as soon as possible as she hated the drive over the mountainous area where Alecos had met with his accident.

Cathy talked animatedly to Marjorie. 'We watched the Olympic Games and the Paralympics that were held in London. I found the Paralympics quite fascinating. So many people who are confined to wheelchairs are tremendous sportsmen and women. They must have incredible strength in their upper body.'

'Do you still swim?' asked Saffron.

'In the summer months Vasilis takes me to a local hotel each day where I can use their pool. Fortunately most people prefer to go to the beach and there are no children around. People often stare a bit at first when Vasilis has to lift me in and out of the pool, but they soon get over it.'

Saffron nodded. 'I'm pleased to hear it. I'm sure swimming is beneficial.'

'So is the sunshine. I always dread the winter. The cold seems to go right through me and I really stiffen up.'

'If you saw the cost of our heating bills!' remarked Vasilis. 'I am walking around in a T-shirt and Cathy is wearing layers of clothing.'

'At least our winter does not last as long as it does in England. I wonder now how I ever managed to cope with it.'

Marjorie helped herself to another keftedes and some tsatziki. 'I do love these,' she said. 'We can buy most Greek food at home in the supermarket but it never seems to taste the same as when I eat it out here.'

'Then you should come out here to live,' smiled Cathy.

Marjorie shook her head. 'I'm too old to think about such a big move now. I'm settled where I am and I have friends. If I came out here I would have to try to make new friends and I'm not sure I have the energy.'

'Whilst you're here I've arranged for Ronnie to take you out with her mother and great uncle. I hope you'll feel able to be friends with them.'

'Are they living over here?'

'As far as I know they have no plans to move here from New Orleans. Ronnie is planning to stay, despite the fire at her house.'

'Will she have enough money to rebuild?' asked Vasilis.

'I understand she's planning to leave it for the time being and convert the extension she had built into an apartment.'

Vasilis nodded. 'That seems practical, but will she be able to let it? We have noticed at the hotel that our bookings are down. It is due to the unrest that is taking place throughout the whole of Greece due to the monetary situation. Visitors do not want to come here and find they are experiencing riots or strikes.'

'Apart from the coach drivers and rubbish collectors going on strike a couple of times we have not experienced anything very drastic in Elounda, thank goodness.'

'You are fortunate.' Vasilis began to talk about the problems confronting the Greek government and Saffron gave a surreptitious glance at her watch. Vasilis, like all Greek men could talk for hours expanding on his opinion of the government, explaining the economic situation and proposing his own political remedies.

'We really must make a move or Vasi will be getting worried,' said Saffron. 'It has been lovely to see you and you must come down to visit us very soon. I know Vasi comes up to Heraklion regularly but I never get to see you. I'm sure you would be interested to see the new items I have in my shop, Cathy. Are you ready, Marjorie?'

Saffron was relieved when she arrived home after a drive without incident. She carried Marjorie's case up to her room and explained that Ronnie was staying in the other bedroom for a few days.

'Is that because her house has been destroyed? I thought she lived in one of Giovanni's self catering apartments.'

'I believe there's some work being undertaken in her apartment and it was more convenient for her to stay here until it was completed.' Saffron did not want to explain to her step-mother that there were bones drying in the apartment. She hoped that by the following day she would be able to pack them in the casket and return them to the family.

'I'll leave you to get settled in. I need to go up to the shop and check that all is well with Bryony.' Saffron realised that she was becoming quite adept at making excuses. Once in her car she telephoned Ronnie.

'Are you in Elounda?' she asked.

'I'm at the hotel. Is there a problem?'

'No, I've just returned from Heraklion and I wondered if it would be convenient for me to check on a few things with you.'

'At my apartment?'

'That's right. I'm on my way and can take you up there in my car.'

'Give me five minutes to make my excuses to my mother.'

'We shouldn't be gone long.'

Ronnie was waiting for Saffron when she drew up. 'Kyriakos had a visit from the police Inspector this morning,' she said as she climbed into the car.

'And?'

'He was a bit shaken up but absolutely nothing could be found to substantiate that man's story.'

Saffron nodded. 'We were very careful to ensure everywhere was clean before we left. When I've packed the bones I'll return the lids and bowl and sterilise them. If the Inspector did decide to pay him another visit I'm sure he won't be able to find anything suspicious.'

'I'd like to know if that man did pay for the taxi or if he found himself abandoned in Elounda.'

'Why don't you ask Kyriakos to 'phone the taxi company and find out?'

'I suppose I could. We're planning to go up there again for a meal tonight. I told Kyriakos my idea for the apartment at Kastelli and we were interrupted by that family arriving. He wanted me to stay up there and talk about it some more, but I refused and said he could have time to think about my proposal. I'm hoping that by the time Mum and Uncle Alex leave he will have decided it's a feasible proposition.'

Saffron telephoned Giovanni whilst sitting in her car. She did not want Marjorie to overhear her conversation and want to know why she was talking about bones.

'I've just been to Ronnie's apartment and the bones are virtually dry. I've turned them over so there won't be any damp spots and I should be able to pack them tomorrow afternoon. I'll call in for the casket on my way up to Ronnie's apartment.'

'Is she going to help you?' asked Giovanni.

'No, she's going to take Marjorie and her relatives up to Plaka and will drop her key in to me as she goes past.'

'There is no need for that. I can give you a master key and you can return it to me when you bring the casket.'

'That would be a great help. I do need to talk to you before I make a start.'

Saffron looked at the casket that Giovanni handed to her.

'Is there any special way I am supposed to pack them?' she asked.

'Well, when I went to the undertaker I asked how all the bones fitted as the container seemed quite small. He said you had to wrap the long bones from the legs individually and lay them across diagonally, top corner to the opposite bottom corner. All the other large bones have to be wrapped then the arm bones lay down flat by the side of the box.'

'Wait a minute. Let me write this down or I may not remember. I don't want to spend hours trying to get them to fit in.'

Giovanni smiled and handed her a napkin. He repeated his

earlier instructions and then continued. 'All the smaller bones are wrapped in two or three bundles to keep them together. Those are usually placed beneath the leg bones and on top of the arm bones. The wrapped shoulder bones and pelvis are placed on the other side. The bones from the spine are wrapped together and so are the rib bones and there should be enough space for them to fit somewhere. The skull is not wrapped and placed in the space at the end of the casket, but it must be facing the bones. Each time you place some bones in the casket you make the sign of the cross above them.'

Saffron frowned. 'Should I make the sign of the cross? It seems somewhat irreligious as I am not of your faith.'

Giovanni shrugged. 'It is more a sign of respect than of faith.'

'Well, I guess I can manage that.' Saffron made a rough sketch on the napkin. 'Does that look right?'

Giovanni gave the sketch a cursory glance. 'How would I know? I have never placed bones in a casket.'

'Nor have I,' replied Saffron. 'What am I supposed to wrap them in?'

'The cotton sheet that we used to move his body in is quite adequate if you cut it into strips like bandages. Do you still have it?'

'It's in Ronnie's apartment with the bones. Didn't the undertaker ask why you were so interested in the procedure?'

Giovanni smiled. 'I told him I was investigating ancient burial customs. That caught his interest and he was very happy to describe the various ways in which bodies had been interred from the Minoan times up to the present day.'

Saffron raised her eyebrows. 'Now I know where John gets his devious nature from.'

Giovanni shrugged. 'It kept him happy and gave me the knowledge I wanted. Do you think you'll be able to manage?'

'I hope so. It was no problem washing the bones, but I don't want to make a mistake that could cause offence when I pack them.'

'I'm sure you won't and I'm equally sure that no one will be opening the casket to check. I'll just be relieved when they have been reburied. John keeps going over and checking that the hole he dug has not been disturbed in any way. He says we'll have to be patient whilst he digs out the stones.'

'Are you planning to have a funeral service?'

Giovanni shook his head. 'Father Andreas conducted Old Uncle Yannis's original burial service and he's no longer with us. The priest who was on the island when we collected him said a special prayer for him and that will have to suffice.'

Saffron opened her purse and took out the broken silver chain with the evil eye charm and handed it to Giovanni. 'I found this amongst the folds of his original shroud.'

Giovanni looked at the item and then held it to his lips. 'Old Uncle Yannis always wore this. After he died Anna threw it down into the tower for him.' He brushed his moist eyes with his hand. 'Thank you, Saffie. I'll show it to Uncle Yannis and Marisa and then we will place it in the casket before it is sealed. It belongs with him.'

Saffron felt a lump in her throat as she witnessed Giovanni's evident emotion.

Saffron took her time as she packed Old Uncle Yannis's bones according to Giovanni's verbal instructions and the sketch she had made. She examined all of them for the tell tale signs of leprosy. His leg and arm bones showed no sign of malformation and his spine was not unduly curved. From this she deduced that the man would not have had too much difficulty walking, despite a certain amount of bone absorption that had taken place in his toes giving them an hour glass appearance.

When she examined his finger and wrist bones they told a different story. Due to the bone absorption his fingers would have been clawed, making every day activities like fastening buttons and picking anything up difficult. No doubt he had adapted to the problems as the deterioration would have been gradual.

At some time Old Uncle Yannis's teeth had been replaced with false ones and the bones of his upper and lower jaw were thinned with a certain amount of pitting. The delicate nasal bones were completely missing. This was not unusual in old bones and she decided they had decayed after he was placed in the tower and not during his life time or someone would surely have remarked on his grotesque appearance.

To her relief the bones fitted snugly in the casket and she packed any spaces with strips from the cloth she had used to wrap the bones before replacing the lid with a feeling of sadness. The man who had contributed so much to bettering the conditions for those abandoned on the island deserved recognition, not an anonymous burial in the floor of his house.

Giovanni accepted the casket of bones from Saffron and made the sign of the cross over it. So far everything had gone according to plan. Now he had to arrange when they would go to the island and which members of the family wished to accompany them.

'Obviously I will go over with you,' declared Uncle Yannis.

Giovanni nodded. He had expected his uncle to wish to pay his last respects.

'What about Aunt Ourania?'

To Giovanni's relief Uncle Yannis shook his head. 'I'm not sure if she would fully comprehend the situation and it could distress her. It would be better if she could stay here.'

Marcus exchanged looks with Bryony. 'Neither of us feel it is fitting for us to be there. We did not know him and this is a close family affair. Besides, if Aunt Ourania is staying here we can look after her.'

'I won't be going over,' stated Nicola. 'I will have to stay here with the girls.'

John gave a slight smirk. Bryony could quite well have looked after the girls as they would be in bed and asleep when they left, but Nicola had confided in him that she thought she was pregnant again. She was not prepared to make a general announcement to that effect until she was completely sure, but she did not want the motion of the boat to upset her. This pregnancy was very different from when she had carried the twins. Most mornings she had to spend some time in the bathroom before appearing for breakfast and she hoped it was a sign that this time she was carrying a boy. She knew how delighted John would be if that were the case.

'I want to come,' announced Marisa. 'He was my uncle and gave me away when I was married on Spinalonga.' She gave a deep sigh. 'I do wish Victor could be with us.'

'Of course you can come, Mamma,' Giovanni assured her. 'John says we may have to wait a while whilst he removes the stones from the hole he dug but we'll take a cushion for you and you can sit on the steps. What about you, Marianne?'

Marianne hesitated. 'I'll come if Grandma Marisa wants me to keep her company, otherwise I'll stay here.'

Giovanni nodded. 'Your decision can be made at the last minute. If there are only four or five of us we won't need to make two trips in the boat.'

'I'll buy some new torch batteries,' promised John. 'I know I can walk around over there in the dark, but I don't expect everyone else to be able to. I don't want anyone to end up with a sprained ankle so we have to carry them back to the boat.'

'I'll take my stick,' announced Marisa. 'If I have that to lean on and Giovanni's arm I will be safe enough.'

'So I propose we go over on Saturday night about nine when it is dark. Most of the fishermen make sure they are back in the harbour by late afternoon. The tavernas are always busy on a Saturday so it's unlikely anyone apart from tourists will be wandering around. Agreed?' asked Giovanni.

Week Three – September 2012
Friday and Saturday

Now Kyriakos was no longer fearful of Inspector Antonakis or the Health and Hygiene department inspecting and closing down his taverna he began to brood again on his mother's words regarding Ronnie's lineage. Finally he decided he would ask Costas to collect him a little earlier from his house and take him to Mavrikiano. He should be able to walk back down to the main road from there and 'phone for a taxi to take him up to his taverna after he had spoken to Soula.

Undoubtedly Soula would tell his mother that he had visited and she would accuse Kyriakos of going behind her back, but hadn't she gone behind his back? She was just trying to make trouble and stop Kyriakos from marrying an American.

Kyriakos knocked on Soula's door and he could hear her muttering as she shuffled across the room to answer it.

'Who is it?'

'Kyriakos, I'd like to talk to you.'

'It's early. I'm not fully dressed yet.'

'I can wait. Take your time.'

Within minutes the door opened and Soula peered at Kyriakos suspiciously. 'What do you want? Is your mother ill?'

Kyriakos shook his head. 'No, she was fine when I left the house this morning. I want to talk to you about all these old wives' tales and nonsense about the Kastelli house that you have been filling her head with.'

'It's not nonsense. I've only told her what my Thranassis has told me.'

'It's village gossip. I know all about Ronnie's relatives, the old man and his daughter, and that her grandmother was born on Spinalonga. You are just making trouble. There's nothing wrong with Ronnie, she's as fit as you or me.'

Soula raised her eyebrows. 'That's what you think. The disease has a way of reappearing down the years, particularly when two people have a history of infection.'

'It was years ago that her family were infected.'

'It may have been for them, but it's not that long for you. Sometimes it skips a generation only to come out in their children.'

'What do you mean? Not that long for me?'

'Your mother has never told you about her father, my uncle. She thought the disease had died out with him but there's no guarantee of that.'

'My grandfather? What about him? He died in the war.'

'That's what everyone believes. He spent his last years on Spinalonga. The family kept it a secret. It was not something to boast about. We told the villagers he had gone up to Rethymnon to work. After the war it was accepted that he had died at the hands of the Germans or Italians like so many others.'

'Poor old man.' Kyriakos crossed himself. 'I suppose he starved to death like so many of the sufferers.'

Soula shook her head. 'He survived the war. He was one of the few whose results had come back to say he was still infectious. That meant your family and mine had to be tested again, but we were all declared healthy.'

'So there is nothing to worry about.'

'The germs can live on for many years before they can be detected,' remarked Soula grimly. 'The doctor insisted everyone should have a full examination every two years. When your father found out he was expected to be tested along with the rest of us he disappeared.'

'My father is dead,' said Kyriakos firmly.

Soula shrugged. 'He may be. Who knows? He went away and has never been heard from since. He had no wish to be associated with a leper's family, or he may have known he was ill, of course, and wanted to avoid being sent to a leprosarium.'

'I don't believe you.'

'Ask your mother to tell you the truth if you think I'm lying. You could be making a big mistake if you insist on marrying this girl.'

Kyriakos leaned against the wall of the house. It could not be true. Surely his mother would have told him if his father had left her and the reason why. His photograph was displayed on the dresser and his mother had always spoken about him with sad affection. Soula must be making the story up.

As he walked down the road he turned the information over and over in his mind. He could not go up to the taverna. He must return home and demand to be told the truth about both his father and grandfather.

Irini looked up in surprise when she saw her son appear in the doorway.

'What's wrong? Are you not feeling well?'

'I need to talk to you, Mamma. I want some answers and I also want the truth.'

'What do you mean?'

'I went up to visit Soula. I was sick of the village gossip she had told you about the family who owned the house in Kastelli. I went to tell her to stop frightening you with her silly stories.' Kyriakos's voice broke. 'She told me my grandfather had been an incurable and that my father had disappeared. I want to know the truth, Mamma.'

'You should have taken notice of my warnings in the first place.'

'That's not a good enough answer. Soula said your father

had spent his last days on Spinalonga and should have gone to the hospital in Athens as he was still infectious. She said you told people he had gone to Rethymnon to look for work and let it be believed that he had been killed during the war. Why did you never tell me?'

'You had no need to know. The rest of the family, including you and me, were all declared healthy and finally they said we no longer needed to be tested. I examined you daily when you were a little boy and you never had any signs. Had I told you about your grandfather every time you had a scratch you would have been worrying that the injury would become infected. Why should I place that burden on your shoulders? There have been no more than three cases in this area in the last fifty years and none of them were related to us.' Irini leaned back against the dresser. She wished she had never have visited Soula.

Kyriakos took a deep breath. 'I think you were wrong not to tell me when I became an adult. Suppose I have developed the first signs and have not recognised them? I could ignore them until it was too late for any medical treatment to help me. When I go to the doctor and have my plaster removed I will ask him to give me a full examination.'

'There is no treatment for an incurable,' stated Irini.

'Yes there is,' insisted Kyriakos. 'Modern medicine has done wonders for those who are afflicted. The disease can be halted if it is diagnosed early enough. The infection does not go away, but nor does it get any worse. People do not end up losing their limbs or having horrendous facial deformities these days.'

Irini pursed her lips. It was still a disease to be dreaded.

'Now I want to know about my father,' continued Kyriakos relentlessly. 'You told me he had died.'

Irini shrugged. 'He may have done for all I know.'

'Mamma, I realise it might be painful for you to talk about him, but I do need to know. Sit down and tell me exactly what happened. Soula said he refused to be tested and went away without a word. Was he ill?'

Irini sat down on an upright chair and looked across at the dresser where the photograph of Kyriakos's father was displayed.

'I don't know,' she said sadly. 'It was time for us to go to the doctor to be tested. I took you and then the doctor said my husband should be tested also.'

'Did Pappa know about my grandfather?'

Irini shook her head. 'I hadn't told him. Our tests had come back clear for years. When I told him that he needed to be tested and why he was furious; accused me of lying to him about my past. I hadn't lied; I just avoided telling him. I was ashamed to admit there had been anyone incurable in our family.'

'So you thought you could get away with deceiving him the same way as did with me,' said Kyriakos bitterly. 'He had every right to know the same as I did. I'm not surprised he was cross and upset with you.'

'I thought he would get over it in a couple of days. We had had disagreements before and settled them. We were happy together. He was proud to be the father of a fine, healthy boy. He was working hard, fishing during the day and we were able to save a little money each week. He said he wanted to buy his own boat eventually.' Irini looked at her son sadly. 'Then he left without a word. He took all our savings with him and left me with fifteen drachmas. How long was that going to last with a small boy to feed and clothe?'

Kyriakos rose and patted his mother on her shoulder. 'I understand how difficult this is for you, Mamma, but I do have a right to know. What did you do?'

'I worked. I took any work that was available provided I could take you with me. I would scrub a floor during the day and wash dishes at night in a taverna. We had little money, but at least I could put food on the table, even if it was the remains from a taverna that would have been thrown away. I always made sure you had the best of the scraps.'

Kyriakos frowned. 'So where did you get the money to help

me when I wanted to open a taverna? You placed all your savings as a guarantee for the bank loan I was granted. You could never have earned that much by washing floors and dishes.'

'That came later from the old man who lived up the road. I had known him since I was a child and he always had a kind word to say to me and a sweet for you. His neighbour told me he had suffered a stroke and needed someone to help him as he had no relatives. She knew I wanted work and thought it might suit me.'

Kyriakos nodded. He remembered the old man with whom his mother had spent a considerable amount of time whilst he was left alone after school and during the school holidays or given an errand to run to save her from having to visit the shops a second time.

'At first I just made a meal for him and took it in each day, but as the time passed he became more incapable. He arranged that I could go to the bank and withdraw five hundred drachmas each month on his behalf. Each week he would give me the money to settle his outstanding bills and leave fifty drachmas on the dresser. That was for cooking his meals and cleaning the house. When he was no longer capable of getting out of his bed I washed him and his soiled bedding, cleaned him and the house; even fed him when he could no longer lift a spoon to his mouth. He still only paid me fifty drachmas a week and whatever was left after paying the bills I had to place in a drawer. It was full of drachmas notes.'

'Where did he get his money from?' asked Kyriakos curiously.

'I have no idea. Each week I selected the notes and held them up for him to see that I had only taken fifty drachmas. I was working for a pittance,' Irini said bitterly, 'and he could well have afforded to employ a trained nurse and housekeeper. When he died I took what was due to me from the drawer.'

Kyriakos looked at his mother in horror. 'You mean you stole his money?'

Irini shook her head. 'I had looked after him as well as if he had been my own father. I took what I considered had become due to me over the years. He had no relatives and I knew there was still sufficient in the bank to pay for his funeral.'

'Didn't anyone wonder why you were suddenly so well off?'

'I didn't flaunt my money and buy new clothes or furnishings. I bought some new trousers and a pair of shoes for you and hid the rest beneath my mattress until I had found more work. Then I opened a bank account and placed a few drachmas into my account each week. It gradually built up and earned interest. I grew a few vegetables and kept chickens. I stood in the market with my basket and usually made enough money to pay our weekly bills and buy any necessities. I didn't touch the money that was in the bank. I was determined that if I became ill and needed to be looked after the burden would not fall on you. The money would be available to pay someone to care for me. That's where the money came from to help you start your taverna.'

'I am grateful, Mamma,' replied Kyriakos humbly.

'So you should be. Had your father stayed around I would not have had to work so hard and you could have bought your taverna without a bank loan. I know you insisted you used some of the profit from the taverna in the first year you were open to make a proper bathroom and have all that nice tiling done in there, but we could have continued to manage as we had done for years.'

Kyriakos smiled. 'I had to put decent modern toilets in at the taverna. It was wrong that we should still have to use an outside privy in all weathers and use a tin bath in the kitchen. My builder said he would give me a decent price for the work if I would pay him cash and allow him to work here at weekends.'

'It meant you could not pay back as much as you would have liked from your bank loan. You should have waited until that was cleared.'

'I wanted to do it for you as a way of saying thank you. It made little difference to the amount of interest I was paying on the loan.'

Kyriakos realised his mother had adroitly turned the conversation away from his father. 'I still need some more information, Mamma.

What did you tell the neighbours when my father went away?' Kyriakos could imagine the shame she had felt when she realised her husband had left her.

Irini shrugged. 'I said he had gone to Aghios Nikolaos where the fishing was more plentiful, then I said there had been an accident and he was drowned.'

'Mamma!'

'What else was I supposed to do?' Irini defended herself. 'If he was living locally why didn't he come back to visit us and bring me some money?'

'So he could still be alive?'

'He could be.'

'Did you ever try to find him?'

Irini gave her son a sour look. 'He knew where to find me. I had no idea where to start looking for him, but even if he came begging at my door tomorrow I'd not take him back.'

Kyriakos sighed. 'I thought you still loved him,' he said sadly.

Irini shrugged. 'I have good memories of when he was with us. Had he stayed we might not even like each other by now. Better to forget him. What's done is done.'

Kyriakos left his mother's house his thoughts in turmoil. He must return to the taverna. Costas would be wondering what had happened to him and there could be customers waiting to be served. What was he going to say to Ronnie? She had made no secret of the illness that had afflicted her family and he felt he would have to tell her about his grandfather. Suppose she decided that marrying him held too much of a risk to her health? What would he do? What would her mother and uncle think? She would certainly tell them and they could advise her to end her association with him.

Feeling thoroughly miserable Kyriakos paid the taxi that had taken him from Elounda to his taverna, hardly listening to the story the driver was telling him.

'That family I picked up from you the other night, remember? I took your advice and asked them for the fare in advance. The man offered me twenty Euros on account and said he would pay the balance when they reached their hotel. I refused and he threatened me with the police. When I reached the taxi rank I parked up and told them to get out. I felt pretty safe there as there were half a dozen other drivers around on the night shift. He started shouting at me and they came to see what the fuss was about. He soon quietened down when he realised he was outnumbered.'

'So what happened?' Kyriakos felt obliged to ask.

'We all drove away and left them there. We cruised around the bars in case anyone genuinely wanted a late night taxi but most places were already closed so we went home. We may have lost some fares, but I didn't trust that man. Better to lose my licence than be hit over the head and robbed.'

'Did he report you to the police?'

'I don't know. Apparently the police inspector called and wanted to see our logs for the previous evening. There had only been about a dozen journeys to Aghios Nikolaos and all of those took place before eleven. He appeared to go away satisfied and we've heard no more about it.'

'Inspector Antonakis interviewed me as the man had complained about the taverna. Said it was unhygienic and should be closed down.' Kyriakos was not prepared to go into details of the man's complaint. 'We decided he was drunk or deranged.'

'That would explain it then.'

Kyriakos handed over ten Euros and the driver smiled in pleasure and did not offer any change.

'Have a good day, and thanks for tipping me off. I usually trust people to pay their fare.'

Kyriakos nodded and hurried towards the taverna where he could see Costas waiting for him.

Week Four – September 2012
Saturday and Sunday

John placed three sacks, a fork, shovel, hand brush and dustpan into his boat along with two cushions and three torches. He looked over the water to Spinalonga, tempted to go over and ensure that his handiwork had not been disturbed and also to see how the workmen had progressed with dismantling the tower and removing the skeletons. Provided their nocturnal visit went as planned he would come over during the week to ensure that Old Uncle Yannis's burial had not been disturbed.

He wished his uncle and grandmother had not elected to go with him and his father. He was not at all sure if the elderly couple were capable of climbing in and out of his boat and then walking up the stony path to the main road. He would have to use a torch to light their way and their progress would be slow. He did not want anyone on the mainland to become suspicious of a light on the island and contact the coastguard.

John jumped ashore and took the fork and shovel from his father as he handed them up, followed by the sacks, one contained the hand brush and dustpan and the other two cushions. He placed the implements over by the arched entrance and unlocked the gate. Giovanni helped Uncle Yannis to his feet and steadied him as he stepped ashore where John was waiting on the jetty.

'Just a couple of steps forward, Uncle and then stand still.

When we've helped Grandma Marisa ashore we'll use a torch so you can see your way up to the main road. Don't want you to fall over into the sea.'

'Where's the casket?'

'Dad will bring that and I'll carry the tools. All you need to do is concentrate on keeping your footing. I'll be beside you and you can grab hold of me if necessary. Dad will help Grandma Marisa.'

The slow, sombre procession made its way up to the main road and John was relieved when the light from their torches would no longer be seen by anyone looking at the island from the shore.

'I've got to open up the hole and whilst I do so I suggest you and Grandma Marisa sit on the steps here. We've brought some cushions so you shouldn't be too uncomfortable and I'll leave a torch with you. We'll be as quick as possible.'

Marisa sank down gratefully on the cushion. She had not walked up an incline and on uneven ground for a considerable amount of time. Yannis sat down beside her, both of them lost in thought.

Yannis gave a deep sigh. 'I remember your wedding day over here. Old Uncle Yannis was so proud and happy.'

'I was happy too. I miss Victor so much.'

Her brother took her hand in his. 'We're both lonely old people. Ourania is no company now.'

'When I die, Yannis, I want to be taken back to Italy so I can be buried with Victor. It may be foolish of me but I want to be close to him again. If I die before you, you'll make sure of that, won't you?'

'It's not foolish and I'll make sure you have your wish,' Yannis assured her. 'We've brought Old Uncle Yannis back so he can be near Phaedra.'

'Do you think her bones will be put on display?'

'It's possible, but we'll never know.'

'I'm not coming over to see them,' said Marisa firmly. 'This island is a sad and lonely place now there is no one living here. I used to enjoy coming over with Aunt Anna and meeting everyone. They were always so cheerful whatever limitations their disabilities placed on them. Do you remember when we used to come over to see the films? We always brought Ourania's mother and she kept saying "I never would have believed it" all the way through. It was a good job they were not like the films you see on the television these days. We would never have been able to hear the dialogue.'

In the darkness Yannis nodded. He had his own memories of visiting his uncle on Spinalonga.

'Even Old Uncle Yannis's house is not the same now they've removed so much of it,' continued Marisa. 'I wish they'd left it as it was, with the stairs leading to the upper floor and the cupboard he built at the side. Even the fireplace has been dismantled. He would have had nowhere to display the pictures little Anna drew. John says the shutters where she carved the boats have been removed and replaced with new ones.' She shook her head sadly. 'When you think of all the time and effort he and the others put in to build their houses and now so many have been pulled down.'

'They were no longer stable. The authorities could not risk a wall collapsing on a visitor.'

'Don't know why tourists want to come here in the first place. It means nothing to them. Their relatives didn't live over here. The island should have been left to decay in peace.'

'Without the summer visitors we'd still be a poor fishing village. They've brought a good deal of prosperity to the area and the main attraction is Spinalonga. I'm sure Old Uncle Yannis would be amused if he knew just how popular his home has become.'

It took John and Giovanni nearly an hour to remove the earth and stones from the hole that John had dug in the corner of Old Uncle Yannis's house. John had swept away the dust and sand from the corner and shovelled it into a sack ready to replace later to hide traces of their work. Giovanni had carried most of the large stones back to the pile as John unearthed them and between them they had filled the other two sacks with the soil leaving a gaping hole.

'Do you think it will be deep enough?' asked John anxiously as he shone one of the torches into the cavity. 'I didn't know how big the casket would be.'

Giovanni nodded. 'It will have to be laid on its side. You certainly can't dig down any deeper or the sides will start to cave in or we could undermine the wall. We don't want that falling down on top of us. Let's collect Uncle Yannis and my mother or they'll think we've forgotten about them.'

Uncle Yannis and Marisa rose stiffly to their feet with the aid of the younger men and were escorted into the remains of Old Uncle Yannis's house.

Giovanni placed the casket into the hole that John had dug. 'I'm not a priest, so I can't say a prayer; but I am sure we can all say our own silent prayers and they will be acceptable.'

The four stood with their heads bowed in silent contemplation. Marisa wiped her eyes on the corner of her shawl, before turning to her brother.

'Can we go now, Yannis? I don't want to be here any longer.'

Giovanni frowned. 'We have to fill in the hole before we leave. I'll take you both back to the steps to wait for us. It should take us less time than earlier.'

Whilst Giovanni helped Marisa back to the steps John commenced work on filling in the hole. He placed a couple of the stones down the sides and packed the earth down as hard as possible between them. He placed a thick layer of earth on top of the casket and then three large stones on top, again filling the cracks between them with earth and compressing it as much as he was able.

John placed a further thick layer of earth on the stones. 'I'm sorry, Uncle Yannis,' he said as he stamped the earth down. 'I'm not being disrespectful, but I don't want anyone to find that you are here and moving you elsewhere.'

'Who are you talking to?' asked Giovanni.

John flushed with embarrassment. 'I was apologising to Old Uncle Yannis for treading on him. I want to make everything as solid as possible. If it started to subside the authorities would probably think the wall was giving way and start digging around.'

'I'm sure he'd understand.' Giovanni shone the torch across the top of the hole. 'A bit more earth over in that corner wouldn't come amiss,' and John dutifully placed another shovel full where his father indicated.

Finally both men declared the hole felt solid when stepped upon and was level with the rest of the floor. John tipped the dust and sand from the sack back across it, scuffing the surface with his shoe so that it would not look pristine. He straightened up with a sigh and crossed himself.

'Goodbye, Old Uncle Yannis. You will never be forgotten. Rest in peace in your home. I wish we could have placed Phaedra here with you.'

Giovanni felt a lump come into his throat. 'We ought to be getting back,' he said gruffly.

'Stay here with Grandma and Uncle Yannis whilst I take the tools back to the boat. I can't manage them and the sacks of soil at the same time. I'll empty the sacks into the sea so that the earth will disperse. There's no reason to take it back with us.'

John walked back along the main road. As he reached the disinfection room he could hear the rhythmical chug of a boat engine and stopped in his tracks. Quietly he placed the tools on the ground and walked silently down the ramp to the jetty where his boat was moored. A small fishing boat was approaching and as it reached Spinalonga the man cut the engine.

John frowned in annoyance. He would have to prevent the man from landing on the island or he would have to explain why he and his father were over there with their elderly relatives at that time of night.

'Hello,' called the fisherman. 'Is that you over here, John? Have you got a problem?'

John stepped forwards onto the jetty. 'Hello, Mikhaelis. Have you been fishing?'

'Just returning when I saw your boat was moored here. Have you run out of petrol and want me to take you back to the shore?'

'No, thanks.' John tried to smile. 'I thought I saw a light over here and came to check there wasn't a stranded tourist.'

'Do you want me to come and search with you?' offered Mikhaelis.

John shook his head. 'I've been through the village and there's no sign of anyone. I'm going to walk up to the flats just to make sure, then I'll be off. It must have been a trick of the moonlight. If you see a light as you return to Plaka it will be me. No need for you to be concerned.'

'Well, if you're happy to be there on your own I'll be on my way. I wouldn't fancy walking around there alone at night, that's for sure.'

'It doesn't bother me,' replied John. 'I'd rather be on land than out at sea. Did you make a good catch?'

'Can't complain.' Mikhaelis's eyes roved over the dark shape of the island. He was pleased John had not accepted his offer to accompany him. During the daylight the island held no fear for him, but he knew workmen had been removing the bodies from the graves and tower. Who knew what evil spirits they had released? He crossed himself and re-started his engine, raising his hand to John as his boat drew away.

John drew a breath of relief. He would return to where his father was waiting before he risked placing the tools into the boat and possibly attracting Mikhaelis's attention to his activity.

Marianne was waiting for them on their return. Uncle Yannis immediately went to his bedroom to check that Ourania was still asleep and returned to the kitchen relieved.

'I've checked on her a couple of times and she hasn't stirred,' Marianne assured him.

'I gave her a slightly increased dose of her sleeping medicine,' he admitted.

'Hopefully that will mean you have a good night's rest also.' Marisa shivered and Marianne was immediately concerned.

'Are you cold?'

Marisa shook her head. 'No, I just had a strange chill pass over me. I'm sure it was nothing. Just a reaction to my uncle's burial and visiting Spinalonga.'

'Some hot milk,' announced Marianne. 'I'll bring it to you and you can drink it in bed. Would you like some whisky with it?'

'No, just some milk would be fine.'

'I'll have a whisky,' announced Yannis and Giovanni smiled as he lifted the bottle from the cupboard.

'That's a good idea. I'll join you. We can raise our glasses to Old Uncle Yannis's new resting place and hope he will never be disturbed again.' Giovanni brushed the dust from his trousers. He had felt obliged to wear his black suit that he always wore to any local funeral he had to attend.

Yannis switched on the low light beside his bed and undressed quietly. He looked over at Ourania. She appeared to sleeping peacefully and he climbed into bed grateful that she would not be demanding to know where he had been and asking why he had not taken her with him.

He lay there, unable to sleep, despite having had the generous measure of whisky Giovanni had poured for him. There was something not right. Was it the unorthodox burial that was on his mind? It had not worried him previously when his uncle had been placed in the tower, although he knew if the act was discovered they were all likely to end up in trouble with both the authorities and the church.

If this latest burial was found they could all end up serving a prison sentence. They would be accused of body snatching, bribery, defacing a National Heritage site along with an illegal burial. What would happen to Ourania if he was sent to prison? He gave a sigh and turned over again.

Sleep still would not come and he crept quietly out of his bed and placed his dressing gown over his nightclothes. He would have another glass of whisky. Stealthily he made his way to the kitchen and poured a second glass and drank it slowly. Maybe he should have accepted the offer of warm milk as Marisa had. The visit to Spinalonga had unsettled her also.

Her request to return to Turin and be buried alongside her husband was disconcerting. He would have to speak to Giovanni and ensure that her wishes were carried out. There was no guarantee that he would be around and permission would be needed to transport her body back to Italy. There would be numerous official forms to be completed and he was not sure if he would be considered as her next of kin or if he would be able to pass the onerous task on to Giovanni.

Yannis drained the last of his whisky and placed the glass on the side. Now maybe he would be able to sleep. He returned quietly to his room and looked again at Ourania. She was very still. He bent closer to her and could not hear her regular breathing. Risking waking her he placed his hand on her head. It felt cold, although the nights were still warm, and she made no response to his touch. He pulled the light bed cover away from her and placed his hand on her heart. He could feel nothing; there was no discernible heartbeat, however faint.

He switched on the main light. Ourania looked as if she was peacefully asleep. Taking her cold hand in his he chaffed it gently. ''Rani, 'Rani, wake up. You have to wake up.'

Ourania did not sir and Yannis felt a rising panic. He pulled the bed cover back over his wife and leaving the light on hastened down to Giovanni and Marianne's bedroom. He banged on the door, tempted to go straight in and wake them.

'Marianne,' he called, 'I need you.'

He could hear movement and Giovanni opened the door.

'What's wrong, Uncle Yannis?'

'It's Ourania. She won't wake up.'

Giovanni frowned. His uncle had admitted to giving her a slightly larger dose of her medication, but that had been hours ago. She should have slept off the effect by now.

Marianne pushed past the men and walked down to her uncle's room. She placed her fingers on Ourania's neck and could not feel her pulse.

'How long has she been like this, Uncle?'

'I don't know,' replied Yannis miserably. 'I thought she was asleep when I came to bed. I couldn't sleep, there was something wrong. I know now it was because I couldn't hear Ourania breathing.'

'Go and wait in the kitchen with Giovanni,' ordered Marianne. She would try artificial respiration, but without knowing how long Ourania had been without a heartbeat she had little hope of success.

Giovanni raised his eyebrows and Marianne mouthed "doctor" to him.

Giovanni returned a short while later. 'The night doctor is on his way. Do you want me to take over?'

Marianne straightened up. 'I think it's useless. Her body is quite cold. She may have been dead when I checked on her. That was hours ago. I just saw she was safely in bed and I thought she was asleep. I should have checked more thoroughly; made sure she was breathing.'

'Don't blame yourself. Uncle Yannis thought she was asleep when he came in to go to bed.' Giovanni placed his arm around his wife's shoulders.

'How much medication did he give her? Do you think he gave her too much?' Marianne looked around for signs of the bottle.

'He probably keeps it somewhere out of her reach. We can ask him about the dosage when the doctor has been. He's in shock at the moment. Make him some coffee and I'll listen out for the doctor arriving. We don't want everyone awake.'

'It must be my fault. I gave her an extra half measure of the sleeping medication.' Yannis dropped his head into his hands and groaned.

Marianne placed her arms around her uncle. 'I'm sure that was not the cause. The doctor said if the measure he had prescribed was not sufficient after a while the dosage could be increased. You say you only gave her a little extra.'

'Half a teaspoon. I didn't want her to wake up and be distressed because I wasn't around. Do you think the doctor will be able to save her?'

'I don't know, Uncle. It will depend upon when she stopped breathing.' Marianne thought it most unlikely the doctor would be able to help her aunt to recover.

'I thought she was asleep. She looked so peaceful. If I had been able to sleep I would not have known until the morning.'

'Where do you keep the medicine, Uncle? The doctor will probably want to know how much she has had since I collected it on Wednesday.'

'Locked in the cupboard beside my bed. The key is on my key ring along with my others. They're on the dressing table.' A look of horror came over Yannis's face. 'I didn't take them out with me. Do you think Ourania found them and took some more medicine?'

'I think that most unlikely. You said she was asleep when you left. Even if she had found your keys she would not have known which one fitted the lock on the cupboard.'

'She could have fiddled around and found it by chance. You know how obsessed she had become with having windows and doors locked.'

Marianne shook her head. 'We'll ask the doctor to unlock the cupboard and see how much has been taken. It should be at least half full. I'm only allowed one bottle a week.'

'What's wrong?' John entered the kitchen. 'I was trying to be quiet and not disturb anyone and I find you are up.'

'Aunt Ourania isn't well. The doctor is on his way. Why are you up anyway?'

'Nick woke up with a dry mouth and wants some orange juice.'

'I would have thought water would have been more suitable.'

John shrugged. 'She said she wanted orange.' He helped himself from the fridge.

Marianne gave a half smile. Over the past two weeks she had been suspicious about her daughter-in-law's condition; her late appearance in the mornings and the fact that she often made a rapid exit from the room when they were having a meal.

'Settle her down and then go back to bed. There's no point in all of us being awake.'

'What time is it, anyway?' asked John.

'Nearly three.'

'I'm glad I'm not a doctor being called out at all hours.' John yawned widely and walked from the kitchen carrying the glass of orange juice.

The doctor arrived finding an anguished Yannis sitting in the kitchen continually repeating that he should not have given Ourania an increased dose and Marianne trying to comfort him.

'Who discovered the lady?' asked the doctor as Giovanni took him to the bedroom where Ourania lay.

'Her husband. His wife appeared to be sleeping peacefully when he went to bed but he woke in the night feeling that something was wrong. When he checked on her he realised she was not breathing. He roused us and whilst I telephoned you my wife tried to give artificial resuscitation but received no response.'

The doctor nodded and carried out a cursory examination. 'In my opinion the lady has been dead for some hours. Has she any known medical condition that could account for her sudden demise?'

Giovanni shook his head. 'Not exactly. She is – er – was suffering from dementia. She was up during the night and my poor uncle was getting hardly any sleep. Our regular doctor prescribed a light sleeping draught for her.'

'This was administered to her this evening?'

'Her husband gave it to her.'

'May I see it?'

Giovanni unlocked the bedside cupboard and handed the bottle to the doctor. He read the label and handed the bottle back. Unless the family had a hidden supply elsewhere there were only approximately four doses missing from the bottle, certainly not enough to cause a person to die from an overdose.

'Do you have any more?'

Giovanni shook his head. 'My wife collects a bottle each week from the chemist. The doctor said it was wiser to have only a small amount in the house at any one time. There are young children around and he assured us that if they inadvertently drank it one bottle would not harm them, although we should take them straight to the hospital to have it flushed from their system.'

'I'll arrange for the lady to be collected and taken to the morgue. You realise I will have to notify the police and an autopsy will have to be carried out before any burial arrangements can be finalised?'

Giovanni sighed. 'I'll explain to Uncle Yannis.'

As Ourania's body was removed from the house Inspector Antonakis arrived. Giovanni took him into the lounge.

'I realise you have to do your duty, Inspector, but please be very gentle with my uncle. I am only too willing to help you with your questions to take the burden off him at this time. He has had a terrible shock and is blaming himself.'

'Why should he do that?'

'He administered the medication to his wife last night.'

'I was told the lady had not been diagnosed with any physical ailments. What medicine was she given?'

'For some considerable amount of time she has been suffering from dementia. During the day we always managed to cope with her when she became confused, but at night she would wake my uncle and demand to be taken out, usually to visit her mother who has been dead for years. Sometimes she would rage at him for hours and he was becoming quite exhausted. The doctor prescribed a mild sedative for her and it seemed to give both of them a peaceful night.'

Inspector Antonakis nodded. He would ask the doctor exactly what had been prescribed and the correct dosage. It was possible her husband had given her more than was recommended and it had caused her to go into a coma from which she had not woken.

'Do you have the medicine? I need to take it as evidence.'

'Evidence of what?' asked Giovanni.

'That it was suitable for a lady in her condition.'

'The doctor who attended earlier was quite satisfied.'

'I'm sure he was. It is just a formality.'

'It is in the cupboard beside the bed.'

'Could Mrs Andronicatis have helped herself to a second amount?'

Giovanni shook his head. 'The cupboard was locked and my uncle kept the key on his key ring in his trouser pocket.'

'It was with him at all times?'

'Always,' confirmed Giovanni. 'He only placed his keys on the dressing table when he went to bed. He said his wife appeared to be asleep when he retired. My wife had checked on her a couple of times during the evening and had not noticed anything untoward.'

'Why did your wife check on the lady rather than her husband?'

Giovanni was annoyed with himself for saying Marianne had checked on her aunt. Now he would have to admit that his uncle was not in the house. 'We went out for a short while.'

The Inspector looked at Giovanni. 'Where did you go?'

Giovanni swallowed nervously. There was no way he could admit they had gone over to Spinalonga.

'We went up to his shop. He's virtually closed down and we wanted to check how much stock he had stored there and discuss how the premises could be used profitably in the future.'

'So he would have had his keys with him?'

'Of course. He needed them to open the shop door.'

'And what time would this have been?'

'I think we left about nine.'

'Rather early for his wife to be in bed, wasn't it|?'

Giovanni shook his head. 'She often insisted on going to bed as soon as we had finished eating our evening meal.'

'So how long did you spend with Mr Andronicatis at his shop?'

'I'm not sure, maybe an hour.'

'And when you returned?'

'We continued our discussion in the kitchen over a glass of whisky.'

'Did anyone see you at the shop?'

Giovanni shrugged. 'Possibly. I'm not sure.'

'The other shop keepers? They would still have been open at that time.'

'I don't know. They may have been busy with customers. We didn't see them.'

The Inspector sighed. He did not disbelieve Giovanni's account of the evening, but depending upon the outcome of the autopsy he might have to visit Plaka and see if any of the shop keepers there had seen the two men and could corroborate the story.

'I'll not disturb Mr Andronicatis today, but I may need to question him after the result of the autopsy, you understand.'

'Of course. I appreciate your consideration. Is there any reason why we should not go about our business as usual? We have guests leaving today and I need to take them to the airport or make other arrangements for their transport. Also we would all like to go to church and say a prayer for my aunt and apprise the Father of her death.'

Inspector Antonakis nodded. He had no reason to put the family under house arrest.

Giovanni showed the Inspector out and returned to the kitchen and sank down in a chair with a sigh of relief.

Bryony patted him on the shoulder. 'Why didn't you wake us?' she asked.

'There was nothing you could do, but I need to ask for your help now.'

'Of course; anything. What's going to happen?'

'There has to be an autopsy as she died suddenly. That won't be carried out until Monday at the earliest.'

Bryony pulled a face. 'Poor Uncle Yannis. It must be awful for him waiting to know what happened.'

'He is blaming himself for not realising earlier that she wasn't asleep when he went to bed. I'm feeling guilty also. I checked on her a couple of times and because she was lying there quietly with her eyes shut I assumed she was asleep.' Marianne shook her head sadly. 'Had I realised we could have called the doctor earlier.'

'What did the Inspector want?' asked Marcus.

'He asked questions about our evening; why Marianne had checked on Ourania and not Uncle Yannis. I had to tell him that we had been out.'

Marianne looked at her husband in horror.

'I told him Uncle Yannis and I had gone up to his shop in Plaka. He wanted to know if anyone had seen us. I didn't mention your name, Bryony, but if he asks are you willing to say that you saw us walk past? I said the shopkeepers may have been busy and not noticed us.'

Bryony shrugged. 'I'll say I thought I saw you, but I was busy with customers and took little notice.'

'Thank you. If John is questioned he will have to admit that he went over to Spinalonga. Mikhaelis saw him on his way back to Plaka and stopped to ask if he had a problem. What about my mother? Has she been told?'

Marianne nodded. 'She's very shocked. She keeps saying Ourania must have died when she felt that cold chill go over her.'

'Can you impress upon her that she must not mention going to Spinalonga if the Inspector should ask?'

'I'll do my best, but I can't see why she should be questioned. If the Inspector asks me I will say she went to bed shortly after you and Uncle Yannis went out and knew nothing of the situation until I told her this morning. That's partly true.'

Giovanni nodded. He could do no more to prevent the Inspector finding out that they had paid a surreptitious visit to the island

'The earliest the autopsy will be carried out is Monday, I expect, but I have no idea how long it takes for the results to be returned.'

'I'll telephone Saffie and tell her I can't go up to the shop today. I'll explain about Aunt Ourania at the same time. I know she'll understand.'

'I can do the airport run,' confirmed Marcus. 'You wouldn't be safe to drive having had so little sleep. You could fall asleep at the wheel.'

'I hope not,' Giovanni smiled for the first time in some hours, 'But I'll certainly be grateful if you do it on my behalf.'

Week One – October 2012
Monday and Tuesday

Although the family had spent some hours on their knees at the church on Sunday they were all still shocked by Ourania's sudden death and concerned about the result of the autopsy.

'I'm sure that Inspector thinks I gave her an overdose deliberately to kill her. I would never have done such a thing. I loved Ourania.'

'We know you would not have harmed her,' Marianne tried to reassure her uncle. 'That Inspector won't be able to find anything against you.'

'If only we hadn't chosen that night to go to Spinalonga,' sighed Yannis.

'I don't think it would have made any difference. I checked on her and so did you. We both thought she was asleep. There was nothing about her to indicate otherwise. You'll feel better when you have been given permission to hold her funeral.'

'The priest was very kind. He said that he would make arrangements as soon as we notified him.'

'Would it comfort you if we went and spoke to him again today?' suggested Marianne.

Yannis shook his head. 'He can't say any more to me than he did on Sunday'

'So what are you going to do with yourself today?'

'I don't know. There doesn't seem to be anything to do without Ourania. I had become so used to ensuring that she was contented during the day or calming her down when she was distressed.'

'You were very kind and considerate to her. Not every husband would have had the patience that you showed.'

'There is one good thing,' Yannis turned distressed eyes on Marianne and she looked at him in surprise. 'She will never become violent and have to be committed like her mother. I was dreading that would happen.'

Marianne patted his hand. 'That is a comforting thought. She may have been worried that would happen to her. It would have broken her heart to have been parted from you.'

'I wish I knew how she died. What do you think they will discover from an autopsy?'

'I have no idea. We will just have to wait as patiently as possible. The Inspector has promised to telephone Giovanni as soon as he receives the report from the pathologist and Giovanni can drive in to Aghios Nikolaos and collect it.'

'When do you think that will be?'

'I don't know. It will depend upon their findings and if they need to make other tests.'

'Giovanni will tell me what the report says, won't he?'

'I promise he will give it to you to read, whatever the content. You have the right to know.' Her uncle had become an indecisive and anxious old man before her eyes during the last two days.

As soon as he received the telephone call Giovanni drove into Aghios Nikolaos and collected the report. He stood in the small waiting room and read it through. Ourania had died of an aneurysm. What was an aneurysm? He rang the bell for attendance and the pathologist opened the glass partition.

'How can I help? I have given you the full report.'

Giovanni nodded. 'I've read it. There's just one thing I don't understand. What is an aneurysm?'

'Put simply it is a blood clot on the brain, a cerebral haemorrhage. If the signs are not spotted and treated immediately the damage can result in a stroke, complete paralysis or death.'

'So if it happened whilst someone was asleep you would not know?'

'Exactly. In this particular case it was the Modula Oblongata, the brain stem that was affected. It is unlikely that even immediate medical treatment could have saved the lady's life for more than a few weeks.'

Giovanni let out a breath of relief. 'Thank you. Now I know I will be able to explain to my uncle what happened to his wife. There's just one other thing, do I have to take this to the police? They came to the house and made enquiries as her death was unexpected.'

'There's no need for that. I have faxed a report through to them. They shouldn't need to trouble you any further.'

Giovanni felt a tremendous sense of relief. He would not have to ask Bryony to tell the police that she thought she had seen the two men in Plaka.

'So we can make arrangements for her funeral?'

The pathologist nodded. 'I will arrange for her body to go to the funeral director. If her husband wants to visit he will be welcome but please let them know in advance. Is there anything else you wish to have clarified?'

Giovanni shook his head. 'Thank you for your help.'

The pathologist closed the window. The result of the autopsy had been obvious as soon as the lady's brain had been exposed and examined. There had been no need to send off tissue samples for analysis or investigate extensively to ascertain the cause of her demise.

Yannis read through the report slowly. There was no mention of the sleeping draught he had administered.

'What is an aneurysm?' he asked and Giovanni explained the word as the pathologist had done to him.

Yannis nodded contemplatively. 'I'm glad it happened whilst

she was sleeping. Had I been sitting beside her at the time I would not have know how to treat her and blamed myself for ignorance.'

'There is no blame at all attached to you, Uncle Yannis. She would not have suffered, her brain shut down and she did not wake up.'

Yannis rose to his feet. 'I think I need to go to the church and speak to the Father. Once Ourania's funeral has taken place the sooner life can return to normal for everyone.'

Giovanni made no comment. Life would never be normal again for his Uncle Yannis.

Marisa sat beside her brother. 'Can I comfort you in any way, Yannis?'

Yannis smiled thinly. 'It will take time for my pain to ease as yours did when Victor died. I have to become used to not having Ourania around to care for.'

'So what will you do with your time?' Marisa did not want to see her brother growing old and senile through inactivity with nothing to occupy his time.

Yannis sighed. 'There is only one thing I can do. I will re-open my shop next week. It has sat idle for long enough. I'll appreciate your help and company if you're willing Marisa.'

Marisa patted his hand. 'I'll be only too pleased to spend the days up at the shop with you.'

Kyriakos washed and dressed in clean clothes. Once the doctor had removed the plaster cast from his ankle he would ask for a thorough examination and he did not want to feel ashamed by wearing grubby underwear. He looked at the white marks on his arms. They had not become tanned after the scabs had fallen off, but that was hardly surprising as he had worn a long sleeved shirt whilst he was working.

He walked into the living room and looked out of the window to see when Ronnie arrived.

'I'm going to ask the doctor to examine me whilst I'm there. I'm sure I'll be told there is nothing wrong with me and then I don't expect to hear any more of this silly nonsense about leprosy germs being passed down through the generations, Mamma,' he said firmly. 'I'm determined to marry Ronnie. We have plans and I will discuss those with you later.'

'She's not welcome to come and live here with me,' declared Irini.

'We have no intention of living with you, Mamma. I just hope that given time you will grow to like her and realise that she is a suitable wife for me.'

'She'll be no help to you in the taverna.'

'I don't expect her to work in the taverna. She is a successful artist and makes a very good living from the sale of her paintings.'

Irini sniffed derisively. An artist! Anyone could put a few splashes of paint onto a piece of paper and call themselves an artist. She watched as Kyriakos closed the door behind him and climbed into his car beside Ronnie.

'I don't know how long I will be,' he warned Ronnie as she parked a short distance away from the hospital in Aghios Nikolaos. 'You could always catch the bus back to Elounda and I'll meet you later.'

'I could if you are going to be kept waiting for hours. I plan to go to the art shop and stock up on materials. If you're not sitting in the car waiting for me when I've done that I can call you and see how much longer you expect to be. I have a book with me so I can always sit and read.'

Kyriakos took the car keys from the ignition. 'I am expecting to be able to drive home,' he said with a smile. 'Don't worry; you will still be able to use the car each day. You will just have to collect it from the taverna instead of my house.'

'I would certainly be grateful whilst my mother and uncle are here. After that I would only want it occasionally to go up to Kastelli to see how Mr Palamakis is progressing.'

'We could drive up there on our way back,' offered Kyriakos. 'I have thought over your idea and I think it is a good one. Provided the extension is ready at the end of the season we could at least live there this winter. If we find it is too inconvenient then we have to think again.'

Ronnie turned delighted eyes to him. 'Do you mean that?'

'Once you have married me I am willing to live anywhere with you.'

Ronnie bit her lip. 'I can't marry you, Kyriakos. No, wait,' she placed her fingers on his lips as he was about to protest. 'I spoke to Nicola and asked her what was needed in the way of official documents to be able to get married in Crete. I would have to produce my original birth certificate with my biological father's name. He would be checked out and when it was found he was serving a prison sentence it is very unlikely the Greek authorities would allow me to marry you. I might even have my passport taken away and be unable to return to Crete.'

'What! Unable to return?'

'It's possible. I wouldn't want to take the chance of that happening. I'm willing to live with you, but I don't want to risk asking for permission to get married. There are other couples here who are in the same position.'

'My mother would disapprove,' remarked Kyriakos sadly

'Your mother disapproves of me to start with,' replied Ronnie tartly. 'This is another thing you have to consider, Kyriakos. Are you willing to live with me rather than get married? Think about it carefully. Would your relatives accept the relationship? I don't want you falling out with all of them because of me.'

Kyriakos shrugged. 'It would be their problem, not mine.'

Ronnie looked at her watch. 'You ought to go or you'll be late for your appointment. You can tell me your decision later.' She leaned over and kissed him. 'I'll call you when I return from the art shop.'

Kyriakos removed his trousers and gritted his teeth as the saw cut through his plaster cast; once removed his skin looked white and shrivelled.

'Don't worry,' said the nurse as she saw his horrified look. 'In a few days your skin will look normal again. Now, I'll take you to the X-ray department and then the doctor will decide whether your ankle has healed completely or if you need a new plaster cast for a week or so. Into the wheelchair.'

'I don't need a wheelchair,' protested Kyriakos.

'A safety precaution. If your ankle is not fully healed you could damage it by walking on it too soon.'

Careful not to put any weight on his injured ankle Kyriakos moved into the wheelchair. 'How much longer will I be? I have someone waiting for me.'

'Probably about half an hour.'

The doctor examined the X-ray and nodded. 'That all seems well. Be a bit careful for the next few days until you have the full strength back then there should be no reason why you cannot go about your business as before. You may find you have a touch of arthritis later on in life,' the doctor shrugged. 'Most people end up with some sort of joint pains.'

'There's something else, doctor, whilst I'm here.' Kyriakos felt both nervous and embarrassed. 'I've recently been told by my mother that her father suffered from leprosy. I'd like you to give me a full examination to put my mind at rest that I am not affected in any way.'

The doctor frowned. 'It's rather unorthodox. I'm not a specialist in the disease.'

'I understand, but if you would just examine me and tell me if I should have any cause for concern.'

The doctor sighed. It would take no more than a few minutes to look at the man's body. He appeared healthy enough. 'Very well. I certainly did not see any indications on your legs or feet. Remove your shirt.'

Kyriakos pulled it off over his head and the doctor looked at his torso. 'What are those white marks on your arms?'

'I was dragged along the ground when my ankle was broken and ended up with cuts and grazes on my arms. I have a taverna and I've been wearing a long sleeved shirt as my arms looked so unsightly. I didn't want to frighten my customers away.'

The doctor nodded. 'Stand up and turn around so I can see your back.'

Still holding the arms of the wheelchair Kyriakos stood and turned his back towards the doctor.

'What's this?' asked the doctor.

Kyriakos tried to turn his head and see what the doctor was looking at.

'Does this hurt?'

'No.'

'Can you feel me touching you?' The doctor's fingers roamed across his upper back.

'Yes, yes, I think so.'

'Hmm. As I said, I'm not a specialist. I doubt that it's anything to be concerned about, but it would be advisable for you to go to the hospital in Heraklion for further tests.'

'What is it?' asked Kyriakos thoroughly alarmed.

'You have quite a large area of white skin on your back. It may have been scraped away when you had the accident, but to be on the safe side it would be sensible to go and have a blood test. It could be done here, but it would take at least a week before the results came through. If you go up to Heraklion they would be able to give you the result in a couple of days.'

The blood drained from Kyriakos's face. 'You mean I have leprosy?' he whispered.

'Not necessarily. As I said, it could be an injury from your accident. Without a blood test no diagnosis can be definite. I'll give you a letter to take with you.'

Kyriakos sat back down in the wheelchair and waited whilst

the doctor scrawled a brief note. He was not sure if he had enough strength to stand up and walk out of the doctor's surgery.

Kyriakos stood outside the hospital building and tried to think clearly. He must make an excuse to Ronnie and drive to Heraklion immediately. There was no way he could see her again until he knew if he was infectious. He took out his mobile 'phone and pressed her number.

'Are you finished already? That's good,' answered Ronnie cheerfully.

'No,' Kyriakos forced himself to speak normally. 'There's a delay here. Probably an emergency admission. I still need to have my cast removed; then I have to have an X-ray and see the doctor. There are others waiting ahead of me so I could be here for hours. You catch the bus or take a taxi back to Elounda and I'll see you later.'

'Oh, we had planned to drive up to Kastelli.' Ronnie sounded disappointed.

'We will have to do that another day.'

'Would you like me to wait with you?'

'It's better that you go back to you mother and uncle and spend the afternoon with them. I must turn my 'phone off and go back inside. I don't want to miss my place in the queue.'

Ronnie sighed in exasperation. Now she would have to walk to the bus terminal and find out the time of the next bus to Elounda. She would probably have just missed one and if so she determined to take a taxi.

Kyriakos waited, leaning against the hospital wall. He must be patient and allow time for Ronnie to leave the area before he returned to his car. In the meantime he must call Costas and tell him that the taverna would have to be closed for a couple of days.

He drove carefully through Aghios Nikolaos and onto the main road to Heraklion, trying hard not to think about the possible diagnosis. If it was confirmed what would he do – what could he do? Would he have to agree to be admitted to a leprosarium for treatment or was it possible to be treated as an outpatient? He would certainly not want his friends to know he was receiving treatment. If only his mother had told him about her father earlier he could have ensured he had regular examinations. Now the disease could be so far advanced that there could be no way of halting its progress.

He would certainly not be would be allowed to run a taverna, he would have to try to sell it so he could repay his bank loan and his mother would have her savings available to cover her living costs. It was nearing the end of the season; no one would want to buy a taverna now. If his illness was confirmed he could not expect Ronnie to be willing to marry or live with him; he would not only be ill, he would also be penniless. The thought of parting from Ronnie brought a lump to his throat.

To Kyriakos's surprise he was not put into an isolation room at the hospital, but sat amongst others who were attending the clinic for blood tests for their various medical conditions and he wondered if he should have declared that he could be suffering from leprosy. Surely he should not have been allowed to mix with people who had other ailments and risk infecting them? He glanced at the waiting men and women; maybe they were all undergoing the same test as him. He sat at the end of the row of seats as far away from the other occupants as possible.

He was trembling when his name was called and he entered the doctor's room. He handed over his letter and the doctor made no comment on the contents.

'You understand I will be taking a sample of blood and sending it to the Pathology Lab for analysis. Once that has been done you are free to go about your business. You should avoid crowded places and intimate relations with anyone until the results are known. Call back in two days. I should have the results by then.'

Kyriakos nodded. His mouth was too dry to speak. He must telephone his mother and tell her he would not be home for a couple of days.

Ronnie walked up to the taverna after spending the afternoon and evening with her mother and uncle. She was surprised to see the taverna was closed. Kyriakos must have been detained far longer than he had envisaged at the hospital and decided it was too late to open up. She had tried to telephone him on a number of occasions, but his mobile was switched off and she felt mildly annoyed that he had not switched it back on when leaving the hospital or called her.

Week One – October 2012
Wednesday

Kyriakos had wandered around Heraklion, bought himself some sandwiches and a bottle of water before finding a sheltered spot to sit and eat. To his surprise had found he was hungry and returned and purchased two more packs of sandwiches. He drove to a car park, selected an empty space at the far end, and resigned himself to spending the next two nights sleeping in his car.

Ronnie walked to Kyriakos's house the next morning and was surprised that his car was not parked outside as usual. It must mean that he had gone up to the taverna early and she cursed herself for not looking there first. She had planned to drive her mother, uncle and Marjorie to Ierapetra and had asked them to be ready shortly after ten. Now she would have to walk back and collect the car from the taverna.

As she approached she could see the establishment was still closed. Had Kyriakos had an accident as he drove home form Aghios Nikolaos? She tried yet again to call him on his mobile and it was still switched off. She frowned in annoyance. His mother would have been informed if he had met with an accident that caused a hospital admission, but it would be useless going to ask her. She spoke only a few words of English.

She debated on her best course of action and decided to 'phone John and see if he was able to help, or if he was not available Giovanni might be willing to visit Mrs Mandakis and ask for news of her son.

'Where are you now?' asked John.

'I'm at the taverna. It's still closed. I'm really worried, John.'

'I'll come up to meet you on my bike. I'll speak to Kyriakos's mother and see if she knows where he is. I can always collect Skele on my way back.'

Ronnie sighed with relief. 'I'll start walking down the road.'

She took a last look around and as she did so a car slowed almost to a halt and there was the sound of clapping. The man leaned across his wife and called loudly from the car window to her.

'I told you I'd get you closed down.'

Ronnie looked at the man in disbelief. Had Kyriakos been arrested due to the man reporting him for having a body in his kitchen? Kyriakos had told her that the Inspector had visited and decided the man's story had been fictitious. What could have happened to make the Inspector change his mind? If Kyriakos was in gaol that would explain why his mobile was switched off, but surely he would have been allowed to telephone his mother.

She hurried down the road now and was relieved when John drew up beside her.

'Sorry,' he grinned. 'Just as I was leaving Mum gave me a shopping list.'

Ronnie hardly heard him. 'I think Kyriakos may have been arrested.'

'What for?'

'That man and his family who came when Saffie was washing the bones have just driven past. He called out to me that he had caused the taverna to be closed.'

'That has to be rubbish,' declared John and passed Ronnie a helmet. 'Put that on and we'll go and see what his mother has to say.'

Irini opened her door as soon as John knocked. She looked pale, dark rings under her eyes where she had not slept the previous night. She saw Ronnie immediately and pointed her finger at her.

'It's her fault. She has contaminated my son. He was healthy until he met her. Leper woman!' she slammed the door shut leaving both Ronnie and John standing in a stunned silence.

'What does she mean? Kyriakos only went to have his plaster cast removed.'

'His mother may well have misunderstood whatever he told her on the telephone.'

'Why didn't he call me? Every time I've tried to contact him it says his mobile is switched off.'

'He may have forgotten to turn it on again after leaving the hospital,' John tried to comfort Ronnie. 'I'll call his number, there may be a fault on your 'phone.'

John frowned in consternation and shook his head as he received a message to say that Kyriakos's mobile 'phone was switched off.

'He can't be ill. He was perfectly well when we drove to the hospital. We'd planned to visit Kastelli on the way back to see how Mr Palamakis was progressing. I know his mother dislikes me because I'm a foreigner but to accuse me of infecting Kyriakos with leprosy is cruel and untrue.'

John placed his arm around Ronnie's shoulders. 'We don't know what is wrong with him and I don't actually know how to find out. My doctor friend certainly won't give me any information about a current patient.'

'There must be some way we can find out.'

John shook his head. 'If I can think of anything I'll let you know. In the meantime all you can do is keep trying his mobile or wait for him to turn up.'

Week One – October 2012
Thursday

Kyriakos awoke after his second night of sleeping in his car. His clothes were creased and he felt decidedly dirty. He would have to find a different taverna this morning where he could use their toilet to have a wash before he visited the hospital for his results. He did not like to use the one he had used the previous day a second time or he would be considered a vagrant.

He checked his mobile 'phone and saw he had twenty or more missed calls from Ronnie's number and another from one that he did not recognise. Could it be the hospital in Aghios Nikolaos telling him there was a mistake and he had not needed to visit Heraklion? He pressed the number in eagerly and waited, expecting to be asked which department he wanted.

To his surprise John answered and he switched his mobile off quickly. Even if he was allowed to return home and attend a hospital for treatment as an outpatient word of his illness would soon spread. John could wait to find out the same as everyone else.

Kyriakos sat and waited in the hospital corridor. Each time the door opened he half rose from his seat, hoping it would be his name that was called. An hour later he was rewarded.

'Mr Mandakis? Please come in. I have your results here.' The doctor held the door open for Kyriakos.

On shaking legs Kyriakos followed the doctor into his surgery.

Coming Soon

My good friend Monique who has the shop 'Hansenmoon' along with her husband in Plaka asked me to write a book using her name as the title. She is known locally as Monika.

I agreed, provided she would be on the cover. She has had some lovely photos taken.

All I have to do now is write Monika's story! I have started – twenty pages completed so far with a publication date of late June - early July in mind.

Her life will start in Rhodes, but, of course, she will go to Elounda so that 'the family' can be included.